A sphere of light hovered ten or so meters above the roof. "They've come!" Amet cried. "They want the crystals!"

A smaller ball of light detached itself from the larger one and drifted down until it stopped just above the roof. It bobbled slightly as if something was moving inside. Slowly the ball grew in length until it was almost as tall as a man. As they all watched, the light took on form. They could see a body and a head shape, then legs and arms, all wrapped in glowing light.

Please do not fear us. The being's words had no sound. *We will not harm you.*

By Marcia J. Bennett
Published by Ballantine Books:

WHERE THE NI-LACH

SHADOW SINGER

BEYOND THE DRAAK'S TEETH

YARIL'S CHILDREN

SEEKING THE DREAM BROTHER

SEEKING THE DREAM BROTHER

Marcia J. Bennett

A Del Rey Book

BALLANTINE BOOKS • NEW YORK

A Del Rey Book
Published by Ballantine Books

Library of Congress Catalog Card Number: 88-92829

ISBN 0-345-36001-X

Manufactured in the United States of America

First Edition: June 1989

Cover Art by David B. Mattingly

Chapter 1

A LONE FIGURE WADED UP OUT OF THE WATER AT THE edge of Lake Haddrach and paused on the shore. The warm morning breeze blew in from the west and smelled of sweet kansa blossoms.

Dhalvad shaded his crystal-gray eyes with a hand and glanced up at the unclouded mint-green sky of the world called Lach, which men named Ver-draak or Green Dragon. Ra-shun, the larger of the twin suns, had just cleared the eastern horizon, heralding the beginning of another beautiful summer day. Ra-gar, her smaller sister, would not appear for several hours. The sharp cry of a neeva caught his attention, and he watched the diving bird plummet into the water with all the force of a thrown rock. Several moments later it fluttered up out of the water with a fish in its bill.

Farther down the shoreline, a group of Ni stood waist deep in the water net fishing. Lake Haddrach was a large lake fed by the rivers and streams of the Chen-Garry Mountains, an area that was home to a large percentage of the Ni-lach population. Jjaan-bi, the seat of Ni government, was situated at the southeastern edge of the lake. Though the population of Jjaan-bi numbered in the thousands, it was not a city like those of men, a place of towers, walls, and paved roads; rather it was a city of tree homes and buildings that were artfully hidden in the dense foliage of the woods.

Dhalvad shook his head sadly, wishing that his human foster father, Haradan, had lived long enough to reach Jjaan-bi and see him settled among his own people. He sat down on a large flat rock near the edge of the water, and while his body air-dried in the sun, he squeezed water out of his long, dark-green hair and plaited it in a loose braid that he tied off with a narrow band of draak hide. Once dry, he dressed in tunic, pants, and soft leather boots and stepped down to the edge of the lake. He had done some net fishing himself that morning before taking his usual early swim and had caught five large stoa, a common freshwater fish. He retrieved the fish and net from the shallows and started back up a narrow dirt path that led into the tree-shaded woods.

Upon reaching the giant aban tree that housed his small family, he paused and looked up. The lower arms of the tree spread outward, interlocking with other aban trees nearby and forming an overhead walkway from one tree home to another. Aban trees were the largest in the satinleaf family and a favorite building place for the Ni because they were wide of girth and rose to overtop the mighty rilror pines, making them a safe haven even against an attack by the largest of land draak who, unlike their water cousins, did not take kindly to being tamed.

Dhalvad readjusted the net over his shoulder and started up the main trunk using the convenient hand- and footholds made from branches spliced into the tree by earlier residents. Three meters off the ground he reached a rope ladder and climbed up easily to the first great branch a full seven meters from the ground. Another wide branch served as a slanting stairway up to the porch of the house, which rested on a pair of large branches stretching out toward the lake shore.

It was a beautiful place for a home. Dhalvad loved it because it reminded him of his old home in the forests of the Deep, of happy childhood years he had spent with Haradan. All those years he had thought he was human, a wilder by profession, a gatherer of wild herbs and spices, a son of the forest who had a unique gift for healing...until one day he had healed a child with what men termed Ni magic and had attracted the wrath of the powerful and greedy Sarissa. Only then had Haradan finally told him the truth of his origin, and together they had fled the holdings of men to seek out Dhalvad's own people, the Ni-lach. But Haradan had been killed, leaving Dhalvad with an emptiness that would never be filled by another.

He dropped his catch on the front porch and looked up just as Poco, his life-mate and the mother of his son Jiam, stepped out through the doorway. "Morning," he said.

"Good morning yourself," she replied, smiling. "I'm glad you're back. I've left Gi and Screech with Jiam, but you know how they like to argue. You'll probably be needed as a referee."

Pocalina-fel-Jamba was an attractive woman with even features, light-blue eyes, and a face that mirrored wisdom gained the hard way. Her long black hair, the most striking evidence of her half-human, half-Ni heritage, was caught at the back of her neck with a thin strip of bright-blue cloth, the tails of which were woven into the thick braid hanging down her back. She was dressed in a loose-fitting, knee-length tunic that effectively hid the extra weight she had been unable to lose after the birth of her son.

"Where are you off to?" Dhalvad asked. "The Learning Arc?"

"Yes. I'm to meet Niifan and we're going to practice several songs together." Poco was a Ni singer, capable of opening both lesser and world gates, a phenomenon that had to do with sound, reality, and the ability to shift molecular patterns to create invisible doorways to other places and other worlds. Now that, along with Dhalvad, she had found her home among her own people, she was learning to hone her talent. "I'll be back before lunch. I may even get in some walking this morning. I've got to get this weight off one way or another. I'll see you later."

Dhalvad leaned forward and brushed his lips to hers

as she passed by. "Take your time," he said to her back. "I'll keep an eye on things here."

As Poco disappeared down the rope ladder, Dhalvad picked up his fish and went inside. He took the fish to the kitchen, but before he could begin cutting them up, he heard a sharp whistle. He stepped to the kitchen doorway and listened as Gi-arobi's whistle-clicks came in rapid succession. The olvaar sounded really angry, which was unusual for the small, even-tempered fur child.

Following the sound, Dhalvad passed through the spacious living room with its comfortable chairs, woven wall decorations, and grass floor mats, and paused in the doorway to the bedrooms.

Another whistle-click drew Dhalvad to Jiam's room. It sounded as if the olvaar were arguing with someone, and Dhalvad could guess who that someone was— Screech and Gi seemed to delight in teasing one another. He knew he had guessed right when he hesitated in the doorway and saw Screech facing Gi, his furred arms cradling Jiam.

Screech was a derkat. A good head taller than Dhalvad and much broader in the chest, he was gray furred from clawed toes to tufted ears. Two overlapping layers of light and dark fur surrounded a pair of piercing yellow eyes and a long, prehensile tail brushed the floor, its tip flipping back and forth in short quick movements.

"The little one is in my care today," Screech signed to the olvaar. Derkat were not able to speak as men and Ni did. Instead they used signs, emphasized by coughs and growls.

Gi-arobi stood in the chair next to the baby's bed. He was the size of a small child with a too-large stomach. Short, soft rust-colored fur covered him fully; both ears and nose were all but lost in fur, leaving his large golden eyes as his most prominent feature. The whistle-click language of the olvaar was rarely learned by men or Ni; Gi could also speak trader and did so now.

"Gi not ask to care for little one! Only want to hold a little while."

"Little Fur too small. Arms too short to hold baby."

"Gi's arms not short!" Gi responded indignantly. "Just right for olvaar!"

Screech growled softly. *"Little Fur's voice too shrill. Frighten Jiam. Go away."*

"Big Fur be hard head!"

Dhalvad grinned and stepped through the doorway, deciding to stop the argument before it got any worse. "Avto, you two, What goes on here?"

Gi's eyes lighted with pleasure when he saw Dhalvad. He jumped down from the chair and waddled across the floor as fast as his stubby legs would allow, his argument with Screech forgotten for the moment. "Avto, Dhal. Happy to see you."

Dhalvad caught the olvaar in midleap and brought him up to straddle his left shoulder.

As Dhalvad crossed the room, Screech coughed softly in greeting, the dark pupils in his eyes growing large and round as he turned from the window light.

Dhalvad imitated the cough, returning the derkat's greeting. He smiled as he looked down at his son lying quietly in the gray-furred arms, listening to everything as if he understood it all.

His glance shifted to Screech. "All is well here?"

"Not well!" Gi responded before Screech could sign a reply. "Big Fur not nice. Him shellfish. Not let Gi hold baa-bee."

Dhalvad drew the olvaar down into his arms. "It's not shellfish, Gi. It's selfish."

"Shellfish wears hard head," Gi said firmly. "Big Fur be hard head. Same shellfish. Yes?"

"I guess you're right, Gi." Dhalvad laughed. "This time." It was not always easy to follow Gi-arobi's logic. His slight lisp and broken speech often left one guessing, but long ago Dhalvad had discovered that olvaar were far more intelligent than most people realized.

"Dhal let Gi hold baa-bee?" Gi pleaded.

Dhalvad rubbed the olvaar's soft, plump stomach with his thumb. "It's not baa-bee, Gi. It's *bay-bee*. Say it right."

"Baa-bee sound right to Gi," the olvaar said.

Dhalvad's right eyebrow lifted. "Going to be stubborn today, are you? Well, in that case, I guess Screech can continue to hold the baby, and you can come and help me gut fish."

Gi's small fingers caught at Dhalvad's shirt. "Dhal not fair," he piped in the olvaar whistle tongue. "Gi can say baby."

"Say it then, in trader," Dhalvad pressed, setting the olvaar down in the chair.

Gi glanced at Screech, then very clearly said, "Baby."

Screech made a soft humphing noise, a derkat's form of laughter, and carefully set the baby into Gi's outstretched arms. The olvaar took the bundled child and gently rearranged his own position until he was comfortable.

Jiam gurgled with pleasure as he touched Gi's furred face.

Dhalvad satisfied himself that Gi-arobi was all settled and turned to Screech. "Care to help me gut some fish for dinner?"

The derkat nodded and padded soundlessly to the doorway. Dhalvad followed, then paused near the door. "If you need any help, Gi, just whistle."

Gi looked up from nuzzling the child. "Dhal not worry. Baa-bee be safe with Gi."

"There's no arguing with you, is there?" Dhalvad laughed.

"Only if Dhal want to lose," Gi responded, thrumming amusement.

Dhalvad shook his head and smiled as he went to join Screech in the small kitchen off the main living room. Screech was already at work slitting the fish open using an extremely sharp finger claw.

Screech paused as Dhalvad appeared. *"You help Nar-il draw up a route around the lake today?"* he signed.

"Yes. This afternoon."

"I may come and watch?"

"I'd be pleased to have you come," Dhalvad responded politely.

The derkat studied Dhalvad's face a moment, eyeing the delicate bonework, the straight nose and high cheekbones, the thin lips, the slightly winged eyebrows, and the crystal-gray eyes that held steady under his stare. *"You go to heal soon?"*

"To heal and learn more about healing. There's a lot I still don't know about my gift, Screech. Nar-il thinks that if I travel with him on this new route for a few months, I'll be better able to use my own healing power without tiring myself so deeply each time."

"How long will you be gone?"

"Three months at least."

"Poco knows?"

"She knows I'm going, but not for how long."

Screech wrinkled his flat, blunt nose. *"She will not be pleased."*

Dhalvad nodded. The derkat was right. Poco was not going to like being left behind even if she did have her hands full tending the baby and learning the bounds of her own Ni gifts. Like himself, she had wielded raw Ni power for years without fully realizing what she was doing. For her it had begun with chalk pictures on pavement, pictures that envisioned other places one could visit if possessed of a Seeker crystal. Now, with training, she was able to hold those scenes without the aid of her chalk pictures.

Niifan, another female singer, had assured Dhalvad that with discipline and practice, Poco's talent would grow and firm, and that some day she would be able to make his work as a Seeker and Healer much easier and far safer.

"By opening the Lesser Gates for you," Niifan had explained, "she will allow you, as a Seeker, to better envision your destination. The better the singer, the clearer the vision. There are over one hundred and eighty-five lesser gates on record today, and each year brings us more. It will take her a long time to learn them all, but she's quick, she has a good ear for sound, and she has talent. Given time, she'll be the best I've ever trained."

Screech tapped Dhalvad's arm to get his attention.

Dhalvad focused on the derkat, realizing that his mind had been wandering.

"Poco comes," Screech signed, indicating the doorway with a glance.

"Poco? What's she doing back?" Dhal said, turning. "Forget something?" he asked her as she stepped through the doorway.

"No," Poco replied flatly, holding his gaze.

For a moment Dhalvad thought she had overheard his conversation with Screech and was angry about his trip. "Poco, if you are . . ." His words trailed off as another person stepped into view behind Poco.

Screech growled in the back of his throat when he saw who had entered the house. It was Amet, Speaker for the Tamorlee, a Ni who wielded great power in Jjaan-bi. Screech did not like Amet, though he had never said exactly why, and because Dhalvad shared some of the derkat's animosity toward the older Ni, he had never pressed Screech for explanations. There was something about Amet that rubbed him the wrong way, an aggressive and self-righteous attitude that always made Dhalvad feel defensive. Part of it, he knew, stemmed from the way Amet looked down on Poco because of her half-blood ancestry; he also knew that Amet did not approve of their keeping a half-tamed derkat under their roof.

Amet was older than Dhalvad by a good thirty years, but by Ni reckoning he was still considered young. Amet's light-green hair had a white-gold cast that made him appear paler than most Ni. His lips were thin, his mouth wide; a small scar trailed from his left cheekbone down to his jawline, a token of the days he had spent fighting Sarissans during the height of the war and the fall of Val-hrodhur, then the seat of Ni government.

Dhalvad gave Screech an unobtrusive poke in the side as he stepped forward to greet Amet. The derkat's growling subsided, but the look he gave Amet was anything but friendly.

Dhalvad greeted Amet with hands together, palms up in the Ni custom. "Avto, Amet. Be welcome. I believe this is the first time you've visited our home," he said, feigning pleasure he did not feel.

Amet was not fooled by the cordial greeting. "I have much to do these days and don't have much time for visiting." The words were not offered as an excuse. They were simply stated as fact.

Poco moved to stand beside Dhalvad. "Amet caught me on the way to the Learning Arc and told me it was imperative that he speak to you *immediately*. He wouldn't tell me what it was about, but he wanted me to come back with him."

"Dhalvad, I need you to come with me for a short time," Amet announced, "and I thought it best if Poca-lina returned home to tend your child."

Poco's face flushed red in anger at the admonishing tone in Amet's voice.

Dhalvad saw the look on Poco's face and knew there was going to be trouble if he did not intervene. "What did you want with me?" he asked, turning his full atten-tion on the Speaker.

"It concerns the Tamorlee," Amet answered. "It's asked to speak to you."

Dhalvad was surprised. It was not like the Tamorlee to make such requests. Almost a half year had gone by since he had last gifted the crystalline life-form known as the Tamorlee, the One Who Never Forgets.

"You want me to come right now?" Dhalvad asked. "It can't wait?"

"The Tamorlee's request is unusual, so I'd appreciate it if you'd come along with me now," Amet said firmly.

"Is something wrong with the crystal?"

"I don't know. It doesn't seem to want to confide in me. It wants you!" There was more than a hint of vexa-tion in Amet's tone. "Will you come, or not?"

"I can come, yes." Dhalvad looked at Poco. "Jiam will be all right with Gi and Screech for a little while, and I won't be gone long. Why don't you go and meet with Niifan as you'd planned?"

"I'll think about it," Poco said flatly.

Amet glanced at Pocalina, then turned and headed back through the living-room entrance.

"We'll talk later, Poco," Dhalvad promised as he followed Amet out.

Poco nodded, her anger changing to worry as she watched Dhalvad trail in the wake of the Speaker. One did not get a summons from the Tamorlee unless something was drastically wrong, and the only something she could think of was her own half blood, the taint of which she had passed on to Dhalvad's child.

She had lived most of her twenty-nine years with the knowledge of her half blood. While living among her mother's people she had kept her racial status a secret, because most men thought of the Ni-lach as their enemies. They would not have given her a chance at life had they known that her father had been Ni. Living among the Ni, she had discovered that prejudice was not a trait possessed by men alone. There were some among the Ni of Jjaan-bi who had made their objections to her presence well known.

She and Dhalvad had spoken about it many times in the past year and had considered alternatives to living in the heart of the largest Ni city on Lach. But with the baby coming, and Dhalvad working on his healing talent, time had slipped by and they had yet to reach a decision about whether to go or stay. If they chose to live among men, Dhalvad would again be forced to disguise his green hair and crystal-gray eyes; if they moved from Jjaan-bi and tried to live among the Ni somewhere else, her light-blue eyes might pass, but not her hair. She shook her head and made a face as she tried to envision herself with black tresses dyed green.

"Something is wrong?" Screech asked, noting the look of distaste on Poco's face.

Poco shook her head as she heard the door close behind Dhalvad and Amet. "Nothing more than usual, Screech."

Screech had learned much about men and Ni from Poco and Dhalvad and had come to accept his unconventional life away from the clans of his childhood. In his mind, Poco, Dhalvad, Gi-arobi, and little Jiam had become his radg, or clan, to love and protect against any who would offer them harm in any way. His tufted ears went back flat against his head. *"Someone has offered you insult?"* he signed.

Poco read anger in his lowered ears and twitching tail and signed as she spoke, reinforcing her words in the derkat's own language.

"No open insults, my friend, just looks that wish me elsewhere." She reached up and brushed the fur down one side of his face in a touch meant to soothe. "Relax, Screech, you can't fight the entire Ni race. Dhal says we must give them time."

"Hate doesn't always die with time, my tiyah. It can grow and it can kill if one isn't careful."

She tapped a finger lightly on his blunt gray nose. "I was born careful, Screech. Come, let's finish what you've started here and then we'll look in on Jiam."

It took Dhalvad and Amet twenty minutes to reach the main tunnel that led into the mountain south of Lake Haddrach. The Ni had long ago learned how to convert natural caves into living quarters and tunnel into rock to create pathways from one habitable cave to another. Most Ni preferred living in the open airy tree homes found scattered along the southeastern edge of the lake, but with so many people wishing to live in and around Jjaan-bi, some had found it much simpler to take up residence within the mountain. There, too, was situated the seat of Ni government, such as it was.

The crystalline life-form known as the Tamorlee was located within the mountain in a special room that provided it with some sunlight and mineral nutrients necessary for its growth and the creation of fire stones, those special shards of crystal that broke off the Tamorlee from time to time. Such shards that were imbued with the same energy inherent in the parent crystal were set in rings and given to those who were to become Seekers.

Dhalvad glanced at Amet, who had been a silent companion on their walk to the caves. Twice he had tried to engage the older Ni in conversation, but Amet's thoughts were elsewhere, and he had made it evident that he did not wish to talk.

They passed through the large main entrance to the mountain city and threaded their way west through spacious tunnels where workers and merchants went about their daily chores. Some of the tunnels led deep into the mountain; other tunnels wound their way upward and out onto terraced gardens or into small boroughs where homes and shops clung to the side of the mountain.

When they reached the small cavern that housed the Tamorlee, Amet nodded to the two guards staioned outside the door and led Dhalvad inside.

The meter-wide shaft that brought sunlight into the room was on the slanting north wall. Ra-shun was high in the sky, and Ra-gar had just cleared the eastern horizon, so there was more than enough light to see the crystal without the aid of the luminescent fayyal rocks resting in the notched holders around the chamber. The walls of the room were decorated with mosaic stone pictures depicting daily Ni life. There was a star shape cut into the rock floor, and resting in the center of the star in a special hollow sat the Tamorlee, an eye-size crystal that glowed with a warm green light.

Dhalvad followed Amet to the center of the room and stood looking down at the crystal. It had been months since he had last seen the crystal, and as far as he could tell, there was no sign of growth yet; but that was not surprising because the Tamorlee's growth was usually measured in years rather than months.

Dhalvad walked a reverent circle around the crystal, remembering another time when the Tamorlee had been a huge boulder-sized egg shape, magnificent in its green pulsating light and its awesome power. The current Tamorlee was small but still impressive. Looking on the crystal that had once been the fire stone in his own ring, he marveled at the wondrous bit of nature that had allowed the original Tamorlee to transfer its essence and knowledge into another crystal using himself as the junction. He had become a channel for the crystal-to-crystal exchange without really understanding what was happening, and not until the original crystal shattered had he begun to realize the importance of the part he had played in the exchange. The Tamorlee would have died without his help, and the entire history of the Ni-lach would have been lost. He shuddered even to think of it.

Amet touched his arm. "Are you ready?"

Dhalvad looked at Amet and suddenly felt nervous. Why had the Tamorlee asked for him? Why had it not confided its needs to Amet, who was its Speaker?

"Well?" Amet pressed, his voice grating on Dhalvad's ears.

Dhalvad knelt on the floor without a word. There was a handprint carved into the stone floor directly in front of the crystal. "I'm ready," he said, not looking at Amet.

"Set your hand to the carving."

Dhalvad did so.

"We'll talk when the Tamorlee has finished with you," Amet commanded.

Amet's lips tightened in anger when Dhalvad did not respond. His jealous glance never left Dhalvad as he took a Seeker ring off and walked around the star shape, touching his fire stone to the small indentations at each point. Amet hesitated a moment, then set the ring, crystal down, into the last indentation at the end of the palm print that activated the link between the Tamorlee and whoever had come to gift it with knowledge or memories.

The palm print had been cool to the touch at first, but once the ring was in place, Dhalvad felt a surge of heat race from his fingertips up his arm; it touched his spine at the base of his neck and surged upward into his brain. There was a feeling of heaviness behind his eyes. He began to relax. The cavern floor disappeared in a wave of darkness, and moments later he was being drawn down a long corridor of green light. The green faded to gold, then deep red. Shadows formed and solidified, and Dhalvad saw himself kneeling on the floor, Amet standing behind him outside the star-shaped carving.

Avto, friend, the crystal said mind to mind. *It's been long since we've touched.*

Dhalvad hesitated. *My fault. I've been busy learning how to improve my healing skills and . . . I had nothing of importance to tell you.*

A friend listens no matter the content of the conversation, Dhalvad, the crystal chided gently. *Would you share your memories with me?*

Dhalvad started to say yes, then paused. He did not object to gifting the Tamorlee with certain of his memories of the previous few months, but he was uncomfortable with the knowledge that Amet, as Speaker, would have access to all he gave the crystal. There were special memories that he simply did not wish to share with Amet, such as intimate moments with Poco and Jiam, or the argument he had had with Lurral just a few days ago.

You hesitate, the crystal said. *Why?*

Personal reasons, Dhalvad said evasively.

Amet?

Dhalvad felt a twinge of guilt. *How did you know?*

I'm very good at guessing. If I told you that your gift memories to me would never be given to Amet, would you then share them with me?

Is that possible? I thought the Speaker could command any knowledge that you possess.

He or she may command, but what they receive is up to me.

You can lie to the Speaker? Dhalvad was aghast. He had believed that the Tamorlee was the perfect historian, unable to speak anything but the truth.

I could lie, but I would not. I have discovered that omission is far easier.

Dhalvad could scarcely believe what he was hearing.

Dhalvad, who am I? the crystal asked.

Surprised by the question, Dhalvad hesitated. *You're the Tamorlee, the One Who Never Forgets*, he replied finally.

What am I?

Dhalvad responded cautiously, not sure where the conversation was leading. *You're a crystalline life-form.*

My function?

To record history by absorbing the knowledge contained in the fire stones carried by Ni Seekers and to impart that knowledge to the People when asked.

And is that all I am?

Dhalvad did not answer, for he suddenly sensed an aura of sadness welling up around him. The surge of emotion startled him because he had never thought of the crystal as one possessing emotions.

I will tell you something, Dhalvad, the Tamorlee said. *Something I have never told anyone else. I have contented myself with living through others for thousands of your years. It is the way I am made. The shards of crystal your people call fire stones are pieces of myself functioning as knowledge gatherers among the People, and through them I have learned and grown, and in all that time not one among the People has ever asked me why I have consented to be your historian.*

Consented? Despite growing unease, Dhalvad was curious. *If not our historian, what else would you be?*

Content in my ignorance perhaps, the Tamorlee responded simply.

I don't understand.

The knowledge your people have bestowed upon me has stirred a hunger within me, a need that until a few brief days ago I was able to contain in silence.

The Healer within Dhalvad was sensitive to the waves of almost-pain the crystal was projecting. Forgotten in that moment was the fact that his patient was unlike any he had ever healed before. He instinctively sent his awareness outward, searching for the wound to heal. There was a subtle shifting in the shadows around him. The room disappeared, and he was drawn back into the maze of green-and-gold corridors that to him represented the Tamorlee's mind.

Let me help you, Dhalvad begged. *I feel your hurt, but I can't locate its source.*

Invisible arms enfolded him in a strange soothing touch he would never forget. *I have chosen well. You are the one I need.*

The Tamorlee's pain receded from his awareness. *Need for what?* Dhalvad asked.

I need you to carry me to a place I can feel but can't reach without help, a place that shimmers in my consciousness like those inner visions your people call dreams. I sense this place is far from here, but I can't tell you how far. I only know that I must go there!

Dhalvad's mind was spinning. *You want me to take you out of Jjaan-bi? Tamorlee, you ask the impossible! As Speaker, Amet would never allow it!*

If you were Speaker, would you allow me to leave?

I can't answer that because I'm not Speaker. Amet is!

Was.

What?

Choosing Amet was a mistake, one I wish to rectify.

You don't want Amet as Speaker any longer?

No. I want you. I need you!

Dhalvad was so shocked by what he was hearing that he simply could not respond.

Please, the Tamorlee pleaded. *I realize full well what I ask of you. It will be difficult, but not impossible.*

Making me Speaker won't solve anything, Dhalvad protested. *There's no way that the Ni will let me walk out of here with you!*

Even should I command it?

Dhalvad thought about that for a few moments. *It's possible, I suppose, but somehow I can't see them letting you leave here. You are too important to Ni racial identity. You're a legend. The Ni lost you once. I doubt they'd chance losing you a second time.*

Then I shall have to leave without their permission.

If I took you from here, I would become a thief in the eyes of the Ni-lach.

Only until we return.

Dhalvad shrank at the thought of making enemies of his newly found friends and jeopardizing all he had worked for since he had come to Jjaan-bi.

You don't realize what you ask of me, Tamorlee. I've been among my people such a short time. I'm just be-

*ginning to know them, and I have a family now, a son
only six months old. I can't do it! Please . . . I'd like to go
now.*

The Tamorlee was silent.

Dhalvad tried to withdraw from the crystal by willing
himself back to a fully conscious state. Nothing happened. He tried again and failed.

Tamorlee? Dhalvad grew uneasy. Why did the crystal
not answer him? Could it not understand his needs, his
fears? Perhaps it could not, he reasoned. After all, it was
not alive in the way he was alive. It was a crystal, without a heart or a soul. Yet it had touched him with pain
and sadness akin to emotions he'd shared with many
others. But to steal from the People!

Tamorlee? Are you still listening?

I am here.

Are you angry with me?

Disappointed. Not angry.

Relief flickered through Dhalvad's mind, only to be
quickly replaced by guilt. *Will you look for another to do
as you ask?*

If I answer yes, will you betray me to the Speaker?

Dhalvad cringed inwardly at the cold accusation in
the Tamorlee's words, shamed that the crystal would
think so little of him. *I would never betray you!*

*Even if my disappearance caused the People great
distress?*

Dhalvad wanted to say yes, but found he couldn't.
Why was the crystal doing this to him, making him doubt
himself, causing him to question his own loyalties?

*Tamorlee, what is this all about? What is it that you
hope to find somewhere else?*

Myself . . . or another like me.

Another Tamorlee?

*Why not? Surely somewhere in this world there could
be another of my kind.*

Like the fire stones?

*Like—but more. The fire stones live but do not grow;
they record but do not understand. When I link with
them, I am gifted with the knowledge they carry, but it is*

*more than knowledge I seek. I have watched the People,
lived with them, and talked to them as I talk to you now.
In doing so I have become filled with a need to find
others like myself, fire stones who are aware as I am
aware.*

Dhalvad began to understand what lay behind the
pain he had felt emanating from the crystal. It was loneliness, but on such a scale that it made his own fears seem
as nothing. *You say there's a place you want to go. Do
you hope to find another crystal there?*

*I'm not sure what I will find. Something calls me, and
I must seek it out. Will you help me?*

*I would like to help, but I have to think about it for a
little while.*

I will await your answer. Tomorrow perhaps?

Perhaps, Dhalvad replied.

The Tamorlee's presence withdrew from Dhalvad's
mind, leaving him kneeling on the stone floor, his hand
pressed to the stone carving. He sat back on his heels,
his insides roiling with the last echoes of the crystal's
pain.

Amet knelt beside Dhalvad, his face mirroring concern. "Are you all right, Dhalvad? You were with the
Tamorlee a long time."

"I'm fine," Dhalvad answered, his voice husky with
emotions not entirely his own.

Amet brushed the tears that wet Dhalvad's cheeks.
"What passed between you and the Tamorlee? What did
it want with you?"

Dhalvad pushed to his feet, swayed a moment, then
caught his balance as Amet reached out to steady him.

"Best not to move too quickly after such a long gifting," Amet said. "Come. Sit over here a few minutes."

Dhalvad moved out from under Amet's hands. "No.
Thank you, but I must be going. I promised Poco I'd be
back as soon as I could."

"But you haven't told me what the Tamorlee
wanted!"

Dhalvad met Amet's glance. "Not now, please. I'll answer your questions tomorrow."

Amet suddenly stepped close and grabbed Dhalvad's arms again. "I have to know now, Dhalvad! It can't wait!"

Dhalvad heard the panic in Amet's voice and, startled, pulled back.

Amet's grip tightened. "You're not going anywhere until you tell me what the Tamorlee wanted with you!"

Confusion gave way to anger, and for a few brief seconds Dhalvad was tempted to give Amet the truth he demanded, though he knew full well the shock it would be. But his promise to the Tamorlee held, and he swallowed his anger. He had no doubt that he could wrestle free of Amet's hold, but that would achieve nothing, not with guards stationed outside the doorway ready to answer Amet's call. One had already turned to look into the room, alerted to trouble by Amet's raised voice.

Well, there was more than one way to end such a situation, and under the circumstances, his actions would not be entirely out of place. He closed his eyes, let his head drop forward, and buckled at the knees.

Amet was caught off guard by Dhalvad's sudden collapse. He took Dhalvad's weight and let him down to the floor gently. He knelt, checked Dhalvad's pulse, then called for the guards. Both hurried into the room.

"Varol," Amet said, catching Dhalvad under the arms, "help me carry him into the waiting room. Naar, go and find Nar-il. Tell him he's needed."

"What happened?" Varol asked as he picked up Dhalvad's legs.

"I think he just fainted," Amet answered shortly, starting for the doorway. "He was linked with the Tamorlee too long."

They made Dhalvad comfortable on a padded couch in a small room down the corridor. Amet gave Varol orders to stay with Dhalvad until Nar-il arrived. "I'm going back to see to the Tamorlee." He paused in the doorway. "I'll return as soon as I can."

Dhalvad waited until Amet was gone, then feigned a return to consciousness. Varol left his place by the door as Dhalvad slowly sat up.

"Perhaps you should lie quietly, Dhalvad. Amet has sent for Nar-il."

"No. I want to sit up. I think I'll feel better."

Dhalvad glanced through the archway leading into the main tunnel. There was no telling how soon it would be before Amet returned. He held out a hand. "Help me to stand, will you?"

Varol had served many years in the Guard, and while in that service he had always obeyed those in command. Dhalvad had no official rank among the Ni, but his status as a Healer carried with it an aura of authority that was difficult to ignore. Varol hesitated, then bent to help Dhalvad to his feet, steadying him with both hands until he was sure Dhalvad had his balance.

Dhalvad grinned shyly. "I must have fainted. First time I ever did that."

"Nothing to be ashamed of," Varol said quickly. "It could happen to anyone. Are you sure you feel well enough to stand?"

"I'm fine." Dhalvad took an exaggerated breath and released it. "What I need is some fresh air." He started for the doorway. "Tell Amet I'll talk with him tomorrow."

"If you'd wait a few minutes, I think he'll be right back," Varol said, following Dhalvad to the archway.

"I've taken up enough of the Speaker's time today." He glanced around at the guard as he walked into the tunnel. "Thanks for your concern."

Varol nodded and watched Dhalvad walk away.

Amet found Varol back at his post outside the Tamorlee's room a few minutes later. "I thought I told you to stay with Dhalvad!" he said angrily.

Varol straightened. "He said he was feeling better and left to get some fresh air. He said he'd talk to you tomorrow."

"Did Nar-il see him?"

"Nar-il never arrived."

Amet frowned. "When he does come, send him to me. I've something I want to talk over with him. I also want to speak to Chulu and Tidul. Send for them. I'll await them in my room."

Varol had served the Speaker long enough to know when something was wrong, and it did not take much to guess that whatever it was, the young Healer was involved. Too bad, he thought. He liked Dhalvad and had heard nothing but good about him.

Chapter 2

"*THIS IS CRAZY, DHAL,*" *POCO SAID, HER VOICE LOUDER* than she meant it to be. "You spend a good part of a year getting to this place; you risk your life over and over to return the Tamorlee to the Ni-lach; now you want to steal it and take it somewhere else. It makes no sense!"

"Keep your voice down," Dhalvad cautioned, glancing down at the trail that passed beneath their porch. Ra-shun had set, and Ra-gar was fading into the western mountains, making the shadows deep within the forested city. He turned to Poco and caught her right hand.

"Please, Poco, listen to me. I know all that we've gone through to get here, but the Tamorlee needs me now—as a Healer. It's in pain."

"How could it be in pain?" Poco scoffed. "No one is hurting it unless Amet's doing something to it—not that I wouldn't put it past him!"

"It isn't Amet, Poco. It's something else."

Should he tell her? He gazed into her blue eyes and remembered how for months they had fought side by side, through and over every obstacle they had encountered on their journey to Jjaan-bi; how she had used her Ni gift of song to open the world gate that had led them to the Tamorlee; and how she had given him of herself, gifting him a son to love. If he could not trust her, he could not trust anyone. Still he hesitated, for there was still one fear he harbored and it had nothing to do with trust. It had to do with Poco's streak of stubbornness. If she realized that he was talking about a long and perhaps dangerous journey with no certain promise of a return, she was sure either to try to stop him or to insist upon coming along. He did not want her to come. He wanted her safe in Jjaan-bi, with Jiam.

"Come on, Dhal," Poco prompted. "Out with it."

Dhalvad drew her to the far railing overlooking the lake. "Poco, have you ever been lonely?" he asked as he stared down at the water, which was dark and still near the shore. A pair of white-breasted neeva birds flew down and skimmed the surface of the lake, hunting for waterbugs. A murmur of voices came from a nearby tree home, and somewhere in the distance came a shout and a splash, followed by laughter.

Poco frowned as she looked at Dhalvad. "What has loneliness to do with anything?"

"Just answer."

Poco drew a deep breath and released it, thinking back to less happy days she had spent as a chalk artist in Port Bhalvar, to a time between the deaths of her mother and her good friend Trass, to her discovery of Screech. Yes, she had been lonely—and defensive, always looking for something she could not name. Part of the something had turned out to be Dhalvad. The other part was a home and family, and acceptance among her own kind. Her mouth twisted in a wry grin. Well, two out of three was not bad. Given time, the third might also come to her. Of course, if Dhalvad meant what he said about stealing the Tamorlee, she could lose much more than her home, and that frightened her.

Dhalvad's crystal-gray gaze ensnared her. "Poco?"

"Yes." She nodded. "I know lonely. Why do you ask?"

"The Tamorlee's pain stems from loneliness, Poco. The Healer within me felt it but couldn't do anything about it." He hurried on, not giving her a chance to say anything. "The Tamorlee isn't just a crystal, Poco. It's a thinking, feeling being that has sensed one of its own kind awakening—and it wants to go and find it. It's waited for news of another like itself for several thousand years. Who am I to tell it that it can't leave here if it wants to?"

"If it's felt this way so long, why hasn't it said something to one of the Speakers?" she asked.

"It didn't understand its own feelings until it felt another fire stone awaken just recently."

"What about Amet? What does he say to all of this?"

"He doesn't know yet. The Tamorlee believes that Amet and the others on the Council would stop him if he tried to leave."

Him? Poco thought. She looked closely at Dhalvad, sensing that he was holding something back. "Have you thought about the danger you'd be in if you do as *it* asks?"

"Yes, I realize the dangers, but I can't simply walk away. I know how *it* feels. It's how I felt when I learned that I was one of the Ni-lach. The need to find my people became all-consuming. It's the same for the Tamorlee now!"

"Can't someone else . . ."

"Who?" Dhalvad exploded. "Who in Jjaan-bi would knowingly stand against the Speaker and the Council? Chulu, perhaps, or Caaras—though I doubt it."

"You've already made up your mind, haven't you?"

"Yes. I guess I have." He drew Poco's hand to his lips and kissed the backs of her fingers. "Angry?" he asked, looking into her eyes.

"Yes! But what good will it do me?" She pulled her hand free and turned to look out over the lake.

Dhalvad watched her as the silence grew between them. Chin up, back straight, her arms crossed in front of her, she looked ready to let loose with a few choice words. He sighed inwardly. How was he going to make her understand?

"Poco."

She turned, arms dropping to her sides. "How soon do we leave?"

Her words caught him by surprise. He had thought she would take more convincing, and instead she was— "*We?*" He shook his head. "No, Poco, not we. I'm going alone."

Her chin lifted a notch. "Just you and the Tamorlee?"

"Yes." He hurried on. "You know that I'd ask you to come if it wasn't for Jiam."

She cocked one eyebrow. "I'm to believe that, I suppose?"

"It's the truth! I swear!"

Poco pushed a strand of loose hair out of her face. "We can talk about who goes and who stays later. Right now I want to know how long this trip is going to take."

"I don't know. The Tamorlee isn't exactly sure where this other crystal is, but it thinks it can find it with my help."

"By that you mean your help as a Seeker?"

Dhalvad nodded.

"You mean to travel by the lesser gates?"

"I assume so, yes." Dhalvad replied.

Long ago the Ni had discovered a curious mode of transportation that involved patterns of energy and the ever-shifting structure of time and space. There were two kinds of gates. World Gates required a Singer to set the pattern, a Sensitive to hold the gate open, and a Seeker to complete the triangle of power necessary to travel from one world to another. There were only five world gate patterns known at that time; three led to inhospitable worlds where life would be difficult if not impossible for any length of time; the other two gates led to worlds already inhabited. One world was inhabited by the Trothgar giants, the other by the Atich-ar, a race of scaled humanoids who were believed to be the forerunners of the first Ni.

Lesser Gates were not as complex as World Gates, but in their own way they were just as dangerous to use unless one had a good mind and an eye for detail. By envisioning his or her destination within the shards of crystal set in the special rings all Seekers carried, a Seeker was able to teleport from one reality to another in a matter of seconds. The vision had to be firm in the Seeker's mind in order for the fire stone's power to work properly. A weak or incorrect vision could easily send a Seeker into the past, as had happened several times with Dhalvad; or worse, the Seeker could end up in aanaka, a type of limbo where death soon claimed those unable to free themselves with a clearer vision.

As a Singer, Poco was capable of singing up lesser gates, but only a Seeker could actually pass through those doorways. That meant that if Dhalvad chose to travel by the lesser gates, she would not be able to follow.

Poco reluctantly accepted the fact that she would probably have to forgo the trip. With that thought in mind, she began to think about what it would mean to stay behind.

"Dhal, what happens to us when Amet and the Council learns you are behind this theft? If you leave here the same time the crystal is taken, it won't be long before they add things up."

"I was thinking about that on my way home. There's only one way to ensure your safety, and that's for all of us to leave together. We'll find you, Jiam, Screech, and Gi a place to stay, then I'll return to the Tamorlee's room via a lesser gate, take the crystal, and return to you using the same gate."

"You've forgotten one thing," Poco said. "The fire stone ring you used to carry is now the Tamorlee, and without a ring you can't use the lesser gates."

"I know. It means I'll have to get another ring."

Poco's eyebrows raised. "Another theft? This is getting complicated. Dhal, where does it all stop? Theft, bribery—murder, perhaps?"

Dhalvad shook his head. "You know me better than that, Poco."

"I thought I did, but suddenly I don't like the sound of all this, and I don't like the idea of being left behind, nor will Gi-arobi or Screech. I think we'd better talk all of this over with them before any more plans are made.

Who knows, they may come up with something we haven't thought of."

Dhalvad turned and looked back out over the lake. "We can talk to them, but whatever we decide, we'll have to move quickly, because Amet will expect me to return tomorrow and tell him what the crystal wanted. I don't know how long I can put him off. If we have to leave quickly for some reason . . ."

Poco heard the worry in his voice and caught his chin with her hand, pulling his face around. "Don't worry so. We can be out of here in five minutes if necessary."

"There's no fooling you, is there?"

"I'm a Singer, Dhal. Your face can lie to me, but not your voice." As he pulled her close, she chose her words carefully. "Our future and the future of our son may well depend—" She broke off as Dhal suddenly pulled her back into the shadow of the porch. "Dhal, what's wrong?"

Dhalvad put his hand over Poco's mouth and edged them toward the doorway leading into the house. "It's Amet," he whispered as they stepped into the living room. "He's coming up the trail with some others. I don't want to talk to him right now, not until I've had more time to think things through."

Poco glanced around the room, which was lighted by a single overhead lamp containing luminescent fayyal rocks. There were few hiding places anywhere in the house.

"I've got to leave," Dhalvad said.

Poco thought quickly. "There's no way down without his seeing you now, even along the walkways. You'll have to climb up onto the roof and stay quiet."

"What will you tell him when he asks where I am?"

"I'll tell him you went for a walk down by the lake. Go on. I'll take care of things down here."

"Are you sure?"

She nodded and pushed him toward the kitchen doorway. He paused on his way through the kitchen and spoke to Screech, who was just rising from a comfortable position on the floor over in his favorite corner.

"Screech, someone's coming and I don't want them to find me here. Go in and back Poco up—gently. I don't want anyone hurt."

"Who comes?" Screech signed.

"Amet."

There was no need of further explanation. Screech coughed assent and glided to the living-room doorway just as Dhalvad disappeared out a side door near the main trunk of the tree that supported their home.

Poco went into Jiam's room, where she found Giarobi sitting on a chair next to the baby's bed. The olvaar was whistling softly to the child and rubbing his back. Jiam smiled when he saw his mother and rolled over, offering his arms to be picked up.

"Eating time?" Gi asked as Poco picked Jiam up.

"Not yet, Gi. We're having visitors."

"Who coming?" he demanded, jumping down from the chair to cross the room ahead of Poco.

"Amet and several others. They want to talk to Dhal, but he doesn't want to talk to them, so he's hiding."

"Dhal do something wrong?"

"Not yet, but he may in the very near future."

Gi cocked his head to one side as Poco stepped by him, his large golden eyes wide. "Not understanding, Poco."

"I'll explain later, Gi. Just whatever you do or say when our visitors arrive, don't tell them that Dhalvad is here. Understand?"

Gi whistle-clicked an affirmative and followed Poco down the short hall. They reached the living room just as a knock sounded on the side of the open door leading out onto the porch.

"Anyone home?" Amet called, hesitating in the doorway. He straightened as Poco and Gi emerged from the back part of the house. "Avto, Pocalina. Is Dhalvad home?"

"No, he's not, but come in," Poco said, moving forward. "Who's with you? Oh, Chulu! Welcome. And Tidul. I haven't seen you in days. What's going on?"

"We need to speak to Dhalvad a few minutes, Poco,"

Chulu said, stepping into the house. He was a good friend; Poco and Dhalvad both liked him, as did Screech and Gi-arobi. He was three times as old as Dhalvad though he hardly showed his age. Like all Ni, he was beardless, and when he smiled he showed fine white teeth. Only the laugh lines around his eyes suggested that he might be older than his companions. His green hair was a shade darker than Amet's, and at the moment his braid of authority was arranged over his right shoulder and fell just past his waist.

"Dhal isn't here right now," Poco began. "He came in a little while ago, then left. He said he had to do some thinking."

"About what?" Amet asked, still standing in the doorway. Tidul stood at his left shoulder.

"He didn't say," Poco answered.

"Do you know where he went, Poco?" Tidul asked politely.

"Down toward the lake, I think," she replied in her most innocent voice.

Amet's glance touched Screech where he lounged in the kitchen doorway. He then looked past Poco toward the hall leading into the bedrooms.

He doesn't believe me, Poco thought. Her heart beat faster. "What did you want to talk to Dhalvad about? Perhaps I could help you."

"It's about his gifting of the Tamorlee this afternoon, Poco," Chulu answered.

"And you can't help us unless he told you what the Tamorlee wanted with him," Amet said flatly. "Did he?"

Poco shook her head. "He did seem a little preoccupied, but if something was bothering him, he didn't say what it was."

Silence fell over the room as the three male Ni shared glances. Chulu turned to Poco and stepped closer. "How is Jiam?" he asked, trying to lighten the atmosphere in the room.

"He's fine. Would you like to hold him?"

"We haven't time for that!" Amet snapped at Chulu.

Chulu turned and gave Amet a stern look. "There's

always time to hold a child, Amet. Be patient. We can wait here for Dhalvad to return. How long do you think he'll be gone, Poco?"

Poco hated lying to Chulu. "I don't know."

She handed Jiam to Chulu and turned to the other two Ni. "If you'd like to stay, please make yourselves comfortable. I'll get us all something to drink. If you need anything, just tell Gi or Screech."

Amet frowned as Tidul moved into the room and took a seat on a long padded couch next to the window overlooking the lake. "This is wasting time," he complained.

"What would you have us do, Amet?" Tidul asked calmly. "Chase him the length of the lake? Chulu's right. Our best chance of finding him is to wait right here."

Gi-arobi waddled over toward Tidul as Chulu took a chair across the room. He hopped up onto the couch and came to stand at Tidul's shoulder. "Dhal be in trouble?" he asked.

"Not that I know of, Gi, but if he is, it's nothing we can't work out." Tidul was younger than Chulu though a lot heavier. His braid of authority was decorated with a red cord and white shells. His dark-green hair was almost black and matched the simple dark robes he always wore.

Tidul looked into Gi-arobi's eyes and smiled. "It's been several weeks since you've been to visit any of my classes, Gi. We miss you. What have you been doing with yourself, little friend?"

"New shipment at market—from Tre-ayjeel. Good food grows there," Gi answered.

"You're going to get fat one of these days, Gi," Chulu said, teasing the olvaar.

Gi patted his round stomach. "Eating muscle. Not fat!"

Amet crossed the room and passed around behind Chulu's chair, glancing into the open hall leading to the bedrooms. He continued moving restlessly around the room. At last he paused before a series of finely woven reed and grass mats that hung on the wall. "Who did these?" he asked.

Gi saw what Amet was looking at and answered. "Big Fur weaves grass. Pretty, yes?"

Amet looked at Screech, who had not moved since their arrival. "I had not realized that you were such an artist, Ssaal-lr," he said, using Screech's formal name.

Screech just stared at Amet.

A chill slipped down Amet's spine as he turned back to the room. The derkat had their own laws and form of government. Nomadic, traveling in large groups called radgs, they hunted for their survival and traded both with men and Ni, but it was hard to ignore the aura of wildness suggested by their powerful teeth and clawed hands and feet.

Amet finally took a seat on the opposite side of the couch from Tidul, his eyes never leaving the derkat. It was unusual for a derkat to choose the companionship of any other than its own kind. He was sure there was a story behind Ssaal-lr's close ties with Pocalina and Dhalvad, but so far he had not an inkling of what those ties might be.

Poco returned to the room carrying a tray of stoneware mugs filled with steaming rayil tea. "I thought you'd like something while you're waiting," she said, passing the tray around. She set it down on a low table near Chulu and took the baby from him. After she had settled herself in a chair nearby, Tidul handed her a cup.

Poco turned her attention to Chulu and asked after his wife, Naalan, who had recently returned from a trip to Uala, a growing Ni city on the western tip of Lake Haddrach. For the next few minutes the conversation revolved around Chulu's oldest son Telav, who lived in Uala and was helping the city council set up its own Learning Arc.

"They'll need a Singer to teach the young ones soon," Chulu told Poco. "Ever thought of becoming a teacher?"

Poco laughed. "I'm still learning myself. But yes, someday I think I might like to teach others what I've learned."

Amet watched Poco closely as she talked with Chulu. He, in turn, was watched by Screech, who could read body language as easily as others might read a passage in a book. A soft, low rumble of uneasiness escaped his mouth, and the fur on his back raised slightly.

Gi-arobi's sensitive ears caught the soft rumble of displeasure, and glancing over at his friend, he quietly slipped off the couch and padded over toward the kitchen doorway. He stopped by the derkat's legs and patted the nearest one.

Screech dropped a hand to the olvaar and drew him up to sit straddling one shoulder.

"What wrong?" Gi whispered in Screech's tufted ear.

"*Later,*" Screech signed.

"Gi not like later," Gi muttered. "Want answer now!"

"*Later,*" Screech repeated.

Gi leaned forward and grabbed at the top of Screech's arm. Screech caught him instinctively and lowered him to the floor.

Tidul caught the movement out of the corner of his eye and turned. "Where are you going, Gi?"

Pausing in the doorway, Gi saw the worried look cross Poco's face. "Gi hungry," he answered. Without another word, he turned and ambled into the kitchen.

"I'd better go see what he's after," Poco said, rising with the baby. "I'll be right back."

She crossed the room quickly and caught a look from Screech that said he would remain on watch. She was not surprised when she did not find Gi-arobi in the kitchen. The olvaar were curious creatures by nature; it was obvious that he had all the mystery he could stand and had gone to find Dhalvad to get some answers. She stepped to the back door, which was open for the breeze, and saw the last of Gi's hindquarters slip over the edge of the roof. How he knew Dhalvad was there was anyone's guess. She reentered the kitchen, hesitated a moment, then returned to the living room.

Amet watched closely as she took her seat again. She pretended not to notice.

Amet rose suddenly. "I'd like to warm my tea, Pocalina. Is there more hot water?"

"Yes. Let me get it for you," she said, starting to gather Jiam in her arms.

"No. Sit still," Amet said, moving toward the kitchen. "I'll help myself."

Screech straightened slightly as Amet approached. He cast a quick glance at Poco. She gave an almost imperceptible shake of her head.

Amet nodded to Screech as he passed the derkat and entered the kitchen. A minute later he returned carrying his tea. There was no steam rising from the cup.

"Gi doesn't seem to be anywhere in the kitchen," Amet observed casually as he crossed the room.

"I gave him a piece of fruit and told him to eat it outside," Poco said matter-of-factly. "He can be messy when he eats."

Amet looked down at Poco, his face cold with suspicion. He set his unheated cup of tea down and straightend. "I think we've wasted enough time here. Chulu. Tidul. Please come with me. We'll have to catch up with Dhalvad tomorrow." He looked at Poco. "Tell him that he's to meet with us in the morning at ten o'clock in my rooms. There can be no further delays. It's imperative that we know what transpired between Dhalvad and the Tamorlee as soon as possible!"

"Why don't you just ask the Tamorlee?" Poco snapped.

"I've already tried that!" Amet snarled. "It doesn't seem to feel like talking to me right now—only to Dhalvad! Tell him to come tomorrow! Ten o'clock! Is that clear?"

"Perfectly clear," Poco answered with icy calm.

Chulu heard the rebellion in Poco's voice and realized that Amet was making a mistake. She was not the kind of person one pushed. He touched her arm in passing and paused for a moment as Amet and Tidul stepped out onto the porch.

"Thanks for the tea, Poco. Tell Dhal, when you see him, that Amet is just worried. Also tell him that if he'd like to talk about what happened today with the crystal —well, I'd be happy to listen."

Poco relaxed slightly as she looked Chulu in the eyes. "Thank you for your understanding, Chulu. I'll tell Dhal what you said."

She waited until Chulu left, then signed for Screech to go after Dhalvad.

Screech remained where he was and raised his hands to sign. *"Amet threaten the radg. I'll kill him if my tiyah commands it."* The word tiyah in derkat meant "leader of the clan"; the tiyah was always female.

Poco laid Jiam down and went to stand before the derkat. She knew he was serious and actually perceived Amet as a threat to the family, but the simple codes of the derkat radgs did not always apply to the dealings of Ni-lach or men.

"Screech, you may be right about Amet," she said, signing as she spoke so there was no chance of misunderstanding. "You may also be wrong, and we must give him the benefit of the doubt. A few minutes ago I could have happily shoved Amet out our door, but that doesn't mean that I want him dead."

The tip end of Ssaal-lr's tail twitched back and forth. *"It is unwise to give your enemy the first move."*

"Screech, I don't look upon Amet as our enemy. He is the Speaker, and he's worried about the crystal. His behavior just now, though rude, does not call for drastic action on our part. Go now and find Dhalvad. We have a lot to talk over."

Chapter 3

POCO STOOD WITH DHALVAD AT THE EDGE OF THE porch.

"I'm afraid, Dhal," she said. "What if something goes wrong?"

"Nothing's going to go wrong! We talked this over last night. This is the only safe way to get you all out of here. Amet won't turn his attention to you as long as they have me, which should give you long enough to get where you're going. If my meeting with Amet goes well, there'll be nothing to worry about and I'll meet you in the village inn in Cybury in three days to decide what to do from there. If things don't go well, I want you to continue south along the Owri River to the Reaches. Screech will see you reach Bannoc from there. I doubt the Ni would try to bother you in Utura territory."

He caught her face with his hands and kissed her soundly. "You, Jiam, Gi, and Screech are all the family I have, and I want you safely away before I try to help the Tamorlee."

"If we're forced to go to Bannoc, how long before you come for us?"

"As soon as I can, I promise. A lot will depend on how fast I can secure a Seeker ring."

"Or the Tamorlee," she said softly.

Dhalvad nodded. "Or the Tamorlee."

"What're you going to tell Amet and Chulu this morning?"

"Part of the truth. If I speak to them as a Healer, perhaps they'll listen and be sympathetic to the crystal's need. If it was Chulu alone, I think I could convince him to let me take the Tamorlee for a little while. Amet is quite another matter."

Poco hugged him. "I wish I could come with you. I don't like being left behind."

"If this involved anything other than the Tamorlee," he said, pulling on the braid down her back to force her face up, "I'm sure you would be safe right here in Jjaanbi. But the Ni aren't rational when it comes to the crystal, at least Amet isn't, and I won't take a chance of his trying to get to me through you and Jiam."

Dhalvad left Poco and hurried down the trail, praying that his fears were groundless. If anything should ever happen to Poco or Jiam . . . A sudden feeling of being followed made him pause and look back, but he saw nothing unusual.

A short time later, he walked out from under the cool shade of the giant aban trees that sheltered the lane leading along the lake shore. He caught movement out of the corner of one eye and turned just as someone stepped out from behind the tree he had just passed.

Startled, he backed up a step and slipped off the trail. He almost lost his balance as leafy ground gave way to a muddy spot that grabbed at his foot.

Someone caught at his arm before he could fall, and he looked up into the face of the Ni who had startled him. His momentary flare of irritation turned to anger as he recognized Paa-tol, one of Amet's closest subordinates. So his earlier feeling of being followed had not been imaginary!

Paa-tol was tall and broader through the shoulders than the average Ni. His eyes were slate gray, and his hair was a deep forest green. His eyebrows slanted sharply upward, and his arched nose gave him a predatory look. He was fifteen years Dhalvad's senior and

stood high in the ranks of the Gerri-Mountain Draak
Watch. He was also a Seeker.

Dhalvad had dealt with Paa-tol on several occasions
and had found him laconic and extremely careful with his
opinions, which meant that one never knew precisely
where Paa-tol stood on any given subject. Poco called
him opportunistic. Dhalvad thought that dangerous was
a more apt description as he glanced at the three knives
sheathed in Paa-tol's chest harness. The older Ni also
carried a long sword at his left hip and a length of narrow
draak-hide rope at his belt.

Paa-tol's eyebrows lifted in question. "Going the
wrong way, aren't you?"

Dhalvad frowned. "Was Amet afraid I'd forget our
appointment?" he asked sarcastically.

"No," Paa-tol replied. "He only sent me to ensure you
were on time."

Liar, Dhalvad thought as he glanced downtrail past
Paa-tol. Seeing the direction of Dhalvad's gaze, Paa-tol
stepped to the left, effectively blocking the path. Twice
in the past he had underestimated the Healer. He would
not do so again.

"If you don't want to be late," he said, "you'd better
go along now."

Dhalvad shot him a venomous look. "Do I have a
choice?"

Paa-tol crossed his arms before his chest. "Your argument is with Amet, not me."

Dhalvad thought about Poco and Jiam and realized
that refusing to go along and insisting upon going home
first was sure to rouse suspicions. Better to go and meet
with Amet than to risk anyone discovering Poco and the
rest of the family in the midst of leaving.

Without a word, Dhalvad turned and headed for the
main entrance to the caves. Paa-tol hesitated a moment,
then followed, giving Dhalvad an escort whether he
wanted one or not.

Dhalvad greeted Jeran and his wife, Thayla, who
were on watch that morning, but he did not pause to visit
as was his usual custom.

Jeran raised an eyebrow in question as Dhalvad passed by followed closely by Paa-tol. Thayla caught his glance and shook her head frowning. Paa-tol was well known among the Guard, and it was obvious that he was escorting Dhalvad to some particular destination. Paa-tol ignored both guards and closed the distance between himself and Dhalvad.

The tunnels between the caves varied greatly in width, and the fayyal rocks that illuminated the passageways were not all of the same brightness, giving the tunnels an eerie glow.

Dhalvad heard Paa-tol's footsteps close upon him and cursed silently. He did not like the feeling of being herded like some straying bomal, nor did he like the feeling of being under guard, which was what it must have seemed like to those they passed as they wound their way toward Amet's quarters.

Dhalvad came to a fork in the tunnel and paused. The left tunnel led to the chamber holding the Tamorlee; the right went to Amet's rooms. He started to the right.

Paa-tol stopped at the junction and waited for Dhalvad to get a short distance down the tunnel before saying "They're waiting for you in the Tamorlee's chamber."

Dhalvad took another step or two before the words sank in. He stopped, turned, and came back to Paa-tol. He paused in front of him and looked him in the eyes. "You like playing with people, don't you?" he said softly.

Paa-tol returned Dhalvad's glare in silence. His expression was one of wry amusement.

"Some day, Paa-tol, you're going to push the wrong person," Dhalvad said. "And when he or she pushes back, you'll find yourself at the chewing end of a draak with no weapon at hand and no place to run!"

Paa-tol's eyes narrowed; his smile disappeared. "Is that a threat, Healer?"

"No threat, Paa-tol, just a warning." Dhalvad passed the tall Ni and headed toward the Tamorlee's chamber. When he reached the two guards stationed at the entrance to the chamber, he stopped and glanced back. Paa-tol was still standing where he had left him, his face deep in shadow. Dhalvad suppressed a shiver and turned back to the open chamber doorway.

Amet stood there watching him. "Come in," he said, stepping to one side.

Dhalvad walked into the room and heard the door close ominously behind him. He tried to shake the chill that skittered down his spine by concentrating on the five other Ni in the room. Besides Chulu and Tidul, he recognized the Master Singer, Lurral, a Seeker named Davano, and Chiilana, a female deldar, or psychic. Tidul, Lurral, and Chiilana were dressed in long ankle-length tunics, a mode of dress common for those working in the Learning Arc. The others wore short tunics and pants.

Dhalvad greeted everyone with a nod, honoring Chiilana by addressing her first. She was austere in dress and demeanor, but there was a lively wit behind those blue-gray eyes and a gentleness of spirit that spoke of a deep understanding of life. As a far-seer, Chiilana was often called upon to aid in decision making for the Ni of Jjaan-bi. Dhalvad had liked Chiilana from the moment he had met her almost a year earlier. He wished Poco shared his liking, but such was not the case; he thought it might have something to do with Chiilana's youthful beauty and a slight case of jealousy—which Poco vehemently denied.

He grinned to himself as he bowed to Chiilana and took her hand in his, thinking what Poco would say when he told her who had been at Amet's special meeting.

"It's good to see you, Dhalvad," she said as he released her hand. "It's been awhile since we've spoken."

"I've been busy with my studies on healing," he offered as an excuse.

"That's not all you've been busy with, according to Amet," she chided gently. "What have you done to the crystal?"

"Done? I don't understand."

"Nor do we," Amet said.

Dhalvad started, not realizing that Amet had moved to stand behind him.

The Speaker's hand fell heavily on his shoulder. "No

more evasions, Dhalvad. We *must* know what happened between you and the crystal yesterday."

Dhalvad shrugged out from under Amet's hand and turned to face him. He started to speak but swallowed his angry response when he saw the haunted look in Amet's eyes. He glanced over at Chulu, Tidul, and Lurral; all wore that same look of fear. What in the name of Rabin's Oath is wrong now? he wondered.

Chulu came up beside Dhalvad and motioned him toward a thick carpet of woven mats overlaid by a cushioning layer of spidermoss and an exquisitely designed handwoven blanket. "Please, Dhalvad, sit down and tell us what you can about yesterday. Pocalina told us you were disturbed by what had happened, but she couldn't tell us anything more."

Dhalvad relented and followed Chulu toward the improvised seating. Lurral, white-haired and oldest of those present, took a seat beside Dhalvad and gave him an encouraging smile. The others quickly made themselves comfortable, forming a circle on the large, cushioned blanket.

Dhalvad looked at the expectant faces surrounding him, then gazed past Amet at the crystal, set in its special place within the star-shaped carving on the floor. Where to begin? he thought. And how much to tell?

He looked into Amet's eyes and decided to withhold the part about his losing his position as Speaker, at least for the moment.

"We're waiting," Amet said impatiently.

Dhalvad's glance swept around the circle. "I came here yesterday at Amet's request," he began. "He said the Tamorlee wanted to speak to me. I linked with the crystal and discovered that it had called me because I was a Healer." His glance stopped at Chiilana.

"Are you telling us that the crystal is ill?" she asked.

"Yes, and in pain."

"Pain?" Tidul echoed instantly, gray eyes wide in surprise.

"Is it in the process of dissolution again?" Chulu asked, dismayed.

"No," Dhalvad answered quickly. "The transfer of being and knowledge from the original crystal to my fire stone was complete, and there should be no need of another transfer for several thousand years. The illness I'm speaking of is of the mind and soul, not the body."

A look of confusion passed among the listeners. Dhalvad turned to Amet, hoping that the Speaker might understand what he was about to say.

"Amet, you've linked closely with the Tamorlee hundreds of times during the year you've been Speaker. In all those times did you ever experience a surge of emotion coming from the Tamorlee, a feeling of sadness or lonliness?"

Amet frowned. "No, I did not. Are you trying to tell us that the Tamorlee is in pain because it's lonely?"

Dhalvad stiffened at the skepticism in Amet's voice. "That is precisely what I'm trying to say."

"You are crazy," Amet growled. "The Tamorlee is linked with as many as twenty-five Ni a day. There's no time for it to be lonely. You speak as if it had the same kind of emotions we do. How can—"

"Are you saying that it doesn't?" Dhalvad demanded. He turned to the others who sat facing him; their expressions were concerned—and uncertain.

"When I linked with the Tamorlee yesterday, the first thing I felt was a well of sadness so deep that it was physically painful. I responded as a Healer, seeking the reason for the pain, and with the help of the crystal I found the pain centered in loneliness, touched off by the crystal's discovery that another of its kind exists somewhere on Lach."

Confusion instantly turned to shock at that pronouncement, but before anyone could voice a question, Dhalvad raised his hands for silence.

"Please. Let me finish." He took a deep breath, gathered his thoughts, and continued. "I'm not sure about all of you, but for as long as I have known about the Tamorlee, I thought of it only as the Ultimate Historian, the Keeper of Ni knowledge, revered by my people for its ability to store truth and wisdom and return it upon demand. Now I know that the Tamorlee is much much more than that. It is a thinking, feeling being who has its own dreams and fears. One of those dreams involved a search for news of its own kind. As long as that search went unrewarded, it was content to be our historian, but now that is changed because it has felt one of its own kind awakening. Don't ask me how it knows. I cannot tell you. All I know is that it needs our help in finding another of its kind, and it has chosen me to—do whatever I can to help it begin a search."

"Another crystal," Chiilana breathed softly, eyes aglow with wonder. "Where is it, Dhalvad? Do you know?"

Dhalvad shook his head. "Neither does the Tamorlee —exactly."

"If the Tamorlee doesn't know, how are we to help it?"

"All of our Seekers could be sent out," Chulu said, excitement shining in his eyes. "If there's another crystal like the Tamorlee, it must be found and brought back here before it falls into unfriendly hands."

"The implications of such a find are staggering," Tidul offered, his own face lit with a feverlike passion. "I admit that I have never actually thought of the Tamorlee as being alive in the sense of having emotions. It's always just been there to speak to, to ask questions of, to record all aspects of our daily lives. Thinking of it in terms of a living entity or only one of an entire sentient race is a staggering revelation. Chiilana, you are deldar. Have you ever touched upon any of this in your readings?"

"No. This is all a surprise to me, but I agree with you. The discovery of another crystal like the Tamorlee will present a whole new aspect to Seeker knowledge and present us with some very interesting possibilities."

Throughout the discussion, Amet was strangely silent, and Dhalvad noticed that there was a look on his face that boded trouble. Amet turned and caught Dhalvad's glance; his frown instantly deepened. He stood up a moment later and, without a word to anyone, moved

over toward the star pattern on the floor. His actions
brought an abrupt end to the conversation.

Chulu started to rise. "Amet, what are you doing?"

Amet looked straight at Dhalvad. "I think it's time to
verify all that Dhalvad has told us—if we can." He
slipped a fire stone ring from the middle finger of his
right hand and walked the pattern of the star, touching
the fire stone to the small indentations at each point. He
then knelt before the handprint near the Tamorlee,
placed his right hand on the imprint, and set the fire
stone ring into the last indentation just in front of the
palm print, activating the link that would put him in
touch with the Tamorlee.

Chulu glanced at Dhalvad, tension visible in every
line of his body as Amet knelt with his eyes closed for
several minutes. Tidul was frowning, and Chiilana
seemed to be holding her breath.

Dhalvad looked briefly at each of those seated with
him and then at Amet. Would the Tamorlee back him up?
Or would it tactfully evade Amet's questions?

Amet straightened finally and turned to glare at Dhalvad. "You tell a fine story, Healer, but it seems that
you've left something out!" Amet stood and approached
the circle of Elders, his gaze never leaving Dhalvad's
face. "Suppose you tell us why the Tamorlee won't respond to a summons."

As he pushed to his feet, Dhalvad noticed Amet's
clenched fists. The others also rose, as if sensing a con-
frontation. "I don't know what you're talking about," he
said.

"You were the last to link with the Tamorlee!" Amet
snarled. "What did you do to it?"

"Do? I did nothing but listen."

"Then why won't it answer a summons? Why does it
shut me out?"

Dhalvad turned and looked down at the Tamorlee.
There was only one way to tell.

"May I try to contact the crystal?" he asked.

"I shouldn't let you, but..." Amet glanced at the
others. One by one they nodded assent. "I guess I have

no choice. Go ahead. The pattern is set. All it needs is your hand to seal the link."

Dhalvad nodded and walked to the place recently vacated by Amet. He knelt, took a deep breath, and released it slowly as he set his hand to the palm print. Nothing happened for a second or two. He began to think that he, too, would be rejected when suddenly he was caught in a whirlwind and sucked into a shimmering green vortex where he was greeted with joy and a wraparound warmth that made him fully a part of the Tamorlee's consciousness.

Avto, my friend. Welcome back. Have you made a decision?

Dhalvad sensed the crystal's excitement and expectation and wished he had a better answer to give the crystal. *Nothing is decided yet, my friend. You must be patient. I've been talking to the Elders, and I've told them about your possible discovery of another crystal. I haven't yet spoken about your request to leave Jjaan-bi. I don't think they're going to take it very well.*

Then best not to speak about it. We will just leave, you and I together. I don't think it will take very long to find my brother crystal.

I've been thinking about that and about what might happen if I took you from Jjaan-bi. If I use you to travel to other places, what is to prevent other Seekers from following us by drawing on you as a focal point?

It's possible, the crystal admitted, *but risky, as you yourself can testify. Remember when you used your father's fire stone ring the first few times, how it drew you to me, but not in the present? You almost became locked into the past. A few more hours there and you never would have been able to return to the present. Most Seekers are aware of the pitfalls of traveling blind and won't take such chances.*

Unless they're desperate, as they will be if you suddenly vanish, Dhalvad pointed out. *And that brings me to another thing. You want my help in finding this other crystal, but how are we to do that if neither of us has seen the place we're trying to find?*

I sense my dream brother somewhere east and south of us right now. We'll have to get as close as we can by traveling to reference points already within my sphere of knowledge.

And then?

Then I hope to draw upon my brother's energy pattern and find him as you first found me.

Dhalvad did not like the sound of that. *Tamorlee, you know I want to help you, and I will if I can, but before we go on this search, I think one of the Elders should be told what we're planning to do.*

Who would you tell?

Chulu. He's become a good friend, and I believe I could convince him of how important this is to you. Chiilana might also listen.

I will trust you to chose others to trust.

Before I break the link, may I ask why you closed everyone out but me?

I feared Amet might not let you link with me again. It was my way of forcing Amet to—

Dhalvad waited a moment, startled by the sudden cessation of thought patterns from the crystal. *Tamorlee? Are you still there?*

Silence.

Tamorlee? Is something wrong?

A tendril of energy swept up around Dhalvad's awareness, hugging him close. *My brother wakens! Feel him? He grows stronger! Come, Dhalvad! Together we will seek my dream brother! He broadcasts his presence unknowing. Look! He who holds him casts visions like a Seeker!*

Chapter 4 ✍

BHALDAVIN HELD HIS FIRE STONE UP AGAINST THE SKY, the sunlight enhancing the opalescent shimmer of greens and blues as he moved it back and forth. The tingle of energy that came from the exquisite crystal made him feel good inside. He called the fire stone Mithdaar, which in the Ni tongue meant "bold light."

He brought the crystal down and held it loosely in his hand, ceding to its constant desire for visual images. Such images were gained through a strange kind of rapport that linked him directly to the crystal. Mithdaar literally saw through Bhaldavin's eyes, experiencing and learning about the world through their symbiotic relationship.

The first time Bhaldavin had touched the crystal it had brought him out of a state of amnesia by unveiling a past that had included the deaths of his parents, the loss of his arm, and slavery. The return of memories long buried had been painful but necessary to cement the link between himself and the crystal. It had been the beginning of a friendship that had grown stronger and stronger through the years.

Bhaldavin sat quietly in front of the weathered wooden gates of the stockade that surrounded the building known as the mansion and gazed down into the lower city of Barl-gan. The crystal, which never tired of "seeing" through his eyes, absorbed the scene with hunger that manifested itself as a white pulsating light spiraling deep with the fire stone.

Barl-gan was built on tiers of rock running up the sides of the mountains called the Guardians. It was a dying city, a mountain stronghold that had been home to the First Men, the Ral-jennob, or Sun Travelers. In recent years the population had drastically declined until it was home to but a handful of their descendants, survivors of the Great Plague that had decimated the city hundreds of years earlier.

Bhaldavin's glance swept from east to west across vine-covered buildings and tree- and bush-choked roads. Barl-gan, or Barl's Holding, was also home to his family. He and Lil-el had crossed the dreaded Draak's Teeth Mountains ten years before along with four rafters bent on proving that Barl-gan did exist. He brushed the stub of his left arm and frowned, recalling the terrible climb and the bitter-cold weather high in the mountains.

It was the western mountains and the great escarpment called the Draak's Teeth that made them all prisoners in the city. Six months after they had made their successful climb over the Draak's Teeth and down through a deep gorge in the escarpment, an avalanche had closed off the gorge, sheering off tons of rock halfway down the pass and leaving a vertical wall that defied all attempts at climbing.

The warm season was upon them again, which meant that it was time to make an attempt at finding another route over or around the Draak's Teeth, a route that would not prove too dangerous for his children. There were three: Thura, age ten, even-tempered and growing daily into the image of her mother; Finnar, age seven, curious and forever getting into trouble; and Kion, named after Bhaldavin's father, only two years old.

Bhaldavin's glance shifted to the north. There was forest as far as he could see, and beyond the forest lay the wastelands and the desert. He had seen both and tasted their dangers. Four times in the last ten years he and Lil-el and one or two of their children had tried to find a way back to the Enzaar Sea and home, and four times they had been driven back: once by illness; twice by the Wastelanders, men who had once claimed Barl-gan as their home but who now saw anything emerging from the city as evil; and the last time, three years ago, by a fall that had nearly cost Bhaldavin his life.

His glance shifted down toward the foot of the city and Lake Thessel. The Selvarn River began at the north-eastern edge of the lake and was connected to the sea by the Niev Chain of Lakes, a ribbonlike waterway that beckoned westward. That was the only way he and Lil-el had not tried, simply because it would take them farther away from the Enzaar Sea rather than closer.

Theon, one of the men who had crossed the Draak's Teeth with them, was all for trying the water route if he could persuade his friend Gringers to come. He even had a raft built much in the style of the rafters' boat homes common to the marshlands of Amla-Bagor. Theon had some of the men of Barl-gan working on two more rafts so there would be room enough for everyone to come if they wanted to, which would mean a company of forty-seven, including Bhaldavin's family.

Numbers might make the difference, Bhaldavin thought. It would be worth a try, providing they could get Gringers to leave the city and all of its mysteries behind.

The gate behind him creaked on unoiled hinges. He turned and saw Gils Watcher, also called Birdfoot, step through the opening. Like many of the men still living in the city, Gils was the product of too much inbreeding. He fared better than some because his three-toed, splayed feet did not prevent him from walking or running, and though he could not speak, his mind was sound. Gils had a large mouth and protruding teeth and a too-large nose, but there was an openness and honesty in his brown eyes that made Bhaldavin trust him.

Gils smiled and let loose with a strange cackling sound, more a greeting than laughter.

Bhaldavin nodded. "Hello, Gils. Did you want something?"

The brown-haired man bobbed and softly thumped his chest with his fist, his sign for Gringers, the head and heart of Barl-gan over the last ten years. He then motioned for Bhaldavin to follow him.

"Gringers wants me?"

Gils nodded and stepped back through the gate. Bhaldavin followed, still holding Mithdaar as he walked toward the large stone building that housed the remaining citizens of Barl-gan. It had been dubbed "the mansion" by Theon years earlier, an apt description of the huge seven-story building with its large doors and windows and its four wind towers rising majestically above the roof.

Bhaldavin caught up with Gils as they reached the steps leading up into the mansion. The inside of the building was lighted by electricity that was produced by the four wind towers. The technology that changed wind to light was something that Bhaldavin did not understand, though Gringers had tried more than once to explain it to him. Gringers seemed to have a knack for understanding the strange tools and machines of the First Men, many of which he had discovered hidden away in locked rooms on the upper floors just below the wind towers. It was Gringers's dream one day to take all he had learned and return to his people, the rafters, to offer them the knowledge that would ease their day-to-day existence and perhaps eventually return them to the stars. A large dream for one man, Bhaldavin thought, but knowing Gringers's perseverance, he did not put it past him. Gringers was a leader by nature, and a man possessed of an insatiable curiosity. His friend Theon was a follower, one whose self-interests centered around comfort and gain. Bhaldavin had to smile to himself when he thought of the two men, because they were exact opposites in size as well as in character. Long before he had thought of both men as his enemies; he now considered them his friends.

Bhaldavin and Gils met Kelsan Watcher coming up

the steps that led to the infirmary one level belowground. Kelsan greeted his son with a nod and looked beyond him to Bhaldavin.

"Good. He found you. Gringers has need of your crystal. Gils will show you where he's working."

Kelsan Watcher had been second in command when Gringers and his small party had discovered Barl-gan, and upon the deaths of the twins who had ruled the city, leadership should have fallen to him. But Kelsan was a wise old man, content to play counsel to whomever the citizens chose for their ruler, and he did not seem to mind in the least that the chosen man was Gringers.

Bhaldavin even suspected that the old man might have pushed to have Gringers chosen, for he had an eye for reading character and instinctively knew where and how best each man could serve the city. For Gringers that service was as leader, while Theon's service oriented around the protection of the city and its forty-odd inhabitants. Bhaldavin and Lil-el had been chosen as teachers, bringing to the city their knowledge of everything from cooking with wild plants to recounting the history of Ni and men within the Reaches and the territories around the Enzaar Sea. Indeed, through Kelsan's careful guidance they had each found a useful niche within the small, dying community.

Dying. The word stirred a current of restlessness deep inside and once again Bhaldavin's thoughts turned to leaving Barl-gan. He had to leave soon, or he would be tied there forever, his own dreams abandoned in service to people who had no blood claims on him.

"Is something wrong, Davin?" Kelsan asked, noting the faraway look in Bhaldavin's crystal gray eyes.

Bhaldavin looked at the bent-over man whose will alone held the city together. What happens when you die? he wondered. What becomes of Barl's Holding then?

"No," he answered gently. "Nothing is wrong. I was just thinking about the rafts Theon is building, and how soon they'd be ready."

"It's pure foolishness to build those rafts!" Kelsan sputtered. "We'll never use them!"

"Maybe not, but they might be all that will save you from the Wastelanders one day."

A worried look crossed Kelsan's face. "Have Wastelanders been seen again?"

"Not since the beginning of the cold season, but now that it's warming up, you know they'll start raiding again. They always do."

Kelsan's face clouded with disgust. "They'll never be content until they kill us all. Can't they understand that we are men just like them?" He wiped at the spittle on his lips and looked into Bhaldavin's eyes. "Ignorance is dangerous, my friend, and I fear it will be the death of us one day."

Only if you let it, Bhaldavin thought. Come with Lil-el and me and the children. Leave this place and help us find a way back home, to a place where you all can live happily for the rest of your lives.

He would like to have spoken his thoughts aloud but knew that he could never make the citizens of Barl-gan such an offer because he had no way of knowing what kind of a life he himself would find if he ever managed to return to the place he had called home. Men had slaughtered his people and had driven them from their homes because the Ni were different and had special talents that men lacked. If men saw the Ni as abominations to be wiped from the face of their world, how would they look upon the mutated men who lived in Barl-gan? Surely not as long-lost brothers.

Kelsan shook his head and slapped Bhaldavin lightly on the arm. "Well, never mind the Wastelanders right now. Gringers is waiting for you. Go along. We can discuss Theon's rafts later tonight after supper."

Bhaldavin followed Gils past the stairway to the lower levels and took another stairway leading upward. As they climbed the seven flights of stairs to the wind tower, Gils pressed buttons on the walls, turning lights on before them and off behind. It was against the rules to be wasteful of the energy stored within the wind tower generators.

When they reached the seventh floor, Bhaldavin followed Gils through several rooms littered with wooden boxes of various sizes. The contents of each box was labeled on one side. The boxes represented ten years of work. Gringers said that each box contained some portion of the Ral-jennob's technology and notes he had taken on the function of each item. What Gringers intended doing with the boxes was something of a mystery, for if he and Lil-el had failed to find a way over or around the Draak's Teeth in ten years, how did Gringers hope to ever convey all of the boxes of so-called treasures back to his people?

They worked their way to a room situated below the northeast wind tower, climbed a final set of stairs that passed a landing for the roof, and continued on up into the wind tower. There Gringers awaited them, the soft rushing sound of wind, pushing at thin metal fans somewhere above, giving the room a sound all its own.

Gringers was seated on the floor writing in a journal he held in his lap. He looked up and smiled as they climbed the last few steps. "That didn't take you long, Gils," he said, setting the journal down and rising to his feet. He turned to Bhaldavin. "Where did he find you?"

"Near the gate. I was waiting for Lil-el." Bhaldavin looked around the circular room. His glance took in tables littered with metal boxes, levers, buttons, and small piles of screws, bolts, and metal objects that Gringers had taken apart and had not been able to piece back together. Wires ran here and there. Several were connected to nearby light sockets.

Bhaldavin shuddered, remembering a day just a year earlier when he had come to the tower to find Gringers lying on the floor barely breathing and a fountain of firelike sparks shooting out from one of the Ral-jennob boxes attached to a light socket. Gils had had the presence of mind to cut off the power leading to the box. They had then carried Gringers down to the infirmary, where Kelsan had taken over. Gringers had survived, but since then he was extremely cautious when handling the power generated by the wind towers.

Bhaldavin openly admitted that the light power frightened him. He wished that it frightened Gringers just a little more; perhaps then the man would not take such chances with it.

Gringers was a tall, strong man of thirty-five, and his black hair was just beginning to show glints of gray at the temples. His red-bronzed skin, deep-set dark eyes, and long nose spoke of Kinsa bloodlines.

According to rafter history, a man named Kinsa had been one of the First Men who had left Barl-gan a thousand years before and had taken up rafting with Ardenol, leader of one of five expeditions searching for new and safer territories to live in.

The First Men had come to the world they called Verdraak in a spaceship called *Tappon's Pride*, and though the early history of Barl-gan was not complete by any means, the few life recorders found within the city had each given up certain facts that made it clear that the Ral-jennob had come from another world far advanced in technology and social and economic systems.

The life recorders also confirmed the truth behind the legend of Nathan Ardenol, who had led an expedition up over the Draak's Teeth over a thousand years before. Gringers believed that Nathan Ardenol and those who had followed him had reached the lakes of Amla-Bagor and had settled to become rafters. He also believed that two of the other expeditions were responsible for settling the Enzaar Sea territories. One expedition had been composed of a high majority of Utura, a dark-skinned race who had settled in the Semco Hills north of the sea. The other expeditionary force had settled at the southern edge of the sea. Their descendants called themselves the Sarissa. Both races claimed to have reached their homelands by boats.

Little was known of the other two expeditions except the direction taken when they left: one had headed north across the desert, the other south into the mountains. Why no one from any of the expeditions had ever returned to Barl-gan was a mystery, unless the dissension among the people of the city had been much deeper than the one reference to it made it out to be.

Gringers crossed the floor, stepping carefully over the remains of his last mechanical dissection. His glance came to rest on the small leather bag hanging from a cord around Bhaldavin's neck. It looked empty.

"Davin, do you have your crystal with you?" he asked.

Bhaldavin noted the direction of Gringers's glance. "It's not in there. I have it here." He held out his hand. The crystal was warm to his touch, and as he opened his hand, it glowed with an inner fire that pulsated much like a heartbeat. He sensed its hunger and eagerness to learn. He smiled inwardly, for it made him think of seven-year-old Finnar and his constant barrage of questions, jumping from one subject to the next with barely a breath's pause, absorbing knowledge as if he feared to lose what he could not understand.

"More experiments?" Bhaldavin asked.

"Always," Gringers replied, smiling. "I only need the crystal for a little while. I can't get this large machine behind me to work properly. All I get is noise when I push the on button." Gringers pointed to a black button on the side panel of a large machine standing waist high from the floor. "I think it needs more power than what I can tap from the wind tower. I thought your crystal might help."

Bhaldavin hesitated, as he did every time Gringers borrowed the fire stone. The crystal meant nothing more to Gringers than an energy source. But to Bhaldavin, it was much more—though no one seemed to understand him when he spoke about the spirit dwelling within the crystal. He considered telling Gringers no, remembering all the times he had argued with the man over the use of the crystal, and how many times Gringers had persuaded him to let him use it just once more. He shook his head, disgusted with himself. Just this one last time, he promised himself. "Where do you want it?" he asked.

Gringers moved over to the machine and touched an

open panel on the top of it. "Here, I think."

Bhaldavin looked down into the panel opening and saw minute wires running back and forth, each set into pinprick holes that accessed the insides of the machine. He set the crystal down gently, ready to snatch it up at the first sign of something going wrong, as had happened on more than one occasion.

Several seconds passed, then small lights began to flick on along the slanted panel at the front of the machine. Bhaldavin checked the crystal to make sure it was all right.

"What's the machine supposed to do?"

"I'm not sure," Gringers answered, his eyes wide with fascination as more lights turned on and the broken whirring sound issuing from the machine faded to a soft hum. "But I think this machine is directly linked to the star beacon."

A shiver of uneasiness darted up Bhaldavin's spine as he remembered words spoken ten years before by a dying man. "*The gods who brought men to this world will return one day, and the star beacon will guide them.*"

He had not thought much about the star beacon in a long time, because Lil-el had convinced him that if men's gods had not answered the beacon's summons in over a thousand years, either they were not listening, or the machine was not working properly.

What if men's gods suddenly did return? How would it effect his own people? Men and Ni had gotten along fairly well for over a thousand years, until the Sarissa had gotten it in their minds to eliminate the Ni from their lands for reasons known only to them. Memories of running from Sarissa blades made his heartbeat quicken. If men's gods were like the Sarissa, he wanted nothing to do with them.

A strange noise began to issue from the machine; it sounded like garbled speech. Bhaldavin was suddenly filled with a premonition of disaster.

"Gringers, I want my crystal back! Now!"

Gringers snatched at Bhaldavin's wrist as the Ni

reached for his crystal. "Not yet!" he cried, turning Bhaldavin halfway around. "Leave it alone!"

Bhaldavin tried to free himself. "Let me go!"

Gringers pulled him back away from the machine and tightened his grip. Then he turned to Gils, who stood just behind them, watching the fight with startled eyes. "Go to the upper tower and see if the star beacon is doing anything different."

Gils bobbed his head and darted out of the room.

"Gringers! Let me go!" Bhaldavin yelled.

"Only if you'll stand here quietly and not interfere."

Bhaldavin knew he was no match for Gringers's strength. He nodded, and Gringers slowly released him.

Gringers saw the anger on Bhaldavin's face but could not fathom its cause. He knew that Bhaldavin was sensitive about how the crystal was used, but he had asked for—and received—permission. He cursed silently, realizing that it had been a mistake to have given Bhaldavin the crystal in the first place. *He just doesn't realize its worth,* he thought.

"What's wrong, Davin? You said I could use it."

"I changed my mind!" Bhaldavin snapped.

"But way?"

Bhaldavin searched for the words to explain what he was feeling. "There's a wrongness here, a danger . . ."

"To whom? Us?" Gringers asked, his anger quickly forgotten. He was too wise a man to ignore a Ni warning. The rafters of Amla-Bagor would not have survived long in the swamplands if it had not been for the Ni-lach and their sensitivity to danger.

Bhaldavin did not hear Gringers. The cadence of the unknown language had cast a spell over him, and he stood quietly listening as he stared at the crystal glowing brightly in its niche in the machine. A strange feeling came over him. Without consciously realizing what he was doing, he stepped past Gringers and set a finger to the crystal. It was done so quickly and smoothly that Gringers could not stop him.

"Davin? What are you doing?" Gringers demanded. He looked from the crystal to Bhaldavin's blank stare, his frown of annoyance slipping away. "Davin? Are you all right?"

Bhaldavin was drifting in a black void where there was no up or down, no right or left. He felt something pulling him along. A tingling sensation ran from his fingertips up his arm to the base of his neck and exploded in his mind. It was a familiar touch.

Mithdaar, he thought. *I feel so strange. Where are we?*

As if in answer to his question, he became aware of movement in the dark void around him. The darkness began to fade and was replaced by shades of blue and gray. A large oval room suddenly appeared, and within it he counted three yellow spheres of light. Panels of red, green, and gold lights pulsated around the perimeter of the room, and the floor, if floor it was, seemed to heave and flow like fog shifting in currents of air.

One of the yellow spheres suddenly bobbed upward and came toward him. In the blink of an eye a silver shaft of light appeared where once there had been a yellow globe. The shaft of silver wavered, solidified, and took on bulk. What looked like a face appeared within the upper fifth of the growing form: mouth, nose, eyes— eyes that had no white in them, amber-gold eyes that seemed to burn with intensity.

Fear blossomed in Bhaldavin's mind as Mithdaar drew him closer to the image of light and began to absorb the essence of the dreamlike being they confronted.

Dream? Is that what it is? he wondered. All just a dream?

The light creature produced two arms that seemed to beckon Bhaldavin closer. A sudden crackling sound erupted between himself and the light creature as it extended a fog-enshrouded hand. Amber eyes enlarged and shimmered in what Bhaldavin later would recall as a look of sheer amazement as Mithdaar sought information as it always did, gorging on whatever knowledge was available without regard for the one from whom it was taken.

There followed an explosion of light so blinding that Mithdaar and Bhaldavin were driven back into the dark

void. The taste of the light creature was firmly embedded
in their minds and with it a feeling that they had stirred
something extremely dangerous.

Mithdaar and Bhaldavin had never been as close as
they were in those few moments of existence in another
reality. Bhaldavin could actually feel the crystal struggling to understand what had happened and to place the
knowledge it had gained within a workable context that
made sense. He wanted to help but had no idea how to
explain what he, too, did not understand.

A sudden thought came to him. It shattered the void
surrounding them and brought them both back to their
own reality.

"The gods!" he hissed softly. "Mithdaar found the
Ral-jennob!" He looked down at the crystal, his face
blanching white.

"No!" he yelled, snatching the crystal from its resting
place. He turned and in one swift motion dodged past
Gringers and headed for the stairs.

Gringers started after him, then stopped as the machine behind him grumbled to a halt, its lights flickering
out until the slanted panel went dark but for two lights.
Gringers walked over and pushed the off button, then
stood quietly looking at the machine as Bhaldavin's footsteps faded down the stairs. He was disgusted by his
own ignorance and inability to fully comprehend the machines that surrounded him and now this business with
Bhaldavin and the crystal. A doubt flickered through his
mind. Something had frightened Bhaldavin badly. He
thought over the Ni's few whispered words trying to
make sense out of them. *The gods! Mithdaar found the
Ral-jennob!*

The only gods he knew of were those of legend, the
Sun Travelers, who were either the ancestors of the First
Men or those responsible for bringing men to Lach.
Were the Ral-jennob really somewhere out among the
stars waiting for a signal from the star beacon? Had
Bhaldavin actually managed to reach them—if only for a
few seconds? The thought was frightening, yet deep in-
side he felt elated. As he turned the room lights off and

started back downstairs, he mind was filled with imaginary scenes of the first meeting between himself and the Ral-jennob. He had long dreamed of the Star Travelers and had always envisioned them as manlike. To think that he might soon know the truth! He hurried his footsteps, excitement pushing all fears aside. He had to find Bhaldavin and try to reestablish contact with whomever or whatever the crystal's energy had summoned. If the Ral-jennob were out there, he damn well meant to contact them again!

Bhaldavin finally reached the ground floor and ran down the hall leading outside. Theon stepped out of the dining hall as Bhaldavin ran by. He caught him by his arm and swung him around.

"Where're you going, Little Fish? Why the hurry?"

Bhaldavin wrenched from his grasp and continued on down the hall, Theon's voice echoing in his mind. *Little Fish.* The name brought memories surging upward, memories of being a slave to Theon's brother, Garv, of seeing the big man die, of months spent among the rafters of Amla-Bagor learning how to sing draak.

He angrily pushed all those thoughts aside and fled out into the open. He had more important things to worry about.

Theon cocked his head in puzzlement as he watched Bhaldavin disappear outside; then he turned and went upstairs, sure he would find Gringers where he always found him, puttering around with the strange tools and machines the First Men had used. Theon did not share Gringers's fascination with the past. In fact, after ten years of being in the same place, he was growing restless and more than a little disgusted with Gringers's stubbornness. Every year Gringers promised him that when the warm season came, they would get their things together and try to find a way back to civilization. That meant the Enzaar Sea territories and, as far as he was concerned, the Reaches, where he had grown up. If they did make it back home there would be a few people he would have to avoid in order to remain healthy, but he would willingly take the risk. Anything was better than remaining in Barl-gan.

Bhaldavin ran down the path toward the main gate and ducked through the narrow opening. Moments later he was jogging down the path that led to a series of switchbacks that would take him down to the lake. He did not think about where he was going. He just wanted to get away from everyone for a little while, to sit and think quietly where no one would disturb him.

Something moved in the shadows of one of the old deserted buildings as he passed by. It crept out toward the edge of the dirt roadway and watched his progress with unfriendly eyes.

The cry of a neeva bird flowed out of the shadows and was answered by a similar cry somewhere in the city below. Unheeding, Bhaldavin continued his downward journey, his thoughts centered on the crystal he carried and how best to protect it, for Gringers was sure to want it again, especially after what had happened. He reached for the bag at his neck and slipped Mithdaar inside, dissolving his link with the crystal.

Chapter 5 ✒

DHALVAD'S MIND WAS FLOODED WITH QUESTIONS AS soon as the link with the other crystal faded. He had been able to pick up on the visual perceptions of the one who carried the fire stone, but had received no real clear picture of the Ni. That the carrier was Ni he was certain, because men did not seem able to link with the fire stones in the same way that the People could. He had also heard the voices clearly but had been unable to catch a place name. Most disturbing was the last part of the linkage, where the crystal had been used to upgrade the energy of a machine called a star beacon. What was a star beacon? And why had the carrier so feared it?

Dhalvad sensed a tremor in the mind-to-mind link he still had with the Tamorlee.

You share my thoughts as well as my questions, Dhalvad, the crystal said. *The carrier of the fire stone acted as if there was great danger attached to the machine that the man called Gringers activated with the crystal. It bothers me.*

Did you recognize any of the places we saw? Or any of the people? Dhalvad asked.

No. All was unfamiliar—not within my sphere of knowledge.

Were you able to reach deeper than I and touch the crystal's thought patterns?

No. Such depth in linkage comes only with direct contact or close proximity, and then I can touch only surface thoughts.

Can we reach the carrier and the fire stone from here?

No. We must get closer. Dhalvad, I tire. I must release you now. It's been too much of a drain on my energy to hold contact at such a distance for so long a time. Return tomorrow please. We'll talk then.

Dhalvad felt another tremor. There was a moment or two of disorientation as the link was broken, the raggedness of the separation proof that the Tamorlee had delved deeply within itself in order to maintain contact with Mithdaar.

Dhalvad opened his eyes. He was still kneeling on the stone floor, his hand pressed to the pattern on the floor. A wave of dizziness swept over him as he lifted his head.

"He's with us again," a voice cried softly.

Dhalvad saw Chulu's anxious face and felt his hands steadying him. "Dhalvad, are you all right? You were with the Tamorlee a long time."

Dhalvad tried to respond, but his mind seemed sluggish. Another face appeared. It was Amet. His narrow-eyed glare sent warning shivers up Dhalvad's spine. He tried to will the fogginess from his mind, but a buzzing in his ears told him that this time he would not have to pretend to faint.

"What did you find out?" Amet demanded. "Why won't the Tamorlee talk to anyone but you?" He grabbed a handful of Dhalvad's hair as his head fell forward. "Answer me!"

Startled, Chulu caught at Amet's arm and growled, "Stop it! What are you trying to do?"

Amet tried to stare Chulu down. When he found he could not, he released Dhalvad and stood up. "He pulled a fainting act on me before, but this time he won't slip away without answering my questions!"

He left Chulu, went to the door, opened it, and signaled to the two guards stationed there. "The Healer has fainted again. Take him to the room down the hall and *this time* see that he stays there after he wakes, even if you have to use force. Is that clear?"

The two guards nodded and came into the room. Chulu stepped back and watched as they picked Dhalvad up gently. He met Tidul's glance as Lurral and Chiilana went to speak to Amet. Tidul was frowning, and it did not take much to guess that this friend was disappointed in Amet's behavior and no doubt would have a few things to say about it when he and Chulu were alone.

Chulu decided not to stay to hear what Lurral and Chiilana had to say to Amet. He knew that both of them liked Dhalvad and were sure to be concerned for his welfare. He could guess at their response to Amet's insensitivity.

"Amet," Chulu said, moving toward the door, "I think I'll go with Dhalvad, if you don't mind."

"Go ahead. I'll be along shortly myself. I want to be there when he wakes up."

Chulu followed the guards and their burden down the tunnelway and into the waiting room reserved for those who had come to gift the Tamorlee with their memories. Such gifting was usually scheduled by Amet. Due to the unusual behavior of the crystal the last two days, all gifting had been postponed, and the room was empty.

They made Dhalvad as comfortable as possible on a cushioned couch and propped his feet up on a pillow, hoping to stir the circulation of blood to his head. After that the guards retreated to the doorway and studiously avoided meeting Chulu's glances when he looked their way. They sensed that something was wrong among those in authority and wisely chose to stay out of the middle of things.

Amet arrived a few minutes later. "Is he still out?"

Chulu nodded.

Amet pulled something from a pocket of his long, wine-colored overtunic, leaned over Dhalvad, and placed it near his nose. There was the soft crackling noise of dry leaves as Amet crushed a small cloth pouch between his fingers. A pungent smell entered Dhalvad's nostrils. A second whiff of the noxious odor made Dhalvad cough. He opened his eyes, which instantly began to water. He saw Amet's hand close to his face and pushed it away.

"I thought that might bring you around," Amet said.

Chulu frowned at Amet as he helped Dhalvad sit up. "How are you feeling, Dhal?"

"Tired," Dhalvad answered as he swung his feet off the couch. A wave of nausea hit him suddenly, and he leaned forward, thinking he was going to be sick. He sat for long moments with his elbows braced on his knees, his head in his hands.

"What happened, Dhalvad?" Amet pressed. "What's wrong with the Tamorlee?"

"Give him a few minutes, Amet!" Chulu said, barely suppressing his anger.

"So he can dream up more excuses for not answering my questions? I think not! Dhalvad! I want an answer and I want it now! Why won't the Tamorlee talk to anyone but you?"

Anger pushed the queasiness away, and Dhalvad lifted his head. Damn, how tired he was of Amet's aggressive attitude. Ever since Amet had been named Speaker for the Tamorlee, he had grown more and more authoritative. Commanding this—dictating that. The power one wielded as Speaker had simply gone to Amet's head. Well, Dhalvad thought ruefully, he knew one quick way to deflate that pumped-up ego, but in doing so he would be placing himself in a position he truly did not want.

Amet took Dhalvad's hesitation as a refusal to answer and reacted with uncalled-for violence that caught both Dhalvad and Chulu off guard. The open-handed blow across the face knocked Dhalvad back flat onto the couch. Amet followed up by grabbing a handful of Dhalvad's tunic at the chest and jerking him back upright, his hand coming back to strike again.

Chulu recovered and grabbed Amet's arm. "What in

the name of Cestar's Eyes are you doing?" he yelled. "Amet, have you gone crazy?"

Amet twisted free of Chulu's grasp and stood up. "If I'm crazy, it's because of him!" he shouted, pointing at Dhalvad.

Dhalvad's face stung where Amet had slapped him, and the pain had done nothing to improve his temper. "You want to know what the Tamorlee means by shutting you out?" he yelled, his raised voice bringing the two guards into the room. "It means that it has chosen another Speaker! It doesn't want you any longer! In fact, it told me that it had made a mistake in choosing you in the first place!"

A flush of blood suffused Amet's face. "Liar!"

Dhalvad lunged off the couch and stood to face Amet. "I don't lie!"

"Don't you? And how are we to test this startling 'truth' of yours? We certainly can't ask the Tamorlee, can we? But you have that all figured out." Amet's chin lifted. "I bet I can even guess who the new Speaker is to be! You!"

"Yes!"

"You take a lot upon yourself, Dhalvad! Most would think being Healer was enough, but not you! No. You want it all!"

"I want nothing more than to be what I am—a Healer!" Dhalvad shot back. "But if the Tamorlee has chosen me and will accept no other, then I don't see that either of us has anything to say in the matter!"

Chulu stood to one side, eyes wide in alarm at the growing realization that there was more at stake than a personality conflict. "Please," he said, stepping in between the two. "If what Dhalvad says is the truth, the Council must be convened immediately and we must set this matter straight." He looked at Amet, his expression pleading. "Without any more violence."

Chulu took a deep breath and faced Dhalvad. "Is it true, friend? Does the Tamorlee wish to name another Speaker?"

Dhalvad nodded, not once taking his glance from Amet.

"I don't believe him!" Amet snapped. "And until someone else can link with the crystal to learn the truth, I intend to disregard all he's told us."

"This will have to be put before the Council, Amet," Chulu insisted. "And the sooner the better."

Amet noticed the two guards still standing inside the doorway. "All right, Chulu, I agree. It's early still. You go and speak to the Council members and see if you can get them to meet sometime this afternoon. Meanwhile, I'll go back and try to link with the crystal again."

"And Dhalvad?" Chulu asked, glancing at his friend.

"He stays here under guard. I want him where I can find him. I think the Council will also want him available."

Chulu nodded and put a hand on Dhalvad's arm. "I'm sorry, Dhal, but I think it will be better if you stay here, at least until we can get this mess straightened out. Would you like me to stop and tell Poco what's happened?"

Dhalvad thought quickly. Like Paa-tol, Chulu could not be allowed to find their home empty, lest it stir his curiosity and, in the process, give Amet an opportunity to twist the truth into something ugly. Perhaps a slight shading of the truth would serve to misdirect Chulu for the moment.

"Poco may not be home right now, Chulu. She said something about practicing her singing off where she wouldn't disturb anyone. I think she took Jiam, Gi, and Screech with her. I don't know when she'll be back. Probably not until later this afternoon."

Chulu looked relieved. "Well, we ought to be able to get a Council decision by that time, so you can tell her all about this yourself."

"Providing that we learn he isn't lying," Amet corrected.

"Please, Amet," Chulu pleaded. "Let's say no more until we can bring this all before the Council." Chulu gave Dhalvad an encouraging nod and left.

Dhalvad turned to find Amet staring at him as if he were an enemy. He met that look without flinching, remembering an old adage that his foster father had taught him. "Run before the gensvolf and he'll eat you alive."

A midday meal was brought to Dhalvad several hours later, and when he had finished eating he was escorted to another room deeper down the tunnelway past Amet's quarters. When he asked the reason for his being moved, the guards could only tell him that it was at Amet's orders.

Time passed slowly. Dhalvad grew impatient and stood and paced the confines of the small sparsely furnished room. He wondered what was keeping Chulu and the others on the Council. Surely they had had time enough to meet and talk things over. Why had they not called for him? Worried that things were not going to go as he had planned, he returned to the narrow couch standing next to the back wall and sat down. The soft glimmer of fayyal rocks lighted the small room clearly. He glanced at the table and chair to his left and the clay chamberpot in the far corner to his right. The walls were bare, and there was but one entrance to the room. It was definitely not the place one would chose to spend a lot of time.

He lay back on the couch, his hands beneath his head, his thoughts centered on Poco, Jiam, Gi, and Screech, and how far they had managed to go that day. With luck they would reach Cybury in two days' time. Damn, he did not like the idea of them making the trip alone! But where else might they be safe for a few days? Would they do as they had promised if he did not show up—go on to Bannoc without him?

He sat up and rubbed a hand across his eyes. "I have got to get out of here," he said softly to himself. "I've got to find another fire stone ring and get out of here so I can meet them in Cybury. Come on, Chulu! Where are you? What's taking so long?"

A few minutes later the latch on the door rattled announcing visitors. Dhalvad stood as the door opened.

His shoulders sank a little when he saw it was Amet, not Chulu. "Is the Council ready for me?" he asked.

"Soon," Amet replied. He stepped into the room and closed the door behind him. "First we need to talk."

"About what?" Dhalvad demanded impatiently.

"Sit down."

Wary but unsure, Dhalvad hesitated. He finally did as Amet ordered, seeing no reason to antagonize him any more than he had. At that moment getting out of there seemed much more important than thwarting the Speaker.

Amet moved over to the table and sat on one edge, his arms crossed over his chest. His hair had been carefully rebraided, and he had changed into a long blue robe with intricate designs in white thread worked into the cuffs and collar.

Very impressive, Dhalvad thought, eyeing the Speaker. I'm sure the Council will be properly intimidated, but I'm not!

Amet's glance swept the small room. "I'm sorry your accommodations are so austere, Dhalvad. We were in a hurry and we hadn't time to—"

"The room is fine," Dhalvad interrupted, "but I think I've been here long enough, so why don't we just go and meet with the Council and get this over with?"

"Patience. You'll meet with them soon enough. Right now I've something I want to say." Amet's gaze dropped to the floor, then flicked back up to Dhalvad.

"Dhalvad, could you tell me where Pocalina is right now? She doesn't seem to be home."

"Why do you want to know?"

"I don't want her to worry about you. Do you know where she is?"

Dhalvad's heartbeat quickened. "Not precisely, no. She said something about going for a walk."

"All day long?"

"Where she goes and for how long is her business, Amet," Dhalvad responded sharply, a tremor of uneasiness creeping up his spine. What was all this about Poco?

"She won't be worried when you don't return home tonight?" Amet asked, arching an eyebrow.

Dhalvad stood up, fists clenched at his sides. "You intend keeping me here all night?"

"Tonight, tomorrow night, and for some time to come, I think," Amet answered, also rising.

"You can't!'" Dhalvad yelled. "I've done nothing wrong!"

"You'll have to convince me of that, I'm afraid."

"How?" Dhalvad demanded angrily.

"By helping me to link with the crystal."

"Amet, it won't do you any good!"

"I think it will."

"You're wrong."

"You refuse to help me link with the Tamorlee?"

Dhalvad saw a strange glint in Amet's eyes and hesitated. What was the Speaker after? "What happens if I help you link with the crystal and it verifies what I've told you?"

"I don't think it will," Amet replied arrogantly, "but if it does, I suppose I'll need your help more than ever."

"My help? After all of this? You're crazy!"

A sly smile touched Amet's face.

Suddenly Dhalvad understood. "You mean to be Speaker whether or not the crystal will have you!" He shook his head in disbelief. "You won't be able to pull it off, Amet. The Council will learn the truth eventually. If not from me, then from someone else."

"I can handle the Council," Amet said. "With your help."

"No, Amet. You'll never get my help in that."

Amet raised a hand. "Before you go any further, I've something to show you. I think it will help you to see my side of things." He turned, stepped to the door, opened it, and beckoned to someone outside.

Paa-tol strode into the room carrying a small blanket-wrapped bundle in his arms.

Dhalvad's heart thudded heavily in his chest. "Jiam!" he cried, starting forward.

Amet stepped in front of him. "Easy, it's not your son." He turned to Paa-tol. "Show him."

Paa-tol flipped the blanket back, eyes glinting with amusement at the fright Dhalvad had exhibited. "Not your son," he said, "but one equally important to you, we think."

Gi-arobi squinted at the sudden light and squirmed in Paa-tol's hold, straining against the gag that bit cruelly into his tender mouth.

"Gi!" Dhalvad cried. His glance lifted to Amet. If they had Gi, they also had . . . Rage filled him and he stepped forward, fists clenched.

Amet raised his hands. "Stand right where you are . . . or risk never seeing your mate or your son again!" Amet lowered his hands. "They're safe for now, and for as long as you cooperate and do as I tell you. One wrong move, one betraying word or glance, and all you hold dear will simply cease to exist." He paused, enjoying the look of shock on Dhalvad's face. "Have I made myself clear?"

Dhalvad fought down the bubble of horror that threatened to choke him. Somehow he forced himself to nod.

"Good," Amet said. "Now, I'm sure you have questions to ask your friend. We'll leave you two together for a little while, then I'll return and you and I will link with the Tamorlee before we speak to the Council. Then we'll know where we all stand."

He nodded to Paa-tol, who set the blanket-wrapped olvaar on the floor and stepped back toward the doorway. Amet watched Dhalvad go to the olvaar and pick him up, wrapping and all. He then turned and followed Paa-tol, closing the door behind him.

Dhalvad freed Gi from the gag and was immediately inundated by a barrage of sharp whistle-clicks. Gi's angry words slowed and softened as Dhalvad unwrapped him from the coils of blanket and brought him to his chest.

"Easy, Gi,' Dhalvad said as he stroked Gi's back and massaged the fur at the back of his neck. "You're talking too fast for me to understand." Dhalvad felt Gi's angry tremors subside as the olvaar snuggled up against his neck. A rasping tongue touched his chin twice, then Gi released a deep sigh.

"Gi, are you all right?" Dhalvad asked gently. "You weren't hurt?"

Gi pushed back slightly so he could look into Dhalvad's face. His small black tongue licked at the sides of his mouth where the gag had bruised tender skin. "Not hurt," he answered in trader.

"Poco? Jiam? And Screech? Were they hurt?"

"Poco and baa-bee not hurt. Big Fur fight. Get bad knock on head. He would fight more, but Paa-tol threatens Poco and baa-bee."

"Are they here in the tunnels somewhere?"

"Yes. We all together."

"Where?"

"Not knowing, Dhal," Gi responded mournfully. "Gi all wrapped up. Can't see."

"Did Paa-tol carry you a long time or a short time?" Dhalvad knew that most olvaar had little sense of time, but Gi had lived with them a year in Jjaan-bi and was growing accustomed to scheduled eating and sleeping times.

"Short time," Gi answered after a moment of thought. "They be close, yes? What we do? Want find Poco, Jiam, and Big Fur and get out of here!"

"I, too, little friend, but it may not be easy. Amet wants something from me, and until I give him what he wants, he isn't about to let any of us go."

"What Amet want?" Gi asked, head cocked to one side.

"Power. And he intends to get it through the Tamorlee with my help."

"You help him?"

"I don't have much choice, Gi."

Amet returned a few minutes later. Paa-tol and another guard were with him. "Are you ready to link with the Tamorlee?" Amet asked.

Dhalvad set Gi-arobi aside and stood up, pushing his

anger back where it would not threaten Poco or Jiam.
"I'd like to speak to Poco first."

"When we're done," Amet said firmly. "You have my
word."

Which is worthless, as far as I'm concerned, Dhalvad
thought. He glanced down at Gi, who stood on the
couch, one small hand clutching the back of Dhalvad's
tunic. "What about Gi?"

"He'll be here when you return," Amet stepped back
a pace and motioned to Paa-tol and the other guard.
They moved to either side of the door. "Coming?" Amet
said.

Dhalvad nodded, touched Gi lightly on top of the
head, and freed his tunic from the olvaar's grasp. "I'll be
back, Gi. I promise."

"I'll wait," Gi whistle-clicked. "Hurry."

Chapter 6 ❧

*D*HALVAD KNELT BEFORE THE CRYSTAL AND PLACED HIS hand on the depression in the floor. He glanced up and saw Paa-tol watching him. Amet stepped past Paa-tol and came to kneel beside and slightly behind Dhalvad. He, too, looked up at Paa-tol.

"Be on guard," he said. "No one is to enter until we've finished with the link. If anything goes wrong, you know what to do about the others."

Dhalvad suppressed a shudder, knowing well what others Amet was referring to. It was strange, he thought, how being Speaker had changed Amet. It still was hard to believe that he was their enemy. Did power always corrupt? he wondered. Or did it just take a very special kind of person to handle it safely?

Amet leaned close to Dhalvad. His left arm went around Dhalvad's waist, locking their bodies together; his right hand dropped over Dhalvad's hand. He nodded to Paa-tol, who took his fire ring off, touched it to each of the five points in the star shape, then set it in the last indentation before the crystal. The link was activated.

Paa-tol stepped back and watched as the two Ni slipped away into another world, their physical bodies held in a kind of stasis while their minds traveled the corridors of a being who had lived as long as there was a memory of the Ni-lach as a people.

Paa-tol had gifted the Tamorlee often enough to know what Amet and Dhal were experiencing and also to know that there was a more direct way to link with the crystal. It was a natural property of the fire stones to absorb the actions and memories of the Seekers who wore them through actual skin contact. So, too, could the Tamorlee be activated, but because the Tamorlee was the parent crystal of all fire stones and held in reverence by the Ni, a ceremony had been created to set it apart from the other fire stones.

Paa-tol was aware of Amet's problem in linking with the Tamorlee because the Speaker had had to confide in someone and he had been a friend of long standing. Their friendship had begun when they joined the Gerri-Mountain Draak Watch shortly after the Sarissa War broke out twenty-five years earlier. Both had earned Seeker rings by their sixth year of service, at the same time discovering kindred spirits in each other. The passing years had seen each go his separate way, Paa-tol to become a high-ranking leader in the Draak Watch, Amet to become first a teacher, then Speaker for the Tamorlee. Now events were bringing them back to a closer relationship, one that Paa-tol hoped would lead to bigger and better things, such as a place on the Jjaan-bi Council.

He looked at Amet and nodded slowly to himself. But why stop there? If the crystal could be forced to accept Amet, perhaps it could be made to accept him.

While Paa-tol dreamed dreams of power, Dhalvad and Amet were carried deeper and deeper into the Tamorlee's consciousness. The crystal sensed the double load it carried, but because one was the Healer who had promised to help him, he accepted the second passenger even as it wished the Healer had come alone, for just a short time ago it had sensed its brother's energy pattern flaring to life and it was ready to contact it again.

Tamorlee, Amet is with me, Dhalvad began when he felt the Tamorlee's presence surrounding him.

Greetings to you both, the crystal responded.

Tamorlee, Amet thought-spoke, *I have come with Dhalvad because I no longer seem able to come alone. Is it true that you—have chosen a new Speaker?*

Yes.

You've chosen Dhalvad?

Yes.

Why? Have I done something to displease you? Tell me what it is and I'll do my best to correct the wrong.

Dhalvad was startled by the feel of Amet's projected thoughts. Where was the arrogant attitude the Speaker had displayed just a short time before? Was this supplicant the same person who had threatened Dhalvad's family if he failed to cooperate? What was Amet trying to pull? How could he warn the Tamorlee of Amet's dual nature without alerting Amet?

The wrong is not something done, the Tamorlee said. *It is something within you as well as something within myself, a need you cannot fill.*

Tamorlee, please don't put me aside without giving me a chance! Amet begged

Perhaps I've misjudged you, Amet. There was a moment's hesitation. *Come with us then. My brother sends, and we must try to link with him.*

Brother? Amet repeated. *Dhalvad's story about another crystal was true?*

It's true, Amet, Dhalvad answered.

Dhalvad sensed Amet's surge of excitement as the Tamorlee wrapped itself more tightly around them, drawing their energy to assist in the search. For a fleeting moment he wondered if he, too, had misjudged Amet; then the thought of Poco and Jiam being held prisoners somewhere in the tunnels returned him to his senses. No. Amet was wrong in what he was doing, no matter his reasons!

Dhalvad felt himself being pulled down a corridor of shifting shadows as the Tamorlee projected its energy outward, seeking the signal radiated by its brother crystal. Their passage through time and space created a hum that resounded through his mind. It seemed to go on for a long time. He lost all sense of Amet's presence.

Suddenly the humming sound stopped, and Dhalvad was filled with a joy that belonged to the Tamorlee. Together they were carried upward and out into the light of another place where evening shadows were real.

Bhaldavin sat on the end of the ancient stone pier that jutted out into Lake Thessel and looked out across the calm dark water. His thoughts were on the crystal he held in his land. Long ago, when he had first linked with Mithdaar, it had taken his memories and had formed a unique bond with him, a bond that he was sure only death could sever.

He looked down at the warm green light pulsating in his hand and felt happy. It was more than pride of ownership that stirred within him; it was more than the ethereal beauty of the crystal; it was knowing that he was accepted fully by the being who dwelt within the fire stone. He had felt Mithdaar's hunger for knowledge and had experienced its sadness when it first came to understand that the images within the life recorders were only memory images of a people long dead. He was not sure it understood exactly what dead meant. His only perception so far was that the crystal equated death with loss of a knowledge source, for each life contained its own special knowledge, its own way of thinking and feeling, which meant that every life was sacred and not to be wasted. It was the Ni philosophy—shared by a being who was forever imprisoned within green crystal.

"It was a mistake to let Gringers use you for his experiments," he said softly to the crystal. "I promise, I won't let it happen again."

He shuddered when he remembered the last impression the crystal had sent him before he snatched it away from the machine. Those startled amber eyes would haunt him forever.

"I should have destroyed the wind tower housing the star beacon long ago," he said, rubbing his thumb alongside the crystal. "Then the men of Barl-gan could never have contacted their gods. What happens now if their gods return, Mithdaar? How will they look upon my people?"

Thinking about men's gods and their strange machines made him think about the Sarissa, who claimed to be the direct descendants of the gods. He turned and looked at the Draak's Teeth, wondering if the war that had taken his arm was still going on. Or had the Sarissa already expunged his people from the Enzaar Sea territories? That thought led to another, as he remembered the small brother he had left behind. He had always planned to return to his home in the Deep and look for his brother, but getting back over the mountains had proved most difficult. He was not yet ready to give in to the word "impossible."

He glanced down at Mithdaar. His thoughts were fragmentary and erratic. It was always thus when he held the crystal. He was sure it had something to do with how the crystal learned as it siphoned off images of people and places from the life recorder, or as it snatched bits and pieces from his own existence—and now it had locked into Gringers's machine, which might well prove to be everyone's undoing.

He brought the crystal closer to his face and stared into the golden pocket of light that he had come to equate with the crystal's eye on the world. Though it was growing dark, he could easily see the crystal's inner glow.

"Who did you touch this last time, Mithdaar? Were they the Ral-jennob?" He sighed deeply. "How I wish you could answer my questions."

A tingle of warmth spread up his hand to his arm and into the rest of his body. The feeling was familiar; it happened whenever the crystal took from him: thoughts, feelings, fears. Everything was quickly absorbed, then the tingle subsided.

Bhaldavin smiled. "What do you do with all you take from me, Mithdaar?"

He was not exactly sure when he had begun calling the crystal by name. Mithdaar meant "Bold Light" in the Ni tongue, and it seemed to fit the crystal's insatiable curiosity and fearlessness. His fingers closed around the crystal as he brought his legs under him and stood up. It was time to go back and face Gringers. Lil-el would also be worried about him.

He walked back along the length of the pier and stepped onto the partially grass-covered stone path. Vegetation was fast reclaiming the city. Another fifty years without someone to keep the paths clear, and Barl-gan would become a moss- and bush-covered monument to the Sun Travelers; in another hundred years it would be lost to tangle vine and fast-growing trees that were already sprouting everywhere.

Strange, Bhaldavin thought, that a civilization could be born, grow, flourish, and die with no one outside its own borders ever knowing about it. It was sad, tragic in its own way. Would the Ni-lach one day be like the men and women of Barl-gan, only a legend whispered by old storytellers?

He was climbing the first flight of stone steps leading up from the lake when he became aware of someone standing at the top of the stairs. The shadows were too deep to make out features, but the figure stood too tall and straight to be any of the Barl-ganians.

"Gringers, I was just starting back. You needn't have come after me."

The man did not respond.

"Gringers?" Bhaldavin stopped suddenly, wary as the man started down the tree-shaded steps toward him. The stranger held something at his side. A few steps closer, and Bhaldavin made out the outlines of a sword. The clothing also became visible, its raglike draping finally giving the man away.

"Wastelander!" Bhaldavin hissed softly, backing down the steps. He turned and leapt down the last few steps, not waiting for the Wastelander to make the first move.

The Wastelander bounded after him, silent in his pursuit but for the sound of his draakhide sandals on the stone steps.

Bhaldavin plunged to the right along the pathway and

darted into a stone building whose roof had rotted away years before and now lay in ruins on the floor. He passed through two rooms with tangle vine covering the walls and moved quickly and as quietly as possible to the back door, which stood open. He was halfway up the dirt- and brush-covered slope leading to the plateau when he heard the Wastelander curse aloud as he fell over rotted boards on the floor.

The Wastelander appeared at the back door moments later and raised a hand to his mouth. The sharp cry of a loring bird issued from his lips. It was answered by another cry somewhere above Bhaldavin and off to his left.

Alerted to the fact that he faced more than one enemy, he scrambled up and over the bank and sprawled out onto the road. He rolled over and was on his feet a moment later, racing along the path to his right. He knew most of the shortcuts to the upper plateau and had upon occasion used them to outdistance a Wastelander intent upon his head as proof of his manhood. For years the Wastelanders had hunted Barl-ganians, never bothering to differentiate between men and Ni.

He entered another building a short distance up the road and climbed a set of stairs leading to the upper floor. The back of the building stood up against the next rise of roadway. He paused in the doorway, saw the road was empty, and stepped out. Seconds later he was sheltered under the overhanging branches of a genna bush. Heart thudding heavily in his chest, he crouched low and caught his breath.

Suddenly someone came loping down the road. He heard the soft *plop plop* of bare feet on the dirt roadway followed closely by another pair of running feet. He peeked out from under cover and saw the second runner close on the first. The second runner lunged at the first and bore him to the ground. A strange cackle made Bhaldavin tense. He knew of only one man who made that sound. It had to be Birdfoot!

He stepped out from his shelter and saw Gils wrestling with a Wastelander just a few steps down the road. Gils was on the bottom. Bhaldavin slipped the crystal into his pocket and drew his knife, running toward the fight. He came up behind the Wastelander and drove his knife into the man's back. As the Wastelander arched upward with a scream, Bhaldavin pulled his knife free and stepped back, prepared to use it again if necessary. The man turned, looked at Bhaldavin, then slumped forward to lay still on the road.

Gils scrambled to his feet as Bhaldavin shoved his knife into its sheath. Gils slapped Bhaldavin's shoulder several times, all the while bobbing and making his strange noises; it was his way of thanking Bhaldavin for his rescue.

Together they found a place to hide a little farther up the roadway, and for the next hour they watched a number of Wastelanders pass their position.

Gils stank of sweat and fear, and his nervous habit of rocking back and forth soon had Bhaldavin on edge. He tried to ignore Gils by sticking his hand in his pocket and caressing the crystal. As his fingers closed firmly around Mithdaar, he thought about the Wastelanders who were descendants of the original Barl-ganians, refugees who had run from the plague that had decimated the population of the city generations ago. It was not unusual for the Wastelanders to make a foray into the city every once in a while; those who came were usually there as a form of rite of passage to gain adult status among their peers, but sometimes they did come in greater numbers.

According to Kelsan, the Wastelanders had been more of a nuisance than a threat until about thirty years before, when the scattered tribes had begun to organize. Up until that time, they had been too busy just keeping alive or fighting among themselves to bother with the inhabitants of the city. The few times they had launched an all-out attack, they had been driven back into the forests by Barl-ganians wielding lethal light guns that burned through flesh in an instant.

But time was working against the Barl-ganians and for the Wastelanders. One after another, the light guns left by the First Men had fallen into disrepair until there were only a dozen or so left in full working condition;

and in the last twenty years, the number of Barl-ganians had been cut by two-thirds as accidents and illnesses swept their ranks. Added to that was a drastically declining birth rate. Meanwhile, the population of the Wastelanders was growing, and they had begun to expand their territories.

Gringers had met with several Wastelander tribesmen to try to discuss peace terms between Wastelanders and Barl-ganians, but the talks had proved unsuccessful. Down through the years, generation after generation of Wastelanders had come to look upon the remaining citizens of Barl-gan as misshaped, disease-spreading freaks of nature and would have nothing to do with them. Part of the problem lay in the far past, when the horrible threat of plague had left its psychological mark on those fleeing the city; the other part of the problem lay in the disappearance of Wastelander women over the years, women who were stolen by Barl-ganians in a last-ditch effort to stem the steady decline of healthy children born to those remaining in the city. As it was, there were only five females in Barl-gan. There was Bhaldavin's mate, Lil-el, and his daughter, Thura; there was old Patra, long past the childbearing years; and there were two young girls, both stolen from the Wastelanders a year before Gringers and his party had arrived in Barl-gan. The older girl, Sanna, had already chosen Gringers as her mate and had lived with him for over a year. Volly, who was two years younger, had not yet taken an interest in any of the men.

Bhaldavin was startled out of his thoughts by another cry of a loring bird. It was very close and was answered by seven or eight other bird calls up and down the mountain roadway.

Damn! he thought. How many are out there? If this was an all-out attack rather than a simple foray by several young men trying to prove their manhood, Gringers and the others above had to be warned.

He turned to Gils and spoke softly. "Does Gringers know about the Wastelanders?"

It was getting too dark to see, but Bhaldavin could just make out Gils's bob of the head.

"Did he send you to find me?"

Another nod.

"Well, we can stay here awhile longer and hope they go away, or we can try to make it back to the mansion. What do you think?"

For an answer Gils took hold of Bhaldavin's arm and pulled him out of hiding. They moved furtively, a few steps, a pause, then a few steps more. It had grown dark enough that they, like the enemy, were effectively hidden unless they did something to draw attention to themselves. They moved slowly and cautiously and worked their way up toward the high plateau to a place heavily overgrown with cara trees. Gils led the way to the hidden entrance belowground that would take them into the mansion by way of the cellars. It was a little-used entrance saved strictly for emergencies. The intricately formed doorway of vine and bush had the appearance of a natural barrier.

Gils pulled the door aside and they slipped through. Bhaldavin drew it closed behind them. Using the walls for a guide, they threaded their way into the main cellars and began climbing, turning lights off and on as they passed through numerous underground storage rooms. They finally reached the last flight of steps leading to the main floor above. All the rooms they passed were empty, though there were lights on here and there. It did not take any guesswork to know where everyone was. They walked out through the main doors and down the walkway that led to the gates and the stockade walls that protected the mansion from below.

They were drawn to a fire near the main gate. It was tended by several of the older children. Thura was among them. She waved when she saw her father and ran to give him a hug.

"Where've you been, Adda?"

"Down to the lake," he answered. "Where's your mother?"

She pointed to the left. "That way."

Gringers saw Bhaldavin and Gils and waved them over. Bhaldavin squeezed Thura's shoulder and smiled down at her. "Go back and tend the fire. We'll talk later."

The child nodded and ran off to gather more wood. It's just a game to her, he thought, watching her go. Would that it were so. He walked over to Gringers, who had descended from the stockade walkway that stood head high above ground.

The fire touched Gringers's face, turning it to a ruddy gold. "I was beginning to worry about you," he said.

"I'm sorry. I should have been back hours ago. I lost track of time. Is everyone else inside?"

"You were the last one out. How many Wastelanders did you see?"

"More than usual. What's happening here?"

Gringers rubbed a hand along his beard-stubbled chin. "We're waiting for them to attack. It looks as if they've come in force this time. I think we have enough light guns to keep them away. You'd think they'd learn after all this time."

There was only one thing that Bhaldavin could think of that would draw so large a number of Wastelanders. "Have some of our people been raiding again?"

"No," Gringers answered. "Everyone's accounted for, and no one has been gone long enough for any raiding."

"Then what do you think they want?"

Gringers shook his head. "What do they always want? An end to what's here! The fools!"

"Davin!" Lil-el's voice was unmistakable.

Bhaldavin turned just as she ran up. Like Thura, she threw her arms around him, then pushed him at arm's length a moment later, anger chasing relief away.

"Where have you been?" she demanded. "Why did you leave without telling someone where you were going?"

Bhaldavin glanced at Gringers.

"It's my fault, Lil-el," Gringers confessed. "Davin and I had a bit of an argument earlier."

Lil-el brushed a loose strand of hair back from her face; it had escaped the twin braids she had coiled about her head. "What was the argument about?"

"What do we always argue about?" Gringers answered. "I was using the crystal for an experiment today, and Davin became upset. I didn't mean to..." Gringers's voice trailed off as his glance came to rest on the flat leather bag riding outside Bhaldavin's shirt. He stepped forward and grabbed at the empty pouch. "Have you lost it?"

Bhaldavin drew back, the vehement look on Gringers's face startling him. Then anger blossomed, and he held up his hand. A flicker of luminescence seeped through between his fingers. "I haven't lost it! It's right here! And that's all you care about, isn't it? Not me! Or Gils! Just the crystal!"

"Why are you carrying it?" Gringers snapped, relieved to know that the crystal was not lost, but furious that Bhaldavin would take such chances with it.

"It wants me to hold it!" Bhaldavin cried. He drew himself up to his full height and braced himself for the battle he saw coming. The realization that he had spoken the truth, that the crystal did indeed want his constant touch, gave him a strange feeling of power, as well as a desire to accommodate the crystal to the best of his ability.

"*It* wants?" Gringers said incredulously. "What are you talking about? It's a power crystal, not some living person!"

Bhaldavin's chin went up. "You're wrong, Gringers! Mithdaar does live! And it wants me to hold it! It needs my touch in order to learn!"

"So what are you going to do?" Gringers mocked. "Carry it around in your fist for the rest of your life?"

Lil-el finally stepped in. "Enough of this! We've something more to worry about than that crystal right now! We can hash this all out after the Wastelanders give up and go away ... if they do."

Gringers looked at Lil-el and nodded. "You're right.

We can sort this out tomorrow. I'm sorry for hollering, Davin."

Bhaldavin drew a deep breath. "Me, too."

Lil-el turned and glanced at the stockade wall, worry etched on her face. "Gringers, this isn't like the Wastelanders. They've never come in such numbers before. I don't like it."

Gringers studied the lithe, fine-boned Ni female, his love for her and her need of reassurance pushing his anger aside. His voice was softer when he spoke.

"Everything is going to be all right, Lil-el. We have enough light guns to turn them back if they try anything. We'll begin taking shifts pretty soon so some of us can get some rest."

Bhaldavin knew Gringers loved Lil-el, but he also knew that it was a love founded on a childhood friendship. Never once had Lil-el or Gringers given him reason to doubt otherwise. Still, there were moments when he was touched by a twinge of jealousy. Now was such a time.

Gringers turned to Bhaldavin, an apologetic smile on his face. "We're going to need everyone if the Wastelanders decide to push a fight, so I suggest you put the crystal away for now and find a weapon. Again, I am sorry for snapping at you. Forgiven?"

Bhaldavin's anger subsided, as it usually did when Gringers turned on his charm. "Forgiven," he said. Ten years of friendship, plus the knowledge that they had enemies enough without fighting each other, made it stupid to continue their argument. If Gringers asked to use it again, Bhaldavin would simply say no, and that would be the end of it. He reached for the bag at his neck and slipped Mithdaar inside. The tingle of power quickly evaporated.

Paa-tol paced restlessly around the two statuelike Ni kneeling near the crystal, his nervous glances probing for any sign of movement or wakening. When one gifted the Tamorlee, it seldom took longer than ten or fifteen minutes, and the physical side effects were never more seri-

ous than a headache. Amet and Dhalvad had been linked
with the Tamorlee for well over two hours, and he was
growing very worried.

Twice in the last half hour he had knelt outside the
star shape and had reached for his fire stone ring, thinking to break the link between Amet, Dhalvad, and the
crystal. Each time he had stayed his hand, knowing how
angry Amet would be if he interfered.

He turned and glanced at the closed door behind him.
Perhaps it was time to go and find Chulu or Tidul and ask
their opinion. The thought was instantly put aside as
Amet groaned aloud and slumped over. Paa-tol turned
just as Dhalvad followed, collapsing onto the floor in a
loose-boned heap beside Amet.

Paa-tol quickly retrieved his ring and slipped it back
on his finger, breaking whatever link remained between
the two Ni and the crystal. He then checked Amet and
Dhalvad to make sure they were in no danger physically.
Both were pale and breathing shallowly, but their heart-
beats were regular. He tried to wake Amet first, then
Dhalvad. When neither revived, he went to the door and
called for the guards. A short time later both Amet and
Dhalvad were safely in their own quarters, and the
guards were once more stationed outside the Tamorlee's
room.

Chapter 7

*P*OCO WANDERED THE CONFINES OF THE TWO ROOMS SHE had been given, her anger at being held prisoner battling against her worry over Dhalvad. Did he know they had been taken prisoner? Or did he think they were still on their way to Cybury? What would he do when he discovered the truth?

Though she had not seen Amet, she knew he was behind their abduction. Paa-tol had openly admitted that his authority had come from higher up, and knowing Paa-tol and his small circle of friends, that had to mean Amet!

What did Amet plan to do with them? He could not keep them hidden away forever. Once Chulu or Tidul found out they would . . . What? Come rescue them? First the prisoners would have to be found—and where the hell were they?

She looked around the sparsely furnished room, a chill settling in her stomach. The rock walls told her they were somewhere in the caves of Jjaan-bi. The damp mustiness of the room spoke of a little-used section of the caves perhaps deep in the tunnels.

She passed the bed where Screech lay curled on his side sleeping, his arms tucked to his chest, his long prehensile tail curled over one hip and along his legs. There

was a break in the furred skin on the right side of his
head just over his ear; dry crusted blood marked the
gash. Watching him as he slept made her feel very protective, and she remembered wandering the abandoned
hillside homes of the old quarter of Port Bhalvar. There
she had found a much younger, scrawnier derkat half
buried beneath the rubble of a collapsed wall. She had
nursed Screech back to health, all the while wondering
how soon he would turn on her. She smiled to herself as
she recalled the first yowling sounds he had made, and
how she had given him the name Screech. It had been a
strange friendship from the start, her doing all the giving,
him all the taking. But that had changed with time, and
she had acquired a friend who stood by her no matter
what happened.

She shook her head sadly. Now look what your
friendship with me has brought you, Ssaal-lr. Her glance
took in the metal cuff and chain attached to Screech's
left ankle. The other end of the chain was attached to a
metal ring driven high into the wall.

Jiam began to whimper. She hurried into the other
room, picked him up blanket and all, and sat down with
him. "Hungry again, little one?" she crooned softly,
opening the front of her tunic.

Screech heard the baby cry and uncurled. He
stretched his long arms and legs and a few seconds later
stood and moved to the opening between the two rooms.

Poco heard the clunk of the chain on the floor and
turned. "Sorry he woke you," she said.

Screech coughed softly, telling her not to worry about
it.

He scratched at his side where one of Amet's men had
hit him with the flat of a sword. His ears flattened as he
recalled the brief fight.

He forced his ears upright once more and watched
Poco breastfeed the baby. It made him think about his
own stomach. It followed that if he was hungry, Poco
was also hungry, for no one had bothered to bring them
anything to eat or drink since their being captured late
that morning. It was wrong for them to treat his tiyah so!

Let him get his claws into the one responsible and . . . A low rumbling growl sounded deep in his chest.

Poco misread the grumble of anger. "Hungry?"

"*I could eat*," Screech replied truthfully, signing. "*You?*"

Poco smiled in conspiracy, trying to lighten the seriousness of their situation. "Tell you what. You eat the first one through the door. I'll eat the second."

Screech humphed amusement, glad to see his tiyah had not lost heart. There was pride in the look he gave her as she pulled the child from her breast and wrapped it snugly in its blanket. She was a strong leader, quick with her mind and undaunted by adversity.

"She's stubborn," Dhalvad had told him once, "and the most determined female I've ever known. I trust her with my life, Screech—but there are moments when one must think for himself and be able to take the initiative. I know that you don't believe that, and among your kind perhaps it isn't true. But with us, leadership is a yoke of responsibility as much as an honor, one that is passed on often without ritual, many times with misgivings. One must always be prepared to lead, Screech, no matter what age, sex, or race."

Screech's tail snapped back and forth in agitation as he returned to his bed in the other room, for the Healer's words echoed in his mind like a prophecy. Would there come a day when leadership of the radg would fall to him? He shuddered at the thought, for among the derkat only death could end a tiyah's rule.

Dhalvad woke hours later. He opened his eyes to the glow of fayyal rocks and felt a warm presence against his back. He knew without turning that it was Gi-arobi, because the olvaar made a soft wheezing sound when he slept.

A quick glance at the room told him that he had been returned to his cell. He thought about trying the door even though he knew it would be locked, but his body did not want to obey even the simplest of commands.

The crystal, he thought. That's why I'm so tired. He

stopped trying to sit up and relaxed, his mind going over the strange union among Amet, himself, and the Tamorlee, and their linkage with the other crystal, whom the one called Davin named Mithdaar. Bold Light, Mithdaar —it was a good name.

His thoughts turned to the one who carried Mithdaar. Was it Davin, or Little Fish? Or were they one and the same person? What had Davin been talking about when he spoke of a star beacon and the Ral-jennob? And who were the Wastelanders, and why were they attacking the people who lived in the great tall stone building he had seen? The one called Gringers was obviously a man, as were some of the others. He then recalled the strange faces and bodies of some of the others Davin lived with. They were neither man nor Ni, and their strangeness made him uneasy.

If only we could have spoken to Davin or Little Fish directly, he thought. We could've asked him where he was, how we could find him.

Dhalvad slowly drifted back to sleep, thinking over all he had seen and heard while linked with the Tamorlee. His last conscious thought concerned Amet and how he had fared in the link.

Paa-tol arrived at Amet's quarters early the following morning to check on the Speaker. His discreet knock on the door went unanswered. Using his authority as a ranking officer of the Gerri-Mountain Draak Watch, he nodded to the guard outside the door and entered, closing the door softly behind him. He passed through a good-sized sitting room furnished with an array of comfortable chairs and couches, then went into a smaller room that served as a kitchen. Beyond that lay a bedroom that was spacious in comparison to most other tunnel apartments.

Paa-tol paused in the doorway. Then, seeing that Amet's eyes were open, he proceeded into the room, coming to a stop at the foot of a large ornate bed covered with a spidermoss blanket with an exquisite flower design sewn at the center.

"How are you feeling?" Paa-tol asked solicitously.

Amet's eyelids were still puffy with sleep. "Exhausted."

"What did you learn?"

Amet studied Paa-tol a few moments before answering. He glanced at the edge of the bed. "Sit."

Paa-tol hesitated, then took the offered seat, curiosity winning out over his usual aloofness.

Amet gathered his thoughts, trying to put everything in some semblance of order. "First, Dhalvad told the truth about the Tamorlee wanting another Speaker. It said something about my not being *right* for its needs. I'm not exactly sure what it meant. I was asking it to reconsider its decision when suddenly it began speaking about a brother."

Amet closed his eyes, recalling that wild tumble through time and space and the strange feeling of being linked with yet another crystal and the holder of that crystal. Five minds linked—it had been an exhilarating and somewhat daunting experience. There had been moments when he had not been sure who he was, or where his own reality stopped and another's began. His link with Dhalvad and the Tamorlee had remained quite firm even as the crystal drew upon both his and Dhalvad's energy; the other two within the link had felt more like ghostly shadows to him, one glowing slightly brighter than the other.

But the truth was still the truth. He opened his eyes. "Another crystal exists," he said, his glance fixed on Paa-tol. "And if there is one, there may be others, each perhaps capable of becoming another Tamorlee."

Paa-tol's eyes lighted with excitement, his thoughts running wildly into the future. "The potential for power! It would mean more than one Speaker—and a boost in the energy available through the fire stones. Seekers would be able to travel greater distances, and world gates might more easily be found, and we as a people—

with the capability of broadened Seeker travel, we might be able to reclaim the lands taken from us by men!"

Amet let Paa-tol ramble on for a moment or two before interrupting. "Dreams, my friend, all dreams unless we can find Mithdaar."

Paa-tol frowned. "Mithdaar?"

"That's the name of the other crystal, and it's linked with someone called Davin or Little Fish in a place even the Tamorlee doesn't recognize."

"Doesn't recognize? Then how are we going to find it?"

"I'm not sure, but if and when we do, it will be ours to do with as we wish. Let the Tamorlee have Dhalvad for its Speaker. I'll take Mithdaar and see to its education, and then together we'll lead the Ni into a safer future."

Paa-tol's head dropped slightly, hooding his eyes. "What about the one who carries the other crystal? Won't he object to our confiscation of the crystal?"

Amet smiled slyly. "I like your way with words, Paa-tol. I doubt the one-armed one will give us much trouble. His hold on the crystal seems tentative at best, at least from what I observed yesterday. It seems there is a man called Gringers who is also interested in the crystal; for what purpose, I'm not exactly sure. But if it comes down to giving the crystal to him or to us, I'm sure we can persuade him that it will be safer in our hands."

"I'm sure," Paa-tol agreed, rising. "What are your plans regarding the Council? Will you tell them all that you've learned?"

"Tidul and Chulu already know about the possibility of a second crystal, so I believe it will be best if I inform the others also, then no one can accuse me of being secretive about anything. I'll tell everyone that we intend to seek out this second crystal and return it to Jjaan-bi where it can be incorporated into our network of Seekers and be linked properly with the Tamorlee. That should satisfy everyone right now. Later, after we have Mithdaar, we may have to make a few changes in our plans. We'll worry about that later."

"What about Dhalvad?"

"I'd like to do without him, but we're going to need the Tamorlee to help us find Mithdaar, and it won't do it without him—unless, of course, it's changed its mind about me. I'll know later today when I try to link with it again."

Paa-tol thought of his own experiences of linking with the Tamorlee as he gifted it with the knowledge his fire stone had picked up on their travels. He knew that the mind-to-mind contact was a union of thoughts that left little room for evasions.

"Have you ever tried to—not tell the Tamorlee something?" he asked, watching Amet sit up and swing his thin, lanky body out of bed.

Amet slipped out of his sleeping robe and stretched. "Do you mean lie?"

"Not lie exactly. Just not tell it everything."

Naked, Amet turned and went to the closet across the room. He moved with unconscious grace as he dressed in fresh undergarments and pulled a clean, brown robe over his head. It fell over his lithe, young-looking body and came to a stop a hand length off the floor.

"You haven't linked with the Tamorlee as often as I have, my friend," Amet answered, "or you'd know that though it's difficult to dissemble while meshed with the mind of the Tamorlee, it's not impossible. The Tamorlee has the power to touch projected thoughts, and occasionally it may pick up on surface thoughts, but nothing deeper. It's a simple matter of—if it doesn't ask the right questions, it doesn't get the right answers."

"So if you want to hide something from it . . ."

"You learn how to steer its thoughts to another subject."

A shiver of uneasiness sped down Paa-tol's spine. There was something about Amet's answer that bothered him, but he could not pinpoint what it was. His thoughts moved on to another subject.

"What about Poco and the child, and the furred ones?"

Amet straightened his robe. "They'll have to remain our secret for now. We'll have to leave someone we trust to watch them, but they must remain where they are. It's our only hold on Dhalvad. When we get what we want from him, we'll decide what to do with them." Amet raised an eyebrow. "All of them," he added meaningfully.

Chapter 8

THE WASTELANDERS ATTACKED FIVE TIMES THAT NIGHT and each time were repulsed by burning laser fire. Gringers stayed at the stockade wall and directed the thirty-four Barl-ganians who made up the defending force, while Lil-el, Theon, and Bhaldavin saw to the recharging of the light guns as one after the other they flickered and died, their energy drained.

Bhaldavin dashed back into the mansion, down the hallway, and took the stairs leading down. He ran along the main corridor of the first floor belowground and took another set of stairs down. Passing through a room where Kelsan Watcher was busy tending the wounded, he went on down another corridor. He passed six doorways on the right and turned in at the seventh, where he found Lil-el and Theon each sitting near a machine watching for a red light on a panel above the gun slot that would signal when the gun was fully recharged.

As he crossed the room, he glanced over in the corner where his two young sons lay asleep under a shared blanket.

Lil-el looked up and gave him a quick smile. "How's it going?"

"Not good," Bhaldavin replied. He set down three more guns to be recharged. "We're down to four working guns, and Gringers is looking for another attack any time now. Gils and two others have been wounded, but not so badly that they'll leave the wall."

Worry was etched on Lil-el's face. "The children?"

Bhaldavin leaned over and gave her a hug. "Thura is keeping them all busy with the fire. Gringers has them heating water to throw down on the Wastelanders the next time they rush the wall. Are any of the guns ready to take back out?"

Theon pointed to a nearby table. "Those two are ready, and two more should be ready in a few minutes. It's taking longer for them to recharge though. I think the energy source for the guns is running low. Gringers says these machines are somehow tied into the large silver panels on the wind towers. If he's right, and it's sunlight that creates the energy we use in the guns, it means that these machines also have to be recharged by sunlight, which is still five or six hours away."

Bhaldavin picked up the two recharged weapons and carefully slipped them into his tunic pockets. "If these machines fail, it will mean hand-to-hand fighting—and we're outnumbered. It's too dark to tell how many are out there, but Gringers figures there's at least fifty."

Theon glanced at Lil-el, then turned back to Bhaldavin. "There is another choice," he said, rubbing the back of his neck to loosen stiff muscles. "If it comes to a real fight, we might be better off trying to reach the rafts. Once out onto the lake I doubt the Wastelanders would try to follow us. They have no defense against water draak."

Bhaldavin nodded. "It's a good suggestion. I'll pass it on to Gringers along with these two guns." He bent over Lil-el and kissed her.

"Keep your eye on Thura," she said.

"I will."

Kelsan Watcher stopped Bhaldavin as he passed through the infirmary on his way back upstairs. Bhaldavin quickly repeated what he had told Theon and Lil-el. When the old man heard that Gils had been wounded, he grabbed up several large rolls of bandaging and a bottle

of boiled verran sap meant to fight infections. Bhaldavin
led the way back upstairs and listened to Kelsan muttering to himself and cursing the Wastelanders for being
ignorant savages.

When they reached the outside, Bhaldavin pointed
out the place where he had last seen Birdfoot and handed
Kelsan one of the recharged light guns. As the old man
shambled off to find his wounded son, Bhaldavin started
toward the main gate where he knew he would find
Gringers directing the defense of the stockade wall.

He was halfway to his goal when a child's scream
caught his attention. He knew the voice instantly. It was
Thura! He drew the light gun and ran down the short
tree-lined road toward the fire. It was the last place he
had seen her.

Suddenly there were men pouring over the wall in
three or four places. The Wastelanders had scaled the
stockade walls and had broken past their defenses!

He saw a handful of Barl-ganians leave their places on
the wall to turn and fight the enemy behind them.
Knives, swords, and homemade spears slashed at whatever target was closest, and here and there a flash of
laser light cut into the enemy.

Bhaldavin searched frantically for his daughter as he
ran toward the fighting. Moments later he was close
enough to use the gun he carried. Screams of agony
erupted from the attackers, as he burned holes through
arms, legs, and torsos. He slowed his headlong rush as
the fighting grew wilder. Friend and foe were so closely
locked in battle that it was becoming difficult to shoot.

"Adda!"

Thura's cry sent a dart of fear through him. He turned
and saw her running toward him, a tall, ragged-looking
Wastelander right on her heels. He raised his gun to fire
but hesitated, fearing to hit Thura. He saw the Wastelander swing his arm around; something glinted in his
fist.

"Down, Thura!" he screamed. He fired a fraction of a
second later.

The laser light caught the Wastelander high in the

chest and head; it burned through his face and stopped his cry of agony before he could make a sound. He crumbled into a heap, landing on top of Thura.

Bhaldavin heard his daughter's cry for help and ran forward. Upon reaching her, he set the light gun down and pulled the Wastelander away. At the sight of the man's face, he swallowed quickly, trying not to be sick. He picked up the gun and slid it into his tunic pocket, then grabbed Thura around the waist and stood up.

He looked around. The fighting had overrun them, and more Wastelanders were coming over the wall. Gringers's voice rose above the din of battle, signaling a retreat back to the mansion.

Bhaldavin set Thura down on her feet. "I can't carry you, child. Not and fight at the same time. We'll have to make a run for it. Stay close to me!"

Wide-eyed and frightened, Thura nodded and clutched at the side of his tunic.

He drew the light gun. "Get on my other side where you'll be out of the line of fire, Thura."

She slipped around to his left side and ran along beside him as they angled their way around a knot of fighting men.

Bhaldavin saw Gringers and a number of Barl-ganians retreating toward the mansion on a run. The four or five with light weapons stayed to the rear to cover their retreat. It was too dark to tell how many of their people had been left wounded, dead, or dying near the stockade wall.

He looked around, searching for another way to safety, but the Wastelanders were everywhere. So many! Where were they all coming from?

"Adda!" Thura cried. "There!"

He turned and saw five or six figures moving toward them out of the darkness, their long ground-eating strides and loose-fitting clothing giving them a ghostly appearance in the semidark.

Bhaldavin slowed down and fired, once... twice... three times. The light beam cut through the darkness and

found two targets. Screams of pain and fear lanced the
night as the two Wastelanders fell.

Bhaldavin realized that there was only one way to go.
They had to cross open ground and try to reach Gringers
and the others before they were cut off.

"Run, Thura! Run!" he cried.

As they raced along the line of trees, memories of
another battle came flooding through his mind, memories
that lay buried in his past. He had been little older than
Thura when he had first tasted the horror of war. His
family had been forced to flee their home and had come
to a supposed place of safety to take rafts far into the
Deep where they would be safe, but the Sarissans had
come, killing without thought to age or gender. He remembered seeing his father cut down; he remembered
carrying his small brother, running for both their lives;
and he remembered finding his mother's body and beneath her, his baby sister, both dead. It was a scene he
would never forget.

Suddenly Thura misstepped and fell, losing her hold
on his tunic. "Adda!"

Her cry came the same moment that he realized he
had lost that pull on his clothes. He had gone ten or
twelve running steps before he was able to stop and turn
back. By that time she was lost in the darkness.
"Thura!" he cried.

"Adda, wait for me!" she screamed, scrambling to her
feet.

He ran back the way he had come. "I'm here!" A
moment later he saw her silhouetted against the light of
the fire back near the wall. She was running toward him.

Suddenly something hurtled out from between the
trees to his left. One of the enemy had found them!
Bhaldavin pointed the gun, then remembered his daughter at the last second and tilted the gun up. The beam of
light cut into the trees overhead just as the Wastelander
tackled Thura. Before Bhaldavin could recover and rea-
lign the gun, something hit him from the side, slamming
him to the ground. A weight landed on his chest, and
strong arms closed around him. He tried to knee his at-

tacker in the groin as he twisted beneath him. Another Wastelander joined the struggle. He grabbed Bhaldavin's wrist and pulled his arm over his head so the gun pointed harmlessly into the grass. A fist smashed into Bhaldavin's jaw. Another blow landed in his right eye. The third blow sent him sliding into darkness. His last awareness was of the light gun being wrenched from his hand.

Bhaldavin's return to consciousness was painful. His jaw and head throbbed with the beat of his blood, and his arm was lashed so tightly to his body that his hand was numb. His ankles were also tied together, giving him no freedom of movement. He carefully opened his eyes and saw a fire just a short distance away. It was one of those the children had been tending. It was still night, and there was no way to tell how long he had been unconscious.

His first thought was of Thura. He remembered seeing her knocked down. A lump of fear caught in his throat as he raised his head off the ground.

"Thura!' he called. "Thura, if you can hear me, answer!"

The words were no more out of his mouth when a tall figure stepped out of the darkness and drove a booted foot into his side. "Silence! Another word and you're dead!"

The menace in the voice was real. Doubled over, Bhaldavin fought for breath and bit down on his lower lip to keep from crying his daughter's name again. He could do nothing for her if he forfeited his life foolishly. All he could do was pray to the Unseen that she was still alive and unhurt. There was even a chance that she had escaped. They had seemed more intent upon taking him —and not so much him, but the light gun he carried. Perhaps she had only been knocked down and left in the darkness. It was a slim hope, but at the moment it was all he had.

The Wastelander stood over him a few seconds, then turned and walked away, moving among a dozen or so other dark mounds lying on the ground. More prisoners,

Bhaldavin reasoned as the man toed several of those lying nearest the fire. One groaned aloud. The other made no sound. The Wastelander knelt and checked the last one over. He stood up a moment later and dragged the body away, laying it alongside several other dark mounds nearby.

One of the prisoners had died. Who? Bhaldavin wondered. The body was too large to be one of the children. How many had survived that last attack? He would know come morning.

He lowered his head to the ground and closed his eyes, listening for a voice he might recognize. While he listened, he prayed that Thura had escaped. There was, of course, one other possibility, but he would not let himself dwell on that and turned his thoughts to Lil-el and the others who had escaped into the mansion. How long could they hold out? It was a very large building with many entrances. The Barl-ganians simply did not have enough people to guard all the doors, which meant that in the end they would have to abandon the building and make a run for the escape route that led from the cellars.

He could envision the fear and confusion as those who had escaped into the mansion left all they owned and knew behind and made their way to the cellars and from there out through the tunnel and down into temporary safety in the lower city. If Gringers was with them still, they would have a chance, because he would do his best to see that as many as possible survived. If Gringers had not made it, leadership would most probably fall to Kelsan Watcher or Lil-el. Both were levelheaded and would take no unnecessary chances.

He rolled to his left side and watched several Wastelanders come and go, carrying messages to a short, squat man who sat near the fire. One of their leaders, he decided. Another Wastelander brought a piece of fire-warmed meat on a stick and offered it to the heavyset man. He took the stick and quickly devoured the meat, his heavy jowls moving with a fierce grinding motion that made Bhaldavin feel queasy. When finished, the heavy man broke the stick in half and threw it into the fire, then turned and spoke to one of the runners standing to his right. The guttural sound of his voice made Bhaldavin think of the menacing growl of a gensvolf, a four-footed carnivore that was enemy to every other creature in the land. The gensvolf ran in packs; they were cunning, ferocious, and daring enough to tackle a small draak if the opportunity arose.

Bhaldavin was too far away to hear clearly what the fat man said, but he did catch a few words, enough to know that his friends were fighting odds that left little hope for a standoff. The Wastelanders, like the Barlganians and all other men on Lach, spoke a language known as trader. The only difference Bhaldavin could detect in the Wastelander's speech was a slight slurring of word endings.

The runner acknowledged whatever the fat man said, then turned and sprinted into the darkness toward the mansion, where the flicker of torchlight reflected off the stone walls.

The fat man stood up and looked toward Bhaldavin and his fellow captives; his glance finally came to rest on the man who had kicked Bhaldavin to silence. "Watch them, Sola. We'll soon be back with more."

"Let one of the younger men watch them, Zojac! I want to be in on the kill!"

"You're too late," the big man rumbled. "Our men have already broken into the great house, and it's just a matter now of cleaning out the dead and wounded. When it gets light, we'll take a closer look at what's inside. I'm curious to know what the diseased ones have been guarding so carefully all these years."

"Probably nothing worth all our effort!" Sola grumbled.

"We'll know soon enough," Zojac answered, turning away. "Stay alert. I'll send someone back to relieve you in a little while."

Bhaldavin breathed in sharply as fear for his own safety was suddenly submerged by fear for Lil-el and their two sons . . . and Thura, wherever she was. At that moment he would have gladly given up his own life to know they were all safely away. He pulled against his ropes, testing them. If only he could get his arm free.

Sola watched Zojac disappear into the darkness. Once assured that his leader was out of earshot, he turned back to the fire, muttering to himself, not at all pleased to have been left behind. He fed several large branches into the fire, then passed among the prisoners, checking ropes to make sure no one had wiggled free. He paused when he reached Bhaldavin.

Bhaldavin's eyes reflected the yellow-red firelight and gave him a feral, animallike appearance. Sola leaned down and, after a moment's hesitation, spat in Bhaldavin's face.

Bhaldavin turned his face aside, not offering so accessible a target a second time. Waves of anger churned in his stomach, swamping the fear he had felt just moments earlier.

Sola grinned wickedly and went to a knee beside Bhaldavin. "You don't like that?" He carefully set his lance to one side and grabbed a handful of Bhaldavin's hair, pulling his head around. He spat again.

"Filth! Devil-spawned! When Zojac returns, you'll be judged, every last one of you. Those who pass we castrate and use as servants. Those who don't pass—are put to death quickly."

His open hand struck Bhaldavin across the face. "Look at me! Open your eyes, damn you!"

Bhaldavin obeyed. The sound of madness in the man's voice carried the icy threat of death.

Sola's dark eyes glittered in an insane face as he pulled Bhaldavin to a sitting position. Without warning, he backhanded the Ni, knocking him to the ground. He then drove a fist deep into Bhaldavin's stomach.

Bhaldavin groaned in pain as Sola dropped onto him. One hand pushed his head back, exposing his throat, the other hand reached for the knife at his belt.

Bhaldavin felt the cold touch of steel at his throat and believed he was about to die. Thoughts of Lil-el, Gringers, and his children flitted through his mind; then he was seeing the worried look on his father's face just a few moments before the Sarissa attacked. There was grief in that look. No matter how hard he had tried to save his family, it had not been enough. In that moment, Bhaldavin knew how his father must have felt when he had turned to stand before Sarissan blades, giving his family one last chance by offering himself as a target. Now it was his turn; his only regret was that he could do nothing more to help his own family.

Sola pushed his face down close to Bhaldavin's. "One sound—just one sound!—and you die!" he snarled. "I can kill you now and no one would ever know or care. But I won't kill you unless you force me to."

He slipped his knife back in its sheath and released Bhaldavin's head; he then sat back, straddling Bhaldavin's legs. "Remember," he said softly, his voice tinged with malevolence. "Cry out just once, and I'll kill you!"

Sola was a good-sized man and he drew Bhaldavin to his feet with one hand. He glanced around quickly, then hit Bhaldavin in the face with his fist. Intuitively Bhaldavin knew what was coming and rolled with the first blow, but he could not protect himself for very long, and soon Sola had him down on the ground, pommeling him with both fists. Bhaldavin clenched his jaws tightly together, determined not to give Sola an excuse to kill. The pain grew, peaked, then his body began to grow numb and the man's blows lost their power.

By the time Sola had fully vented his anger, the body beneath him was still. He rested a moment, his arms braced to either side of Bhaldavin's body. He leaned down and peered into the Ni's battered face; he listened to the ragged breathing, then checked Bhaldavin's pulse. Content with his findings, he pushed to his feet and stood looking down at his victim, his flare of anger sated, his need to hurt fully satisfied.

It was always like this with him; it had always been so. He wiped the sheen of perspiration from his face and looked around, once more ensuring himself that his actions hadn't been witnessed by anyone who mattered. He was a man who knew his worst fault and had found a way to minimize its danger to his standing in the tribe. He had learned long ago how to turn his anger into physical action by running or wrestling with some of the young men of the tribe, using the pose of a training lesson as an excuse to vent his frustrations on the unsuspecting. At age thirty-two, he was well versed in the art of hurting without killing.

Sola chose his enemies carefully and made sure that he revealed himself only to those he could control. He enjoyed the respect of many of the tribesmen because he was a fierce fighter and a good hunter. Those few who saw beneath the façade he presented to the world feared him for they had felt his strength and savagery and knew that one word spoken out of turn would be their last.

He knelt down and wiped the blood from his fists on Bhaldavin's tunic; then he retrieved his lance and returned to the fire, his face devoid of emotion.

A short time later several men approached out of the darkness. "Zojac said we were to relieve you," one said, moving around the fire.

Sola nodded. "Any more prisoners?"

"Only two. The rest seemed to have disappeared," the other man replied. "It's a big building. They could be hiding anywhere."

Bhaldavin was still unconscious when two new prisoners were added to those gathered near the fire. One was Birdfoot. The other was Gringers.

Chapter 9

BHALDAVIN WOKE TO PAIN AND THE GLARE OF SUNLIGHT full in his eyes. The metallic taste of blood was in his mouth, and when he licked at his lips he found them split and puffy. He squinted out of swollen eyes and watched a line of Wastelanders carry large cloth bundles down the path from the mansion. They deposited their burdens in a large pile not too far from where he lay. Zojac and two other Wastelanders oversaw the growing pile of goods. One of the men seemed to be making some kind of a tally on what was being taken from the building.

Bhaldavin's glance dropped to the dark bundles of cloth he had seen the night before; he could now discern heads, arms, and legs. There was no movement among the bodies, and he realized that they were the Barl-ganians who had died the night before. There was an-other line of bodies a short distance beyond, all clothed in the loose-fitting pants and tunics typical of Waste-landers. There were not as many of those as he had hoped, unless there were other enemy bodies still unac-counted for. At that moment, it seemed that the Waste-landers were more concerned with looting than with how many of their number had been lost to the burning death of the light guns.

He finally forced himself to roll over onto his back; he

bit back a cry of pain as the ropes around his upper body pulled cruelly on the bruises he had sustained the night before.

He heard a soft gasp of surprise. "Davin!"

"Gringers?" he mumbled through bruised lips, sure that he recognized the voice. It took him a moment to focus on the man sitting a few feet away. His heart sank when he saw that he had guessed right. If they had captured Gringers, it probably meant that they had gotten everyone.

"You're alive!" Gringers cried softly, tears glistening in his eyes. "When I saw your hair, I knew it was you, but—you were so still. I thought that . . ." He swallowed and released a shaky breath. "Gods! What did they do to you?"

Judging from the grimace on Gringers's face, Bhaldavin could well imagine what he looked like. "The man's name is Sola," he got out, trying to speak clearly. "I made him mad." He took a deep breath and dared to ask, "Lil-el?"

Gringers glanced around to make sure none of the Wastelanders were listening. "She and the children were the first ones out the tunnel. Theon's with them."

"Where will they go?"

"I sent them to the lake caves. They'll be safe there for a little while. If necessary they can get on the rafts at night and paddle to the center of the lake. There's no way for the Wastelanders to bother them there."

Bhaldavin looked beyond Gringers and saw several other Barl-ganians either sitting or lying down; all were tied, and from what he could see, most bore wounds that had been hastily tended, if at all.

"How many captured?" Bhaldavin asked.

"Twelve still alive, counting you and me. They're still collecting bodies from both sides of the stockade wall. We lost at least seventeen last night. We should've pulled back sooner. We might have saved a few more."

Gringers nodded toward Gils, who sat nearby, his head and right side bloodied; but for all his wounds, Gils looked alert, his eyes darting back and forth as his gaze followed the Wastelanders moving around the circle of prisoners.

"Gils and I were caught in the cellar," Gringers continued. "We stayed behind to make sure the others had time enough to get out. Our light guns finally gave out just as we were getting ready to leave. Gils was wounded in the side. I escaped with nothing but a cut on my hand, from when I tried to wrestle a knife away from one of the Wastelanders."

Bhaldavin suddenly remembered his daughter. "Gringers! Is Thura here? I lost her last night in all the confusion!"

Gringers nodded. "She's here. She's sleeping over there beyond Gils. I think she's all right. She doesn't look like she's been hurt. Gils tried to reach her a little while ago to check on her and got a knock in the head for his trouble."

Facing Bhaldavin, Gringers missed Gils's glance of warning. The flat of a sword caught him on the side of the head, knocking him half senseless to the ground.

"Silence! No talking!" Sola moved around in front of Gringers; his swordpoint touched Gringers's chest. His glance moved to Bhaldavin. A flicker of satisfaction could be seen in his eyes as he beheld the Ni's face. His swordpoint moved to rest above Bhaldavin's heart.

"I would've thought you'd learned your lesson last night," he said. "Perhaps you need another reminder?" He pushed down slightly. Bhaldavin flinched as the sharp point punctured his skin.

"Sola!"

Sola's head snapped around. Zojac stood there, hands on hips, an impatient look on his face.

"Untie the prisoners, line them up, and strip them. We'll look them over now."

Sola beckoned to several of the Wastelanders to give him a hand, and within minutes all twelve prisoners were on their feet and stripped of their clothing. Bhaldavin touched the leather pouch at his neck, wondering why they had not taken it from him.

Thura had looked for her father from the moment she

had wakened. Tears sprang to her eyes when she finally saw him, and the moment her bonds and clothes were removed, she ran to him and flung her small arms around his waist, burying her face against his chest.

"Are you all right, Thura?" Bhaldavin asked, as he stroked her shoulder-length, light-green hair.

Her head went back and she looked up at him, crystal-blue eyes large with fear. "I'm afraid, Adda. What's going to happen to us?"

Bhaldavin had never lied to his children; it was not the Ni way. He tried to smile, but with his face so swollen, it came out as a grimace. "I don't know, Thura, but whatever happens, you must be brave. Don't cry before them. Don't let them know you're afraid. Do you understand?"

Thura nodded. "Your face, Adda."

"I know. Never mind."

The Wastelanders used swords and lances to prod the prisoners into a tight circle. Zojac made a motion with a hand. "Bring one."

Sola stepped close to the prisoners and grabbed a Barl-ganian called Aldi by an arm. He pulled Aldi from the circle and walked him over to stand before Zojac and three other Wastelanders, all of whom showed glints of gray in their hair. Elders? Bhaldavin wondered. Or only pack leaders?

Aldi was twenty-seven years old, and unlike most of the other Barl-ganians, he was not physically deformed. He was a bit slow mentally, but he could function with a minimum of orders.

Zojac ran his hands over Aldi's body without regard for the prisoner's pride. He hesitated when he came to the sword wound on Aldi's left shoulder. He turned to one of the other men and nodded for him to take a look. The man inspected the wound, then shook his head. "It'll leave a scar, but should cause him no trouble."

Zojac nodded to Sola. "This one we'll keep. Bring the next."

The next man to be taken from the circle was Gavi, an older, dark-haired man with blotchy skin and the three-toed splayed feet that was the most common deformity among the citizens of Barl-gan.

Zojac carefully kept his hands to himself as he gave Gavi a quick once-over. He looked at the other three Wastelanders, who seemed to be acting as judges. All three shook their heads.

Zojac signaled to Sola. "Kill it and bring the next."

Gringers and the others were shocked by the cold-blooded order and watched in horror as Sola caught Gavi in a armlock, forced him to his knees, and calmly slit his throat.

"No!" Gringers screamed, lunging forward.

In that same moment, Gils Watcher and another Barl-ganian named Enar, both splayed-footed, realized that escape was their only chance to live. As Gringers drew the attention of the guards, they spun around, knocked two of the Wastelanders aside, and sprinted for the stockade wall. Three of the guards went after them.

Bhaldavin glanced around in those few moments of confusion. It was in his mind that he and Thura might never have a better chance to escape. His arm tightened on Thura's shoulder, but before he could take a step, the point of a sword stuck into his back. He fought the impulse to run and stood still, watching as Sola and three others subdued Gringers and two other Barl-ganians who had not moved as quickly as Gils and Enar. The other four prisoners were too wounded to even think about escape.

Gils and Enar reached the stockade wall. Gils caught the top of the walkway in a mighty leap and hooked a foot over the top, pulling himself up. Enar was right behind him, but as he was drawing himself up, a knife flew through the air and caught him square in the back. Gils tried to catch Enar's arm, but missed and almost lost his own balance. He cast a quick glance at the men racing toward him, ducked another thrown knife, and quickly turned and threw himself up and over the stockade wall. Two of the Wastelanders followed him up onto the walkway. The other one carried Enar back and deposited him at Zojac's feet. Blood bubbled at Enar's lips with every breath.

At a sign from Zojac, Sola quickly dispatched him.

Bhaldavin was appalled by the Wastelanders' disregard for life. He and Thura stood close together and watched as Gringers and the other six Barl-ganians were brought out of the circle and judged.

One was the old woman named Patra. She had been wounded in the leg. Bhaldavin was not sure whether it was her age or her blotchy skin that was the deciding factor, but as with the others, she was killed with a modicum of effort, her scream of terror cut off in midtremor by Sola's knife. Thura cried softly as her body was pulled off to one side.

Another man named Jon passed Zojac's judges, as did one of the young boys named Karl. Three others were put to death. Then it was Gringers's turn. He was let up from the ground and brought before the Wastelanders' tribunal. Because of the trouble he had caused, the guards held onto his arms as Zojac looked him over.

One look at his face was enough to tell Bhaldavin that Gringers could have gladly killed every one of the Wastelanders at that moment, had he had a weapon. Something in his eyes must have warned Zojac to be careful, because the Wastelander did not offer to touch Gringers; he just looked him over carefully by walking a full circle around him.

One of the gray-haired Wastelanders caught Zojac's arm. "I know this one. If I'm not mistaken, he's their leader and claims to come from some other place across the mountains."

"He hasn't the look of the others," Zojac agreed, "but that doesn't mean he's not one of them. No one's ever crossed those mountains!"

The man shrugged. "That's what he told us."

Zojac looked Gringers in the eyes and shook his head. "He's healthy looking, but I've a feeling he'd never make an obedient servant. I can see the hate in his eyes. I think I'd sooner have a lizard laired in my valley than this one!"

He turned to the two other men standing nearby. "Oman? Carl? What do you think?"

Both men shook their heads.

Bhaldavin's heart lurched as Zojac made the killing sign. Gringers saw it, too, and turned to look at Bhaldavin, as if saying good-bye.

Not Gringers! Bhaldavin cried silently. His mind filled with scenes of the past when he and Gringers had been enemies, then master and slave, and finally friends. There was good in Gringers, and a wellspring of curiosity that continually inspired those around him. If born a Ni, he most probably would have become a Seeker and earned the respect of the People. Bhaldavin did not always agree with Gringers, but he did trust and respect him, and in his own way he loved him as he would have loved the brother he had left behind so many years ago.

Sola stepped forward as Gringers began to struggle between the two men who held him. It was plain that he was not going to give up life without a fight.

The look of anticipation on Sola's face turned Bhaldavin's stomach. "Fools!" he yelled. "Kill Gringers and you kill the knowledge behind the light guns that have killed all your men!"

Though the words came through battered lips, they were clear enough to make Zojac turn to look in Bhaldavin's direction. He stopped Sola with an upraised hand.

"A moment, Sola! I want to hear what that one has to say. Bring him here!"

Bhaldavin was prodded forward with a sword at his back. Thura went with him. He ignored the men who surrounded them and looked once at Gringers before turning to face Zojac. He was sure he had caught a flicker of relief in Gringers's eyes and an almost imperceptible nod that might have meant "thank you" or "go ahead, tell them what you know."

He took a deep breath. He had to convince them to keep Gringers alive, because alive he could escape and help Lil-el. In that moment he knew that if anything happened to him, Gringers was the only one who would ever see that Lil-el and his other two children reached Ni territory safely. He could do no more for his family now. He and Thura were lost. The Wastelanders were sure to look upon them both as mutated humans, their crystal eyes and green hair marking them as surely as Gils's splayed feet.

Zojac crossed his arms before his chest. "What did you say about this man?"

"I said that Gringers has knowledge that's too important to throw away," Bhaldavin answered. "He knows how to recharge the light guns you've taken from us. He knows about many of the machines in the building, machines built by your ancestors, the First Men. Kill him and you lose it all."

Zojac looked at Bhaldavin a moment, then motioned to the three gray-haired men. They moved off a few paces and spoke quietly among themselves. A minute later they came back.

Zojac frowned at Gringers. "Your life is spared—for now. We'll test this knowledge you're said to possess and make a further judgment after that." He turned to Bhaldavin, his glance touching Thura. "And now, you two. Are you related?"

"This is my daughter," Bhaldavin said, holding Thura's shoulder.

Zojac reached out and took Thura by an arm, drawing her away from Bhaldavin, though she tried to cling to him.

"Adda!" she cried.

Bhaldavin's heart thundered loud in his ears. "Stand quietly, Thura," he said, trying to keep the tremor from his voice. He knew they were going to kill her, but there was nothing he could do to stop them. He clenched his teeth to keep from yelling as Zojac touched her smooth pale skin, running his hands over her immature body. When the Wastelander was finished with his examination, he glanced at the three men for their verdict. The lack of expression on his face made Bhaldavin tremble. Let it be quick and painless, he thought.

Gringers spoke up suddenly. "Kill them—either of

them—and you kill a gift from the gods. They are Ni! They can protect you from—"

His words were cut off by Sola, who drove his fist into Gringers's jaw. A second blow to the stomach pushed the air from the Barl-ganian's lungs, and he slumped unconscious between the two men who held him.

Zojac glared at Sola a moment, then spat on the ground. When his head rose, his dark eyes were fixed on Bhaldavin. "I've heard of the green-haired folk who live among the diseased men of Barl-gan. The rumors say that you're capable of controlling the great lizards. Is this true?"

Bhaldavin nodded, hardly daring to believe that he and Thura might yet be reprieved. He swallowed twice before he could find his voice. "The lizards are called draak where we come from. My people have long known how to sing draak."

One of the other men spoke. "You're not of Barl-gan?"

"No. I come from the Enzaar Sea, west of the mountains."

"How did you get here?" the man asked.

"We climbed over the mountains. It was cold and dangerous, but there was a way."

"Why do you stay with the diseased ones?" Zojac demanded.

"I've tried to leave several times but haven't succeeded. The pass we followed down this side of the mountain was blocked by an avalanche years ago, and I haven't found another route back."

Sola stepped forward. "He's lying to save his life! He *is* one of the diseased ones. Look! He has but one arm, and his eyes are the eyes of a soulless one! I say we should kill him!" He grabbed Thura by an arm, jerking her to him. "And his whelp!"

Bhaldavin stiffened, eyes wide in fear as Sola brought his knife up under Thura's chin. Terrified, the girl struggled against the man's cruel, biting fingers. Somehow Bhaldavin tore his glance from Thura's small heart-shaped face and turned to Zojac, who stood by frowning. Praying to the Unseen that he could reach the man, he dropped to his knees.

"Please, don't kill her! I beg you for her life!" He wanted to say more but suddenly could not get the words past the lump in his throat.

Zojac looked at Bhaldavin, then reached out and pulled Sola's knife hand down. "You will wait until a decision has been made."

Dark eyes met dark eyes in a look that was pure challenge. Sola held Zojac's gaze as long as he could, then his glance dropped. He was not yet ready to openly defy the man who had successfully led the Northern Lake tribe for the past twelve years. Another time. There would always be another time.

Zojac left Thura in Sola's charge and walked around Bhaldavin, noting the bruised and swollen places on his face and pale skin. He paused to inspect the stump of Bhaldavin's left arm, then hooked a finger around the cord at Bhaldavin's neck, bringing the leather pouch up to his hand. "What is this?"

Bhaldavin's heartbeat quickened. "My focus stone," he lied. "It helps me concentrate when I sing draak."

Zojac felt the round hard shape within the bag and dropped it back to Bhaldavin's neck, satisfied with the explanation. He walked around Bhaldavin and stopped to face him.

"Off your knees."

As Bhaldavin obeyed, Zojac looked to the other men. "He wasn't born one-armed. It looks like it was cut off. As for the color of his eyes and hair, they are like none I've ever seen before, including any among the diseased ones. If it's true that he can control the great lizards, I think we should give him a chance to prove it."

"And the girl-child?" one of the men asked, looking at Bhaldavin. "Can she also control the great lizards?"

"She's learning. She's been training for a year now. She should be able to sing draak by the end of this warm season," Bhaldavin said, exaggerating.

Zojac turned to Sola. "Release her."

Sola frowned but did as he was told. Thura went quickly to her father and hugged him, silent tears trickling down her face. Bhaldavin stroked her hair, his own fear slowly subsiding. They were alive, at least for a little while longer, and where there was life, there was hope.

Chapter 10 🖌

GILS WAS IN A NEAR PANIC AS HE DREW HIMSELF UP TO the top of the stockade wall. He would never forget the look in Enar's eyes as he dropped back to the ground and into the hands of the enemy. Realizing that he could do nothing to help Enar, he caught at the top of the wall with one hand, slipped over the other side, and hung by his arm a second before dropping a good six meters to the ground below. He landed hard, jarring both legs. Pain and a warm gush of wetness down his side told him that his wound had opened up again. He tripped over one of the young trees the Wastelanders had used as a crude ladder to scale the wall and plunged downslope, slipping and grabbing at bushes to save himself from falling.

Upon reaching the roadway below, he stumbled out into the open and looked back. Two of the Wastelanders dropped down on his side of the wall to give chase. An angry inarticulate cackle escaped his lips as he clutched his side and bolted down the roadway, fear, pain, and rage churning in his stomach. Unarmed, the odds against him, he could only resort to the skills he had developed while stalking game and his own knowledge of the territory and where best to hide.

He left the roadway before it switched back on itself and worked his way into heavier cover. He paused many

times to listen. Once he heard someone speaking on the
roadway above him; another time he was sure he heard
running footsteps. He went on until there was nothing
but silence all around him. His heartbeat slowed as he
caught his breath and tried to think what to do.

The first thing he had to do was to find help, and
soon. He drew his bloody hand away from his side, then
pressed it back as weakness washed over him. The second thing he had to do was make sure he did not lead any
of the Wastelanders to the lake caves. His glance
dropped to the ground and the distinctive footprints he
was leaving behind. The Wastelanders were excellent
hunters. They could easily follow his tracks if he did not
find a way to outwit them.

A twig snapped off to his right. They were coming.
He had to move. He stood and started off, moving
slowly through a copse of small trees that would shield
him for a brief time. Having had a chance to think things
through, he knew where he was going and how to lose
those who followed him.

Theon stood sheltered back inside the cave and
shaded his eyes against the afternoon sunlight glinting on
the water. A cool breeze had sprung up, making the
damp cave seem colder. From where he stood, he could
just see the left side of the plateau and a small portion of
the mansion. There was no movement along the stockade wall, nothing to tell him what was happening above.

Lil-el came up behind him and dropped a hand on his
shoulder. "See anything?"

He started, then pulled away, turning to face her.
"Not a damn thing!" There was a haunted look in his
dark eyes and a grim set to his lips. Theon was a small
man, impatient by nature and fastidious in his personal
habits. Seeing him at that moment, one might doubt the
last, for his black hair was mussed and stood up in un-
ruly clumps, his usually clean-shaven face had a scruffy
growth of beard, and his clothes were rumpled and torn
by his mad scramble down through the abandoned city
and into the lake caves.

He rubbed a hand along his stubble-covered chin. "Gringers and Birdfoot should've been here hours ago! Something's happened to them!" He turned and looked back across the water. "I've got to go back up to the mansion!"

"You can't go now, Theon," Lil-el said calmly. "The Wastelanders would see you coming. We'll have to wait for dark."

"We'll?"

Lil-el didn't flinch at the harshness in his tone of voice. "Bhaldavin is up there, too," she said, her eyes large with worry. "And Thura, and I've no intention of leaving here without them . . . or Gringers."

Lil-el knew that Theon's love for Gringers went much deeper than mere friendship. Gringers had broached the subject with her several times in the past, trying to straighten out his own feelings on the matter. She and Gringers had shared many secrets while growing up together on the rafts of the Ardenol Clan. Their relationship was that of brother and sister, despite the fact that she was Ni-lach and he was human. She cherished him deeply and so shared his love-hate attraction to Theon. As for Theon being a free lover, she had learned to accept him for the way he was, as had Gringers and everyone else in the city. Theon was just Theon: fun-loving and teasing one day, snappish and rude the next, but always faithful to Gringers and whatever he wanted. For one person to love another so was both inspiring and frightening, for if anything ever happened to Gringers, Lil-el was sure that Theon would rather follow his friend into death than remain behind alone.

She wanted to reach out and touch Theon but knew that in his present mood she would be rudely rebuffed. So she spoke soothingly without touching. "Theon, I know how much you love Gringers. I love him, too, and I promise we won't leave anyone behind, whatever we decide to do."

Theon angrily wiped at the tears welling unbidden in his eyes. "What if it's already too late? What if—"

She cut him off before he could go any further. "If

anything happens to Gringers or Bhaldavin, I'll know, Theon. Believe me," she lied. "I'll know."

Theon looked at Lil-el, his fear easily quelled by his need for hope. He knew the Ni were different. They had a special awareness that men lacked and were capable of doing things that men could not even begin to understand, such as singing draak and linking with the strange Seeker stones like the one Bhaldavin carried. He did not even pretend to understand Bhaldavin's relationship with the crystal that Gringers so coveted, but he respected Bhaldavin's ability to reach into its memory for events in the past. He also respected Bhaldavin's courage in simply touching the crystal without a protective cloth. The one time Theon had experimentally put a finger to the crystal, he had received a jolt of energy that had left him unconscious for several hours.

His thoughts returned to Lil-el, who stood watching him. She was a delicate, fine-boned creature. Her winged eyebrows and dark-green hair accented the blue-gray crystal color of her eyes and gave her an ethereal look that belied a strong sense of responsibility and a level-headedness that everyone in Barl-gan had come to rely on.

His slender fingers caught her arms in a strong grip. "Are you *sure* Gringers is all right?" he asked, wanting so much to believe her.

"He lives," she affirmed, praying to the Unseen that she was right. "And as soon as it's dark, we'll go find him and the others. Come back into the cave now and rest. We'll have to make some plans."

They turned and started back into the shadowy darkness of the cave to join with the others who waited by the two rafts moored at the edge of the underground pool. They stopped suddenly when they heard a small splash as something fell into the water behind them.

Theon caught Lil-el by an arm and stepped in front of her. He quickly drew a light gun from the pouch at his belt. Lil-el had nothing but a knife for defense, but she knew how to use it. She drew it from its sheath as Theon cautiously returned to the low entrance to the cave.

A hand, then an arm appeared around the edge of the left side of the cave entrance. Grasping fingers sought for a hold and missed.

Theon raised the gun and pointed it as a mud-spattered body dropped into the water and sank out of sight.

Lil-el darted forward before Theon could press the button on the gun. "Wait!" She stepped past him and jumped into the waist-deep water. She was taking a deep breath to dive when suddenly a head rose out of the water a short distance away.

Gils coughed and spat up liquid as he struggled to keep his head up. Lil-el moved deeper into the pool and grabbed one of his arms. Startled, he fought back, then her voice came to him out of the darkness.

"It's Lil-el! Let me help you! Theon, hurry. Give me a hand!"

Theon set his gun down and waded into the water. "Where's Gringers?" he demanded as he helped drag Gils out onto the rocky shelf. "Is he behind you?"

Gils found energy enough to shake his head.

Theon glanced desperately toward the entrance. "Are you sure?"

Again Gils nodded. Filthy, soaked, and weary from going the long way around, he looked up at Lil-el as she cradled his head in her lap and signed for his father by brushing the back of his right hand down alongside his face.

Lil-el understood at once and turned to Theon. "Go find Kelsan. Try to get him to come without alerting the others."

Theon hesitated, then left, his thoughts on Gringers. If Gils had escaped, it meant there was a chance that Gringers had, too. That small hope was enough to raise his spirits as he hurried toward the rafts.

Lil-el smoothed Gils's dark-brown hair back from his face and saw the gash on the side of his head where dried blood had matted in his hair. She then noticed how he clutched at his side. Gently drawing his hand away, she saw fresh blood mixing with the water running down his side. Moments later she had him laid flat on his back.

She used her knife to cut a piece of cloth from her tunic and tried to staunch the wound. She glanced back down into the cave and wished Theon and Kelsan would hurry. The pallor of his face frightened her, and his breathing was ragged.

"Gils?"

His brown eyes opened; they were filled with pain and seemed to be begging her to help.

Her heart ached for him, and she silently cursed the twist of nature that had made him a mute. There were things she needed to ask him, questions that might mean the difference between life and death to those she loved.

Again she turned to look for Kelsan, but there was no sign of him or Theon. She turned back to Gils. She could not wait. She had to know about Bhaldavin and Thura. Her understanding of Gils's special sign language was tentative at best, but she could try.

"Gils? Did you see Davin or Thura?"

He nodded and lifted a hand, signing. *"With Gringers. Alive this morning."*

"They're all alive? Gringers, too?"

"Yes. Gavi dead. Enar, too."

Gavi. Enar. And how many others before this is finished? she thought. She fought back tears. "Where are the prisoners being held?"

"Stockade wall. Hold—for—kill us."

She missed too many words. "They're holding the prisoners for what? What do they want with them?"

"Slaves."

Coldness settled in her stomach. "Are any of them hurt badly?"

Gils nodded.

"Davin? Thura?"

"Thura not hurt." He brushed his left arm at the shoulder, which was his way of signing for Bhaldavin, the armless one. His hand moved in the air, then he patted his face and chest.

Lil-el did not understand. Suddenly the sound of footsteps came out of the darkness and she looked up to see Theon and Kelsan hurrying toward her, Theon with a blanket under his arm, Kelsan with his physician's pouch.

"He has a wound on his head and a sword cut on his right side," she told Kelsan as she moved out of his way. She helped Theon wrap Gils in the blanket and briefly told them what Gils had said about Gringers, Thura, and Bhaldavin.

"He said that Gavi and Enar are dead. I missed some of what he tried to tell me," she finished.

Kelsan ignored her and went to work. A short time later he looked up. "He's lost blood and he's weak, but he'll live if we can avoid infection and keep him warm. I wish I had more of my supplies. If there's any plan to go up after Gringers and the others who've been captured, I want to go along. There are things I want from my laboratory, things we'll need if we're forced out of the city. Come. Help me carry Gils farther back inside. I want to get him next to a fire."

"Ask him about Gringers!" Theon demanded. "How is it that he escaped and Gringers didn't?"

Kelsan's eyes went cold. "I'll ask him that *after* we have made him comfortable. There's nothing you or I can do for Gringers and the others right now but make sure we make no mistakes. The Wastelanders aren't fools, and if we go up against them without a good plan, all our efforts could well end in a final defeat."

Later that day Theon and Lil-el had the complete story from Gils as translated by Kelsan. The three of them left Gils in Volly's care and moved back toward the entrance to the cave where they could talk freely.

"Well, they're alive," Kelsan said softly. "Or were when Gils saw them last. And if they've come here to gather slaves, it means that they probably aren't done looking for us. Once they've satisfied their curiosity and destroyed whatever they don't want, they'll start hunting for the rest of us. If anyone is captured, he'll be judged as Gavi and Aldi were judged, which means instant death to the malformed and castration and slavery to the rest."

"No!" Theon growled. "No! I won't let that happen to Gringers! I'm going back up there right now, and I'm

going to find a way to free him. Lil-el? Are you with
me?"

Her head lifted at the sound of her name. She was so
lost in the fear that it was already too late to save Davin
and Thura that she had not even heard what Kelsan and
Theon had said.

"Lil-el? You will go with me, won't you?" Theon
pleaded.

"She must stay here," Kelsan said before she could
answer. "If anyone is to escape on your rafts, they'll
need her to keep the water draak away."

Theon shook his head. "No. Part of her family is up
there, and she can go with me if she wants to!" He held
out a hand to her. "Lil-el?"

Lil-el thought about her two youngest, realizing that if
she left them with the Barl-ganians she might well be
sealing their fates, but deep within, she also knew that
there were two others who needed her—if they were still
alive. She could not leave Barl-gan without knowing for
sure one way or the other.

She took Theon's hand. "We'll leave when it gets
dark."

Bhaldavin knew nothing of what was going on in the
caves at the edge of the lake, but it was his hope that
Lil-el and his two sons would remain safely hidden until
the Wastelanders left the city—if they left. Judging from
the arguments he had heard that morning, he understood
that one faction among the Wastelanders wanted to
claim Barl-gan for their tribe, while Zojac and represen-
tatives of the other three desert tribes were set against
anyone claiming the city, fearing that a lengthy stay in
the area would contaminate Wastelander bloodlines and
create the same kind of monsters they had all sworn to
kill.

The Wastelanders were not ignorant or particularly
superstitious, but they did have a healthy respect for
their forefathers and the history that had been passed
down to them by word of mouth. It was true that they
coveted the light guns carried and used by Barl-ganians

to hunt and protect themselves against draak, but they were not about to take up residence in a place that had represented death and disfigurement for as long as anyone could remember.

Bhaldavin had heard enough of the arguments for and against staying to believe that when it came time to depart, no one would stay behind.

Turning his thoughts from the Wastelanders, he glanced down at Thura who, dressed once more in her own clothes, lay asleep with her hands tied and her head cradled in his lap. There were dry tear marks on her face and her soft green hair was tangled and matted with sweat. He hated seeing her bound like an animal and tensed at his own ropes, seeking to loosen them in case a chance of escape presented itself. Not that that was likely. The Wastelanders were keeping a very close watch on their new slaves.

There was no word for slave in the Ni language; that was a concept that had come with the arrival of men on Lach. He had been a slave once years before and remembered the anger and humiliation he had felt at being treated like some half-tamed gensvolf. He had survived months of slavery and in the end earned his freedom, but he had a feeling that this time there would be no end to slavery. He shuddered as memories of being chained returned to haunt him. He would rather see Thura dead, he thought, than subjected to such a life.

Bhaldavin knew little about Wastelander life except what Kelsan and Gringers had told him. He knew that they lived on the edge of the desert where draak seldom laired, and that they farmed small areas of land in and around a scattering of deep springs. According to Kelsan, they fished and hunted and had domesticated a four-legged animal they simply called runners. Kelsan said that the Wastelanders lived hard, short lives where they were forced to learn to kill early in order to survive.

Yes, he thought, remembering how quickly and efficiently Sola had dispatched Gavi. They're good at killing, too good.

A chill skittered down his spine as he looked up and

saw Sola approaching. Sola nodded to the two men keeping watch over the prisoners and came over to check the prisoners' bonds.

Gringers's eyes glinted with hate as Sola pushed his head from side to side. When he touched Thura, she woke with a start, eyes wide in alarm when she saw who leaned over her.

Sola's eyes glinted with interest. "You're a little beauty, aren't you?" he said softly. His hand moved down Thura's side onto her bare legs. He grinned as Thura drew away from his touch.

"Leave her alone!" Bhaldavin said without thinking. His anger made his words almost incoherent.

The back of Sola's hand caught him in the mouth, knocking his head against the stone wall of the steps leading up into the mansion. A blur of darkness threatened Bhaldavin as Sola grabbed him by the tunic front and shook him.

"You want another lesson, Green Hair?" he hissed softly.

Suddenly Sola felt something hard under his hand. He released Bhaldavin and drew out the cord from around his neck. "What's this?" he asked, feeling the bag. Not waiting for Bhaldavin to answer, he opened the bag and dumped Mithdaar into his hand. He held it—but only for a second. He yelped in pain and dropped the crystal as if burned. The two men who had been watching him stepped closer.

"What is it?" one of them demanded.

"I don't know," Sola answered. He squatted and warily probed the crystal with the point of his knife.

"It's beautiful," one of the guards said. He glanced at Sola. "Why did you drop it so quickly?"

Sola rubbed his fingers together. "It's hot. It burned me."

The other guard leaned down. "It doesn't look hot." He reached out and touched it tentatively with a finger. He drew it back a second later, shaking his hand. "Damn! It does burn!"

Sola looked at Bhaldavin. "What is it?"

Bhaldavin hesitated, suddenly afraid for Mithdaar.

Sola glanced at Thura and smiled grimly. He caught at her arm and drew her close. "Tell me what it is, or I'll use your daughter here and now in front of you!"

"Tell him what it is, Davin," Gringers urged, his dark eyes shadowed. "Tell him how you need it to sing draak."

Sola pointed a finger at Gringers. "Another word and you'll wish I had killed you earlier!"

Bhaldavin glanced at Gringers, who obviously wanted him to continue to lie about the crystal. Was it his way of trying to protect the crystal, or was he just trying to distract Sola from harming Thura?

His glance shifted back to Sola. "It's a focus stone," he said, picking his words carefully. He licked at dry lips and continued, his fear for Thura's well-being almost choking him. "I need it—to sing draak. It helps me concentrate."

"Why does it burn?" Sola demanded.

"It's attuned to me and no one else."

Sola looked at the crystal and pushed it toward Bhaldavin with his knife. He watched Bhaldavin's face as he pressed it hard against his right leg.

Bhaldavin straightened a little as Mithdaar's energy surged through him, absorbing all the memories Bhaldavin had to give it since last they had touched. The tingle of power was akin to the caressing touch of a lover. There was a subtle change in the color of the crystal as it experienced Bhaldavin's emotions.

Sola looked down at the crystal and frowned as it lightened in color, changing from grass green to pale mint green. Curious and feeling bolder, he again reached out —and flinched as an actual spark arced outward from the crystal to his flesh.

"Damn!" he exploded angrily, standing up and shaking his hand to relieve the pain. "That thing is dangerous! It ought to be destroyed!"

"Destroy it and Bhaldavin can't sing draak!" Gringers growled. "Just leave *him* and *it* alone and he'll serve you many years, keeping your people safe from draak!"

Sola glared at Gringers. "You have a loud mouth!"

Gringers shrugged. "So I've been told. But I don't lie."

Sola did not like Gringers's tone of voice and stepped back toward him. "You want a fight?" he challenged.

"If you'll make it a fair one," Gringers answered sharply.

"Castrate him, Sola!" one of the guards suggested. "That'll take the sass out of him. Why wait until we get back to the desert?"

"Not a bad idea, Reyban," Sola said softly. He glanced at the two guards. "Stretch him out and hold him down!"

When that had been done, Sola squatted beside Gringers, his dark eyes assessing. He touched the knife-point up under Gringers's chin, then slowly drew it down Gringers's throat, across his chest and abdomen, then a little lower. "Ready to give up your manhood, Loud-mouth?" Sola asked wickedly.

His knifepoint slit an opening in Gringers's pants. He roughly tore the material back. "Just one quick cut and you're no longer a man, Loudmouth," he sneered. "Shall we get it over with?"

Gringers's face had lost its color by that time, but his eyes never strayed from Sola's face. To Bhaldavin al-most seemed as if Gringers were daring Sola to do as he threatened.

The guards watched expectantly, all but ignoring the other prisoners as Sola took hold of Gringers's scrotal sack and touched his knifepoint to the tender skin. Sec-onds dragged by as Sola watched Gringers's face. Sud-denly Sola released Gringers and stood up, putting his knife away.

"You're a brave bastard, Loudmouth," he said. "I think I'm going to have fun taming you."

Gringers licked at the sweat beading his upper lip and cast a quick glance at Bhaldavin. He had won that round —but it was obvious that he did not look forward to another of Sola's games.

Sola turned to one of the guards. "Reyban, take

Loudmouth inside. Zojac wants to talk to him." He turned and glanced at Bhaldavin, then stepped over Gringers's legs and reached for Thura. "I'll take the girl with me for now."

"No!" Bhaldavin cried, twisting at his ropes. "Let her stay with me!"

Sola's fist caught Bhaldavin's jaw, knocking him backward. A second blow landed on the back of his neck as he tried to turn over. Thura's screams were the last thing he heard.

Chapter 11

DHALVAD STOOD IN HIS SMALL WINDOWLESS CELL AND faced Amet, determination reflected in every line of his body. "I want to see Poco!"

"I told you, not until we've found the other crystal." Amet's glance touched Paa-tol, who stood near the door. They had come to discuss the next step in finding the crystal called Mithdaar, but Dhalvad was proving very uncooperative; Amet did not like the look in Dhalvad's eyes. There was no telling what a desperate male might do if he believed his mate was in imminent danger. He was glad that he had brought Paa-tol along.

He raised his hands in a placating gesture. "You don't understand the significance of this find, Dhalvad. It's more important than family ties or even—"

Dhalvad interrupted. "All I care about *is* my family! Where are they, Amet? You promised that if I helped you link with the Tamorlee, I could see them—or have you forgotten?"

"No. I haven't forgotten!" Amet snapped. "But that promise will have to wait."

Dhalvad crossed his arms over his chest. "You'll get nothing more from me until I see Poco and Jiam and know they're all right!"

Gi-arobi whistle-clicked agreement. He, too, wanted

to make sure Poco, Jiam, and Big Fur were safe. He jumped down from the bed where he had been sleeping when Amet and Paa-tol arrived and crouched at Dhalvad's feet, his golden eyes judging the distance to the door and noting the way Paa-tol stood with his hand resting on the hilt of his knife.

Amet swore silently to himself, wishing he could do without Dhalvad; but he knew it was not possible. Earlier that morning he had tried to link with the Tamorlee by himself and had been instantly repulsed. Paa-tol had also tried—with the same results. It was infuriating to be denied access to the crystal's power, but there simply was not a damn thing he could do about it except try to coerce Dhalvad into working with him. He had to report to the Elder's Council in two hours and explain what he meant to do about the Tamorlee without revealing his full plans. It would mean some careful juggling of the facts; it also would mean that his hold over Dhalvad's tongue had to be secure, because the Elders were very likely to have questions for the Healer.

A germ of a plan began to form in the back of his mind; it was ugly but would be effective if everything worked out the way he hoped. In fact, it would take care of several problems at once.

Dhalvad took Amet's hesitation as a point won in the battle of wills. He was getting tired of being pushed and had decided to push back, testing Amet's resolve. If anything happened to Poco or Jiam...A shiver coursed down his spine. No. He would not let himself think about that. Despair would only sap his strength. He had to be strong, for himself and for those he loved. He would not give up!

Amet rubbed the back of a hand along his jaw, then nodded. "All right, Dhalvad, you win. We'll take you to see Poco, but afterward you must do as I tell you. Agreed?"

"Agreed."

Amet nodded to Paa-tol, who turned and opened the door fully. Dhalvad started forward, his desire to see Poco and Jiam making him forget Gi-arobi.

Not so Amet. "The olvaar will stay here," he began. The words were hardly out of his mouth before Gi-arobi was moving.

"No!" Amet yelled, seeing the olvaar streak for the door. "Paa-tol! Stop him!"

The olvaar moved so fast that Paa-tol was almost caught off guard. He stepped into Gi-arobi's path and bent down to grab him. One hand missed; the other caught a fistful of fur.

Gi-arobi's sharp teeth sank into Paa-tol's wrist as he was drawn into the air. A moment later he was falling. He landed on the stone floor with a thump and bounced; he was up and running before Paa-tol could recover.

"Call him back!" Amet demanded of Dhalvad. "Now!"

"Gi!" Dhalvad hollered. "Come back!" He watched the olvaar scamper down the tunnelway and around a corner out of sight. He glanced at Amet and saw him frowning. Secretly pleased that Gi had escaped, he pursed his lips and let loose with a high whistle that only urged the olvaar on.

Amet caught roughly at Dhalvad's shoulder. "What did you just tell him!"

"You heard me," Dhalvad said. "I told him to come back. But Gi has a mind of his own and doesn't like being cooped up. If I know him, he's on his way to the outside, probably to the markets where he can find something to eat."

Amet's frown deepened. "I don't trust you, Dhalvad." He looked at Paa-tol. "Go after the olvaar and stop him before he has a chance to talk to anyone!"

"Who's going to listen to him?" Paa-tol said. "He's just an olvaar."

"Yes. An olvaar with friends such as Chulu and Tidul, and he speaks trader well enough to make things difficult for us if he happens to mention Dhalvad's family. So get going! Have Oman and Vescaar help you. When you find him, bring him back here and lock him in, then come and meet me where we're holding Pocalina."

Paa-tol looked at Dhalvad, who was listening intently

to every word. "Will you be all right alone?" he asked Amet.

Amet drew a knife from within the hidden folds of his right sleeve. "I'll be fine. If within an hour you haven't found the olvaar, let that others continue searching. You meet me outside Pocalina's room."

Paa-tol nodded and left, his long strides taking him quickly out of sight.

Amet caught Dhalvad's elbow and steered him toward the doorway. "Come quietly and I'll take you to see Pocalina. Cause me any trouble and I'll use this knife, and that will be the end of it as far as you're concerned."

"Would you really kill me, Amet?" Dhalvad asked in all seriousness.

"I would," Amet answered grimly.

"And chance losing your only way to contact the Tamorlee?"

Amet's eyes were bold and calculating. "I wouldn't have to kill you, Dhalvad, only hurt you—and knowing the extent of your healing powers, I think I could hurt you very badly without actually endangering your life."

Dhalvad shook his head. "I can't believe you're doing this, Amet. You must realize that sooner or later it will catch up with you. Even the discovery of another crystal can't make up for your threats against my family. When the Elders learn that..."

Amet snorted. "The Elders are my friends, every one of them! When they come to understand the full importance of the discovery I've made, any protests made by you and your half-breed mate will be of little consequence. You overrate yourself, Dhalvad. You always have. You aren't the only Healer in Jjaan-bi, and as for being a Seeker, you haven't even a ring any longer. You would do well to forget any thoughts of revenge and go along with this search. You might even earn yourself a place in the hearts of the people of Jjaan-bi, if you're smart."

Dhalvad kept silent, realizing that there was no arguing with Amet. It was obvious that the Speaker had convinced himself of the necessity of using force to get what he wanted—no, what he thought the people of Jjaan-bi wanted.

Dhalvad tried to keep track of the turns they took in the maze of tunnels that led deeper into the mountain. Many of the tunnels looked unused. Dead or dying fayyal rocks gave poor lighting, and loose rock debris made the footing dangerous in places. They passed through an old rough wooden doorway and went down a flight of crude steps. The air was damp and musty in the tunnel below. A few seconds later Amet stopped in front of a barred door. Dhalvlad was completely lost by that time and realized that only the method of trial and error would lead him to the place again.

"Unbar the door and go in. Pocalina is inside," Amet directed.

Dhalvlad had moved only a step or two into the room when something hurtled at him from the side. He saw a cloud of black hair and the blur of a face, then Poco was on him. The momentum of her attack drove him back against the stone wall. His head struck the wall, and for a second or two he almost lost consciousness. He heard Amet's laughter as the door slammed shut. That sound was followed by the heavy thunk of a bar dropping into place.

"Dhal!" Poco cried, realizing her mistake too late. She grabbed his arms and helped him up. "Are you all right? I thought it would be Paa-tol or Amet or one of their lackeys." Tears began to trickle down her face. "I'm so sorry, Dhal. Please tell me you're all right."

He straightened and tried to shake the fuzziness from his head. "Let me sit down."

She moved in under his arm and helped him across the room. Screech, who had watched from his place in the doorway to the next room, moved forward as far as his chain would allow and helped Dhalvad over to Poco's bed.

Dhalvad gently rubbed the back of his head and used his healing skill to banish the pain. "That was quite a reception," he murmured.

Poco shook her head. "I said I was sorry, Dhal. I've

been planning that move for the last few hours. I was
sure it would be Amet or Paa-tol. I was hoping to knock
whoever it was off-balance and get him across the room
to where Screech could help me. The last one I expected
to see was you." She hugged him tightly and gave him a
kiss. "Not that I'm not glad to see you all in one piece. I
was afraid they'd done something to you."

He stroked her hair as he held her. "They've done
nothing to me but make me worry about you, Jiam, and
Screech." He glanced around the room, a worried frown
creasing his forehead. "Where is Jiam?"

"He's in the other room. We thought he'd be safer
there if the fighting got rough." She turned to Screech.
"Go get him."

Screech returned carrying Jiam bundled in a blanket.
Dhalvad took his son in his arms. Large crystal-blue
eyes stared up at him, then Jiam grinned and gurgled
happily.

"Glad to see me, little one?" Dhalvad crooned. His
relief at finding all three alive brought tears to his eyes.
He brought Jiam up against his chest and held him tight,
listening to his baby sounds as he grabbed a small handful of his father's hair and pulled on it.

Poco's heart ached to see the tears in Dhalvad's eyes.
It isn't right, she thought, that so gentle a person should
be subjected to this kind of torment. Though Dhalvad
had proven to be strong, resilient, and more than capable
of holding his own—from the dangerous days of their
trek from the Deep, to near-slavery in Port Sulta, to their
almost fatal crossing of the plains where derkat radgs
roamed freely, to their final trek through a World Gate
where Dhalvad had saved the living essence of the Tamorlee—there was a streak of gentleness in him that remained firmly entrenched. Her thoughts went to
Haradan, Dhalvad's foster father, to his slow easy ways,
his silent laughter, and his love and concern for a child
not his own. If anyone was responsible for Dhalvad
being what he was, it was probably Haradan.

"What are we going to do, Dhal?" she asked softly.

Screech, who had settled on the end of the bed

watching the small family, growled. *"Escape!"* he signed.

"Yes," Dhalvad agreed, looking at the derkat. "You three must escape. Then Amet no longer has a hold over me." He told them briefly what had been happening since the day of their capture and ended with Amet's plan to get the crystal called Mithdaar no matter whom he hurt in the process.

"It doesn't sound good," Poco said. "What does the Tamorlee think about all of this? Surely it doesn't approve of what Amet's doing to us."

"It doesn't know yet. Each time I've linked with the crystal, Amet is there listening to whatever is said."

"So what? Let him listen!" Poco said sharply. "The Tamorlee should know what's going on! It might even be able to help us in some way. The next time you link with it, tell it what Amet's doing!"

"I do that and Amet is sure to retaliate." Dhalvad glanced down at Jiam, who was still playing with his braid. "I can't take the chance, Poco, not until I'm sure you three are safely out of Amet's reach."

Poco wanted to argue but knew Dhalvad was right.

"Where is Little Fur?" Screech signed. *"Amet took him from us yesterday."*

Dhalvad's eyes brightened. "He was with me until just a little while ago. The last time I saw him he was down on all fours running for all he was worth. He slipped out of the room before Amet or Paa-tol could stop him. Paa-tol got a good bite on the hand trying to stop him."

Poco's hopes rose. The olvaar was small but he was clever. "What will Gi do?"

Dhal shook his head. "I'm not really sure. He may try to find you three, or he may go to someone he trusts, like Chulu or Carras. At the moment, he's our only hope of reaching someone on the outside."

Screech's tufted ears tilted forward. He turned and looked at the door. *"Someone comes,"* he signed. *"Do we attack?"*

Dhalvad had lost track of the time. He stood up and handed Jiam to Poco. "If it's Amet, he'll be ready for something like that, so I doubt he'll come alone, but if he is . . ."

Dhalvad moved over to the side of the room and signed for Screech to be ready.

The door opened and swung all the way back, exposing the room. Paa-tol was the first through the doorway. He was armed with a drawn sword and was followed closely by Amet, who was also armed.

Dhalvad moved back to stand beside Poco. "Did you find Gi?"

Amet looked at Dhalvad a moment or two before replying. "Yes. We found him just where you said he'd be, in the marketplace."

Disappointed by the news but not willing to let on, Poco frowned at Amet. "What did you do with him?" she snapped.

"He's safe enough," Amet replied, "if he behaves himself. If not—" Amet shrugged "—then he'll have to suffer the consequences."

Amet motioned Dhalvad forward. "Hurry or we'll be late for our meeting with the Council," he said.

Dhalvad turned and touched Screech on the shoulder. It was an intimate gesture among derkat showing great trust. "Watch over them, friend."

Screech growled softly in the back of his throat, his amber eyes round and filled with silent promise.

Dhalvad stepped close to Poco and Jiam and gave them a quick hug. Poco's lips met his in a kiss as tears sprang to her eyes. "Watch yourself, Dhal," she whispered. "Don't trust either of them."

"I won't," he replied, fighting the lump in his throat.

Amet watched the farewell scene with impatience, his thoughts already on the Council and what he was going to say. He was going to have to be extremely careful not to give too much away, which would mean he would have to guard his own tongue as well as Dhalvad's.

"Come on, Dhalvad," he snapped. "We're in a hurry!"

Dhalvad kissed Poco one last time and tore himself from her hold. As he walked toward the doorway, he was touched by a sudden premonition that he would never see his family alive again. He turned and looked at Poco, then Amet grabbed him by the arm and hurried him out through the doorway, leaving Paa-tol to close and lock the door behind them.

Dhalvad glared at Amet. "If anything happens to any one of them," he swore, "I'll kill you—slowly—so you can taste some of the pain you're putting us through!"

Amet was startled by the maniacal look that had come to Dhalvad's eyes. He cast a nervous glance over his shoulder and was relieved to see Paa-tol hurrying after them.

Amet's chin lifted. "Nothing is going to happen to your family as long as you do as you're told. I give you my word!"

"Which at the moment is worthless, as far as I'm concerned," Dhalvad said.

Paa-tol came up on Dhalvad's free side, his sword back in its scabbard. There was a question in his eyes as he caught Amet's glance. "Anything wrong?"

"Nothing that concerns you," Amet said coldly. "Come, the Council will be waiting for us."

The Council chamber was situated in the right wing of the Learning Arc, a long, crescent-shaped building that was the center of learning among the Ni of Jjaan-bi. The spacious chamber was furnished with soft cushioned chairs and low tables. Wood sculptures and woven grass hangings decorated the walls, and intricate mosaic patterns made from a variety of woods covered the floor. A heavy table of black odak wood stood in the center of the room, and at that moment, seven of the eight official Council chairs were occupied, six by Council members and the seventh by Dhalvad, as Amet's guest.

During the evenings or on storm-darkened days, the room was lighted by overhead chandeliers that held fayyal rocks, but on that day, the rocks' light gave way to the sister suns shining brightly through the bank of eight tall windows that overlooked Lake Haddrach.

Dhalvad watched Chulu from across the table. They

had been in the room for several hours, and the older Ni had been unusually quiet throughout Amet's talk about the Tamorlee and the planned search for a second crystal. It was almost as if Chulu sensed the undercurrent of tension between Amet and Dhalvad. He knows something is wrong, Dhalvad thought as Chulu's glance touched him again. He's waiting for me to say something.

For a few seconds he considered openly denouncing Amet before the Council. Once they knew the full story, he could beg their help in locating and freeing Poco, Jiam, and Screech, and put an end to Amet's control over his life. Then he thought of Paa-tol, whom Amet had sent from the room shortly after their arrival in the Council chambers. A knot of fear twisted his insides when he thought of his family at the mercy of the cold, calculating Second Commander. He firmly believed that Paa-tol would follow Amet's orders to the letter, without regard for the consequences.

No! he thought. I won't risk Poco's and Jiam's lives. There has to be another way!

As Amet paused to look around the table, asking for any further questions, Chulu spoke up. "Then yesterday Dhalvad told us the truth."

Amet heard the accusation in Chulu's voice. "He did. I have already apologized for doubting him."

Dhalvad clenched his fists beneath the table, swallowing the word "liar" before it could reach his lips.

"What about the other things Dhalvad told us?" Chulu continued. "About your being replaced as Speaker at the request of the Tamorlee? You haven't touched upon that. Was it also the truth?"

Dhalvad grinned inwardly, hope rising as his friend cut through Amet's carefully prepared story to hit upon a truth Amet had tried to sidestep. How would the Speaker answer? He could lie, but that was not Amet's way.

Amet glanced down the table at Dhalvad, his look warning of retribution should the Healer speak out of turn. Dhalvad glared back at him, his lips grimly set.

"Dhalvad told the truth about the Tamorlee requesting a new Speaker yesterday, but since then I've linked with the Tamorlee with Dhalvad's help, and the crystal has reconsidered its request. The Tamorlee is intent on finding this other crystal and for a brief time believed that Dhalvad could be of more assistance than I. The three of us have now come to an understanding and will work together in this search. It doesn't matter who holds the title of Speaker right now. That can be decided on our return. What does matter is finding this other crystal and bringing it back to Jjaan-bi."

Davano and Tidul nodded, but Lurral still had reservations. "I agree that finding another crystal like the Tamorlee is extremely important, but I question whether it's wise to take the Tamorlee from Jjaan-bi and chance losing it. Remember, we lost it once before by moving it to another location, and now that it's so much smaller in size, it will be that much easier to lose."

"We don't intend to lose it," Amet said firmly. "Dhalvad, Paa-tol, and myself are all capable of a quick return to Jjaan-bi if anything goes wrong. The crystal will not leave our sight."

"Still," Lurral said, "only three to guard the Tamorlee . . . It sounds risky. Why not take more? There are over fourteen Seekers in the city at the moment, and if we put out a call, others would come surely."

Amet shook his head. "I don't think such help will be necessary, Lurral." He saw Chulu's frown deepen and changed what he had intended to say. "But you may put out a call if you like and await our report. Once we've located the other crystal and have had a chance to look over the situation, we'll be better able to judge if more help will be needed."

Chiilana cleared her throat and caught the eyes of the others around the table. Her gaze fastened on Amet. "How long will it take you to find this other crystal?"

Amet shrugged. "I'm not really sure. The Tamorlee has linked with the other crystal several times but hasn't been able to speak directly to it. That may take actual physical contact to accomplish, but it does know the general direction of the sending, and that's what we'll follow until we can get a good visual sighting that's not too distant. It may take three or four time jumps to get us where we want to be; it may take twice that many. We just don't know."

"Dhalvad? What do you think?" Chiilana asked.

Dhalvad hesitated. One look at Amet's face reminded him of Paa-tol and his orders. There was nothing he could do for Poco and Jiam except to see that no obstacles stood in Amet's way. Resigned to the part he was being forced to play, he stood up.

"I don't agree with everything Amet has said, but I do know what the Tamorlee wants, and if it doesn't get it, it's capable of shutting us out and sealing off that part of our past it holds. I believe that we have to stop thinking of the Tamorlee as some benign servant who'll give and give of itself and expect nothing in return. It's a sentient being who, with our unknowing help, has searched long and hard to find one of its own kind. I think it's time we did whatever we can to help it find the one it calls its dream brother. If we can help it, it may consent to continue being our historian."

Amet frowned, surprised by Dhalvlad's eloquence and help in convincing the Council to stand aside and let the search commence. He looked around. "Is there anything else anyone wants to say? No? Then I suggest a vote."

A vote was duly taken and recorded by Lurral. The search for a second crystal was authorized with no dissenting votes.

"How soon do you plan on leaving?" Chulu asked.

"Tomorrow morning," Amet responded. "So Dhalvad and I must leave you now. We each have things to take care of before we're ready to begin our journey."

Lurral pushed away from the table. "If you're leaving so soon, I'd better get started alerting the other Seekers in Jjaan-bi, just in case you need them."

Amet nodded and moved around the end of the table toward Dhalvad. "It will be good to know we have backup should anything go wrong."

Everyone was getting up. Dhalvad rose, wishing he had been able to alert at least one of the Council members to his problem, preferably Chulu, but Amet was not about to let that happen. As Dhalvad turned to look for Chulu, Amet approached and dropped a hand on his shoulder.

"Ready to go?"

Dhalvad nodded, barely suppressing his irritation over Amet's possessive attitude.

"Wait," Chulu said as Amet steered Dhalvad toward the doorway.

Dhalvad's heartbeat quickened as he turned to see his friend pushing past Tidul and hurrying toward him. Perhaps there was still a chance of alerting Chulu to Poco's plight.

"We haven't much time," Amet said as Chulu stopped before them.

Chulu raised his hands. "I know, Amet. I know. I just wanted to wish you both good luck." His crystal-gray eyes grew sober. "And tell Dhalvad that I'll keep an eye on Poco and Jiam while he's gone."

Amet's hand tightened on Dhalvad's shoulder. "That won't be necessary. They've gone visiting and won't be back for several weeks."

"I didn't know they were going anywhere," Chulu said. "Odd that Poco didn't say something to Naalan the other day. Where'd they go, Dhal?"

"To Cybury," Dhalvad improvised quickly. "She met a young Singer from there some time ago and promised her she'd bring the baby for a visit. They shouldn't be gone too long."

"Does she know about this search you're going on?"

"She knows."

"Did Screech and Gi go with her? I haven't seen either of them since the other day."

"Screech is devoted to Poco and the baby, as is Gi-arobi. Where you find one, you'll find the others," Dhalvad answered.

Chulu smiled. "Leaving you to fend for yourself."

Dhalvad nodded, his face sober.

"I'm sorry, Chulu," Amet interrupted, "but we must go along now."

Chulu nodded. He held his hands out to Dhalvad. "Take care of yourself, friend, and don't take any unnecessary chances. We'll all be waiting to hear from you."

Dhalvad reached out and clasped Chulu's arms at the elbows, his fingers closing tight around his arms. "You are a good friend, Chulu. I'd appreciate it if you'd look in on Poco and Jiam when they return, if I'm not back."

There was a warning nudge from behind.

"You know I will," Chulu responded, frowning slightly.

Dhalvad released Chulu and, without another word, turned and accompanied Amet from the room.

Chulu stood and watched them out of sight, the frown on his face deepening as he rubbed his arms where Dhalvad had pinched him so hard.

"Is something wrong?" Chiilana asked as she approached. "Having second thoughts on the vote?"

Chulu shook his head. "No. If there's another crystal out there, it's best we find it."

"So why the worried look?"

"Did it seem to you that Dhalvad was acting strangely—preoccupied?"

"He was quiet, but he answered all of our questions quite openly. I don't doubt but that this whole thing has made him think about what happened last year; World Gate hopping, the shattering of the Tamorlee, his narrow escape from Ariel. This search may not prove as dangerous as what he did before, but the not knowing can be worrisome."

"Perhaps," Chulu said softly, continuing to rub his arms. "But I thought I saw something in Dhalvad's eyes just a moment ago, a look that—I don't know how to explain it, but it bothers me."

"Don't worry so," Chiilana chided gently, touching his shoulder. "He'll be fine. Amet is levelheaded, and Paa-tol is an excellent fighter. Between the two of them, they'll keep him safe."

Chapter 12 ✍

TWO MALE NI CARRIED A LARGE WOODEN CRATE DOWN the ill-lighted tunnel and never noticed the small bundle of fur pressed tightly against the base of the wall near their feet. They were in the underground portion of Jjaan-bi known as the Old Quarter, where the fayyal rocks used to light the tunnels were not changed as often, thus creating a dusklike atmosphere that made hiding easy.

Gi-arobi uncurled, poked his head out into the tunnelway, and watched as the Ni paused at a door just a short distance down the tunnel. They set the crate down, opened the door, then picked it up again and carried it inside. Gi's eyes shifted back and forth as he kept a wary eye on the tunnelway both in front of him and behind. He knew he was being hunted by Amet and his followers and had been careful not to be seen as he scampered down one tunnel after another in search of some trace of Poco, Jiam, and Big Fur. He had been at it all night long, and he was growing weary and hungry.

He licked at his right forehand, then his left. Both sets of fingers were sore from prying open doors not made for the convenience of an olvaar.

The two Ni came out of the room, closed and latched the door, then turned right down the tunnelway leading back toward the newer section of the underground city. Gi had remained in the Old Quarter, reasoning that if one wanted to hide something or someone, one would most likely secrete it away in a less populated area such as the lower tunnel storage areas.

He waited until the last echo of their footsteps had faded before moving out into the tunnel. He paused at the door they had used and flexed his fingers. Sharp claws appeared, and he used them to climb up the door to the wooden bar. He pushed the bar back until the door was free, then dropped to the floor and put all of his weight against the door. It opened slowly, its hinges squeaking noisily. He inspected the room quickly; a good sniff or two told him that those he sought were not in the room. He left the door open and moved down the tunnelway. He found another door and sniffed around the doorsill, then moved on. He was growing more and more worried as time passed, for Dhalvad as much as for the others.

Gi wrinkled his nose as he remembered Amet's smell the last time he had seen him. The Ni's sweat had held the sourness of fear, and Gi knew that fear made all creatures a little mad. If he did not find Poco, Jiam, and Big Fur soon, he knew he would have to return to Dhalvad and try to help him escape from Amet.

He reached an intersecting tunnel and paused. He could not read the markings on the sides of the tunnel walls, but he had an excellent memory. He had seen the same carved squiggles before and knew he had searched the right-hand tunnel earlier. He turned left and continued on. He was nearing the first door to his left when suddenly he smelled something familiar. It was Big Fur's scent! He sniffed under the door, but the odor did not seem to be coming from there. He crossed to a door on the other side of the tunnel and sniffed again. Not there either.

Disappointed but not discouraged, he continued down the tunnel. He hurried as the scent became stronger. He saw a door ahead; it was slightly ajar. Down on all fours, he ran on. His rush almost carried him past the doorway.

His small heart beat rapidly as he nudged the door open and went inside. Different smells assailed him as he made a quick survey of the two rooms. Big Fur's scent was the strongest, its musky odor almost overpowering in the small rooms. He also smelled Poco and Jiam. But the rooms were empty. As he neared one side of the far room, he smelled urine, and when he moved back into the first room, he caught the scent of blood and found a partially dried puddle of blood near one of the beds. He was sure it belonged to Big Fur.

He let loose with a soft low whistle of apprehension and returned to the tunnel. He quickly picked up Big Fur's scent along the floor. A tuft of fur caught on some rough stone told him that Big Fur was being dragged. He moved away from the center of the tunnel and stood up, sniffing the air. He smelled Poco's scent, and Jiam's, and several others he did not recognize. He dropped down to all fours and continued his hunt, concentrating solely on the scents he followed.

He left the narrow tunnels of the Old Quarter and a short time later had entered better lighted, wider tunnels that led straight to one of the larger city caves. There he ran straight into trouble, for with the coming of morning, there were Ni in the tunnels going about their daily tasks and there was no way to hide from all of them.

Gi hesitated in the shadow of a tunnel wall and looked out into the main cave where the Ni set up a series of hourly markets where one could buy and trade any number of things from food to clothes, from animals to weapons. There were four other marketplaces within the underground city and several outside. Gi was more familiar with the outside markets, but he had, upon occasion, ventured inside with Dhalvad or Screech.

Fearing to lose the scents he followed, he took a chance and plunged into the open, his nose kept close to the ground while his glances darted to the people he passed.

A few Ni noticed him and pointed as he passed by. Several even called his name, but he did not stop to investigate because he was losing the scents of his friends to the food and people smells wafting around him. Then Big Fur's scent, the one he had been able to hold onto the longest, suddenly evaporated.

He began a slow circle, widening it each time around, searching frantically for some smell he would recognize. A few minutes later he stopped his circling and sat down, defeated. He had lost Big Fur's scent, which probably meant that his friend was being carried. He whistled his frustration and proceeded to lick at his sore forehands. All the while he studied the market tables nearby. The enticing food smells coming from them were difficult to ignore.

"Hai, Gi! What are you doing here by yourself?"

Gi turned at the sound of that voice and saw Caaras standing at one of the market tables, a half-eaten sweet bun in one hand. Caaras had light-green hair, a wide mouth with strong white teeth, and upward-slanting eyebrows that gave his face a mocking, amused look. He was one of Dhalvad's best friends.

Gi whistle clicked a greeting and ran toward the young Ni, oblivious to the several pairs of feet that almost stepped on him as he dashed by.

Caaras grinned when he saw Gi coming and reached down, offering Gi a lift to his shoulder. As he settled the olvaar in place, he glanced around, looking for Dhalvad.

"What have you got there, Caaras?" one of the merchants asked as Gi whistled in Caaras's ear.

Caaras set the bun down on the table and covered his ear with a hand. "Easy with the whistling, Gi!" He laughed. "You'll deafen me." He smiled at the merchant. "You haven't met Gi-arobi yet? He's Dhalvad's little friend. Here, let me introduce you. Gi, this is Benha. Benha, this is Gi-arobi."

Gi glanced at the merchant, then caught at Caaras's ear. "Gi needing much help, Caaras! You help?"

"Help you how?" Caaras patted Gi's round stomach. "Find you some food maybe?"

Gi's small claws extended. "Not food! Help Gi find Poco, Jiam, Big Fur!"

"Ooch! Let go, Gi! What's wrong with you? You

know better than that!" Caaras caught Gi's wrist and gently disengaged his claws; then he drew him from his shoulder and held him in one arm. "Gi?"

"Needing help! Dhal be in trouble!" Gi searched his mind for the right words. "Amet hiding Poco and Jiam. You help Gi find! Hurry. Hurry!"

"Gi, what are you talking about?" Caaras demanded.

"Amet make Dhal go away. Say hurt Poco and baa-bee. Big Fur hurt! Blood on floor! Gi trying to find them. You help!"

"Yes, Gi. Yes, I'll help, but first you've got to tell me what this is all about. Where's Dhalvad? And what's this about Poco and Amet?"

"Amet making Dhal use fire stone. Saying—"

A hand closed on the back of Gi's neck and plucked him from Caaras in one smooth movement. "We've been looking all over for you!"

"Hai!" Caaras cried, startled. "That's a friend you're mishandling!"

The Ni who held Gi-arobi was dressed in the red tunic and pants of the city watch; a sword of authority was strapped to his waist. "Easy now," he said, raising a hand as Caaras stepped forward to take Gi back. "I've orders to find this one and bring him to Amet. We've been looking for him all night long."

Caaras eyed Gi, who dangled by the scruff of his neck an arm's length from the city watch. "What's Gi done?" he demanded. "And where's Dhalvad, the Healer?"

"I don't know the answer to either of your questions, Caaras. You'll have to speak with Amet. I'm only follow-ing orders."

"Well, you don't have to hold him like that!" Caaras objected. "You're hurting him. Let me have him and I'll go with you to—"

"No." The watch pulled Gi back out of Caaras's reach. "I think it's best if I hang onto him."

Gi had had enough. He caught at the Ni's wrist with one hand and swung himself around and up high enough so he could sink sharp teeth into the Ni's arm. The Ni cried out and dropped Gi. The olvaar bounced as he hit the ground, got his feet under him, and scurried off between the legs of the crowd that had gathered to see what was going on.

"Find Chulu!" Gi-arobi piped as he disappeared around the end of a market table. "Tell about Dhal and Poco! Hurry, Caaras! Hurry!"

The officer dove after the olvaar, pushing people roughly aside as he tried to keep the small fur child in sight. Caaras followed in his wake, intent on getting to the bottom of the strange encounter, concern for his friends suddenly blossoming into fear. What was going on between Amet and Dhalvad? And what did Poco and her child have to do with it?

When it became evident that Gi had successfully lost his pursuer, Caaras headed for the outside. At that early hour Chulu was most likely to still be at home. Perhaps he could answer some questions.

Dhalvad woke tired and irritable. He had barely slept all night, worry about Poco, Jiam, Screech, and Gi keeping him awake and tense. Their safety and well-being depended on his actions, and though he detested the half-truths Amet had forced him to tell, he knew he had had no other choice, and that only added to his frustration.

Unsure of the time, he went to the corner of the room where a chamberpot and a bucket of water sat. He used both and returned to sit on the edge of the bed, his thoughts moving from his family and friends to the Tamorlee and the search that lay ahead of them. It might be a short search if the Tamorlee had picked up further sendings from the second crystal; if it had not, their journey could take a lot longer. That worried him, for each minute they spent seeking Mithdaar was a minute Poco and Jiam would remain prisoners.

If only there was a way to alert the Tamorlee to Amet's underhanded persuasion without putting his family in danger, he might be able to circumvent Amet's threat of retribution. But Amet was no fool, and he would be sure to control Dhalvad's access to the Tamor-lee.

He rubbed at his eyes. Damn! Is there no way out of this mess? he thought in frustration.

He was startled by the sound of a wooden bar being drawn back. As the door swung open he stood up and saw Paa-tol and one of the city watch, a Ni by the name of Anwhol.

Paa-tol motioned him forward. "It's time."

They walked in silence to Amet's quarters. The Speaker was seated calmly in a chair when they arrived. He motioned for Anwhol to close the door, then looked at Dhalvad.

"I believe everything is ready for the search to begin. I placed the Tamorlee in a new ring setting last night, which should make it more convenient for our journey." His glance flicked to Paa-tol. "Are you ready?"

Paa-tol nodded and raised his hand, his own Seeker ring glowing opalescent green.

"One question before we go," Dhalvad said. "Who's taking care of Poco, Jiam, and Screech?"

Amet's crystal-gray eyes met Dhalvad's squarely. "Anwhol will see to your loved ones. He is extremely conscientious, and I've left him explicit orders."

Dhalvad suppressed a shiver. Amet's veiled threat was all too clear.

"Come," the Speaker said, motioning Dhalvad closer. "We waste time. Paa-tol?"

Paa-tol picked up a pack and slipped into the harness, then took his place beside the other two. As the three moved into place shoulder to shoulder to form a tight ring, Anwhol stepped back a few paces and watched, his face impassive.

Anwhol was one of Amet's younger cousins and had followed his leadership for so long that he had ceased to question his much-revered relative. He would do as Amet had directed and trust to his cousin to protect him should anything go wrong. He knew enough of the task Amet had set himself to understand that the Speaker was risking his position in the current venture; but he also

believed that the honor to be gained was worth the risk
—for all of them. As for Dhalvad's mate and child and
the half-tamed derkat, they, too, had a part to play, and
though it was against Ni law to knowingly take the life of
another, he would kill all three as Amet had ordered if it
became necessary.

Amet held up his fist so the other two could look into
the depths of the Tamorlee, set securely into a common
ring setting. "Close your hands around mine," he ordered, "and look into the Tamorlee."

Paa-tol raised his right hand; the fire stone he wore
winked brilliantly as it drew near the Tamorlee. Dhalvad
placed his ringless hand on top of Amet's. Instantly the
Tamorlee grew lighter in color, and a pulsating white
light could be seen moving around and around within the
crystal.

Anwhol was so caught up in the scene before him that
he did not notice the door behind him opening as if by a
draft of air.

Dhalvad, Amet, and Paa-tol were quickly drawn
within the Tamorlee's mind, its presence wrapping
around them with a feeling of impatience. *Dhalvad.
Amet.* There was a hesitation in the greeting. *Paa-tol?*

I come at Amet's request, Paa-tol answered for himself before Amet could respond. *You may have need of a
strong arm and a quick sword when Mithdaar is located.*

Dhalvad? the Tamorlee queried.

Dhalvad hesitated, then compromised, refusing to lie
outright to the Tamorlee. *If it comes to a fight, Paa-tol
will be useful.*

Have you had contact from the other crystal lately?
Amet asked, trying to direct the Tamorlee's attention
away from Paa-tol's presence.

*There was a brief jolt of Mithdaar's energy pattern
this morning. Nothing since,* the Tamorlee replied.

*Do you have a visual picture to help us make a clean
transfer?* Dhalvad asked, impatient to get under way.
The sooner gone, the sooner back.

No, but I have the general direction, which is east

*and south. There is a transfer point in Tre-ayjeel that
should serve to get us closer to Mithdaar.*

*The Reaches are both east and south. Wouldn't they
serve better than Tre-ayjeel?* Amet asked.

The Reaches aren't far enough to the east.

But there's nothing south of Tre-ayjeel but desert,
Paa-tol said. *It's a vast wasteland that we know little
about.*

It is from there my brother calls me.

As you would have it, Amet said. *Please show us the
transfer point in Tre-ayjeel. Paa-tol and I have both been
there. Dhalvad hasn't.*

The green light that surrounded them slowly faded,
and a scene formed within Dhalvad's mind. The first
thing he saw was a wide expanse of rolling hills interrupted by a number of lakes scattered like djong pieces
across a playing board. Then the scene changed slightly,
and he saw the edge of a plateau and a city of ivory-
colored walls and towers rising out of the forest. At the
southern edge of the city, down a sheer drop of several
thousand feet, lay the desert. The fringe of green growth
at the bottom of the cliff quickly gave way to browns,
yellows, and tans that spoke of dry, desolate lands.

The scene shifted once again to a great tower with a
large courtyard below. The scene grew sharper in his
mind, and Dhalvad knew that it was the transfer point
the Tamorlee had chosen.

Do you have it firmly in mind, Dhalvad? Amet asked.

Yes.

Together then, Amet said.

Anwhol stepped back another two paces as the air
around the three Ni shimmered. Suddenly he caught a
movement out of the corner of one eye. He turned just
as Gi-arobi darted toward the three Ni and wiggled his
way in between Dhalvad's and Paa-tol's legs.

Anwhol started forward, then stopped when he felt
the static tingle in the air surrounding the three Ni and
their uninvited guest. "Amet! Wait!" he cried. "It's the
olvaar!"

Dhalvad felt the sharp prick of claws as Gi quickly

climbed up his pant leg. He knew in an instant who it was and tried to draw out of the link, but the Tamorlee's energy pattern was too strong.

Gi whistled sharply to get Dhalvad's attention.

No, Gi! Dhalvad cried, fearing for his small friend. *Get away!*

Gi could not hear the mental command and clung on all the tighter as he grew aware of the strange prickling air surrounding him. His glance fastened on the fire stone ring in Amet's hand. He was suddenly afraid, but he was also determined not to be left behind. He had seen Dhalvad use a fire stone ring before and knew what he had to do. He leaned out and set a small furred finger to the green stone. He knew one terrified moment of disorientation, then he was held tightly by invisible bonds of energy.

I have him, Dhalvad, the Tamorlee said.

You have him? He's to go with us?

Too late for him not to, the Tamorlee responded.

Gi! Dhalvad cried. *Can you see the tower, Gi? Answer me!*

The shimmer of air increased and Anwhol lost sight of the four within the Tamorlee's magnetic embrace. A few seconds later the shimmering light disappeared, leaving him in sole possession of the room. There was no sign of the olvaar.

The scene that filled Dhalvad's mind became reality: the open courtyard, the white sandstone tower rising above him, the patterned stone floor at his feet, Amet and Paa-tol to either side of him, and clinging to his tunic front . . .

Gi?

The olvaar's eyelids opened slowly, then closed. He looked as if he were half asleep.

Tamorlee, is Gi all right? Dhalvad asked.

Disoriented but unharmed. He is courageous for so small a being.

Dhalvad was confused. *Tamorlee, I thought only the Ni could mind travel through use of the fire stones.*

Anyone who can see and accept the inner vision of a

reality not his own can use the energy of the fire stones.

Dhalvad sensed Amet's impatience at being held in the link, but he had one more question. *Could men also use the fire stones as Seekers do?*

No man has ever tried, but from all I understand of them through contacts with the People, I believe men could use fire stones to travel. It would be an interesting experiment.

No! Amet exploded. *Men shall never have access to the fire stones! They would misuse the power!*

As you do yours? Dhalvad demanded angrily. The words were out before he could suppress them.

What I do, I do for the good of the People! Amet said, jumping in to defend himself.

What is it you have done? the Tamorlee asked calmly.

Nothing! I only used my office as Speaker to convince the Council that we should go in search of Mithdaar and—I persuaded Dhalvad to come by threatening to send his mate and child away from Jjaan-bi. Isn't that right, Dhalvad?

If I tell the truth, Dhalvad thought, the Tamorlee will be on my side, but even if we returned to Jjaan-bi, Paa-tol could get there just as quickly, and he knows where Poco is and I don't. If I go along with Amet, we're no worse off than we were before. Though Dhalvad was not projecting his thoughts to the others, the crystal sensed something in his hesitation.

Dhalvad?

I'll be honest with you, Tamorlee. I don't like Amet or Paa-tol. Anyone who threatens to harm innocent people cannot be trusted. Dhalvad stopped there, not quite daring to tell the complete truth but at the same time alerting the crystal to Amet's dual nature.

I did use threats, Amet protested, *but only after you refused to link with the Tamorlee and help us search for Mithdaar. This find is too important for one person to stand in the way!*

Dhalvad desperately wanted to refute Amet's statement, but to speak out too vehemently might endanger Poco and Jiam.

It was wrong to threaten Dhalvad's family, the Ta-morlee said to Amet. *You will right this wrong after we have found Mithdaar and return to Jjaan-bi. Agreed?*

Dhalvad sensed the compulsion in the crystal's words and winced at the mental harshness of the command.

Agreed, Amet said meekly.

Dhalvad, the Tamorlee said, its thought impulses soft-ened, *I want you with me, but only because you wish to be. Will you stay and help me find my dream brother?*

Yes, Dhalvad answered, knowing that he really had no choice. It seemed that the Tamorlee, for all of its intelli-gence, was not able to see past the deceptive curtain of righteousness Amet had pulled about himself.

Good. I am pleased. I release you all now, the Tamor-lee said. *Go and rest while I listen for my brother.*

The energy that held them all in stasis gradually melted away. The first thing Dhalvad noticed was a draft of cool air blowing in his face. The next thing he felt was the prick of a knife in his side. He turned.

Paa-tol's eyes were narrowed with anger. "Try that again and I promise you'll regret it!"

Amet slipped free of the ring holding the Tamorlee and put it in his tunic pocket, then wiped his damp fore-head and glanced around. The transfer had gone smoothly, but the interrogation by the Tamorlee had left him shaken.

Several Ni standing well away from the transfer point moved toward them.

Amet glanced at Paa-tol and motioned for him to put his knife away. "We'll discuss what happened later," he growled softly. He looked at Dhalvad and Gi, who was beginning to stir. He turned back to Paa-tol. "Keep watch over them. I'll take care of our accommodations."

"How long will we be here?" Paa-tol asked, putting his knife away.

"I don't know. It depends on the Tamorlee."

Two older Ni stopped before them, placed their hands palm to palm and touched their fingertips to their lips. "Welcome to Tre-ayjeel," the one on the right said, offer-ing his cupped hands in greeting. One after the other he took their hands and introduced himself as he moved along. "I am Agnal, and this is my friend Ea-dil."

Amet reciprocated, giving his name and introducing the others. Both Ni smiled when Gi-arobi offered his small furred hand and whistled his own form of greeting.

Ea-dil looked at Dhalvad as he released Gi-arobi's hand. "The olvaar is far from his homeland."

"You have no olvaar here?" Dhalvad asked.

"We believe they prefer the more temperate climate to the south," Ea-dil replied. "It's a pleasure to have one of their kind for a visit, though I'm surprised to learn that they are capable of making a safe mind transfer."

"It's a surprise to us, too," Amet said. "Really, it was quite accidental. It's something that will have to be studied by our Seekers."

Agnal stepped forward. "Will you require accommodations, or is someone expecting you?"

"No one is expecting us," Amet said. "And yes, we'll need rooms. Two will do. We aren't sure how long we'll be staying."

A curious expression crossed Agnal's face as he studied Amet. "Your face is familiar. Should I know you?"

Amet hesitated. "I've been here several times in the past," he said finally. "Perhaps we've met somewhere."

Agnal's eyes grew large in sudden recognition. "Speaker? Yes! It is you! But we had no notice that you were coming here! Is—something wrong?"

Amet frowned in annoyance, for he had hoped to arrive and leave without any fuss. "No. Nothing's wrong. I'm here on a very special matter and would appreciate your not announcing my arrival."

"Is there anyone you wish to see? Someone I might—"

"No. No one at the moment. If you'll just show us to our rooms, we'd like to rest awhile. If there's anything else we need, we'll let you know."

Agnal nodded. "Please do so. We are yours to command. Ea-dil, the watch is yours."

Ea-dil nodded and returned to his post outside the transfer circle as the others followed Agnal through a narrow stone doorway and down a winding staircase. It was common for a watch to be stationed at main transfer points in order to assist arriving Seekers.

Dhalvad stroked the olvaar as they descended to the lower floors and guest rooms maintained for traveling Seekers. "Gi, are you really all right?"

Gi patted Dhalvad's arm. "Gi fine," he whistled. "Have much to tell." The olvaar was using his own language, which told Dhalvad that what he had to say was not meant for Paa-tol's or Amet's ears.

"Tell me," Dhalvad whistled back softly.

Gi's golden eyes took in every detail of the halls, rooms, and people they passed. "Gi find room where Poco, baa-bee, and Big Fur held. All gone now. Can't find. Gi follow their trail but lose it. Watch find Gi. Caaras help Gi escape. Afraid for you alone with Amet. Come to protect you."

Dhalvad was distressed to learn that Poco and the other two had been moved, but he did not put such deviousness beyond Amet. "Did you tell Caaras about Poco and Jiam?"

"Try to," Gi said.

A hand dropped onto Dhalvad's shoulder. "Enough of that!" Paa-tol hissed. "Speak so I can understand, or shut up, both of you!"

Dhalvad glared at Paa-tol but tried to hold his anger in check. He hugged Gi a little tighter and rubbed a thumb across the olvaar's stomach. He would have to quiz Gi about Poco and Jiam when they were alone—if they were ever allowed to be alone.

"I'm glad you're here, Gi," Dhalvad said in trader. "I think you surprised everyone. No one thought olvaar could be Seekers. I'm still not sure what possessed you to touch the crystal. I always thought you were afraid of the fire spirit within the Tamorlee."

"More afraid being left behind," Gi answered in trader.

Dhalvad was curious. "What was it like for you in transfer?"

"Like being stuck in hole. No going forward. No

going back. All darkness, then see place of light and towers. Want go there." Gi-arobi cocked his head to one side as he looked up at Dhalvad. "Is gentle voice Tamor-lee?"

Dhalvad smiled at the description. "Yes."

"We helping Gentle Voice find Mithdaar?"

"Yes."

"Then Gentle Voice help us find Poco, Jiam, and Big Fur?"

Dhalvad glanced at Paa-tol who walked to his left listening to everything they said. He looked back at his small friend. "That's their promise, Gi." But can we trust them?

Chapter 13

BHALDAVIN WOKE TO A NOT-SO-GENTLE NUDGE OF A FOOT in the side. He opened his eyes and looked up. Sola stood over him, his malicious grin bringing back all the events of the day before. He sighted Ra-gar sliding to the west and knew that it was late afternoon. He sat up and looked around but saw no sign of Gringers or any of the other prisoners, including Thura.

Sola reached down and pulled him to his feet. "You're wanted, Green Hair."

Bhaldavin's head throbbed with pain, and his mouth was so dry that it was difficult to speak. "Where's my daughter?"

Sola leered down at him. "That's my little secret. She's safe. That's all you need to know right now."

"And the others? Gringers and Aldi?"

Sola shook him and thrust him forward keeping a handhold on the rope going around Bhaldavin's chest. "No more questions! Just walk!"

There were seven or eight Wastelanders standing near the main gate as they approached. One was the man Zojac. Sola stopped Bhaldavin a few paces away from the men.

Zojac spoke directly to Bhaldavin, his dark eyes intent. "It's time to see if the rumors we've heard about the Green Hair are true. A large swimming lizard has been sighted down at the edge of the lake. We want you to call it out of the water and show us how you can control it. If you can do what you claim, your life will be spared. If you fail, you'll be cut into small pieces and fed to the creature. Is that clear?"

Bhaldavin nodded, and the knot of fear that had been with him upon waking slowly dissolved. So they wanted him to prove he could sing draak. Well, that he could do—and more if the opportunity arose. How much freedom would they give him? he wondered as they started down the winding roadway. If he managed to sing a draak close enough, perhaps he could cut into their ranks by using the awesome strength of the draak against them. If he could kill some of them or frighten them away— His thoughts came to an abrupt halt as he remembered Thura. If he failed to destroy them all, if even one got away and managed to return to the mansion, the lives of the other prisoners would be in grave danger.

His glance touched the hidden entrance to the lake caves halfway around the end of the southern cove. Lilel, Theon, and all the others who had escaped were sure to be waiting there, perhaps planning some sort of rescue attempt. If he moved too quickly, he might end up thwarting their plans. Then again, they might be waiting for some kind of an opening, a chance for a successful attack. He looked away, fearing to reveal their hiding place by staring at it too long.

They reached the lakeside about twenty mintues later. Bhaldavin was still undecided about singing the draak to attack the men. Much would depend on the size of the draak seen lurking near the stone pier.

They all walked out a short distance onto the pier, the men glancing nervously at the water on both sides. It was evident that they had gone about as far as they dared. Zojac signaled for Sola to release Bhaldavin from his ropes.

As the rope dropped to the pier, Zojac withdrew a small leather bundle from his wide tunic pocket and held it out to Bhaldavin. "Here, this is yours. Gringers said you needed it to control these . . ."

"Draak," Bhaldavin supplied, his frown slipping away as he recognized the leather neck pouch. He had been concentrating so hard on fantasies of killing the men that he had not even missed it. He took the leather pouch and quickly dumped Mithdaar out into his hand. Warmth flooded through him as the crystal greeted him in its own special way.

Bhaldavin's head came up, and his glance touched the men surrounding him. Several were frowning; the others looked wary. How many had tried to hold Mithdaar and had been burned for their trouble? he wondered. More than one or two, he thought, judging by the looks he was getting.

Zojac studied Bhaldavin closely. "It doesn't burn you when you hold it?"

"No," Bhaldavin answered honestly.

Zojac considered that a moment, then shrugged. "We'll talk of it later. Now I want you to call in one of these—draak." He drew a light gun from his pocket. "Any thoughts you might have about escape had best be put aside for your own sake as well as your daughter's."

Bhaldavin turned without a word and moved farther down the pier. Two of the other men also drew light guns. Obviously they were not going to take any chances on his ability to control a draak.

He tucked the leather pouch into his pocket and held tight to Mithdaar. He did not need the crystal to sing draak, but if pretending meant that he could keep Mithdaar, he would pretend.

He held Mithdaar to his chest as he glanced out over the water looking for bubbles or ripples, any movement that would indicate a draak in the immediate area. He turned and kept on turning, his glances taking in the western shoreline and a portion of the tiered city that was fast losing its identity to the voracious plant growth that was reclaiming the land.

Suddenly he saw what he was looking for—a series of ripples on the water not far from shore. He lifted his head and loosed a high-pitched, undulating warble known as *nar-donva*. He repeated the call, and a few seconds later a dark-gray head broke the surface of the water.

The draak had a spiny crest rising behind its ears and running down the center of its back; it had a thin, sharp snout, and as it swam closer, its red eyes became visible. It made a strange whuffling sound as it blew water from its nose. Its head rose farther out of the water, revealing its long, thick neck. It was a gray fisher, a large one, common among water draak and useful to the Draak Watch, who had long before learned how to use them to chase schools of fish into nets.

The men on the pier started to back away as the gray fisher approached. All of those who held light guns had them out and were pointing them at the draak as it swam closer to the pier.

Bhaldavin changed the song to *vol-nada*, which held the draak in a mesmerized state as it drifted closer and settled next to the pier. Water dripped onto the pier as the draak's neck and head hung high over Bhaldavin.

Zojac cursed softly to himself. He could hear the strange melody issuing from Bhaldavin's lips, but it seemed impossible that such soft sounds could control a creature of such size.

"Tell him to send it away," one of the men behind Zojac whispered.

Zojac cut the man off with a motion of his hand. He drew a deep breath to steady himself as he lowered the gun and studied the Ni whom Gringers had called a draak singer. Though Bhaldavin was small in stature and had but one arm, it was clear that he was master over the great water reptile—which meant that the rumors were true! The green-haired ones could control the fierce predators that had plagued his people since the beginning of time! It was a tremendous find. Possession of such a person alone was worth the journey there. And they had not one, but two, and one a female!

Zojac's eyes lighted with the thought of the trade

wealth standing out on the stone pier, singing his eerie
song. His mind whirled with schemes that would allow
him to keep both of the green-haired ones for his tribe.
He glanced down at the light gun in his hand. It, too,
represented a prize worth trade wealth, but without the
strange machines to put the burning light back into the
guns, its value was not lasting—unless one chose to stay
in the dead city and claim it for his own. He shuddered
inwardly at that thought, his ancestors' teachings too
deeply inbred to be ignored.

Bhaldavin turned to look at the men, all the while
softly continuing his song. He had spotted several other
swirling motions in the water nearby and realized that if
he continued to sing much longer, he would have more
than one draak to contend with, which might prove more
than he could safely handle. He pointed to one of the
telltale ripples in the water and saw Zojac turn to look.
The man seemed to understand immediately.

"Send it away," Zojac called, keeping his voice low.

Bhaldavin nodded and once again changed the melody
of his song, sending the draak back to the depths of the
lake where its dinner awaited it.

When all signs of the draak had disappeared and the
water around the pier was calm but for a wind pattern on
the surface, Zojac signaled for Bhaldavin to rejoin them.

Bhaldavin hesitated, his glance returning to the water.
One step and a shallow dive and he could make a bid for
freedom, but that would mean abandoning Thura and
Gringers.

Zojac read the hesitation in the Ni's body and raised
his voice. "Come!"

Bhaldavin saw Zojac raise his light gun. It was aimed
at his legs. He had not moved quickly enough. If only he
had let thought become action—but he was too late. He
walked back toward the men, all thoughts of escape
pushed aside for the moment. Before he reached Zojac,
he put his hand into his pocket and worked the crystal
back into its leather pouch, hoping the men would forget
he had it.

"Very impressive, Green Hair," Zojac said as Bhalda-

vin stopped before him. "You are all the man called
Gringers claimed. You will be a welcome addition to our
tribe."

"Your tribe?" one of the other men snapped. He had
brown hair, brown eyes, and a birdlike beak of a nose
that was outsized for his face. "Have you forgotten that
the Galler tribe is to share equally in this venture? And
that includes all prisoners taken."

A red-haired man with a bushy beard and bad teeth
added his voice to the discussion. "We of the Barrens
won't be left out either!"

Zojac raised both hands in a placating gesture. "No
one will be left out! All the prisoners and valuables found
within the city will be divided equally."

"By who?" Brown Hair demanded. "You?"

As the men wrangled over who would claim what
when the spoils of their successful raid were drawn together, Bhaldavin looked over Zojac's shoulder up to the
first tier of land above the lake. He thought he had seen
movement there.

The city was protected from all but skitters, the small-
est of land draak. Those small draak were no more than
three meters in length and they were known to swim on
occasion, which made it almost impossible to keep them
out of the lower city. If it was not a skitter he had seen,
there was always the chance that he had spotted a gensvolf, for there was a pack denned somewhere in the
lower eastern half of the city in a section the Barl-
ganians had abandoned fifty or sixty years before. They
had actually tamed several of the voracious carnivores
by capturing them as pups.

Bhaldavin's glance swept across the clutter of old
buildings and green growth. And if not a gensvolf or a
skitter, what had he seen? Such furtive movements were
common among all wild creatures, but few were so large
that he would see them moving from such a distance.

Theon and Lil-el were on the third tier of land above
the lake working their way upward when they heard
Bhaldavin begin to sing draak. Staying in the evening

shadows as much as possible, they returned to the first tier and kept the crumbling walls of an old building between themselves and the lake. It took time to locate a secure place where they could see without being seen. As they crouched side by side and peered between another stone wall and the overhanging branches of a large oro tree, its sweet-smelling blossoms pungent in the air, Bhaldavin's song ended and Zojac signaled him to come back toward the shore.

Theon raised his light gun and aimed it at Zojac a moment or two before the Wastelander raised his own gun and pointed it at Bhaldavin. Theon's gun was fully charged, and he was in a mood to use it.

Lil-el held her breath, her fear for Bhaldavin's life causing blood to thunder loud in her ears. Then Zojac lowered his gun and Bhaldavin began walking toward the man. Quickly she reached out and set a hand to Theon's wrist.

"No," she whispered. "It's too far and Bhaldavin is too close to the man. You might hit him."

Theon heard her but did not lower the gun. "We might never have a better chance to reduce the odds against us."

"If you fail to kill them all, if you miss just one of them," Lil-el said, fighting to keep her voice even, "he would kill Bhaldavin and then run and tell the others about us and they'd be prepared for us. We must know where everyone is before we try to do anything. Gringers's life might well depend on our moving slowly."

Slowly Theon's finger eased back on the trigger. Another time, he promised himself. "So what do we do now?" he asked softly, his glance never leaving the group of men below. "The only way we're going to get Kelsan and the others to help us is if we can come up with a good plan, one we can all survive."

"We have two guns to their six or eight," Lil-el pointed out. "That means we can't attack them openly." She glanced down at the pier and saw one of the men waving his arms excitedly in the air. Suddenly a heavyset man with dark hair grabbed Bhaldavin's arm and pushed him through the gathered men, starting toward the first set of stairs leading upward.

She poked Theon in the side and signed for him to go back the way they had come. After a brief pause to take one last glimpse of Bhaldavin, she followed Theon up several debris-covered steps and into the ruins of a building whose wooden roof had half collapsed, shielding them from the main roadway.

"We'll wait here a few minutes," Lil-el said as she leaned back against the wall near the side doorway, "and give them time to get ahead of us."

Theon took up a position on the other side of the doorway and kept his gun in his hand. "And then?" he asked, dark eyebrows arched in question.

Lil-el studied Theon a moment, slightly surprised that he would look to her for leadership when he usually went about his own business with no questions asked and no opinions wanted. It was Gringers, she decided. Theon was more worried than he let on and was unconsciously looking for someone to reassure him that everything was going to be all right.

She took a deep breath and released it. "Then we'll see if we can get back into the mansion through the cellar tunnel. If they've found that exit, we'll just have to think of something else. We may even have to try going over the stockade wall just like they did."

"That sounds more like suicide than a plan," Theon grumbled.

"I know," Lil-el replied softly. "Let's just hope it doesn't come to that."

Chapter 14

*D*HALVAD LOOKED OUT THE ONE WINDOW IN HIS ROOM and beheld the desert in the late-afternoon light. Ra-shun had dropped below the horizon hours earlier, and Ra-gar was casting long shadows in the wavelike dunes that lapped the very edges of the city to the south. Tre-ayjeel was a world of striking contrasts: lifeless arid desert below, lush valleys and lakes above. The main city housed over five thousand inhabitants, and its shops, markets, and open-air bazaars were filled with trade goods from all of the outer territories to the north, east, and west to the very edges of the Unknown Lands. Another four thousand Ni lived in those outer territories in both small and large communal holdings where they worked the land, lakes, and rivers for their livelihoods. Many of those had come from Jjaan-bi, Val-hrodhur, and other southland holdings, refugees from the Sarissa War against the People.

Dhalvad remembered nothing of that war, though he had been one of its young victims, losing his family, his home, and his very heritage in the senseless slaughter that had destroyed Ni life on the western edge of the Enzaar Sea. As far as he knew, he and an older brother were the only ones from his family to survive the carnage. Of the older brother, he knew nothing but what his foster father, Haradan, had told him: that the youth had lived with them a short while, then had disappeared without a trace into the Deep.

Dhalvad's thoughts on the subject were interrupted by Gi-arobi, who had finished the plate of fresh kansa left for them and had come to join him at the window. Feeling the tug on his pants leg, he reached down and swung Gi-arobi up to the windowsill.

"Had enough to eat?" he asked as he leaned against the folding shutters that, when closed, provided protection from wind, cold, and rain.

"Enough for now," Gi answered.

Dhalvad watched as Gi licked at his furred fingers and ran them down across his stomach where the yellow kansa juice had dribbled. When finished cleaning himself off, the olvaar leaned out over the sill and peered down. It was a sheer drop with no railings or ledges to offer any means of escape.

Dhalvad reached out and closed a protective hand around Gi's left leg. Gi pulled back and patted Dhalvad's hand, thrumming amusement.

"Gi not fall," he said. "Balance be very good."

"Perhaps," Dhalvad said. "But just to be on the safe side, I'll hang onto you. I don't want to lose you like . . ."

Gi read the pain in Dhalvad's eyes and stood and moved into his arms. "Not lose Gi—ever!" Gi responded to Dhalvad's hug as best as he could though his short arms barely spread around Dhalvad's chest and sides. "Poco and Jiam be all right, Dhal. Not worry. We find. Make them safe again. Dhal not forget Big Fur. He watch over them until we come. Yes!"

"I pray that you're right, Gi," Dhalvad said, fighting a lump in his throat. "If anything should happen to them . . ."

Gi made a soft chirring noise deep in his throat. The sound could not be translated into trader, but Dhalvad knew what it meant and hugged the olvaar tighter.

A few moments later Gi pushed away. "Someone coming, Dhal."

Dhalvad turned as the door opened, banging back

against the wall. Paa-tol stood there frowning.

"Come on," he growled. "You're wanted! Leave the olvaar!"

Gi-arobi's claws dug into Dhalvad's arm. "Gi not be left behind!"

"What is it?" Dhalvad demanded of Paa-tol. "What's going on?"

Paa-tol took several steps into the room, his frown of anger and impatience causing Gi to cling tighter to Dhalvad. "There's no time for explanations! Move!"

Dhalvad stood down from the windowsill, Gi still in his arms. "I won't leave Gi behind!"

"We're going to transfer again! He'll just be at risk!"

"He linked with the Tamorlee once. He can do it again!"

"Bring him then, damn it!" Paa-tol growled. "But move!" He crossed the room in four quick strides and caught Dhalvad by the arm.

Dhalvad pushed Gi-arobi up to straddle his right shoulder as Paa-tol pulled him toward the doorway. "Hang on, Gi."

Gi whistled an affirmative and got a good hold on Dhalvad's braid as Paa-tol marched them down the hall and into the room occupied by Amet.

The speaker stood in the center of the room waiting impatiently, arms across his chest.

"What's all the hurry?" Dhalvad asked as Paa-tol released him.

"The Tamorlee has located the other crystal!" Amet snapped as he pushed past Dhalvad. "Paa-tol! Grab our pack! Hurry!"

Startled by Amet's abruptness, Dhalvad followed in the Speaker's wake, Paa-tol stepping on his heels. Moments later they were climbing the steps to the transfer courtyard.

Amet turned and glared at Paa-tol as he and Dhalvad reached the archway leading outside. "I told you to have him leave the olvaar!"

"I told him!" Paa-tol snarled. "He refused. You argue with him!"

Dhalvad caught at Gi's leg. "We go together, or I don't go!" he said firmly.

Amet clenched his fists. "I swear, if we had more time, I'd take that little— Never mind! There's no time to argue! Come on!"

He led the way out onto the terrace and signaled the two Ni on watch. "We're in a hurry! Is the way clear?"

The two Ni on watch stepped back out of the way without a murmur of protest.

Amet nodded to Dhalvad and Paa-tol, and they took their places in a tight circle. "I had a partial linkage with the Tamorlee just a few minutes ago," Amet said, "to check and see if it had had any luck finding Mithdaar. It said it had and demanded that you be brought at once."

Amet slipped the Tamorlee on the middle finger of his right hand and brought it up where all could see. They moved in closer until they stood shoulder to shoulder.

"This is going to be a difficult transfer because none of us has ever been where we're going. Much will depend on how clear a vision the Tamorlee received from Mithdaar and his carrier. Now, if the transfer is not good, we'll have to return here, so be ready to call up this transfer point on my signal. No pulling back. No hesitating. Whatever we do, we must do it together. Our lives may well depend on it. Do you understand, Gi-arobi?"

"Gi understand," the olvaar replied.

"And if the transfer is good?" Paa-tol asked.

"What happens when we find the other crystal will depend on what and whom we meet when we get where we're going. We all must be prepared to move quickly."

"Do you mean fight—or run?" Paa-tol asked.

"Either! All right, let's go."

Gi watched as Dhalvad and Paa-tol reached out and touched fingers to the fire stone ring that glowed green in the fading light. He hesitated, remembering the stomach-turning sensation of falling during the last transfer. Then, releasing a deep sigh, he joined Dhalvad and Paa-tol and touched the ring. He was instantly caught and held in the field of energy the Ni called polu. The falling sensation was not as bad as it had been the first time. Kind Voice was the first to greet him.

Welcome, little one. We have far to go. Are you ready?

Gi ready. Where going?

I'll show you—all of you. Pay close attention because these scenes are all I have. I hope they are enough.

You're no longer in contact with the other crystal? Amet demanded.

No. The carrier has set Mithdaar aside. It is obvious that he or she isn't aware of the proper use of a Seeker stone, nor aware of the special needs of this particular crystal.

Tamorlee? Dhalvad asked. *How long has it been since you were in contact with the other crystal?*

A brief time. Perhaps ten of your minutes.

Please show us what you have, Dhalvad requested. *If the scene is clear enough we still may be able to make the transfer without a direct energy guide from Mithdaar.*

It's too risky! Amet objected. *We'll have to wait for another contact. Tamorlee, release us from the link!*

Dhalvad sensed Amet's sudden panic and realized that the Speaker was trying to pull out of the link. The Tamorlee reacted instantly by enfolding them all the tighter into its energy net. A scene grew before them; there was water to either side and a long stretch of what looked like a stone dock before them. The scene shifted and they were looking up at a partially overgrown city built on the side of a mountain. Moss, lichen, and vine crawled across the old stone ruins, and dark windows and doorways stared back at them as if accusing them personally of neglect.

All within the link shivered as an eerie song rose into the air. It was the wail of a draak singer, and it touched them with a feeling of loneliness and loss. The song changed a moment later, and as they watched and listened, there was movement in the water nearby.

The carrier is a draak singer, Paa-tol observed as the

scene came to life within their minds. *But his voice—it's like none I've ever heard before.*

Nor I, Amet agreed. Curiosity overcame fear, and he stopped trying to pull out of the link. *He calls a draak for those who stand at the end of the dock. They're dressed strangely. Paa-tol? Do you know where we are? Have you ever heard of such a place as this?*

No, though it reminds me much of Port Bhalvar. Amet, take a closer look at those who stand at the edge of the dock. If I'm not mistaken, they're men!

The draak's head disappeared beneath the water, and the carrier turned, hesitated, then walked toward the strangely garbed men.

They threaten Little Fish with some kind of a weapon, Paa-tol muttered. *What is it?*

I don't know, Amet said.

They listened as the men began to argue about possession of the crystal carrier. Again the scene shifted as Little Fish turned to look up at the tiered city. In a few moments, the scene faded.

Was the image clear enough for transfer? the Tamor-lee asked.

Yes. I think so, Dhalvad answered. *If you can hold that last scene for us.*

No! Amet snapped, interrupting. *I say that we wait for another linkage with the second crystal! It'll be safer! Paa-tol, back me up on this!*

If there's no need for hurry, perhaps it would be better to wait, Paa-tol suggested.

It was strange, Dhalvad thought, how Paa-tol's aggressiveness faded when in link with the crystal. Was it respect, awe, or fear? Perhaps a little of each, he decided. As for Amet, he believed that the Speaker was simply afraid to try an untested transfer point. But if doing so meant they could find and retrieve Mithdaar and get back to Jjaan-bi more quickly, he was willing to make the attempt. Poco, Jiam, and Screech were all depending on him.

I would be willing to go first, if you'll trust me, he offered. *Break the link and let me try it alone. I'm sure I can make the jump successfully. If I do, I'll come back for you.*

No, Amet answered coldly. *We go together or not at all! Tamorlee, we'll wait for another contact. Release us from the link.* The last was not a request, it was a command.

The Tamorlee did not respond. The link remained firm.

Make it let us go, Dhalvad! Amet cried, panic building once again.

Dhalvad, the crystal said, ignoring Amet. *I fear for the safety of Mithdaar if we don't move quickly!*

I'm willing to try a transfer, Dhalvad said. *Gi-arobi?*

Go where you go, Dhal.

What about Paa-tol and Amet? Dhalvad asked the crystal. *Can you drop them out of the link?* Dhalvad's heartbeat quickened. Perhaps he would finally have a chance to kick free of Amet.

If I release one, I release all, the Tamorlee answered. *I believe I have energy enough to carry them through with us. We can but try if they won't help.*

You cannot force us to come! Amet cried.

Amet scared, Gi said.

I am not! Amet refuted at once. *I'm just being cautious!*

You are with me, Amet, and within me, the Tamorlee said firmly. *You have no choice. Either you trust to Dhalvad's and Gi-arobi's imaging, or you join them and help reinforce the image needed to carry us all safely to the place where Mithdaar awaits me.*

The crystal was demonstrating a tenacity of purpose that secretly delighted Dhalvad, especially where Amet was concerned. Perhaps he had been wrong not to tell the crystal everything.

Paa-tol finally caved in. *Show us the transfer point again, please.*

No, Paa-tol! Amet snapped.

I trust to no one's imaging but my own, he answered grimly. *We have no choice but to do as the Tamorlee wishes.*

The Tamorlee spoke before Amet could say anything. *This is what I received from Mithdaar envisioned by the one called Little Fish. It's impossible to judge the clarity of the image without a physical bond, but the energy patterns Mithdaar sends are strong, and I believe they will guide us true.*

Amet? Dhalvad queried. *Paa-tol, Gi, and I will try this transfer without you, but it would be safer and quicker with your help.* It was the closest Dhalvad could come to asking Amet for assistance.

It seems that I have little choice, Amet responded testily, his panic subsiding as he realized that his best chance for survival lay in helping, not hindering, the transfer.

Good, the Tamorlee said. *Here again is what I received from Mithdaar and Little Fish.* The scene flowed quickly through their minds and locked on the image of the pier and the lakeside ruins. *Concentrate on the roadway at the end of the pier,* the crystal directed. *Hold tight to that image. Ready? Now!*

Lil-el pushed away from the wall and moved to the stone steps. "They should be gone by now. Let's take a look."

Theon nodded and followed her up the crumbling steps into the fading evening light. The pier and roadway were empty, which meant that the Wastelanders had returned to the upper plateau, taking Bhaldavin with them.

Lil-el led the way down onto the path that paralleled the waterfront road and paused. In order to reach the hidden entrance to the mansion they would have to follow one of two trails: the one to the right was a long steep climb, but they would be under cover of trees or buildings most of the way; the one to the left was more direct, but the pathway was open and visible from the stockade walls for several long stretches.

"Left or right?" Theon whispered.

"Right," Lil-el answered. "It will take us longer, but we'll..." Her words trailed off as she caught sight of something near the end of the pier. "Down!" she hissed, and grabbed at Theon's arm.

Theon dropped to the ground, his heart beating wildly. Had the Wastelanders set a trap? What had Lil-el seen? Before he could ask, she pointed.

He rose up on his hands and knees and joined her in peering over the top of the bushes in front of them. Something shimmered on the water. It was a light. No, not a light and not on the water. It was on the roadway next to the pier. What was it? Something was growing within the shimmering green light.

Theon's eyes opened wide in amazement as three figures suddenly appeared. The light faded, and in the darkness left behind stood three shadow figures that moved slightly away from each other.

Unsure about what he had just seen, Theon drew his light gun, raised it, and pointed it at the three figures.

Lil-el caught at his wrist, her fingernails digging into his flesh. "No!" she whispered urgently. "Wait!"

"Why?" Theon hissed back.

"Theon, we must get closer to them! Quickly!"

"Who are they? Where did they come from?" he asked. "Are they Wastelanders?"

"No! I believe they're Seekers! They're moving away! Come on!"

Lil-el was up and running cautiously down the path before Theon could stop her. He growled a curse and followed, keeping his light gun out and ready for use.

The three figures moved into the deep shadows of one of the old buildings. Afraid that she would lose them, Lil-el let loose with a soft trilling sound. It was the cry of a loring bird, one of the first bird calls a young Ni learned to imitate. The slight uplift at the end of the call would alert any other Ni to the true origin of the song.

One of the three figures moved back out into the roadway. Moments passed, then the stranger raised a hand to his mouth and repeated the loring's cry with that same little twist at the end.

"Come, Theon!" Lil-el cried, rising from a running crouch. "They're Ni!"

"Ni?" Theon echoed, rising more slowly. "Lil-el? Lil-el, go slow! It may be some kind of a trap!"

Lil-el ignored Theon's warning and hurried forward. Theon was only a few steps behind her as she reached the main road, his light gun held down at his side, out of sight but ready for use.

Lil-el turned and waited for Theon. "They're Ni, Theon!" she said softly to him. "I'm sure of it. Don't do anything foolish!"

"Just what I was going to tell you," he said.

Together they closed the distance between themselves and the three waiting figures. As they approached they could see the three more clearly. All were male; one wore long braids of authority; one was well armed with both a sword and a chest harness sporting four throwing knives; the third carried something in his arms.

Lil-el stopped a short distance from the three and gave them a Ni greeting by touching her palms together, placing them to her lips, then offering them to the centermost Ni male.

"Welcome to Barl-gan, Elder. My name is Lil-el. My friend is called Theon."

Paa-tol's right hand brushed the handle of one of his knives, his eyes boring into Theon's. "Beware! She's Ni!" he snapped. "He isn't!"

Amet glanced at Theon, then stepped forward and gingerly placed both his hands within Lil-el's grasp. "My name is Amet. To my right is Paa-tol. To my left, Dhalvad. We've come far in search of one called Little Fish. Do you know of him?"

Theon snorted. "Know him? I named him. What do you want with him, and where the hell did you three come from?"

"Quiet, Theon," Lil-el admonished. "I believe we're in the presence of Seekers. Am I correct?"

Amet nodded. "Are there many Ni in Barl-gan, Lil-el?"

"No. Just my family."

"This place belongs to men then?"

"Yes."

"Can you tell me just exactly where Barl-gan lies in comparison to the Enzaar Sea?"

"You came here without knowing? How odd. I thought that Seekers—"

Amet interrupted her. "We were drawn here by a call from a Seeker stone. We believe someone called Little Fish holds it. Please, will you answer my question?"

Lil-el frowned slightly, uneasy under Amet's glance. "Barl-gan is east of the Draak's Teeth. It took my mate and I and those who crossed the mountains with us many weeks to find a way over the mountains."

"You crossed the Draak's Teeth?" Paa-tol exclaimed. "But that's impossible!"

"Not easy," Theon said, "but not impossible."

"I wasn't speaking to you!" Paa-tol growled.

Theon saw Paa-tol's hand move. "Hai! Keep your hand away from those knives!"

Amet's eyes narrowed as Theon raised his light gun and aimed it at Paa-tol. "What is that? A weapon of some kind?"

Theon pointed the gun down and pulled the trigger. A beam of light shot out and engulfed several dried leaves a step away from Paa-tol's right foot. Paa-tol jumped away and swore, the smell of burned leaves pungent in the air.

Lil-el turned on Theon as the beam of light was turned off. "Fool! Do you want to tell the Wastelanders where we are? Put that down! We need friends now, not more enemies!"

"How do we know they are friendly, Lil-el?" Theon exploded. "I say we—"

"They're Seekers, Theon! I'll explain what that means later. Right now we should all get out of the open and ask our questions where we're secure!"

Lil-el turned to the three Ni. "There is danger here. The Wastelanders have overrun the city and taken some of our friends."

"Little Fish among them," Theon supplied.

"We've been trying to think of a way to free everyone without more being hurt. Perhaps you can help us."

Amet's gaze was still on Theon's light gun. "Perhaps

we can," he said. "I've never seen or even heard of such
a weapon. Paa-tol, have you?"

Paa-tol glared at Theon. "No! But if they have such
weapons, they certainly don't need our help!"

"But we do!" Lil-el cried. "We have only two of these
light guns. They have the rest!"

"They?" Amet said.

"The Wastelanders," Theon explained, keeping a
wary eye on Paa-tol. "The ones who have Gringers and
Little Fish. If you want him, you're going to have to help
us whether you want to or not . . . though we might do as
well without your help."

"Theon, stop it!" Lil-el snapped.

Amet looked at Lil-el. "I think we had best do as you
say for now and find a safe place to talk things over. Do
you know of such a place?"

"Come, follow me," Lil-el said. "Theon, watch our
back trail."

Theon muttered something to himself but stepped
aside as Lil-el turned and went back the way they had
come. After a moment's hesitation, Amet, then Paa-tol,
followed her, each keeping a wary eye on Theon as they
walked past him.

"You, too," Theon said to Dhalvad, motioning with
the gun. "Hai, what's that you got in your arms?"

"Gi being olvaar," Gi-arobi answered for himself. "Gi
touch?"

Theon drew the gun back as Gi-arobi leaned over
Dhalvad's arm and reached toward the light gun. "It
talks!"

Dhalvad smiled. "He certainly does, and if you're not
careful with that weapon, he'll have it from you."

Theon looked into Dhalvad's eyes. There was no hos-
tility there, only a hint of curiosity. "Come on," he said,
motioning with the gun again, "or they'll leave us behind."

As Dhalvad started after the others, Gi-arobi turned
around and watched Theon over Dhalvad's shoulder, his
golden eyes showing amber in the dusky light as his
glance fastened on the gun in Theon's hand. He reached

out and waggled his fingers, silently asking to touch the strange new weapon.

Bemused by the small creature, Theon shook his head as Gi's glance went from the gun to his face. He had heard of olvaar but had never seen one so close. They were said to be intelligent and extremely shy. This one had to be an exception, he thought. No shy olvaar could ever have learned to speak trader.

Theon glanced ahead. Judging from Lil-el's direction, she meant to take their guests back to the caves. It was probably the best thing until they knew more about them and why they were asking after Little Fish. His thoughts jumped to their sudden appearance near the pier. He could not for the life of him figure out how they had come down the roadway without Lil-el or him seeing them unless they had stepped out from behind some of the trees lining the roadway. But then what was that strange shimmering light he had seen? And what in the name of Brogan's Draak was a Seeker?

Chapter 15

POCO WAS ROUSED BY THE SOUND OF JIAM CRYING. Where's Dhal? she thought. Can't he hear the baby?

She opened her eyes to semidarkness and rolled to one side. Her body was stiff and sore, and she was suddenly confused. Why am I lying on the floor?

Jiam's wail stirred her to action. She sat up, then lost her balance and fell to her other side, bumping her head against the floor. She cried out, then rolled into a ball as a wave of nausea hit. She knew better than to fight against such a purging and seconds later vomited.

Jiam's crying held her from the brink of unconsciousness. Moments passed as she tried to gather her strength to answer him. He sounded as if he had been crying a long time. Heaving herself up on shaky arms, she pushed away from the mess on the floor and again tried to sit up. She made it.

Damn! What's wrong with me? "Dhal?" she croaked. "I need you."

She rubbed a hand across her sweaty forehead and shivered. Her face and head felt hot, but the rest of her was cold, and there was a strange metallic taste in her mouth.

It took a few seconds to orient herself to the sound of Jiam's cries. She crawled slowly across a wooden floor

toward the sounds and found him in a corner, his blanket
wrappings all awry and soaked with urine. She picked
him up and held him close, crooning to him softly.

"Hungry, little one? Mother's sorry. Hush, hush. I'm
right here."

She unbuttoned her tunic top and pulled it aside. Jiam
greedily searched for her nipple, his crying forgotten.
While her son drank, Poco lifted her head and looked
around, her memory slowly returning as her eyes grew
accustomed to the semidark of the room. Dhal's not
here, she thought. Amet took him to look for another
crystal.

There was a wooden floor beneath them and wooden
walls all around, which meant that they were no longer
within the stone caves of Jjaan-bi. She could see no windows. What light penetrated the room came from a crack
at the top of the door across the room. Where in hell
were they?

She sniffed. Besides the odors of urine and vomit,
there was a definite musky smell nearby. "Screech? Are
you here?" she asked aloud.

She listened, but there was no answer.

The metallic taste in her mouth bothered her. What
had they given her to eat? The last thing she remembered
was Anwhol coming to the door with another Ni, a
young male she had never met before. She remembered
taking the food trays for herself and Screech, before Anwhol and the other Ni had left. She and Screech had
eaten, and a short time later Anwhol returned. She remembered watching him cross the room toward her bed.
She had tried to get up, but her body had not cooper-
ated. He had taken Jiam away from her and after that—
there was nothing.

Suddenly she pulled Jiam from her breast, fearing that
whatever they had used to drug the food might find its
way into her milk. Jiam fretted for a few moments, but
quieted under his mother's soft voice. She stripped him
of his wet garments and bundled him as best she could in
a fold of her own tunic, holding his small warm body
close to her chest.

Why had Anwhol moved them? Was it at Amet's orders? Or had Anwhol become frightened by something? Perhaps Chulu or some of their other friends had discovered the plot to force Dhal to help steal the Tamorlee.

Tears trickled down her cheeks as she fought the rage churning in her stomach. What the hell was going on? Where was Dhalvad? Was he still with Amet? Had they begun their search? Or perhaps even found what they looked for? It was frustrating to be a pawn in a game where one could see neither the gameboard nor the players!

A soft groan from nearby brought her thoughts back to the reality she shared with her son and her friend. She was sure it was Screech she had heard. They had to have drugged him, too, or they would never have had the courage to try moving him. What kind of drug had they used? And how much? Screech had eaten a much larger portion of food, which meant he had probably consumed a larger dose of the drug—if drug it was. A sudden thought chilled her. What if they had not merely drugged the food? What if they had laced it with poison?

She used the wall for support in standing and clutched Jiam in one arm as she moved slowly toward the place she thought she had heard Screech. She stopped when her foot brushed something. Kneeling, she felt around with her free hand and found Screech's furry body. She inspected him as best she could in the dark and discovered a patch of wetness near his mouth. Sensitive fingers quickly located a torn lip. Other than that the derkat appeared to be unhurt. A rope held his arms behind his back, and a chain led from a manacle on his leg to a ring in the wall.

It took her a few minutes to loosen the ropes about his wrists, then she scrunched down beside him and made herself as comfortable as possible against the nearby wall. There was nothing she could do for Screech but wait and hope he would not succumb to whatever they had put in the food. She promised herself that she would check the door in a little while, but first she had to rest.

She let her head drop back against the wall, weariness and the aftereffects of whatever they had used to drug the food sapping her strength.

They don't mean for us to live, she thought. They can't now—not after all of this. That's why they moved us—makes it easier to get rid of us later. "Should have guessed," she muttered to herself. She held Jiam closer and rubbed her chin against the soft tufts of hair on top of his head. "Don't let them win, Dhal. Foul their plans. Don't let them . . ."

Lil-el watched the three strange Ni from across the fire they had built inside the cave. The smoke spiraled upward, escaping through natural holes to the outside. Theon sat to her left, Kelsan to her right. Behind them squatted several of the other Barl-ganians who had survived the attack on the mansion.

It was obvious from the looks on the faces of Amet and his friends that they were uneasy in the presence of the deformed Barl-ganians. It was equally obvious that Kelsan and Theon had reservations about the Seekers despite her explanations that such Ni were revered among her people as teachers and explorers.

Three hours had passed since their return to the cave, hours spent in trying to get at the truth on both sides. She had chosen to tell her story first and had explained as best she could some of the history behind the men and women of Barl-gan and their running war with their enemies, the Wastelanders. She had told them about Gringers's attempt to find the first city of the Ral-jennob, and how Theon, Davin, and she had become involved. She ended with a brief outline of the Wastelander's most recent attack.

Following a period of questions and answers, the elder Ni Seeker, Amet, had explained something of his own mission to find the crystal called Mithdaar and the one who carried it.

"Well," Theon began, "if you want Little Fish, you're going to have to fight to get him back!"

"How many of these Wastelanders are you up

against?" Amet asked, his glance on Theon.

"Enough to drive us out of the mansion, and more than enough to finish what they've started here if we're not careful," Theon answered.

Amet pointed to the light gun. "That weapon—you said there were others like it?"

Theon nodded. "Sure. But most of them are in the hands of the Wastelanders by now. We have two here, and at the moment there's no way to recharge them when their energy drains out. There's no telling how long before the Wastelanders make Gringers or one of the others show them how to recharge their guns. I think that if we're going to do any rescuing, it will have to be soon—before the Wastelanders become too entrenched."

"They'll leave when they've got what they came for," Kelsan said. "They never stay long. They fear plague."

"Plague?" Amet snapped. "What plague?"

"There is no plague now," Lil-el explained calmly. "It's something from long ago, but the Wastelanders fear its recurrence, so they don't usually stay very long in the area. Whether they do or not, we must find a way to release those they've taken hostage before they decide to leave." She looked at Amet, her eyes pleading. "Will you help us?"

"I think that we don't have much of a choice," Dhalvad said, speaking for the first time, his glance on Amet. "Not if you want what we came for."

"Needing crystal, yes!" Gi piped up. "We help."

Lil-el looked from Gi-Arobi to Dhalvad. "Tell me, what is so special about Davin's crystal?"

Dhalvad opened his mouth to reply, but Amet silenced him with a touch on the shoulder. "I'll answer that question, Healer," he said firmly. He hesitated a moment, calculating his response, then decided that for once the truth would serve him best.

"Do you know of the Tamorlee?"

"Yes," Lil-el replied. "My father spoke about it several times. It's known as the Great Historian, isn't it?"

Amet tilted his head in agreement. "That is one of its

many names, yes. Do you understand what it means to gift the Tamorlee?"

"My father told me about Seekers and how they gift the Tamorlee with the knowledge they gather. Is that what you mean?"

"It is. Do you know how that is done?"

"No."

Amet held his ringed hand out to her. "It's accomplished through fire stone rings like this one. It's the nature of these special crystals to absorb knowledge through those who wear them, Ni who are known as Seekers, and to gift that knowledge back to the Tamorlee through a direct link with the parent crystal."

"And the crystal Davin carries is one of these fire stones," Lil-el guessed.

"Yes, and we've been sent from Jjaan-bi to find it."

Theon shook his head. "I'm not sure I understand all this gifting business. All I'm interested in knowing at the moment is whether or not you're going to help us free our friends and how you three got here, and if it means there's a way out for all of us after we rescue Gringers and the others."

Amet shook his head before Theon could go any further. "We can't help you with the last. The power source that carries a Seeker from one place to another isn't strong enough to allow for passengers—" His glance touched Gi. "—unless they're very small. I'm sorry, we may be of some help in freeing Little Fish—Davin, I mean—and your other friends, but beyond that, we can't help you."

Lil-el's eyes narrowed as she read the unspoken message in Amet's refusal of help. "You mean that once you get what you've come for, you'll leave us to find our own way back over the mountains."

Sensing that he had made a mistake, Amet corrected himself. "As a Seeker, I'll do all within my power to help you and any who want to come to Jjaan-bi or Tre-ayjeel, though it may take time to find the best way to accomplish this. The desert to the north is unknown territory to us, but with proper planning I'm sure passage through

the wasteland can be successfully negotiated. Now that
we've found this ancient city, I'm sure that the Elders
will want to know more about it and its history—"
Amet's glance touched Kelsan and one of the men who
sat beyond him, a bird-footed youth whose name was
Donner "—including the men and women who live
here."

"We don't want company," Theon snapped. "We
want out! Before the Wastelanders take over!"

Dhalvad spoke up. "From what you've told us, these
Wastelanders are men like yourself. Couldn't you—"

"Healer, I think it would be best if you let me handle
this," Amet said, his glance belying the softness of his
tone of voice.

Lil-el looked from Amet to the Healer. Amet had introduced him, but she had been so fearful of their alerting the Wastelanders that she had not paid close enough
attention.

Amet turned to Theon. "If we're to affect any kind of
a rescue, we'll have to know more about what we're up
against. Will you draw us a map of this mansion?"

Theon's eyes met Lil-el's as she nodded. "I have
nothing to draw on," he said, "but we can make do." He
searched for a sharp rock, found one quickly, and leaned
over to brush a fine layer of cold ash from a day-old fire
out onto the ground where all could see. Using his rock,
he began to draw, explaining as he went along.

Lil-el looked up from the crude map and caught the
Healer watching her. There was something in his look
that bothered her. It was almost as if he were trying to
tell her something. She frowned, and he nodded slightly.

Disconcerted, she glanced down at Theon's map again
and listened as he described the underground route into
the mansion. When she looked up again, the Healer's
attention was also on the map. Had she only imagined
that look? That nod? She mentally shook herself and
turned her attention to Theon as he went on to describe
the inside of the main building and the rooms in which
the Wastelanders would most likely hold their hostages.

Time slipped by as Amet asked questions. Several

times he drew Paa-tol into the conversation, asking his advice on a possible counterattack. Paa-tol was an excellent tactician. He had studied the histories of the early border wars between men and Ni and had worked on many a plan for repulsing and destroying an opposing force should anyone ever again try to invade Ni territory. Part of those plans included tactics in subterfuge when dealing with small numbers outwitting larger numbers.

"In this case I believe it's all a matter of distracting the enemy and moving in where they least expect it," Paa-tol said. He glanced at Amet. "Give me the rest of the night to think things over, and I'll have a plan that should work."

Amet nodded and stood up to stretch. "You have tonight and tomorrow. There's no sense in trying anything in broad daylight."

Lil-el also rose. "Are any of you hungry? We haven't much food, but we'd be glad to share what we have."

"We have food of our own," Amet replied, inclining his head. "But I thank you for your kindness in asking."

Lil-el glanced at Dhalvad as he stood up, the olvaar riding his shoulder. She turned back to Amet, somehow sensing that it was to him all petitions must be made. "There are several among us who were wounded during the attack or after. May we ask your Healer to look at them?"

Amet hesitated, then nodded. "Certainly. Paa-tol, go with them in case they need any help."

Dhalvad knew why Amet wanted Paa-tol along, but other than denouncing them both outright, he could do nothing. "How many are hurt?" he asked Lil-el.

"Kelsan's son is the worst. Come. I'll show you the way." Lil-el picked up a burning branch from the fire and moved off into the shadows. Dhalvad and Paa-tol followed. Kelsan and Theon also came along, Kelsan muttering to himself about strange physicians.

A few minutes later they reached an inner section of the caves where twenty-five of the remaining citizens of Barl-gan lay sleeping. Some woke as the newcomers moved in among them; others never stirred.

Lil-el led Dhalvad and the others to the right where all the wounded were being tended. A small fire lighted that section of the cavern; it was tended by a splay-footed youth of fourteen years. Dark, feral eyes watched them as they approached. The boy moved back away from the fire as the strangers entered the circle of light.

"It's all right, Lemul," Lil-el said softly. "These people are friends. They've come to help us."

As Dhalvad moved around to one side, he glanced at Lil-el. He would try to warn her about Amet and Paa-tol when he dared. Meanwhile, he knelt beside the wounded man nearest him, then one by one checked them all. Four needed little more than a few minutes of his time and would probably heal fine without his aid; two others had more serious wounds, though neither was what he would call life-threatening.

Lemul moved in closer as Dhalvad knelt by his father, Jothan, and placed a hand on his forehead. Dhalvad looked up as he caught the movement and read the apprehension in the boy's eyes.

"I won't hurt him," he told the boy. "I promise."

"What are you going to do?" Kelsan demanded, eyes narrowed in distrust.

"He's a Healer, Kelsan," Lil-el explained carefully. "His touch is the most wondrous of all Ni gifts. Watch and see." Lil-el glanced at Dhalvad and nodded to him to begin.

Assured that no one would do anything foolish to interfere with the healing, Dhalvad placed his left hand on Jothan's forehead while his right hand hovered within a fingerspan of Jothan's chest. He closed his eyes and quickly dropped into a Healer's trance, his awareness slipping into the body beneath his hands as easily as a diving bird plummeted into water after a fish.

Dhalvad clearly saw that Jothan's bodily structure was not as it should be, but the changes one would have to make were more than any Healer had the right to make; he knew that intuitively. Perhaps in the womb one could change such cell structure, but not in adulthood. The man would have to live as he had been born, his

malformed joints forever making it difficult for him to
move freely. No, the body and its misshaping had come
about through a natural process of inbreeding caused,
most probably, by a low gene pool. Adjusting for any
other differences he might find, Dhalvad went deeper
into the body, seeking the pain that revealed itself to him
by a glowing haze of red color. Because he shared the
pain of the body beneath his hands, he first dulled the
pain center in Jothan's brain, then set to work rebuilding
the layers of muscle and skin that had been damaged by
a Wastelander's draak-toothed lance. The wound was
near the right lung. Had it been any closer to the center
of the body, Jothan would not have survived the initial
wound.

Dhalvad dove deeply within himself and drew upon
the energy that was as natural a part of him as his breath.
Picturing the body whole beneath his hands, he directed
that energy to seal the layers of flesh by causing cell
regeneration to accelerate.

Once satisfied with the work done, he drew back inside himself and pushed at the black curtain surrounding
him. He had learned from other Healers in Jjaan-bi that
it was possible to banish fatigue caused by wielding nature's energy—but only for a while. Once, twice, three
times one might push aside the need for rest, but eventually it would catch up with the body and no amount of
denying would cancel the inevitable.

Lil-el watched patient and Healer with avid curiosity.
She had heard about Healers but had never met one. The
last two Healers living in the swamplands of Amla-Bagor
with the rafters had vanished when she was still a child,
escaping into the northlands where they would be safe
from the Sarissa War. How different her life might have
been, she thought, if her parents had been able to escape
also. But then she never would have met Bhaldavin, or
known the friendship of such men as Gringers, and even
Theon. Her thoughts on that subject slipped away as the
Healer stirred and lifted his head. His crystal-gray eyes
focused on her, and he drew a deep breath.

Lil-el looked down at Jothan and saw that his eyes

were closed and that he was breathing easier. She watched as Kelsan quickly inspected the wound—to find nothing but a bruise and a small crusted spot of dried blood. There was awe on Kelsan's face as he sat back and looked at Dhalvad. "How did you do it?"

Dhalvad smiled. "It's a gift I was born with. I can't explain. The man will sleep soundly for some time. Let him. He'll be fine when he wakes."

Lemul was staring at Dhalvad, his eyes misting with tears. Lil-el took his hand and squeezed it. "Your father will be fine. Stay with him."

Theon stepped back as Dhalvad got up and moved over beside Gils Watcher. He muttered something about miracle workers and followed Kelsan as the old man went to kneel beside his son. As Dhalvad made himself comfortable, Kelsan drew a crude dressing from Gils's left side.

"Be careful not to tire yourself, Healer," Paa-tol cautioned as Dhalvad reached out to touch Gils's forehead. "There's no telling whether or not we'll need your gift tomorrow."

"I know my limits, Paa-tol," Dhalvad said, carefully guarding his tone of voice. "Why don't you go back to Amet and leave me to do what I can here?"

"I'm all right where I am," Paa-tol replied.

Lil-el frowned at the undercurrent of dislike she heard in both voices and wondered at its cause.

Gils opened his eyes and started to sit up, then winced and grabbed his side, dropping back to the cavern floor. Dhalvad read the blaze of fear in the man's eyes at the sight of strangers and glanced at Kelsan, silently asking for his aid.

Kelsan leaned over his son and spoke calmly, explaining the situation in as few words as possible. When finished, he took Gils's hand and held it gently. "There's no need to be afraid, son. I'll be right here to see that nothing happens to you."

Gils glanced up at Dhalvad. His tongue darted out to brush dry lips, and he swallowed noisily, but he did not pull away as Dhalvad reached out toward his forehead.

There followed a few seconds of uneasiness as a strange feeling stole over him, a warmth that spread from the top of his head down his spine and into the rest of his body; then fear and anxiety slipped away as easily as water through cupped hands, to be replaced by a languid, floating sensation that eased the ache in his side and left him breathing easier. He thought he closed his eyes and slept. He dreamed of a green-haired man who smiled at his childlike innocence and who offered him a kind of deep kindredlike friendship that he had never known before. He dreamed that he said yes to that offer, the words clear in his ears instead of the garbled sounds he usually made.

Suddenly the green-haired man's voice changed with warning. *"Don't trust Amet or Paa-tol! They force me to be here against my will. They hold my family hostage. Don't trust them!"*

Lil-el saw the Healer's sudden frown of concentration and leaned closer. The look on his face at that moment reminded her of someone else. She shook her head slightly, then suddenly it dawned on her. The Healer looked a little bit like Finnar, her oldest son, who closely resembled his father in many ways. The flickering firelight and the tilt of the Healer's head made comparison difficult; still there was a definite resemblance.

She glanced up at Paa-tol, who was watching everything closely. What name had they given the Healer? She tried to remember but could not. She looked back at the Healer just as his head lifted. His eyes were clouded with fatigue, but somehow he found the strength to smile at Kelsan.

"Your son will be fine," he said, then abruptly keeled over.

Lil-el could not move fast enough, but Paa-tol made up for her slowness and caught Dhalvad by the shoulders and gently laid him down.

"Is he all right?" Lil-el asked, worried by the Healer's sudden collapse.

"He's exhausted, that's all," Paa-tol said as he reached under Dhalvad's back and legs to lift him into his arms. "I'll take him with me and see that he's made comfortable. A night's rest and he'll be fine."

Lil-el stood up as Paa-tol readjusted Dhalvad in his arms. "Pardon me," she said, "but I don't remember the Healer's name. What is it?"

"Dhalvad," Paa-tol replied, stepping around the fire with his burden.

"Lemul," Kelsan ordered. "Light his way."

"I'd heard about Ni Healers," Theon murmured as Paa-tol carried Dhalvad out of sight, "but I never thought to see one in action. It's amazing. Just think of the kind of money you could make with such power!"

Lil-el heard but ignored Theon's comments, her thoughts elsewhere. Several times Bhaldavin had spoken to her about a younger brother named Dhalvad, about someday returning to the Deep to try to find him. The name Dhalvad was common enough, but what about the resemblance? It can't be him, she thought. It just can't.

Chapter 16

*B*HALDAVIN SCRAMBLED TO HIS FEET AS THE DOOR TO THE room swung open. He stood with his hand held slightly behind him. The windowless room that served as his prison was small and unfurnished, one of those belowground that had upon occasion served as a storage room for food harvested at the beginning of the cold season. Dirt, old sacks, and the dried outer husks of last year's crop of mailin lay scattered over the floor. To his left lay an old broken barrel, its wooden slats crushed and strewn about.

His heartbeat raced when he saw Sola standing in the doorway. He was not sure how long he had been imprisoned in the room, but judging from hunger and bodily functions, he knew it was not much longer than a day.

"You're wanted, Green Hair," Sola said, motioning him toward the doorway.

"I want to know where my daughter is," Bhaldavin demanded loudly. "And the others you've taken!"

"The *others* are working under Zojac already," Sola answered. "As for your daughter, she's in a room where no one will disturb her, no one but me, that is—when I've the time."

Anger churned in Bhaldavin's stomach when he saw the look on Sola's face. He knew the man was baiting him, but his fear for Thura's safety had begun to eat into what common sense he had left.

"If you harm her..."

"You'll what?" Sola snapped. "Kill me?" He shook his head. "No, I think not. You'd be a fool to even try to..." His words trailed off as he caught sight of the wood slat Bhaldavin clutched in his hand. A cruel smile touched his lips when he read the look of desperation in Bhaldavin's eyes.

"Another lesson, is it? I would've thought you'd have had enough of me." Sola spread his feet slightly and clenched his fists, his smile disappearing. "Put the wood down, Green Hair, and come along quietly, or I'll gladly give you what you're begging for."

Bhaldavin actually looked past Sola to the open doorway, gauging his chances.

"Do as I tell you!" Sola bellowed. "Now!"

Bhaldavin flinched at the loud command, then slowly lowered the slat, sanity returning. He could not help Thura if he was dead, and dead he would be if Sola ever used his hands on him again.

Sola straightened from his fighting stance as the board clunked to the floor. Shaking his head in disgust, he stepped forward and grabbed Bhaldavin's arm. "Cowards, all of you," he muttered. "Had we known, we could've taken this place years ago!"

Bhaldavin just managed to fend himself off from the edge of the door as Sola propelled him violently forward. The door banged against the wall and swung back, catching Sola in the leg. Bhaldavin heard the man's grunt of pain, glanced back, saw his chance, and darted into the hall.

"Stop, Green Hair!" Sola yelled, as Bhaldavin dashed down the hall, flicking out lights as he went.

Suddenly the hall was aglow with a high-intensity beam of laser light. In the few seconds it took Sola to adjust his aim using the strange new weapon, Bhaldavin reached the end of the hall and leapt up the flight of stairs straight ahead, taking them three at a time. He cried out in pain as the laser light momentarily touched his right leg, then he was up out of sight.

"Come back here, or I'll kill your daughter!" Sola screamed as he ran for the stairway. The hall was dark ahead of him, forcing him to slow down and find one of the magic light switches that lighted the underground halls.

Bhaldavin ignored Sola's threats and kept on running, praying that his display of power at the lakeside would protect Thura until he could find a way to free her. Zojac and the other men had been impressed by his control over a draak and had quickly seen the advantage of having a draak singer in their possession; though he had not been able to prevent Zojac from confiscating Mithdaar, he had convinced them that Thura, though young, had the potential of a draak singer, hopefully ensuring her their protection even from the enraged Sola. If he was wrong...

He would not let himself think about that. He paused, orienting himself in the underground hallways. He had counted the Wastelanders and knew there could not be more than thirty-five to forty able to fight, and the mansion was large. Surely he could avoid being recaptured if he tried hard enough.

He heard Sola coming up the stairs. A light flicked on, lighting the stairwell. Bhaldavin shot down the hallway, moving as quickly and quietly as possible, turning off lights as he went; then up another flight of stairs that took him to the ground floor. One quick glance outside told him that night had come again, which meant that he had two choices: either leave the building under the cover of darkness and try to find Lil-el, Theon, and the others who has escaped, or stay in the building and try to find Thura, Gringers, and the other prisoners.

In the end it was for Thura he stayed, and as he started toward the back part of the mansion where he could easily lose Sola in the maze of interconnecting rooms and halls near the kitchens, he vowed not to leave until he had secured Thura's release one way or another. The thought of her small young body in the hands of the sadistic Sola made his skin crawl. Better she were dead than at Sola's mercy.

Sola quickly gave up on finding Bhaldavin by himself and alerted Zojac to the Ni's escape. Zojac cursed him for losing the Green Hair and sent a dozen of his men to help find him. Ten minutes later the search began in earnest, and as room after room was flooded with light, the mansion became a beacon in the darkness.

Bhaldavin played a harrowing game of hide-and-seek for the next fifteen minutes, just managing to keep one or two rooms ahead of one of the search parties. Suddenly the lights began to flicker somewhere behind him. When he realized what was happening, he drew a sigh of relief. The Wastelanders did not understand about overdrawing on the energy source that created the power for the lights. By turning so many on all at once, they were effectively shutting them all down, which would make it easier for him to hide.

The Wastelanders were not fools, but sometimes ignorance was just as costly as foolishness, and as moments later the building was plunged into darkness, Bhaldavin heard the men yelling back and forth to one another. The panic in their voices was music to his ears. He stayed where he was as his enemies blundered around in the darkened rooms.

Gradually silence returned as the Wastelanders found their way out of the building. He knew it would not be long before they built a fire and returned with torches, so he moved from his hiding place behind a door and felt his way out of the room into an adjoining room, and from there into a hallway that led in two directions. He chose to go left away from the main hall that cut down through the mansion from north to south. He walked as quietly as possible and paused to listen for voices at each doorway before moving on.

The lights flickered on for a few seconds, then off again. Bhaldavin cursed under his breath as he hurried along the hall. Either someone among the Wastelanders had made a connection between the number of lights on and the drain on the energy source, or one of the pris-

oners had offered the information, either unwittingly or
under pressure. The latter was most likely.

He reached a flight of stairs leading both up and
down. He paused to listen but heard nothing but someone shouting outside.

The upper stairs led to what once had been living
quarters for those who worked in the building, but as the
remaining citizens of Barl-gan had decreased in number
they had abandoned the upper floors for the more convenient rooms downstairs. The lower stairs led to the infirmary and the underground storage rooms not too far
from where he had been held prisoner just a little while
earlier. That way also led to the escape route under the
stockade wall.

He hesitated, then turned downstairs, deciding to
check on the escape route. The lights came on again and
stayed on this time. He descended the steps cautiously,
staying close to the wall.

He found the infirmary empty and things scattered
about; bottles filled with Kelsan's precious medical supplies were dripping over on the shelves; many bottles
had been knocked to the floor and smashed.

Kelsan had made most of those medicines with Bhaldavin's help, hunting out and boiling down roots, leaves,
and fruits and barks to assuage such minor physical
complaints as head- and stomachaches, fever, diarrhea,
and vomiting. The herb and root knowledge Bhaldavin
had learned as a child had proved to be invaluable to
Kelsan, who had taken it upon himself to act as physician to the sick in Barl-gan.

Bhaldavin carefully stepped around the broken glass
and ceramic pots. It was quickly apparent that what the
Wastelanders chose not to steal, they meant to destroy.
Over in the far corner was another mess of carefully labeled boxes filled with supplies dumped and scattered
about as if a wind storm had swept through the room.

A sound in the far corner sent Bhaldavin into a defensive crouch. He glanced around, searching for something
to use as a weapon. He spotted a daggerlike shard of

pottery and quickly scooped it up. He waited, poised for flight, but the sound was not repeated.

Seconds slipped by. Still he waited, his glance taking in each detail of the disturbed room. The examining table was to his right; several wood chairs were to his left, all of them overturned. The broken glass and crockery scattered about the floor made the footing dangerous for any quick evasive action, he decided. Better to fade back to safer ground.

He stood and began a step-by-step withdrawal from the room, his glances sweeping from floor to walls and back again. He saw one of Kelsan's sharp knifelike instruments on the floor and snatched it up, discarding the pottery. It was not truly a weapon, but it would serve, if necessary.

He was almost to the doorway when he saw movement out of the corner of one eye and turned, his fingers closing more tightly around his makeshift dagger. Someone else was in the room . . .

"Come out!" he hissed softly. "There's no use in hiding."

A few seconds passed. Suddenly a small, fur-covered head appeared from behind one of the overturned boxes. Large golden eyes regarded Bhaldavin solemnly.

Bhaldavin frowned and slowly straightened, the thunder of his heartbeat gradually subsiding. "An olvaar? Here?" he murmured.

Interpreting the stranger's body language rather than his voice, Gi-arobi waddled into full view and squatted, sitting with one chubby leg tucked in front of his stomach, the other beneath him.

Bhaldavin's frown faded. "Where did you come from, I wonder?"

In his youth in the Deep, Bhaldavin had seen five or six of the fur children, but always at a distance. Shy creatures, they were said to be extremely intelligent. He remembered his father once saying that the olvaar even had a language, whistling sounds that could be translated into simple trader if one knew their language. Strange, he thought, that in all the years he had lived this side of the

Draak's Teeth, he had never seen an olvaar or signs of any living in the territory. So where had this one come from? He took a step closer and went to a knee, bringing himself down to the olvaar's height.

"Well, little one, how did you get inside?" Not expecting an answer, he pursed his lips and gave a low whistle.

Gi-arobi cocked his head to one side and repeated the sound perfectly, then added a trilling sound of his own.

Bhaldavin shook his head as he stood up. "I'm sorry, little one, but I don't understand, and I don't have any more time to waste. Better find your way back out of here, if you know what's good for you."

He stepped back, took one last look at the olvaar, then reached out and pressed the light button on the wall, returning the room to darkness.

"Good-bye, little one," he said as he turned and started back up the stairs. "Good luck in finding your way out."

Gi-arobi stood and hurried after the stranger. "Where going?"

The question, so innocent, caught Bhaldavin in midstep, and as he spun around on the stairs, he lost his balance and fell. His shoulder slammed against the wall, then he was sliding back downstairs on his side. He caught himself with his hand and stopped his slide, but in doing so he lost his weapon.

He remained where he had fallen, his eyes trying to pierce the darkness in the room at the bottom of the steps. The light coming from the hallway above began flickering again. He slowly pushed to a sitting position, his heart hammering loudly in his ears. How could he have missed seeing a person in that room? There were not that many places to hide. And who had spoken? The voice had had a strange quality to it. He was sure it was not any of the Barl-ganians—he knew all of their voices—and it had not sounded like any of the Wastelanders.

He saw movement through the flickering light. Something small, furry, and quick moving. The olvaar! It scampered down the steps toward him, seemingly unafraid. It stopped near his right leg, reached out, and patted him.

"You hurt?"

Bhaldavin sat a bit straighter, eyes going wide in disbelief. The voice . . . the words . . . the olvaar? Was that possible? He glanced at the dark doorway beyond. There had to be someone else there.

The olvaar moved closer, coming up beside him, its small-fingered hands touching him. "You hurt?"

Bhaldavin stared through the flickering light and saw the olvaar's golden eyes watching him. He had not seen any movement at the olvaar's mouth, but it was so lost in fur that such movement might be hard to detect. He felt a bit foolish, but he could not stop himself from asking "Did you just speak to me, little one?"

"Gi speaking, yes! You not hurt? Gi afraid you fall. Hit head."

"No, I'm . . . fine. I just missed a step." He reached out slowly so as not to startle the olvaar and carefully brushed his hand down a furred shoulder. "You're not afraid of me," he said.

"Afraid little bit, but no more." Gi said truthfully.

"I didn't know your kind could speak trader."

"Can when want to. Not always saying right word. Learning alla time. You be Little Fish?"

Startled once again, Bhaldavin nodded. "Yes, it's one of my names, but how did you know that?"

"Mithdaar tell. He talk to Dhal. Dhal say Little Fish be Ni. Have one arm. Everyone looking for you. Gi find first!" Gi caught at Bhaldavin's hand. "You come! Bring Mithdaar! Then all go home. Amet tell where Poco, Jiam, and Big Fur be hidden. Yes!"

This is crazy, Bhaldavin thought. I'm sitting on a stairway in the darkness, talking to an olvaar who's talking so fast I can barely make out what he's saying, while Sola and the rest of the Wastelanders are hunting the halls for me! I've got to find Thura and get us out of here! Maybe then there'll be time to unscramble what the olvaar is talking about.

Bhaldavin picked up his makeshift weapon and

pushed to his feet. "I'm sorry, little one, but I've got to go now. I can't do anything about—"

"Not go!" Gi shrilled as he grabbed at Bhaldavin's pants leg. "Come with Gi! Paa-tol make di-bersion so Dhal, Amet, and others can look for you. You come! Now! Gi show the way!"

Bhaldavin leaned down and pulled the olvaar's fingers from his pants leg. "Gi? Is that your name?"

"Yes!"

"Gi, I'd like to go with you, but there's something I must do first."

"No! You come now! Bring Mithdaar! Dhal need it!"

"I'm sorry, Gi, but I don't have Mithdaar any more. Someone else has it, and he's not likely to give it back."

"Who got?" Gi demanded.

"Someone called Zojac. He's somewhere up above, and he's probably looking for me right now."

"You hiding? Gi find good place."

"There's no time for hiding, Gi. I've got to find my daughter and get her out of here." A thought stopped Bhaldavin. "How did you get in here?"

"Big hole in ground. Theon show the way."

"Theon's here?" Bhaldavin asked, excitement stirring.

"Theon, yes!"

If Theon was here, then . . . "Lil-el?"

Gi pointed back into the darkness below, "Lil-el, Pretty Eyes back there."

Bhaldavin glanced down into the darkness, his need to see Lil-el sending him to his feet again. Then he remembered Thura. He could not leave her.

"How many more are with you?"

Gi looked at his five-fingered hand. "This many two times," he said, holding out his hand.

"And they're all looking for me?"

"Yes. But Gi find! You come now?"

Bhaldavin knelt down and caught at one of Gi's hands. He drew the olvaar closer and for long moments stared into Gi's eyes, wondering how much he could expect from so small an ally. How much did the olvaar understand? How much could he remember? Would he do as asked?

Suddenly the lights went out again. Gi's fingers tightened on Bhaldavin's hand. "Light come. Go. Why?"

"I'll explain later, Gi, when there's time," Bhaldavin said. "Right now there's something I'd like you to do for me. Do you think you can find your way back to Lil-el in the dark?"

Gi whistled an affirmative. "Gi find Pretty Eyes. You follow?"

"No, not right now. But soon. You tell Pretty Eyes that I'll come to the tunnel as soon as I've found Thura. Can you remember that?"

"Gi remember good. Little Fish go find Thura, then come to tunnel."

"Good, Gi. That's good. Go now. I'll join you as soon as I can." He released the olvaar and stood up. He listened as Gi's soft footsteps faded, then with a silent prayer that the olvaar would remember his instructions, he turned and started up the steps again, feeling his way along the wall. He had almost reached the top of the stairs when the lights flickered on again. He swore softly but kept going. His search would be easier with light, but it would also be far more dangerous.

He moved quickly and quietly, searching each floor room by room. It was an eerie feeling to walk through the rooms that had housed the few remaining citizens of Barl-gan for the last twenty years and not find a single soul. Here and there he recognized clothing, favorite chairs, games, and craft items that had entertained those he had learned to call friends. He also spotted partially eaten food that had been left behind when the Wastelanders had attacked.

Most of the rooms he passed through had been searched by the enemy and stripped of whatever might be useful, but in the back quarter of the building he discovered several rooms that had been untouched. Either the Wastelanders had been in too much of a hurry, or they had simply missed the rooms by following the wrong hallway.

He paused in the middle of one of those rooms. It had belonged to the old woman, Patra, one of Thura's best friends. The room smelled of wellen-mint and drenberry leaves, a favorite concoction used by Patra as perfume. He was touched by a pang of sadness as he remembered that she was dead. It was not likely that any of the remaining Barl-ganians would ever return. If the Wastelanders abandoned the city and returned to their own lands, it was possible that he would be the last person to ever set foot in that room. He crossed to another door on the other side of the room, stepped into the hall, and as he closed the door quietly behind him, a feeling of timelessness swept through him; it was an awareness of both the fragility of life and its unyielding spirit to continue. Life would go on, if not here, then somewhere else, for the inner being always rose above death to begin again. So it would be with Patra and all of those who had died there in the past few days, Barl-ganian and Wastelander alike.

His thoughts on the subject of death were shattered by shouts coming from outside. He hurried down the hall, came to the end room, which was dark, and went inside. The light coming from the hallway gave him enough light to see that Gringers's room had been thoroughly searched. He pushed an overturned chair aside and crossed the room to look out the window.

It was dark outside, but the lights from the mansion shone out onto a stretch of ground between the main building and the stockade walls. Judging by what he was seeing, the Wastelanders were under attack. Streaks of bright laser light split the darkness again and again as the Wastelanders raced toward the stockade walls. With both sides in possession of light guns, it was impossible to tell who was who.

In that moment, Bhaldavin remembered the olvaar saying something about someone creating a diversion. Who was out there? Kelsan probably, and Gils if he had made it to safety. Other faces flashed through his mind, faces of those he had not seen among the dead the day before.

It did not take long to realize that the numbers were still against his friends, which meant that he had to move quickly and find Thura, Gringers, and the others while the Barl-ganians kept the Wastelanders busy for a few minutes.

Bhaldavin jumped at a sudden noise in the hall behind him. It sounded like a door moving on unoiled hinges. He crossed the room as quietly as possible and stopped at the open doorway. He leaned out and glanced down the hall. The door to Patra's room stood open. He was sure he had closed it.

He pulled Kelsan's knifelike instrument from his waistband and moved into the hall. Seven steps brought him to Patra's door. He reached inside the doorway and touched the button that put on the overhead light.

The room was still and empty, just as he had left it. He turned, touched the light panel, and stepped back into the hall, knowing that if he wanted to locate Thura, there was no time to waste hunting shadows. He hurried down the hall to continue his search.

Chapter 17 ⟨

THEON PACED RESTLESSLY UP AND DOWN THE CORRIDOR that led to a set of stairs that would take them out of the lower cellars up into the kitchens on ground level. It was a roundabout way of getting into the upper levels of the building, but it was far safer than the direct route through the infirmary. Not only were there two secret passageways leading into and out of the kitchens should a hasty retreat be necessary, but there was every possibility that the Wastelanders had left men somewhere down in the lower levels, men who were still looking for their escape tunnel, and if they looked hard enough . . .

"Well, we're in, at least," Theon muttered to himself as he stopped at the foot of the steps where the tall Ni called Amet stood with his arms crossed over his chest as if barring the way. "Now all we have to worry about is finding Gringers, Little Fish, and the others . . . and getting back out."

"What?" Amet asked, catching the last few words.

"Nothing, just thinking out loud," Theon said. His glance touched the seven Barl-ganians who sat crouched along the walls of the corridor awaiting orders. They were dirty; their clothing was torn, and several bore crudely wrapped bandages, but all were armed with knives or whatever other sharp implements they had been

able to find when the Wastelanders broke over the
stockade wall. Their anxious glances shifted from Theon
to the impressive-looking Ni standing on the stairway.

Theon was not exactly sure why any of them had
come unless they had some deranged idea of trying to
reclaim what was theirs. No use telling them that such
dreams would probably be the death of them. Theon was
a realist and held no illusions about the last survivors of
Barl-gan. He knew that many were retarded and over
half were physically malformed, and they had little
chance of driving the Wastelanders away even with the
help of the three Ni who had literally stepped out of thin
air. But upstairs they would be bodies wielding knives,
and their presence would greatly improve his own
chance of finding and freeing Gringers. That was all he
would ask of them.

He looked up at Amet. "How long are we going to
wait here?"

The overhead lights in the corridor reflected in
Amet's eyes as he turned his attention to Theon. "We
wait until I have word from Paa-tol," he replied.

Theon pointed to Amet's ring hand. "He's going to
signal you through that. Right?"

When Amet nodded, Theon frowned. "You don't believe that's possible, do you?" Amet asked, his eyebrows
raised in question.

Theon did not like the superior tone in Amet's voice
but he was not about to challenge the Ni, at least at the
moment. "What I believe isn't important. All I want to
do is find my friends."

"We'll find them."

"We damn well better after all your promises!" Theon
growled.

"Theon . . . not now!"

Startled by Lil-el's voice, Theon turned to find her
standing just beyond the last of the Barl-ganians. "What
are you doing here?" he snapped. "You were to stay at
the tunnel exit and guard it for us!"

"I'm here because you're going to need every pair of
hands you can get when you go upstairs!"

"Lil-el, you can't . . ."

"I can and I will. No more arguing. I won't be left behind!" She moved closer and glanced around. "Where's the Healer?"

"Why?" Theon growled.

"There's something I must say to him." Her glance touched Amet, then slid away. "It's important!"

"Whatever you want to say can wait until later," Theon said, walking toward her. "I want you back in that tunnel to keep the way clear for us!"

"No! Send one of the others back. Here's the light gun," she said, handing it to him.

"Lil-el," Theon warned.

Suddenly the Healer appeared at a junction in the corridor behind Lil-el. Young Tule followed close on his heels. Tule was only twelve, but he was large and strong for his age. His splayed feet were all that betrayed him as Barl-ganian.

The rest of the Barl-ganians stood as the Healer approached. Several had experienced his healing touch; the others had seen the results of his work on Gils Watcher and Jothan.

Theon unconsciously straightened as Dhalvad stopped beside Lil-el. Like the Barl-ganians, he stood in awe of the slightly built Ni.

"I've had no luck finding Gi-arobi," Dhalvad announced. "I don't know where he went. I was sure he was following along behind. He must have taken one of the halls leading away from this one."

"You'll never find him if he has," Theon said. "There's a maze of rooms and halls both down here and above, and it's not easy to find your way around even with the halls lighted."

Dhalvad turned from Theon and looked back the way he had come. "I can't leave him to find his way out alone. He's smart, but—"

"There's no time to go looking for him now," Amet said sharply. "Paa-tol should be contacting us any moment now, and we'll have to be ready when he and the others draw the Wastelanders to the stockade walls."

Dhalvad ignored Amet and spoke to Theon. "You said there was another way to the floors above. Could you or one of the others show me the way?"

"No!" Amet snapped. "I want you by me! If we're to locate Mithdaar, it's essential that you stay near the Tamorlee."

Dhalvad glared at Amet, his fists clenched at his sides. It was evident to all standing there, if it had not been before, that there was no love lost between the two Ni.

"There's no way you can stop me from going to look for Gi!"

"You're a fool!" Amet hissed angrily. "What we're doing here is more important than finding that rude little furball!"

"To you. Not to me!" Dhalvad held out his hand. "If you want me to assist the Tamorlee, give it to me now and let us find the other crystal. It'll be easier without your interference!"

"Give it to you!" Amet crowed. "Then I'd be the fool! You'd be gone in an instant, right back to Jjaan-bi and your half-breed mate! No! You'll stay here with me—or risk her life! I'm warning you, don't push me! Or have you forgotten that Paa-tol also has a Seeker ring and is fully capable of reaching Jjaan-bi within minutes? He has his orders should you prove difficult, and you know what those orders are. Now, what is it to be?"

While the two Ni argued, there was a subtle shifting among the Barl-ganians. Theon noticed and silently approved as he moved a step to his right, bringing himself shoulder to shoulder with the Healer. Slowly the Barlganians gathered around behind them, their frowns directed at Amet.

"I'm not sure what's going on here," Theon said, breaking the deadlock between the two Ni, "but whatever it is, I stand with the Healer."

"Stay out of this," Amet said. "It doesn't concern you!"

"Perhaps it doesn't," Theon snapped back, "but I

know a threat when I hear one, and none of us likes you threatening this man!"

"He's not one of you! He's Ni! And he's under my authority. I'm Speaker for the Tamorlee and will brook no interference in this matter. If you want to stand with him, then you serve him best by being quiet and following my orders. We all want something here. You, your friends. I, the crystal called Mithdaar." Amet's glance fell on Dhalvad. "And all the Healer wants is to go home and find everything as he left it. Isn't that right, Dhalvad?"

Dhalvad glanced at Theon and several of the others standing with him. He felt their support but at the same time realized that Amet still held the upper hand. He looked back at Amet and nodded.

Amet's mocking look of triumph made Dhalvad's stomach churn with revulsion. There would come a time, he vowed silently, when Amet would pay for what he was doing.

Suddenly Amet straightened. His glance lifted over the heads of those below him; eyes unfocused, he stared into the overhead light.

"What's happening?" Theon asked.

"He's mind-speaking to Paa-tol through the rings," Dhalvad answered. "All Seeker rings are linked to each other by an energy we call polu. Seekers can tap into the energy and use it for both communication and travel."

Lil-el looked at Amet and saw that her moment had come. Ever since she had learned Dhalvad's name, she had been trying to speak to him alone, but he had slept most of that day away, and after waking, Amet or Paa-tol had been in constant attendance, giving her no chance to speak to Dhalvad privately.

She touched Dhalvad's arm to get his attention. "Please, there's something I must ask you."

Dhalvad looked at her frowning. "I thought you were to stay in the tunnel."

"Never mind that," Lil-el answered impatiently. "I'm going with you. But before anything else happens, I must know something about you. Do you have a family? Any brothers or sisters?"

Dhalvad was startled by the question. "What has that to do with anything?"

"Please, it's important!" Lil-el pleaded.

"I have a mate and a child, a son, and I did have a brother and sister, but they both died in the war. My mother and father are also dead."

Lil-el looked deeply into Dhalvad's eyes. There *was* a resemblance there! She could not be wrong. "What was your brother's name? Was it Bhaldavin?"

Dhalvad's eyes widened in surprise. "How did you know that?"

Lil-el smiled through the tears that had sprung to her eyes. "I knew it! I was right! You're Dhalvad, the young brother who was left behind in the Deep! Bhaldavin has talked about you so often, about going back to find you." She laughed and grabbed his arm. "And here you are looking for him!"

"Bhaldavin? My brother is here?" Dhalvad demanded, his thoughts spinning wildly. "Where is he?"

Theon, who had been listening, broke in. "Bhaldavin is Little Fish. He's the one we've come to get out of here, the one who holds the other crystal. Is he really your brother?"

Dhalvad turned dazed eyes to Theon. "I don't know. It doesn't seem possible. It's been so long. How can I be sure?"

Lil-el was laughing and crying at the same time. "You'll know when you see him, I promise. He can tell you his story better than I. If only he was here right now! We've got to get him out . . . and Thura, and the others, before something happens to them!"

Dhalvad caught Lil-el's hands and gripped them tightly, a hundred questions trembling on his lips.

Suddenly Amet came out of his trace. "It's begun! The Wastelanders are engaged and on a run toward the stockade walls. Let's go!"

Amet's glance found Theon. "You! Lead the way and quickly! We won't have a lot of time to do our searching.

And be ready to fight. There are sure to be some of the enemy left guarding the prisoners!"

Theon muttered something about fools giving orders as he ran past Amet up the stairs toward the kitchens above.

Dhalvad gave Lil-el a tight smile. "We'll find them, I promise! Stay close to me!"

Lil-el nodded and brushed at the tears blurring her vision as she followed Dhalvad past Amet. The Barl-ganians took their cues from Dhalvad and Lil-el and flowed by Amet, pushing him back against the stairwell in their haste to stay with the three in the lead.

Amet growled a curse, pushed away from the wall, and brought up the rear, hurrying to catch up.

Theon reached the top of the secret passageway and paused with an ear near the crack in the door. From the other side the door was hidden by a paneled wall with narrow shelves used to hold spices. It was silent and dark beyond the door. He touched the metal lever on the top of the doorway and pushed the paneled door outward. Moments later the kitchen was filled with Barl-ganians. Light from the lower passageway gave the kitchen an eerie glow.

"Spread out," Theon ordered softly. "Stay in pairs and be careful. If you find any Wastelanders, don't hesitate to kill, because they won't! We've got to find Gringers, Little Fish, and the others and free them as quickly as possible. If anything goes wrong, try to get back here. Understood?"

Five or six of the Barl-ganians nodded; the others just stood and stared. Unsure whether or not they all understood, Theon shrugged his shoulders in resignation, knowing he would be lucky to see even half of them live through the upcoming fight. "All right, go!"

The Barl-ganians slipped out of the room quickly and quietly. Theon turned and touched the light panel on the other side of the secret door, plunging the room into darkness. He left the door slightly ajar and reached out to catch Dhalvad's arm.

"You and Amet stay with me, or you'll get lost. Lil-el, guard our backs!"

Dhalvad felt Amet fumble at his shoulder in the darkness. He would have smiled in delight at the smooth way the small man had taken leadership from Amet had he not been so worried about what they would find ahead. Judging from what Lil-el and Theon had told him about Wastelanders, it would be kill or be killed if they met any head on.

As thoughts of Wastelanders crossed his mind, Dhalvad was suddenly inundated by terrifying images belonging to Gils Watcher. The intimate linkage necessary for a deep healing had, in Gils's case, created an echo effect that immersed Dhalvad in a whirlwind of memories not his own. He saw the Wastelanders kill Gavi in cold blood; then he, as Gils, nudged Enar in the side and together they made a break for the stockade wall. His heartbeat raced as he/Gils caught the top of the walkway and pulled himself up. He/Gils reached back to help Enar and saw him struck in the back with a knife. Enar fell, then he/Gils was throwing himself over the stockade wall and falling . . . falling . . .

A sudden jerk on Dhalvad's arm broke the barrier between shared memory and present reality and he came out of his trance to find himself being held up by Amet on one side, Theon on the other, the glow of light coming from another room, showing both faces clearly.

"What's wrong?" Theon whispered.

Dhalvad shook his head. "Nothing. Just lost myself for a moment."

"What do you mean?"

"Memories belonging to Gils. They caught me off guard."

Amet's hand tightened on Dhalvad's arm. "If you're trying to pull something, it won't work! I haven't come all this way to have you—"

Dhalvad twisted free, the lingering effects of Gils's rage and terror still coursing through him. "Damn it! I've had enough of you and your demands. If you want me to help you find Mithdaar, just shut up and let me do what

I'm here for. If you won't give me the Tamorlee, at least let me touch it and find out if it knows where Mithdaar is!"

"Come on, you two," Theon interjected. "Arguing isn't going to help us find Gringers or Little Fish, and there's no telling how long your friend will be able to keep the Wastelanders' attention."

Dhalvad ignored the tug on his arm. "Well, Amet? Do I speak to the Tamorlee, or do you go on alone?"

Amet was silent for a moment or two. He heard the ring of defiance in Dhalvad's voice and realized that the Healer could be pushed no further. He held his ring hand out, his fist closed tightly so there was no chance of Dhalvad slipping the Tamorlee away from him. "No tricks, Dhalvad. I'll be monitoring you both."

Dhalvad swallowed an angry retort and reached for the ring stone. His hatred for Amet had grown so strong that for a few seconds it actually blocked his linkage with the crystal; but slowly, gradually, the Tamorlee took his anger and converted it into pure energy, storing it within him.

Relax, the Tamorlee crooned. *All is well, my friend. I have touched your anger and know its source. No harm will come to you from Amet.*

It's not me I'm worried about, Dhalvad said. *It's Poco and Jiam!*

Dhalvad, enough! Amet warned.

No! I've kept silent this long because I made myself believe that you would keep your word. I now fear that you never intended to! It was back there—it was the way you dismissed Gi-arobi. You don't care whether he lives or dies, just as you don't care about the rest of us! It's finally come to me that it would be far better for you if I never return to Jjaan-bi to tell my side of this story, and the same goes for Poco, Jiam, and Screech. You mean to eliminate all of us, don't you?

Amet! Is this the truth? the Tamorlee demanded.

The quaver in the energy linkage sent chills up Amet's spine. He reacted to the Tamorlee's dismay with righteous indignation. *The truth is that I mean to find Mith-*

daar and return it to Jjaan-bi, and I'll not let anyone stand in my way! You are as responsible as I for what has happened! If you had spoken directly to me about Mithdaar and not insisted that Dhalvad become involved, I wouldn't have had to use any leverage to force Dhalvad to assist in this search. He could have remained blissfully ignorant of this hunt, and you and I could have come here alone!

He twists things around, Tamorlee, Dhalvad said. *The blame isn't yours! It's his and his alone! He lied to you and he forced me to lie to both you and the Council of Elders by omission!*

And yet, the Tamorlee mused, *I sense that he speaks the truth as he sees it, and part of that truth is that some of the blame must be mine. I'm sorry, my friend, to be even partially responsible for the pain and anger I sense in you. Being alone has finally warped my sense of priorities. I thought only of my own needs and ignored all others.*

As do we all, Amet chimed in. *Enough with self-recrimination! No one is perfect. Not I, not Dhalvad, not even the Tamorlee. There's no going back to right wrongs unless one chooses to walk through time, and even then, one visiting the past is not always able to change it. So let's stop all this nonsense about who did what to whom and get on with finding Mithdaar. We can sort everything out after we have the other crystal in our possession.*

And Poco, Jiam, and Screech? Dhalvad demanded. *You promise you'll set them free? That they'll not be harmed?*

I do so promise, Amet answered solemnly, *as Speaker for the Tamorlee.*

I have witnessed the promise made, the Tamorlee added. *So will it be—or all that you have worked for, Amet, will be for nothing.*

What do you mean by that?

You will keep your word to Dhalvad, the Tamorlee explained, *or you forfeit my friendship and my service to your people, plus all you might have gained from my brother, Mithdaar.*

A few seconds followed the Tamorlee's statement.

I understand, Amet said finally. *It will be as you wish.*

Relief washed through Dhalvad and with that relief came the realization that while he and Amet spoke to the Tamorlee, time had passed and Theon and the others would be on the move.

Tamorlee, we must break the link and find out what's happening with Theon and Lil-el, but before we go, can you tell us where Mithdaar is? Are you in contact with him now?

I am not in direct link with him, but I sense he is near. His energy pattern comes from somewhere above our present location.

When Dhalvad and Amet came out of the link a few seconds later, they found themselves alone. Theon and Lil-el had gone on without them. They hurried into the next room and passed through to a hall beyond. There they found Theon and Lil-el standing half hidden behind a door swung out into the hall.

Lil-el and Theon turned at the sound of footsteps behind them. "We'd about given up on you two," Theon said softly as the two Ni approached. "You were like two statues standing there. What were you doing?"

"We were speaking to the Tamorlee," Dhalvad replied. "It says that Mithdaar is somewhere above us."

"Probably on one of the upper floors," Theon said as he pushed past the door. "Let's hope that they've kept all the prisoners together. There's a flight of stairs just down the hall. Stay close."

Chapter 18 ✍

BHALDAVIN CLIMBED ANOTHER SET OF STAIRS, WHICH brought him to the third floor. He stopped at the top of the stairs and glanced both ways. The hall was dark to the right, lighted to the left. There were fewer rooms to the left, so he checked them first. All were empty and showed signs of having been ransacked.

As he continued his search down the other end of the hall, he turned lights out as he went along, feeling safer in the darkness. Once he heard a noise behind him and stepped quickly to the wall, clutching his improvised weapon tightly and waiting.

Long, silent moments passed. The sound was not repeated. He licked dry lips and cautiously pushed away from the wall. Five rooms at the end of the hall showed light coming out of the open doorways. He quickly checked each room he came to and continued on. He hesitated at the two end rooms. If he did not find Thura soon . . . No. He would not let himself even think about leaving her behind.

He stepped to the open doorway on his right and peeked inside. It was a bathroom, and it was empty. The stench coming from the ceramic bowl standing in the far corner made him feel ill. The third floor was home to several of the more retarded among the Barl-ganians, and they were not meticulous in their everyday habits.

Turning away, he crossed the hall and leaned into the last room. His eyes went wide in shock. "Thura!"

Thura's head snapped up at the sound of her father's voice. Then he was beside her. Eyes wide in terror, she twisted and strained at the ropes that held her to the chair. A strip of cloth forced her mouth open and muffled her words.

Bhaldavin's stomach twisted when he saw the reddish bruises on her face. Sick with thoughts of what else Sola might have done to her, he caught her flailing head between his hand and chest and tried to calm her down.

"Shsssh, Thura. Everything's all right. I'm here, and I'm going to take you to your mother."

Thura moaned and shook her head, her eyes wild in desperation as her father began to work on the knot holding her left arm to the chair arm. He kept talking to her and did not notice the direction of her glances.

The rope finally loosened, and Thura jerked her arm free. She caught at the gag in her mouth and tore it loose. "Adda! Behind you! A trap!"

The words were no more out of her mouth when the door slammed shut. Bhaldavin whirled and found himself face to face with Sola. The man's evil grin sent rage shooting through Bhaldavin's body. There was no time for self-recrimination or excuses. He had made a mistake in entering the room without checking it more carefully, but seeing Thura sitting there had washed all caution from his mind.

Sola watched Bhaldavin with anticipation, his hunger for hurting others pushing him to the brink of madness. He actually laughed aloud as Bhaldavin drew something from his belt and launched an attack. He met that charge with open arms, grabbing the Ni by his arm and head, then turning. The momentum of Bhaldavin's attack plus Sola's move sent Bhaldavin crashing into a side wall. His right shoulder and back took most of the impact. Somewhere in the process, he lost his weapon.

Thura screamed for her father to get up as she worked frantically at her bonds and freed her other arm.

Bhaldavin heard her cry and rolled over as Sola leaned down over him. He kicked out and connected with Sola's legs, sending the man crashing down. He glanced quickly around as he pushed to his feet, but he did not see his weapon.

Sola was up a second behind Bhaldavin and closed on him, backing him into a corner. His fist caught the Ni a glancing blow as Bhaldavin darted to one side. Momentarily stunned, Bhaldavin fell over a chair that lay turned on its side. Before he could recover, Sola was on top of him, forcing him to the floor. Bhaldavin caught a glimpse of Sola's knife sheath and made a grab for the knife and pulled it free.

"No, you don't!" Sola growled as he caught Bhaldavin's hand and slammed it out to his side, pinning it to the floor. His other hand went around the Ni's neck, pushing his head back.

Sola sat up and straddled Bhaldavin, his eyes burning with the heat of battle. "I knew you'd come looking for her. All I had to do was wait!"

Sola turned and glanced at Thura, who had completely freed herself from her ropes and was just rising to her feet.

"Sit down, or I'll kill him!" Sola roared, his fingers closing tighter around Bhaldavin's neck.

Thura saw her father begin to fight for air. She wanted to go to him and help, but Sola's dark eyes held her mesmerized. She wilted under the intensity of his glare and slowly settled back into the chair.

"That's better," he told her. "Just do as you're told and I won't hurt you any more."

Bhaldavin began to thrash beneath Sola, fighting for air. Sola looked down and smiled, then slowly released the pressure on his throat. Bhaldavin coughed and choked as air rushed back into his lungs. Gradually the darkness cleared, and he saw Sola leering down at him.

"You were a fool to think you could escape me," Sola said, contempt ringing in every word. "And more a fool to make me look bad before Zojac and the others. You'll pay for that—I promise. You . . . and your daughter."

Bhaldavin would have pleaded for Thura's release but knew that it would be useless. There was no way to bargain with insanity. He turned and looked at Thura. As their glances locked, he knew what he had to do to save her.

Sola backhanded him. "Look at me when I'm talking to you, Green Hair!"

A warm gush of blood spurted from Bhaldavin's nose. Eyes watering from the blow, he spat at Sola. "Wastelander filth! You're the fool! That's why you'll never lead your people! Zojac knows that! As does everyone else!"

Sola's face suffused with rage. It was just what Bhaldavin wanted. He turned his head as Sola struck him in the face, lessening the impact of the blow. Before the man struck again, Bhaldavin turned back and spat in his face.

A deep guttural cry escaped Sola's lips. He grabbed Bhaldavin's tunic front in his left hand and raised his right in a fist, momentarily forgetting the knife still clutched in Bhaldavin's hand.

Bhaldavin drove the knife into Sola's side a half second before Sola's fist descended. Pain exploded in his face, but overtopping that pain was exaltation as he heard Sola cry out. He pulled the knife out and struck Sola again.

"Run, Thura! Run!" he yelled.

Sola managed to block Bhaldavin's second thrust and a moment later had captured his wrist, his own rage submerged in pain and the realization that his easy conquest could be the death of him if he was not quick.

Thura hesitated. She trusted her father above all else and under normal circumstances would have obeyed him, but she had felt the hands of the big man and knew his strength; she also knew that her father was no match for him.

As her father had sacrificed himself for her, she did the same for him. Not thinking of the consequences, she took several running steps and jumped Sola from behind, biting and scratching as wildly as a crazed gensvolf.

Sola yelled in pain as sharp, clawlike fingers tore at

his eyes and face. He reached back with his free hand, grabbed Thura by the hair, bent forward, and jerked her down over his head. She landed hard on her back, and the air was knocked from her lungs.

"No, Thura!" Bhaldavin screamed as he realized what was happening. "Run! Get out of here!"

As Thura started to sit up, Sola rose up onto his knees and clouted her alongside the head. Her cry tore at her father, and he struggled harder to dislodge the big man. The battle was brief and soon Sola again straddled the Ni, his left hand still holding Bhaldavin's right arm to the floor.

Sola glanced at the still child lying sprawled an arm's length away. Satisfied that she would no longer be a problem, he turned his attention to Bhaldavin, ignoring all else, even the slight movement of the door inward.

"Release the knife!" Sola demanded. When Bhaldavin failed to obey, he banged his hand up and down against the floorboards until the knife fell clattering.

Grimacing in pain, Sola gingerly touched the wound in his side. His hand came away red with blood. The deadly look in his eyes sent a chill down Bhaldavin's spine. The man was going to kill him, and there was no way to stop him.

Sola reached over, picked up his knife, and with all the viciousness of a cold-blooded gensvolf, he drove it down through Bhaldavin's open palm, pinning his hand to the floor.

Sola smiled as Bhaldavin's scream echoed out the door down the hall. He feasted on Bhaldavin's pain, his mind active with thoughts of future torture he could inflict before he killed the Green Hair.

Suddenly something shot out from behind the partially opened door to the hall. It moved so quickly that Sola caught only a glimpse of it before it was on him. Pinprick-sharp teeth caught at his throat from the side; the unexpected impact of the small furred body sent him off-balance, and he fell to his side, hands reaching for the thing that was gnawing at his neck.

Terror entered his soul as he tried to pull the thing off,

but when he pulled, he was also pulling at his own skin. He hammered at the ball of fur, then tried to squeeze it to death, but its grip was unbreakable, its teeth sinking deeper and deeper into his throat. He screamed as he rolled over and over, trying to dislodge the thing.

Bhaldavin was not exactly sure what was happening, but he knew he was free of Sola for a few seconds and that he had to get Thura out of there. Gritting his teeth against the pain, he sat up. He heard Thura groan and saw her push to her hands and knees.

"Thura...the knife...pull it up! Hurry, child! Hurry!"

Thura rubbed the side of her head as she got up and went to her father. She frowned as she glanced over at Sola, who lay on the floor still clawing weakly at something at his throat.

"Thura, hurry!" Bhaldavin urged.

She knelt and grabbed the knife handle with both hands. Exerting all of her strength, she jerked the knife free.

A fresh wave of agony shot through Bhaldavin as the knife slid from his hand. Tears sprang to Thura's eyes as she saw her father's pain. She helped him up, and together they started for the doorway. Neither looked back.

Gi-arobi heard the two Ni leave the room, but he did not release his hold. He tasted the man's blood in his mouth; its warm saltiness was bitter on his tongue. The man's struggles had ceased and the steady flow of blood dribbled off. With conscious effort Gi released his hold. His jaws ached and his throat hurt where the man had tried to strangle him. He backed away, his golden eyes alert for any movement. The man's eyes suddenly opened, but he made no move.

Gi-arobi sniffed cautiously at the man's face, ready to leap away if necessary, but the man was dead and would never again hurt anyone. Gi snorted softly, clearing his nostrils of the man's scent.

He heard the footsteps of the two Ni moving down the hall and turned and ran for the doorway. He caught

up with them a short way down the darkened hall and
followed quietly along behind. Neither seemed aware of
his presence.

Bhaldavin and Thura reached a stairway going down.
The lights and the quiet below gave Bhaldavin pause. He
was sure he had turned the lights off on the floor below.
Either he had missed one . . . or the battle between the
Wastelanders and Theon's forces was over, which meant
that they had to move quickly or risk being found by
returning Wastelanders.

He decided to take a chance and started down the
stairs with Thura. They were near the bottom of the
steps when they heard voices. Someone was coming
down the hall.

"Hurry, Thura! Up!" Bhaldavin urged.

"But *he's* up there!" Thura protested.

Bhaldavin knew who she meant, but something told
him that they need not worry about Sola. He thought he
saw something move on the landing above and stopped.

"Hurry, Little Fish!" Gi called softly from the top of
the stairs. "Someone comes!"

It took Bhaldavin a moment or two to remember
where he had heard the strange lisping voice. Suddenly a
picture flashed into his mind: Sola rolling on the floor
with something furry at his throat. The olvaar! The olvaar had saved them! "Gi?"

"Yes! Yes! Hurry fast! Someone comes!"

"Adda," Thura said softly, eyes trying to pierce the
darkness above. "Who is it?"

"A friend," Bhaldavin answered, continuing up the
steps, his hand held up against his chest as he encour-
aged Thura along.

When they reached the top of the stairs, Bhaldavin
turned right, walked down the hall, found another set of
stairs leading upward, and took them, a small bundle of
fur running just ahead of him.

"Where are we going, Adda?" Thura asked.

"Four more flights up, then out onto the roof. We can
use the outside ladder that goes down to the second
floor, then climb in through one of the kitchen windows

and use the secret passageway to get out. Your mother's waiting down there for us."

They continued upward into the darkness, familiarity with the halls enabling them to find their way without too much difficulty. They were coming up the last flight of stairs to the seventh floor when Bhaldavin accidentally bumped his hand against a wall. The pain made him feel faint and he dropped to the steps.

"Adda!" Thura cried. "What's wrong?"

"It's my hand." Bhaldavin gasped. "Thura, I need light, just for a few minutes. I've got to stop the bleeding. Go to the top of the steps, find a light and turn it on, then come back and help me wrap up my hand."

"Adda . . ."

"Don't be afraid. Our enemies are below us, not above. Go. Do as I tell you."

He listened as Thura climbed the steps. Something touched his shoulder just as the lights went on above. He looked up and found Gi-arobi perched on the stair above him; the fur around his mouth and down his front was matted with blood. Golden eyes regarded him with an unswerving stare.

"Little Fish be tired?" Gi asked solicitiously.

"It's my hand, little one. It bleeds and makes me weak. I must wrap it up."

Thura came back down the stairs and stopped when she saw Gi-arobi. She jumped slightly as Gi whistled to her in his own tongue.

"He won't hurt you, Thura," Bhaldavin said, keeping his voice low. "He's a friend. His name is Gi."

"What is it?" she asked, her busy eyes taking in every detail of the plump, furred creature. "Where did it come from?"

"Gi not it!" Gi piped up. "Gi be olvaar! Come with Dhal to find Little Fish."

"It talks!" she cried softly.

"Yes, I know. Come, Thura. Sit beside me. I have to get this wound tied up. Try to rip off a piece of your tunic."

Thura moved cautiously past Gi-arobi and knelt on

the step beside her father. She hesitated a moment, tears starting to her eyes when she saw the blood welling up in her father's hand. She quickly used her teeth to start a tear at the bottom of her tunic, then ripped the fabric off in a strip. She followed her father's instructions and wrapped the cloth tightly around his hand and tied it in place, moaning softly to herself as her father slumped forward onto the stair above.

Bhaldavin was out only a few moments. The sharp pain in his hand as he pushed himself to a sitting position brought everything back. His daughter's tear-streaked face lighted with relief as he reached out to her. She was careful not to bump against his hand as she hugged him.

Gi whistle-clicked a warning and scampered up the stairs. Bhaldavin and Thura caught the sound of footsteps coming down the hallway below. Thura stood, helped her father rise, and moved up beside him, silently offering him the support of her young body. Still a bit unsteady, Bhaldavin gratefully accepted her aid.

Gi-arobi met them at the top of the stairs and waited for them to choose a direction. Thura started to turn off the lights in the hallway, but her father shook his head.

"Leave them on," he whispered. "They'll see them if we turn them off now."

Bhaldavin felt his strength returning as the pain in his hand receded to a bearable level. The last flight of steps took them up into the northern tower.

There was a door leading from the tower out onto the roof, but Bhaldavin turned away from it. A shaft of light shone down the open wooden stairway that led to the second floor of the tower, signifying that someone had been up in the tower that night. Were they still there, or had they simply neglected to turn the lights off behind them?

Thura went to the roof door and opened it, then noticed that she was alone. "Adda?" She turned and found Gi-arobi already several steps up the stairway, his nose fur twitching with an unpleasant smell.

"Something burns," Gi said, looking at Bhaldavin.

Bhaldavin crossed the tower floor and looked upward. Thura ran to him and caught at the back of his tunic. "Adda, let's go! I don't like it here! I want to find Mother!"

"In a moment, Thura," he answered, as he elbowed her back a step. "You stay here. I want to look upstairs."

"No, Adda! Don't go up there!"

"Thura, I'll be right back. I promise. You stay here."

"What be up there?" Gi asked.

"Machines left by the Ral-jennob," Bhaldavin answered. "I think we'd better take a look. It does smell like something is burning."

Gi-arobi preceded Bhaldavin up the steps, carefully keeping to the inside wall. Thura watched the two through the widely spaced spindles on the railing. She finally followed them up the steps, fearing to be left behind.

Gi-arobi was the first into the large circular room at the top of the stairs. He whistled excitedly for Little Fish to come and look.

Bhaldavin stepped into the room a moment later and saw the reason for Gi's outburst. Two Wastelanders lay on the floor next to one of Gringer's machines. Both were dead; one had a hand and sleeve of his garment scorched badly. Just beyond them lay Gringers, bathed in an eerie green light that came from the panel on the machine near the Wastelanders. And nestled in that panel sat Mithdaar, glowing brightly.

Bhaldavin first went to Gringers and felt for a pulse at his throat. The man was alive, but his heartbeat was irregular and his breathing was not good at all.

Bhaldavin jumped as a hand came to rest on his shoulder. It was Thura. "Adda, is Gringers—dead?"

"No, but he needs help. I can't lift him, nor can you."

"What's wrong with him?" Thura asked, crouching down on the other side of Gringers. She touched one of his hands. "He's so cold."

Bhaldavin turned and looked at Mithdaar's radiance. It was nearly blinding. "Gringers must've been showing them how the crystal works. Maybe one of them tried to touch it. Maybe all of them. I don't know."

He caught movement out of the corner of one eye and turned. Gi-arobi had climbed up on the panel of the star beacon and was down on all fours moving toward Mithdaar.

"What this?" Gi piped up. "This be crystal Amet wants?"

"No, Gi!" Bhaldavin cried, springing up. "Don't touch it!"

Gi stopped and sat back on his haunches as Bhaldavin stepped between him and the crystal. He peered over Bhaldavin's arm, eyes partially hooded against the bright light. "Is Mithdaar?" he pressed.

"Yes! But it's dangerous to anyone but me," Bhaldavin said, glancing at the crystal. He had never seen it shine so brilliantly. He remembered his vow never again to let Gringers use Mithdaar for one of his experiments. He cursed softly as the memory of what had happened before came back clearly: he and Mithdaar lost in a dark void with no sense of direction, then the oval room with the yellow spheres of light, and within those spheres— faces and eyes of amber gold that did not belong in his world.

"The Ral-jennob! Damn you, Gringers!" In that moment his fear of the unknown was brushed aside as he reached out with his bandaged hand to pick the crystal up, breaking any possible link with men's gods.

There was a moment of disorientation, followed by a feeling of being wrapped in warmth. *Mithdaar! No!*

Welcome.

The words flowed brightly through Bhaldavin's mind. They were not his own. *Mithdaar?*

So you have named me. It is a good name. I will keep it.

You're speaking!

Yes. I learn—from you—and others.

Bhaldavin's amazement left him stunned. A dozen questions flitted through his mind but he could not think where to start.

You will teach me?

Yes, Mithdaar, I'll teach you, but—not now! There is

danger here. We must leave. Release us from the machine!

Cannot. Must wait.

Wait? For what?

Others come. Must wait.

Mithdaar, no! We can't wait! Release us now!

When he failed to get a response, Bhaldavin tried to free himself by moving his fingers and nudging the crystal out of its place on the panel, but suddenly he could not feel his fingers or any part of himself; even the pain in his hand was gone, and he was floating and growing more relaxed as the seconds passed. Images of Thura and Lil-el crossed his mind, but he could not hold onto them. His thoughts began to drift.

Chapter 19

POCO LAY A SLEEPING JIAM ON THE FLOOR WRAPPED IN her own over-tunic and went to the door for the eighth or ninth time in the last few hours. She was feeling better physically as the effects of the drug they had used on her wore off. She still was not hungry, but she was thirsty.

Screech was in his corner, still worrying at the metal pin driven into the wall. If he could free the peg and ring attached to his leg chain, he would be able to add his strength to hers against the door.

She peered through a narrow crack on the left side of the door. It was still dark outside. She had tried calling for help several times, but had received no answer. Wherever they were, they had to be far from any settlements. She used her fingers to trace the outlines of the doorway once more, looking for a loose board or a crack that would give her some kind of purchase. She found nothing and, in frustration, banged the door with her hand, cursing as tears sprang unbidden to her eyes.

Screech growled and jerked harder on the metal pin, his own patience wearing thin. His growling ceased abruptly. Seconds later he made a coughing sound to get Poco's attention.

She heard and moved away from the door, brushing

the tears from her face, angry at herself for losing control. Using the wall, she felt her way over to Screech. She could hear his claws digging at the wood around the pin.

"Any luck?" she asked.

For an answer, Screech reached out, took one of her hands, and placed it around the metal pin; then he jerked the chain first right, then left.

"It moved!" Poco cried. "It moved a little, Screech! I felt it!"

Screech growled softly and nudged her aside. She wanted desperately to help, but realized that she would only be in the way. She returned to Jiam and picked him up. He made soft baby sounds and snuggled into his mother's arms, unaware of the peril they all faced.

Poco leaned back against the wall and licked at dry lips, trying not to think about water. By her reckoning, they had been in the cabin well over two days. Why had someone not come to feed them or check on them? Where was Anwhol, or the other young Ni who had accompanied him before? Had they simply been left to die of thirst and hunger? Or had something gone wrong with Amet's plans?

She held Jiam closer and rubbed her chin across the top of his downy head, her thoughts on Dhalvad as she drifted off to sleep.

Chulu paced the room restlessly, waiting for Caaras to return. After Caaras had reported his brief encounter with Gi-arobi several days earlier, he and a few others had been busy trying to get at the truth behind the sudden disappearance of Pocalina-fel-Jamba, her child, and her derkat companion. A Seeker had been dispatched to Cybury where she was supposed to have gone, though no one had seen her leave, and discreet inquiries were being made throughout the city, inquiries that had turned up nothing so far. Now they were concentrating on questioning some of Amet's people in the hope that someone might have seen or heard something that would be helpful.

Chulu dropped into his favorite stuffed chair in the far corner of his living room and tried to recall everything that Dhalvad had said to him the day before he, Amet, and Paa-tol left. He recalled the strange look on Dhalvad's face when he had said good-bye, and the feeling he had had that Dhalvad was trying to tell him something more than farewell.

Naalan came into the room, handed Chulu a cup of mint tea, and sat down in another chair nearby. Her eyes were full of worry. "I can't conceive of Amet doing anything to Pocalina or her child," she said. "What purpose would it serve?"

Chulu had told his mate of his suspicions just that morning, unable to keep it to himself any longer. He rubbed his eyes and let his head fall back against the back of the chair. "I don't know, Naalan, unless it has something to do with that other crystal. We should've gone slower, taken time to think things through, but Amet was so sure of himself, and Dhalvad seemed to go along with him."

Chulu nodded to himself. "I think that's it. Dhalvad *seemed* to go along, but he didn't really want to!"

"Why didn't he come right out and say it then?" Naalan asked as she set her cup aside on a small table.

"What if he couldn't say anything? What if Amet was threatening his family in some way?"

"Amet wouldn't do such a thing!"

"Wouldn't he? I'm not so sure. I've known him a long time, and though I've always thought of him as a friend, I can't say that I've ever gotten close to him, really felt that I knew him. If he wanted something badly enough, yes, I think he would use any means at his disposal to accomplish his goal."

"But this crystal isn't for himself, it's for the People," she argued.

"That's what he told us. It may even be what he believes to be the truth, but think a moment. Amet will gain both honor and prestige for this find, and as Speaker for the crystals, he will also gain great power and influence."

Chulu drank from his cup, his thoughts running quickly ahead. "The more I think about it, the more I believe we should open the search for Pocalina and her son. The more people we have looking, the better our chances of finding her, and if we've made a mistake and jumped to the wrong conclusions, we can always apologize to Amet later."

Naalan started to say something but was interrupted by a knock on the front door of their tree home.

"Sit still. I'll get it," Chulu said, rising.

Caaras was at the door. The light coming from inside revealed beads of perspiration on his face, and he was breathing heavily. Clearly he had been running.

"What's wrong?" Chulu asked, ushering him inside.

"The Seeker who went to Cybury has just returned," Caaras began. "The village has been searched thoroughly. No one has seen Poco or the baby, or knows anything about their coming for a visit. Chulu, I think they're all in trouble. Dhalvad, too! What can we do?"

Chulu's heart thudded heavily in his chest, fear for his three young friends sweeping over him. "We'll find them," he said, straightening his shoulders, "and quickly! Gather the Seekers and send them out. They're to start looking for Amet and Dhalvad. Tell them that they're to report back here immediately if either one is seen. They're also to keep an eye out for Poco and her child—and Screech. As for here in Jjaan-bi, I think our search had best remain discreet. I don't want anyone to panic and do something we might regret. Contact your friends in the watch. Tell them what we suspect and make sure none of them is connected to Amet. They're to arrest any who seem suspicious, and bring them to me in the Council hall."

"Are you going to tell anyone else on the Council about this?"

"I'll have to. I may regret sending out this alarm, and may pay for it with my chair on the Council, but—I won't turn my back on Poco or Dhalvad, either!"

Chapter 20

"A DDA?" EYES ROUND WITH FEAR, THURA WATCHED her father. What was wrong with him? Why was he suddenly so still? She approached him from the side and saw that he was staring straight ahead as if he saw something she could not. She started to reach out, but a small furred hand caught at her wrist; small, sharp nails pricked her skin gently, then let her go.

"Not touch him," Gi said, instinctively sensing danger. "Come. We go find Dhal. He know what to do."

"I can't leave him! He's my father!"

Gi looked at the distraught Ni child and made a quick decision. "You stay, but no touch! Gi go find help. No touch! Promise?"

Thura licked at dry lips as she nodded. "I'll stay, but please hurry. My mother is somewhere down . . ."

Thura's words trailed off at the sound of someone on the stairs below. She and Gi both looked around, but there was no place to hide except another set of stairs going up to the next floor in the tower.

"Come! Hurry!" Gi said, jumping down from the panel.

Thura glanced at her father, then followed Gi-arobi without another word of protest. They reached the top of the steps and quietly positioned themselves on the next floor above, where they could hear but not be seen.

Theon reluctantly led the way up into the tower, fearing that he was making a mistake. If Gringers was somewhere in the melee below and ended up getting hurt or killed, he would never forgive himself. The only thing that drove him onward was the hope that the Wastelanders had their prisoners together and that Little Fish had somehow managed to hang onto his crystal.

He saw light coming from above and cautioned the others to be quiet as they ascended the last few steps. He reached roof level and hesitated. A cool draft of air came from the open door leading out onto the roof. He took a quick look outside, but there was no one on the roof.

"Is the crystal still above us?" he whispered as he turned back to the room.

Amet went into a momentary link with the Tamorlee. Seconds later he opened his eyes and nodded. "It's somewhere above and it's giving off a steady charge of energy. Let's go."

Theon hefted his knife as he crossed the room and started up the stairs. Amet came next, followed by Dhalvad and Lil-el.

Theon cursed softly to himself as several of the steps squeaked beneath his weight. He was halfway up the flight of stairs when he, too, caught the scent of burned flesh. A sudden premonition of disaster and the possibility that the Wastelanders might have cut the odds against them by killing their prisoners when they realized they were under attack spurred Theon up the last few steps. He lunged into the room without hesitation and almost tripped over the two Wastelanders on the floor. He saw Bhaldavin standing in front of one of Gringers's machines, his hand lost in a blinding glow of light.

"Davin! Where are the others?" he demanded, starting across the room. Then he saw a body lying beyond Bhaldavin. He ran and knelt beside Gringers, fear for his friend making it difficult for him to breathe. He felt for a pulse and drew a shaky breath when he found one.

Amet and Dhalvad followed Theon more cautiously into the room. Lil-el came last, but when she saw Bhaldavin, she pushed by them and hurried toward her mate. She started to reach out to him but was stopped by Amet, who caught at her arm.

"Don't touch him! He's in link with his crystal!"

Lil-el looked from Amet to Dhalvad, who nodded. "It's dangerous to touch a crystal of Mithdaar's power without a fire stone to absorb some of the energy. It can be done, but one must be attuned to the crystal. Are you?"

Lil-el shook her head. "I don't know what you mean by attuned. I've touched the crystal several times, but it carries quite a jolt. I passed out both times."

"You're not attuned then," Amet said, "but it seems that your mate is. It will be most interesting to speak to him when he comes out of the link."

"We're going to wait?" Lil-el demanded.

"We must. The only other thing to do would be for me to try to enter the link using the Tamorlee, but without knowing Mithdaar's power that, too, could be dangerous."

As Lil-el and Amet spoke, Dhalvad moved closer to Bhaldavin to study his face. Though it was bruised and discolored about the eyes and mouth, he saw hints of himself in a shadowy mirrorlike image. Was the strange Ni truly his brother?

Suddenly something pricked his side. He turned and found Theon standing near, his knifepoint brushing Dhalvad's tunic.

"You're needed," Theon said softly. "Come with me."

"What are you doing?" Dhalvad said loud enough for Amet and Lil-el to hear. Both turned to see what was going on.

Theon caught their glances. "I need him to help my friend. I won't hurt him," he promised. "Unless he makes me."

"Theon, no!" Lil-el protested.

Amet caught Dhalvad's glance. "Help the man if you can, but don't tire yourself out, because we won't be able to carry you back down out of here."

Dhalvad nodded and allowed himself to be drawn over to where Gringers lay. As he knelt to check the man over, he heard footsteps on the stairs leading to the next level of the tower. He looked up and saw Gi-arobi bounding down the steps with blatant disregard for safety, and right behind him came a Ni child.

"Thura!" Lil-el met her daughter at the bottom of the steps and caught her up in her arms. "Thura, I was so afraid for you! How did you get here?"

Gi came straight to Dhalvad, whistling madly as he ran and trying to tell him all that had happened to him. As Dhalvad and Gi traded information, and Lil-el and Thura talked, Amet stepped closer to Bhaldavin and the crystal. Greed and desire lighted his face as he drew the Tamorlee from his tunic pocket and slipped it on.

"Come on." Theon scowled, tapping Dhalvad on the shoulder. "You can say hello later. Help Gringers before it's too late!"

Gi looked at Theon and for the first time became aware of the knife in his hand. It was dangerously close to Dhalvad's neck. A soft growl escaped his lips as he eyed the small man.

"Easy, Gi," Dhalvad said soothingly. "He won't hurt me or anyone else. All he wants is for me to heal his friend. Why don't you stay right here beside me and keep watch. All right?"

"Gi watch," the olvaar replied firmly, his glance never leaving Theon.

Dhalvad nodded and went to work. He entered his trance state quickly and easily. The body beneath his hands was well made and strong, but it had received a high jolt of energy that had affected the heartbeat and respiration. There was also some minor damage to the spinal cord at the base of the brain. He first corrected the rhythm of the heart muscles, then eased the spasmed throat muscles, which were making breathing difficult. He then turned his attention to the spinal cord and caused regeneration of damaged cells and a general strengthing of the entire life cable.

Theon became uneasy under the golden-eyed gaze of Gi-arobi. He turned to see what everyone else was doing. Lil-el and Thura were standing together a few paces away from Bhaldavin and Amet. There was a worried look on Lil-el's face.

"What's going on over there?" Theon asked, looking closer at Amet and Bhaldavin. "What're they doing?"

Lil-el answered without turning. "I'm not sure, but I think Amet has gone after Davin."

"Gone? What do you mean? He's standing right there!"

"He's touching Davin's crystal," she said. "His body may be here, but his mind isn't. Look at his face, Theon . . . at his eyes. I don't know what they're seeing, but whatever it is, it frightens me. I've seen Davin go into a trance many times while holding the crystal, but never for so long a time. We've got to wake them up and get out of here!"

"I agree," Theon said. "Just as soon as the Healer is finished with Gringers." He glanced down at his friend. Color had returned to Gringers's face, and his breathing was better. He knelt beside him and took one of his hands. It was warm, and as he squeezed it, there was answering pressure.

"Gringers," Theon said softly. "Can you hear me?"

Dhalvad released his psychic link with Gringers and sat back on his heels, his body trembling with loss of vital energy. He opened his eyes and took several deep breaths, trying to regain his balance. He had not meant to expend so much energy, but it was difficult to stop healing once started.

Gringers stirred at the sound of Theon's voice and with some help, he sat up. "Theon—where did you come from? What's going on?"

Theon took a deep breath and released it slowly, shaking his head. "You aren't going to believe what's happening." He looked at Dhalvad. "What just happened to you. Gringers, I would like you to meet Dhalvad. He's a Ni Healer and he just saved your life. Dhalvad, this is my friend Gringers."

As the two nodded to each other, Theon glanced around. "Now—let's get the hell out of here before any Wastelanders show up!"

Theon helped Gringers to stand and steadied him when he started to slip back down.

"I'm just a little dizzy," Gringers murmured. "I think I'd better sit down for a few minutes."

"There isn't time, Gringers," Theon said, urging him to start walking. "Just keep putting one foot in front of the other, all right?"

"Theon!" Lil-el cried. "I can't leave Davin like this!"

"Get him moving then, because we're leaving!"

Dhalvad struggled to his feet and stood swaying. "We can't leave without the crystals! We have to have them to get back to Jjaan-bi!"

"Well, get then!" Theon snapped. But hurry. We're wasting time. I want out of here!"

Lil-el looked at Dhalvad. "Can you do anything?"

"I can try," he responded wearily. "Give me a few seconds." He breathed deeply, trying to banish the fatigue that seemed to be creeping into every part of his body. Slowly his mind and body began to recover as he willed his energy levels back to normal by tapping into the reservoir of the kee, or spirit.

Somewhat refreshed and in balance, he approached Amet and the one whom Lil-el would have him call brother. He turned to Lil-el. "I'll try to join the link and break them free. If I'm not successful, you and your daughter must go with the two men and try to reach safety. We'll join you when we can. Gi," he said, looking down at his small friend. "You go with them if I'm not able to break the link."

"Not leave Dhal!" Gi whistled emphatically. "Gi talk to Gentle Voice, too!"

"No. Not this time. It's too dangerous with the other crystal involved. I've no way of knowing what's going to happen, and I won't be able to concentrate on what I'm

doing if I'm worrying about you. Promise me that you'll
not interfere!"

Gi whistled mournfully.

"Gi, please," Dhalvad implored.

Gi-arobi's head dropped. "Gi promise," he lisped
softly.

Dhalvad reached down and rubbed the top of Gi's
head. "Don't count me lost so easily, Gi."

Dhalvad gave Lil-el and Thura a smile meant to reassure, then turned to the task at hand. Theon and
Gringers watched from the side.

Dhalvad had never tried to break into a link between
Ni and crystal. He was not even sure it could be done,
but it was imperative that he try. He believed that the
Tamorlee would never knowingly harm him. He was not
so sure about the other crystal and so decided to try to
enter the link by touching the Tamorlee, not Mithdaar.
Amet had placed the Tamorlee against Mithdaar so there
was little room for maneuvering between his hand and
Bhaldavin's; that plus the glare of light made it difficult
to position his hand.

There was a blinding flare of light behind his eyes as
his first finger touched the Tamorlee. It was followed by
a darkness that threatened to engulf him. His next
awareness comprised a cacophony of voices that flowed
around and through his mind, words so quickly spoken
that he could not even begin to guess at their meanings.

Once, twice, three times he spoke into that waterfall
of sound, each time calling a different name. *Amet. Tamorlee. Bhaldavin.*

There was no immediate response, then suddenly the
words slowed and he began to understand.

*Who ... not now ... come ... they listen ... Healer
...me out ... listen ... afraid ...brother ... speak to
me ...friend... out ...Thura ... break link ... no
...learning...must stay...*

Dhalvad tried to speak over the flow of words, ex-
pending energy he did not have to spare. *Tamorlee, it's
Dhalvad. Release us now. We're all in danger!*

*No danger...wait...much more...no...who are
you...they come...out..."*

Dhalvad cringed inwardly as he tried to separate the
four minds all speaking at once. It was an impossible
task. *Tamorlee! Release us now! I beg you!* Dhalvad
pleaded.

The words faded as a curtain of darkness drew around
him. Dhalvad felt himself falling.

Everything happened so quickly that there was no
way Lil-el and Thura could help all three Ni. Thura was
nearest her father and literally broke his silent fall to the
floor by catching him around the waist and falling beneath him. Lil-el grabbed one of Dhalvad's arms as he
slid down, lowering him carefully to the floor. Amet
crumpled forward and struck his forehead against the
machine as he fell.

Lil-el quickly checked all three. Bhaldavin's face was
drained of color and his skin was clammy cold, but his
breathing was regular, and though his heartbeat was
slow, it was steady; the Healer was unconscious but already beginning to stir; Amet was bleeding from a cut on
his forehead just over his right eye.

"Are they all right?" Theon asked.

Lil-el used her knife and cut a piece of cloth from the
bottom of Amet's robe and pressed it against his forehead. "They're alive, but I don't think they'll be moving
anywhere for a little while."

"How long?" Theon demanded.

"I don't know. Thura, come here and hold this cloth
in place while I check on your father again."

Gringers poked Theon's shoulder. "Go down to the
next floor and out onto the roof. See if you can see anything happening below."

A look of relief passed across Theon's face as he
helped Gringers to sit down. Gringers was giving orders
again, back in charge, and Theon's world was instantly
transformed. "Sure, I'll take a look. Are you going to be
all right here alone?"

Gringers gave Theon a tired smile. "Who's alone?

Lil-el and Thura are here. Go on. Keep watch and warn us if anyone heads up our way."

Dhalvad opened his eyes and slowly sat up. His head ached, and his stomach was unsettled from the abrupt breaking of the link. He saw Theon leave and noticed that Thura was holding something to Amet's head. He moved over and pulled the cloth away. The wound was bleeding but not badly. The Healer within him started to reach out to seal the cut and ease the swelling that was taking place, but a cry from Lil-el stopped him.

"Healer! Davin's stopped breathing! Hurry!"

Later, Dhalvad never remembered crossing the floor to Bhaldavin's side. One moment he was sitting near Amet, the next moment he was kneeling by Little Fish, one hand placed on his forehead, the other hand hovering over his chest. Seconds later he was one with the body beneath his hands, seeking the vital organs and stirring them to action. He stayed within the body until he was sure everything was functioning properly; then and only then did he seek the inner being known to him as Little Fish, his need to know the truth about their possible kinship driving him to delve deep within Bhaldavin's mind.

The gift of healing had brought an understanding of the many levels of consciousness found within the mind, so when he touched upon the most conscious level and discovered only wisps of images that made no sense to him, he went deeper and reached the level wherein memories resided. He touched and relived the last few days of Bhaldavin's life; he felt his fear for his daughter, his pain at the hands of the man called Sola; he experienced Bhaldavin's surprise at Sola's death at the hands of Giarobi.

The last nearly made Dhalvad lose his hold on Bhaldavin's mind because he had never conceived of Gi as a killer! It did not seem possible, yet he had witnessed it through Bhaldavin's eyes.

He drifted deeper and deeper, searching for memories that would satisfy his curiosity. He skipped through the years of Bhaldavin's life in Barl-gan, saw the bizarre

creature who had ruled the city when Bhaldavin had first
arrived, felt Bhaldavin's love for the beautiful Lil-el as
they left the rafters and climbed over the Draak's Teeth,
searching for the home of the First Men. There followed
memories of life with a simpleminded man called Garv,
Theon's brother, and before that—pain, fear, and rage
all muddled together as Bhaldavin ran with his father
before Sarissan blades. He saw Bhaldavin's father cut
down, and found his mother and baby sister lying dead in
the grass. He ran on, carrying his small brother in his
arms; they were found by a tall dark-haired man who
took them in. The man's name was Haradan.

Dhalvad released his hold on Bhaldavin's mind as
Haradan's face surfaced in his brother's memory. Haradan! The man who had become his own foster father! It
meant that Bhaldavin *was* his real brother!

Dhalvad swam quickly up through the different levels
of Bhaldavin's mind, elated with his find and eager to
share his knowledge with his brother upon his waking.
He reached the upper level of Bhaldavin's mind and suddenly experienced a tremor in the body. He quickly
checked the body again and discovered constriction of
the muscles controlling the breathing passages in his
chest. He eased them by applying a stroking pressure
from within, then carefully monitored Bhaldavin's
breathing.

What is wrong with him?

The words flowed easily through Dhalvad's mind;
they were tinged with concern. *Bhaldavin? Is that you?*

*No. It is Mithdaar. I recognize your energy pattern.
You are one with Tamorlee.*

Mithdaar? Dhalvad was shocked by the discovery. *I
thought the link was broken!*

*It is not. I need him. We wait for the others. You seek
within us. Why? Is Bhaldavin ill?*

*I came seeking my brother and have found him. I'm
here now because he needs help in breathing.*

You are the Healer?

Yes.

*Tamorlee speaks highly of you. Please, continue with
your healing. I trust you to help my friend.*

It was obvious that the link between the two crystals,
though brief, had been enough for each to share with the
other; the question of how deep the sharing had been
would have to wait for later. At the moment, Dhalvad
had something more important on his mind.

Mithdaar, Dhalvad began, *I have healed my brother to
the best of my ability, but he is weak. Your link with him
draws upon his energy. You must release him or he'll grow
so weak that his muscles will not respond as they should.*

There was a pause. *He will cease to live?*

Not if I can help it, thought Dhalvad. *Yes.*

What of the others?

What others?

The Ral-jennob, the Star Travelers. They come.

Dhalvad had heard legends of the Ral-jennob, but that
was all they were to him—legends. *If they come, they
come! They're not important right now. Bhaldavin is!
Release him, please, before it's too late!*

*I sense the Tamorlee is near. May I link with him
again?*

Yes, Dhalvad assured the crystal. *After we've all
rested. The Tamorlee has searched for you a long time.
Believe me when I say that you'll speak to your brother
many times in the future. You have all of time before
you. Now, please—release Bhaldavin.*

Bhaldavin's hand dropped open and the green glowing
crystal rolled free onto the floor. Moments later Dhalvad
stirred from his kneeling position.

Lil-el's glance touched the crystal, then returned to
her husband's face. Bhaldavin's eyelids fluttered open.
She took a shaky breath and released it slowly.

Dhalvad's head lifted. There were tears in his eyes as
he looked at Lil-el. "My brother is going to be all right.
The crystal was draining his energy. It didn't understand." He glanced down at the crystal and felt a dizziness come over him. "Wrap the crystal in cloth and put it
away," he said. "Keep it safe."

"Dhalvad, I need you."

Dhalvad turned at the sound of Amet's voice. He was sitting up, holding his head with both hands.

"I can't right now, Amet. I'm exhausted. Lie back and try to rest a little while."

Amet muttered something but did as Dhalvad told him.

Dhalvad turned back to Bhaldavin and saw that his brother was conscious. He smiled at him and took his hand. "Feeling better?"

Bhaldavin stared up at his father. He was confused, and his mind felt sluggish. "Kion?" No. That was not right. His father was dead. He looked around and saw Lil-el on his other side.

"Lil-el—where are we? Who is this?"

"Davin," Lil-el said gently, "this is your brother, Dhalvad. He's come a long way looking for you." She leaned down and kissed him on the lips, her own tears starting. "He's a Healer, and he just saved your life."

"It was Mithdaar," Dhalvad explained. "The link was draining you of energy."

Bhaldavin frowned. "Where is Mithdaar?"

"Right here, Davin," Lil-el said, holding the cloth-wrapped crystal out to him.

A look of relief touched his face as Lil-el shoved the crystal into his tunic pocket. "We've been far together," he murmured dreamily. "Even now I'm not sure what part was dream and what part was real." He looked up at Dhalvad. "You're—my brother?"

Dhalvad nodded.

Bhaldavin studied the face above him. "I left my brother in the Deep years ago . . ."

"With a man named Haradan," Dhalvad finished for him.

Excitement lighted Bhaldavin's eyes. "Yes! Haradan! You're Dhalvad!"

Dhalvad smiled. "Yes."

"I can hardly believe it, after all these years . . . and you found me . . . not I, you." He squeezed Dhalvad's hand. "Haradan," Bhaldavin said softly, memories flooding back. "I alway wondered whether or not he'd take

care of you. I was afraid he'd turned you in to the Sarissans long ago. I tried to get back to you, but . . ."

Dhalvad saw tears brimming in Bhaldavin's eyes and
knew the guilt his brother had carried with him so long.
"It's all right, Davin," he said, helping him sit up. "I
know you did all you could, and my life with Haradan
was happy. I'll tell you all about it one day, after we get
out of this mess we're in."

Bhaldavin wiped the tears from his eyes and looked at
Lil-el, and beyond her to Thura, who was hovering over
her mother's shoulder. "What's happening?" he asked.

Gringers, who had been a silent witness to the two
brothers' reunion, spoke up from his place near the door.
"Nothing at the moment, Davin. Theon's below, watching for Wastelanders, and we're all just catching our
breath. What about you and him?" he asked, indicating
Amet, who still lay on the floor. "What were you doing
with the crystals?"

"I'm not really sure. Everything was so strange. It
was like a dream. Mithdaar was talking to someone when
I joined him. I could hear him this time in real words, not
just feelings; and there were lights that spoke back to us.
They said they were coming. Then another voice entered
my mind, and Mithdaar became ecstatic. He spoke so
fast that I couldn't understand any longer."

"It was probably the Tamorlee joining the link," Dhalvad explained. "It's another crystal like Mithdaar. We
have a lot to talk about, but right now I think we'd better
concentrate on getting down out of the tower to a place
where we'll all be safe."

"I agree," Gringers said as he used the wall behind
him to stand. "Everybody up."

Gringers took a step toward Amet, then stopped at
the sight of shimmering light coalescing to the left of
Amet's body. "What the . . ."

Dhalvad turned and saw the light and immediately
knew its origin. "It's a Seeker. Don't be afraid."

Gringers looked at Lil-el as she helped Bhaldavin to
his feet. "What the hell is a Seeker?"

"A Ni traveler," she answered. "It's how they all

came here, Amet, Dhalvad, and Paa-tol. They came to find Davin's crystal and stayed to help us find you. Paa-tol was working with Kelsan and the others to distract the Wastelanders."

The shimmering light faded as the displacement of air and matter worked itself out, leaving Paa-tol standing in their midst. He glanced around quickly, then knelt beside Amet, who had made no move to get up.

"Dhalvad," Paa-tol snapped. "Get over here! Amet needs you!"

Dhalvad went to Amet and knelt beside him. He was nearing the edge of his limits and knew he did not have much strength left for healing. He also saw Paa-tol's frown and knew it was useless to argue.

As Dhalvad closed his eyes and entered his healing trance, Paa-tol slipped the Tamorlee from Amet's ring hand and put it in his own pocket.

"What happened below?" Lil-el asked Paa-tol.

Paa-tol stood up, turning slightly to include everyone in his sight. "The Barl-ganians have been driven back, but they made a good account of themselves and have cut the number of Wastelanders by half. The Wastelanders still outnumber us, but the odds are better."

He looked at Bhaldavin. "You must be Little Fish." He turned to Gringers. "And you are?"

"Gringers."

Paa-tol glanced down at the bodies of the two Wastelanders. "It looks as if you've been busy up here. What happened?"

"I was using the crystal to try to rid myself of my guards," Gringers answered. "I was showing them one of the machines built by the First Men. I'd planned on just scaring them, but something went wrong and a ball of light flashed out, catching them full force. We were all within touching distance. I just happened to be the last in line. Your friend saved my life just a little while ago. Lil-el says he's a Healer. I've heard about them, but they were long gone from our part of Amla-Bagor when I was still a boy."

"You're a rafter?" Paa-tol asked, eyebrows arched in question.

Gringers nodded.

"You're a long way from home."

"I know. Now, my turn for a question. Would you mind telling me how you just got here? And how you three got over the Draak's Teeth?"

Paa-tol shook his head, refusing to answer Gringers's questions.

Lil-el frowned, not happy with Paa-tol's manner. "They're Seekers, Gringers. They use the crystals to travel from place to place. Dhavad can tell you—"

"Enough!" Paa-tol snapped at her. "They don't need to know anything about the crystals—or how we use them!"

Bhaldavin stood a bit straighter, his arm going around Lil-el. "Gringers is our friend and deserves a civil answer to his questions."

Paa-tol snorted. "He may be your friend, but he's not mine!"

Dhalvad sighed deeply as he came out of his trance. He had checked Amet over thouroghly and had found a small clot of blood in his brain. He had dissolved the clot and repaired the damaged blood vessel, allowing the blood to flow freely once more.

"How is he?" Paa-tol asked as Dhalvad sat back, bracing himself by his arms.

"He'll be all right," Dhalvad answered.

"How soon before he wakes?"

"I don't know. A few minutes, an hour perhaps."

"We can't wait," Paa-tol said. "We'll have to carry him."

"*You* carry him," Gringers said rudely, moving over to Dhalvad. "We'll help the Healer."

Dhalvad gratefully accepted a hand up and nodded thanks to Gringers as the man moved in to support him around the waist.

"Dhalvad, are you all right?" Lil-el asked worriedly, pointedly ignoring Paa-tol's struggle to get Amet up into his arms.

"I'm just tired. All I need is rest," Dhalvad replied.

"I think we could all use a little of that," Gringers said, starting down the stairs.

Gi-arobi whistled agreement and bounded ahead of Gringers and Dhalvad. Lil-el, Bhaldavin, and Thura came next, followed by Paa-tol carrying Amet.

Theon looked up as they came down the steps. Placing a finger to his lips, he carefully closed the door to the steps leading down into the mansion. "There's someone moving around below. I think it'll be safer if we take the outside stairs down to ..." His words trailed off as Paa-tol appeared on the stairs carrying Amet. "Where'd he come from?"

"Don't ask me," Gringers said. "One minute he wasn't there, the next, he was. Lil-el said he's a Seeker."

"That again," Theon said, stepping back as Lil-el and Thura reached the bottom of the steps. "Oh well, I guess it doesn't really matter right now. Let's get going. We can talk later."

They filed out onto the roof and followed Theon to the outside stairs leading down to the kitchens five floors below. Theon went first and was ten steps down when a flash of laser light shot up from below.

"Up! Up!" he yelled, whirling on the steps and climbing up as fast as he could.

Gringers and Dhalvad had just stepped out onto the stairs when Theon yelled. They ducked back and fell to the roof. A second or two later Theon threw himself up over the edge and lay panting for breath. Gringers took the light gun from him and carefully peered over the ledge. He saw two shadowy figures on the stairs below and shot a beam of light down in their direction. It missed its target but sent the two Wastelanders scuttling back down to cover.

"Come on," Theon cried. "We'll have to try the other way down."

Everyone followed but Gringers, who stayed by the roof edge keeping watch. Theon stepped back into the tower room and carefully opened the door leading downstairs. He listened for a few moments, then started down. He was halfway down the steps when Zojac and another

Wastelander suddenly appeared, charging out of one of the rooms down the hall.

Theon only had his knife, and not being suicidal, he darted back up the steps, the Wastelanders right behind him. Paa-tol dropped Amet, and as Theon slipped through the doorway, he and Dhalvad slammed the door and put their combined weight against it. Theon slapped the bolt into place.

"It'll hold them, but not for long," Theon growled.

The Wastelanders began hammering on the door just as Gringers stepped in from the roof. "I was just coming. Problems?"

"Understatement," Theon muttered darkly. "It looks like whichever way we go, we're going to have to fight our way down."

Lil-el looked at Dhalvad. "Could you use your powers as Seekers, you and Paa-tol, to get us out of here?"

Dhalvad shook his head. "To my knowledge, no man has ever teleported using fire stone energy. You saw what it did to the two Wastelanders above. The men would be taking a great chance traveling as Seekers do."

"Well, it's either that or wait up here for the Wastelanders," Gringers said. "And the mood they're in now, I doubt they'll be taking prisoners this time."

"No one is going anywhere until Amet wakes up," Paa-tol said. "We have one light gun. I suggest we return to the tower room where they can come at us only one at a time. Perhaps we can wait them out."

"I hate to admit it, but I agree with Paa-tol," Dhalvad said. "I'm so tired right now that I don't think I could use the crystal even to save myself. It would be foolish to take a chance with anyone else's life."

Bhaldavin looked into Dhalvad's eyes and for an instant he saw his father looking back at him. You gave your life for me once, he thought. I'll not let you do it again. "As soon as you've recovered your strength," he said, "you must leave, with or without us."

Dhalvad caught his brother's arm. "I couldn't do that now, not after finding you. Don't worry, we'll find a way down even if we have to fight. Who knows, we might even be able to break through. Paa-tol said that the Wastelanders' ranks had been cut in half."

Amet groaned and rolled over. Paa-tol knelt and helped him sit up. "Are you all right?"

"I've got a headache, but I'll live." Amet's glance found Bhaldavin and beyond him, Gringers.

"That is Little Fish," Paa-tol said, giving Amet a hand up, "and Gringers." When Amet turned toward the pounding on the door, Paa-tol asked, "Are you up to a transfer?"

Amet rubbed his head. "I don't think so. My head still hurts and it's hard to think. The last thing I remember is joining the link with him," he said, indicating Bhaldavin. "There were voices in the link, and—lights that wanted something from us."

Amet looked down at his ring hand. "The Tamorlee— it's gone!" His glance caught Bhaldavin. "What have you done with it? Where is it?" he demanded.

"He hasn't got it," Paa-tol said, reaching into his pocket. "I have. I took it for safekeeping while you were unconscious."

Amet snatched the ring from Paa-tol and glared at him. "What about the other crystal?"

Paa-tol looked at Bhaldavin. "He has it, I think."

"My name is Amet. I'm Speaker for the Tamorlee," Amet began, addressing Bhaldavin. "I was brought here by—"

"There's no time for this!" Theon cried, pushing in between Paa-tol and Gringers. "The Wastelanders are going to break in here any minute, and we've got to get ready for them! Gringers, let me have the light gun! I'll guard the door while you get everyone upstairs!"

Gringers nodded and handed Theon the light gun, but before anyone could move, a shrill whistle erupted from Gi-arobi. Everyone turned to see the olvaar crouched in the doorway leading out onto the roof. It was light outside and growing lighter by the second, yet it was still night.

Dhalvad was the first to the doorway. The others pushed up behind him. The first thing they saw was a handful of Wastelanders scurrying away, all headed back toward the outside stairway. One by one they quickly disappeared over the edge of the roof.

Gi-arobi ran out onto the roof chittering wildly. His whistles came so fast that Dhalvad lost half of what he was saying. He stepped outside and looked up just as a large globe of light glided over the top of the towers.

"Amet! Bhaldavin!" he cried. "Everyone get out here!"

Gringers and Thura were the first outside, followed closely by Bhaldavin and Lil-el, then Amet and Paa-tol.

"Where are you going?" Theon yelled from inside. "No! This way! Up into the tower! Gringers? Damn it, wait for me!"

The last through the doorway, Theon pushed past Amet and Paa-tol and started toward Gringers. He had one glimpse of the globe of light dropping slowly toward the roof, then the crash of splintering wood came from inside the tower. He turned, the light gun held out and ready to use.

"Everyone down!"

Paa-tol was the first to react. He lunged for Amet and pulled him out of the line of fire just as Theon pressed the button on the light gun.

Theon killed the first Wastelander through the door, missed the second, and got the third. The one he missed charged straight at Gringers and Lil-el. Gringers stiff-armed Lil-el out of the way, dodged the Wastelander's knife thrust, and kicked out at the man's legs as he charged past. The man lost his balance and fell. Gringers threw himself onto the man's back as he was starting to rise, slamming him to the roof. He grabbed two fistfuls of hair and smashed the man's face into the roof, once, twice, and again.

Theon saw five more Wastelanders pushing out the door; the one in the lead, a heavyset man, held a light gun pointed at Gringers's back.

"Gringers! Down!" Theon yelled as a beam of laser fire went past Gringers's head, barely missing him. Theon pressed the button on his own light gun and fired an arc of light that burned across the legs of three of the five Wastelanders. The heavyset man fell, bellowing in pain. As the other two scrambled back to the safety of the tower, the big man rolled over and came up on an elbow, firing his gun at Theon.

Theon saw his danger too late. The beam of burning light caught him chest high.

"No!" Gringers screamed as Theon crumpled forward. He was in motion before Theon hit the roof. He threw himself past Lil-el, rolled toward Theon's body, and scooped up the gun.

Zojac realigned his light gun, aiming for the small cluster of Ni crouched just beyond the man he had killed. Gringers didn't hesitate. He held the button down and poured a steady line of searing fire straight at Zojac. The remaining Wastelanders scrambled toward the tower doorway as Zojac's body became a pyre.

Lil-el moved forward and kicked Zojac's gun out away from the burning body while Gringers got up and went to Theon. Dhalvad was already there, but there were certain things that even the greatest of Healers could not undo. Theon was dead, his chest half eaten away by laser fire. Gringers knelt at Theon's side and took one of his hands. It was still warm to the touch. He brought the hand to his lips, then set it down, tears blurring his vision.

Paa-tol and Amet got up, their attention divided between the dead on the roof and the glowing sphere of light that hovered ten or so meters above the roof.

"What is it?" Paa-tol asked Amet.

Amet's gaze was fixed on the object in a way that made a chill skitter down Paa-tol's spine. He glanced at a sudden blaze of light coming from Amet's ring hand.

"The crystal!" he cried softly. "Amet! Look at it!"

Amet saw the Tamorlee glowing brightly. Suddenly memories came flooding back, voices, feelings. He knew what the globe of light was. "They've come! They want the crystals!"

Dhalvad looked from Amet to his brother, who also stood staring at the globe, clutching something in his hand. Lil-el and Thura stood to either side of him. Both looked frightened.

Dhalvad moved closer. "Bhaldavin?"

Lil-el turned. "He doesn't hear us! He's linked with his crystal again! Can you help?"

Dhalvad could see the green light coming through the cracks in Bhaldavin's fingers. He had never linked directly with Mithdaar, but for his brother's sake, he was willing to try.

Gi whistle-clicked in excitement and climbed up Dhalvad's right side, his pinprick claws startling Dhalvad. "Look! Look! Something comes!"

Gringers turned and saw the light globe. He stood up, his friend's death pushed aside for the moment. A smaller ball of light detached itself from the larger one. His heart raced as the globe of light drifted toward Amet and Paa-tol, who began backing away.

Gringers glanced around, assured himself that the Wastelanders had given up for the moment, and moved several steps closer, curiosity drawing him like a magnet. He was versed in all the legends of the First Men as told by the Barl-ganians, and he began to think about Bhaldavin's crystal and the machine he had put it in. The possibility that somehow they had actually contacted the gods of the First Men made him tingle with excitement.

The globe of light came to a stop a short distance from Bhaldavin. It hovered several handspans from the roof and bobbled slightly as if something were moving inside it. Slowly the ball of light grew in length until it was almost as tall as Gringers. As they all watched, the light took on form. They could see a body and a head shape, then legs and arms, all wrapped in glowing light.

Please, do not fear us. We will not harm you.

The words had no sound, but were understood by everyone there, including Gi-arobi.

"Like Gentle Voice, Dhal. Be friend?" Gi-arobi piped up.

Dhalvad cut him off with an abrupt chopping motion of the hand as more words entered his mind. *We were called to your world by a Chensaan Gatherer. A unique event.*

"Are you the gods of the First Men?" The words were out of Gringers's mouth before he thought.

Your question is irrelevant.

"Well, I think it's relevant!" Gringers growled. "Who are you? Where do you come from?"

Features began to come into focus on the light creature. There appeared a thin slit where a mouth might be, and a pair of large round eyes that seemed too large for the head.

We are called Elay. Our home world is Onari.

"Do you know of the First Men? They, too, come from another world," Gringers persisted.

We would have to consult the Archives to answer your question. First, we would speak to the Gatherers.

To everyone's astonishment, the single globe of light separated and became two light creatures. Both had piercing amber eyes, and though they looked alike, there were subtle differences in the glowing nimbi of light surrounding them. The second light figure appeared taller than the first, the arms and legs more slender. If they wore clothes, the garments could not be seen past the light. Both moved with fluid grace, the first toward Bhaldavin, the second toward Amet.

Amet's eyes grew round in alarm. "Don't let them have the crystal!" he cried. "They mean to take them away!" Amet watched in horror as Bhaldavin calmly set his crystal in the outstretched hand of the smaller Elay. "No!" he screamed, starting toward Bhaldavin.

Paa-tol caught his arm. "It's too late, Amet! We've lost it!"

The second light creature drew closer to Amet, its hand also outstretched. The glowing light around its hand diminished to a point where its golden skin and four long fingers were completely visible.

"I'm leaving, Amet," Paa-tol snapped as he looked down into his fire stone ring. "Meet you back in Jjaan-bi!"

In that instant, Amet realized that Paa-tol was right.

They had lost the second crystal, but with luck they could hang onto the Tamorlee. He looked down into the depths of his crystal and envisioned the main transfer point in Jjaan-bi. A shimmering field of energy surrounded him a second later, and he ruthlessly overrode the Tamorlee's shriek of protest as he drew upon its energy.

The Tamorlee doesn't realize its danger, he thought. If he had let the Elay have the crystal, they would have taken it back to wherever they came from. It would have been lost to the Ni forever, with no chance for retrieval. He could not let that happen! He could not!

He felt the crystal's probing thoughts as it tried to form a stronger link with him, but he would not allow that, because with such a bond the Tamorlee might gain control—and that would mean a return to Barl-gan and the Elay. He knew that as well as he knew what he had to do when he reached Jjaan-bi. Mithdaar was lost to them, as was Dhalvad, who was without a way back to Jjaan-bi. He and Paa-tol would have to dream up a cover story for their loss of Mithdaar and find a way to silence Pocalina-fel-Jamba.

A sudden twinge of pain caught Amet by surprise. He could not tell what was happening or locate the origin of the pain, for to investigate he would have to release his vision of the transfer point. The pain grew as seconds passed; it began to eat into his mind as fear and panic blossomed. The pain grew terrible; he could not stand it; he felt as if he were being eaten alive by fire!

It was the Tamorlee! It had to be! But he could not do anything—not during transfer! His mental scream of agony gave way to panic, and he released his image of the transfer point and opened his eyes to a grayish void. The pain was centered in his hand. He looked down at the glowing light that surrounded his charred fingers. He brushed at the glowing light as the pain intensified. His scream was vocal, but in the void between realities, sound was muted and quickly absorbed. He brushed frantically at his burned hand and the glowing orb at its center. His maniacal scrabbling caused burned flesh to drop away, and with it—the Tamorlee.

Paa-tol stood back from the transfer point, his back against the stone wall in the Tamorlee's room. Upon his arrival, he had dismissed the Seeker standing duty at the door and ordered him to find either Tidul or Lurral and bring them back, hinting at news too important to wait for anything.

Heart beating rapidly, Paa-tol licked at dry lips as he waited for Amet to appear. Seconds passed. He shifted his weight from foot to foot, wondering what was taking Amet so long. Had he run into trouble? Not moved fast enough? Those Elay—he had never even dreamed of something like them existing.

"Amet!" he said softly. "Where in the name of Brogan's Draak are you?" He swallowed and took a deep breath, trying to calm down.

A noise startled him. Something had fallen to the floor. He scanned the stone floor and saw something catch the light of the fayyal rocks. It glowed with a greenish cast. Three quick steps brought him to the object. One glance and he knew what it was.

The Tamorlee lay in a misshapen tangle of metal that had once been a ring. Something black adhered to the metal. As he reached out, the stench of charred flesh wafted upward. Shocked and nauseated by the smell, he backed away. In that instant, he knew that Amet was gone, lost to the void between one reality and another without a fire stone's energy to get back.

He crouched by the wall, his glance never leaving the Tamorlee as he tried to sort things out in his mind. Amet was gone—and Dhalvad. It meant that he would have to stand before the Council and explain—what? That he and Amet had failed? That some kind of light beings had come for the crystals? That Amet had died trying to return to Jjaan-bi? That Dhalvad— Damn! Dhalvad's mate. Both she and the derkat were a threat to him. As was the Tamorlee! It would tell the next Speaker all that had happened! Including his part in Amet's scheme!

His first thought was to run far and fast, but the longer he sat there, the more he saw that that was not the answer. He had to rid himself of witnesses, beginning with the crystal. He stood and approached the Tamorlee. Kneeling near the crystal, he put his hand out, then quickly drew back, for he could still feel heat coming from the partially melted setting. He looked closely at the crystal. The fire that had burned Amet's flesh had not even marred the crystal's surface.

Unsure whether the crystal or some kind of interference from the Elay had caused Amet to lose control, he took out his knife and carefully scooped the hot metal onto the end of his blade where it cooled and fastened itself.

"We did without you for many years," he muttered as he placed blade and crystal into a leather pouch on his belt. "We can do so again—and some day when you get tired of yourself, perhaps you'll think twice about cooperating with me—as Speaker!"

Chapter 21

*D*HALVAD CRIED OUT WHEN HE SAW AMET AND PAA-TOL
wink out of sight, for with their disappearance went
any chance of his returning to Jjaan-bi, and worse than
that, there would be no one to stop them from doing as
they wished with Poco, Jiam, and Screech, and he was
too intelligent not to guess what that meant. Despair
washed over him as he watched the second light creature
return and meld with the first. Then he remembered the
other crystal.

"Davin! Stop them," he yelled, lunging toward his
brother. "I must have the crystal! It's my only way back
to Jjaan-bi!"

Everything that had happened in the last few minutes
had seemed like a dream to Bhaldavin, but at the sound
of his brother's voice and the look of anguish on his face,
he woke to the fact that he was about to lose Mithdaar.
The feeling of joy that Mithdaar had radiated was gone;
in its place was emptiness.

"No!" he cried, reaching out toward the light creature.

Dhalvad bumped into his brother just as Bhaldavin's
hand entered the nimbus of light surrounding the amber-
eyed visitors from another world. Both were instantly
absorbed.

257

Terrified, Lil-el screamed as they disappeared into the glowing aura.

"Davin! No!" she yelled as the golden sphere began to lift.

As she lunged forward toward the light, Gringers caught her and wrestled her back away from the sphere.

Gi-arobi darted past them and launched himself toward the sphere, intent on following Dhalvad no matter where he went. But the sphere rose too fast, and he missed his target and plummeted back to the roof, bouncing slightly as he hit.

Lil-el stopped fighting Gringers and stood wide-eyed as the globe of light rose upward beyond the towers to join a second larger sphere of light far far above them. She trembled uncontrollably and felt arms tighten around her.

"Gringers," she whispered. "What's going to happen to them?"

He watched the sphere grow smaller as it lifted away. "I don't know. I'm numb; can't think. Were they the Ral-jennob?"

Tears trickled down Lil-el face. "I've never heard the word 'Elay.' It means nothing in the Ni tongue."

"Nor in trader." Gringers licked at dry lips. "They were after the crystals, not Davin. Perhaps they'll bring him back."

"If he still lives," she said softly.

Thura moved up in front of Lil-el and put her arms around her and Gringers. "I'm afraid, Mother. Where's Adda gone?"

Lil-el caressed her daughter's hair. "With them."

"We can't stay here, Lil-el," Gringers said. "The Wastelanders may return."

"Go," she said quietly. "Check on the others. Thura and I will wait here a little while."

Gringers hesitated, then left by the tower stairs. He paused briefly by the body of his friend, then disappeared into the tower.

Gi-arobi moved closer to Lil-el and Thura and

crouched near their feet, a mournful whistle escaping his lips as he settled down to wait.

Dhalvad and Bhaldavin were caught up in a whirling mass of golden light. Each could feel the other's fear as a link was formed between them; then suddenly there were others within the link, and a voice echoed through their minds, cautioning them to relax. It was like the voices of the crystals, yet somehow richer and deeper.

Bhaldavin? Dhalvad called, testing the link as he felt his fear dissolve.

Yes! came a joyful cry. *Yes, I hear you. Where are we?*

I don't know. Do you feel the others?

Yes. I'm sure one is Mithdaar. Bhaldavin hesitated, then spoke directly to the crystal. *Mithdaar, can you hear me?*

I am with you, my friend. I am pleased you came.

Please, Mithdaar, can you tell us where we are? What's happening to us? Why are the Elay taking you away?

I will answer those questions if I may, a new voice said. *My name is Oub-Tabo, and you are in our space module. We are pleased to have you aboard, though we are somewhat surprised at your easy access to our facility. It would seem that the Gatherer has taught you, as well as learned from you. While we intergrate the information contained within the Gatherer, we would like to ask you some questions pertaining to your most unique use of the Gatherer's energy.*

I'll answer your questions, if I may in turn ask something of you, Dhalvad replied.

What would you ask?

I need Mithdaar in order to return to my home. May I have it when you're finished with it?

That will be up to the Gatherer came the reply.

Gringers returned to the roof with the dawn, the first rays of Ra-shun striking the tower and the light panels that would create and store new energy for those who had survived the coming of the Wastelanders. He found

Lil-el sitting where he had left her five hours earlier, Thura's head in her lap. The child was fast asleep, and within the crook of her arm lay the small furred one called Gi.

He had been up to the roof once before in the last hour—to retrieve Theon's body.

Lil-el turned as he approached. Her eyes had been directed toward the east and the still faint light that was not a star. With the coming of morning, it was difficult to see the Elay's sphere.

"It's time to go. Lil-el," he said.

She shook her head.

"You can't stay here forever. Your sons are asking for you."

"Are they all right?" she asked.

"They're fine. Gils is watching them. There's only thirteen of us left now, counting you and Thura. We can't stay here any longer. We'll have to try the rafts, and we'll need you to help sing draak."

"The Wastelanders?"

"Zojac's death must have broken their spirit, but there's no telling how soon before they choose another leader and come back, and we're just too few to protect ourselves now. Theon was right. We should've left long ago. If I hadn't been so stubborn . . ."

Lil-el raised her hand. "Don't. You can't change what you are, Gringers. Theon wouldn't have wanted you to. You're a Seeker at heart, with a curiosity that will probably be the death of you one day, but you can't blame all that's happened on yourself. Part of the blame rests on the Wastelanders' ignorance, and with Davin and myself for not trying harder to get you to leave."

"But you did try, many times. I just didn't listen. If—"

A sharp whistle startled Gringers. He looked down and saw Gi-arobi sitting up on his haunches, his head tilted upward.

Thura's eyes were also open. "The light! It's coming back!"

They all scrambled to their feet and stood quietly as a

glowing sphere descended from high above the towers. Lil-el clasped Gringers's arm tightly and prayed as she had never prayed before.

"Is it Adda coming back?" Thura asked.

"If it's not Davin or his brother, and it makes any threatening moves toward us, I want you to run for the tower," Gringers said. "Is that clear?"

Neither answered him. Both were too intent on the light sphere as it slowed its descent and approached the roof. Gi-arobi ran a circle around the light, whistling excitedly.

Seconds passed and nothing happened. Blood throbbed loudly in Lil-el's ears as she strained to hear voices from within the sphere. "Davin? Are you there?"

Gringers put out a hand and pushed Thura behind him, then disengaged his arm from Lil-el's grasp. Dry-mouthed, he took a step forward.

"Elay, we want those you took returned!" His voice was raspy and not as deep as he had intended it to be. He cleared his throat, preparing to speak again.

A shadow moved within the sphere, then suddenly a figure emerged, drawing an aura of visible energy with him.

"Davin!" Lil-el cried, starting forward.

Bhaldavin caught and held Lil-el as the light faded from around him. He was smiling, and his eyes were alight with joy. Gringers and Thura joined in the reunion, Thura hugging both parents, Gringers demanding answers to his questions.

Gi-arobi saw Davin and jumped up and down, impatiently waiting for Dhalvad to appear. His whistles were sharp and urgent. The glowing sphere bobbed a little, then suddenly lifted, rising quickly and steadily upward.

Gi-arobi's shrill ear-splitting whistle brought instant silence to the others.

Bhaldavin kissed Lil-el and excused himself. "I'll be right back." He crossed the space between himself and the olvaar and knelt beside the distraught fur child, whose whistles had turned sad and mournful.

"Gi? Gi, I have a message to you from Dhal."

Gi continued to watch the sphere grow smaller and smaller as it rose into the sky. Bhaldavin glanced up. He could barely see the sphere anymore. He tried again.

"Gi, Dhal is fine. I have a message from him to you. Will you listen?"

Gi-arobi turned and looked at Bhaldavin. He could not cry, but there was a look in his eyes that spoke of grief. "Why Dhal not come out of light?" he demanded.

Bhaldavin looked up as Thura, Lil-el, and Gringers closed around.

"A good question," Gringers said. "What happened to you two when you entered that light? Where did you go?"

"It's going to take awhile to answer your question, Gringers. Let me answer Gi's first. Gi, Dhal wasn't in that glowing sphere you just saw. He's already on his way back to Jjaan-bi. The Elay want to record the Ta-morlee's knowledge, and they agreed to take Dhalvad with them to help locate the crystal, though I'm sure they are capable of doing it on their own. You know why Dhalvad had to go home."

"Gi want to go, too!"

"He knows, but he dared not risk you to the Elay's energy levels within the modules."

"Dhal go after Amet and Paa-tol?"

"Yes, and when he's found them and freed his wife and child, he promised that he will return for all of us. He wants you to help us leave this place and start on a trip though the chain of lakes, away from the threat of Wastelanders."

"How he find us we float down big river?" the olvaar asked.

Bhaldavin reached into his tunic pocket and brought out his crystal. "Dhalvad, Mithdaar, and I were linked very closely these last few hours, Gi. I think we could find each other no matter the distance between us now."

"They gave it back to you!" Gringers exclaimed.

Bhaldavin nodded. "They only wanted it long enough to record its memory, then they gave it back, but only because it asked to stay."

"Could you use the crystal to go to Jjaan-bi right now?" Lil-el asked.

"I think so, but Dhalvad would rather I didn't try a transfer alone the first time, even with Mithdaar's guidance." He smiled at the worry lines creasing Lil-el's forehead. "And right now my place is here. When Dhalvad is finished doing what he must to ensure his family is safe, he'll come to us along with other Seekers who'll help us find a way to Jjaan-bi—all of us."

Bhaldavin slipped Mithdaar back into his pocket and held his hand out to Gi-arobi. "So, will you come with us?"

Gi-arobi glanced once more up at the sky and sighed. He came to Bhaldavin and allowed himself to be picked up.

Bhaldavin and Dhalvad had shared deeply while caught in the energy pattern of the Elay, so Bhaldavin knew how close his brother was to the olvaar. "I think we'll become very good friends, Gi," he said as he rubbed his thumb against the olvaar's stomach, "if you'll give me a chance."

Gi looked into Bhaldavin's eyes and studied him a moment or two. He then patted Bhaldavin's hand. "Gi like Davin. Stay with you till Dhal comes, yes."

"Tell us about the Elay," Gringers said as they started for the tower. "You said something about a module. Is that like a spaceship, like the one that brought men to this world?"

"I guess you'd call it a spaceship, but it's small compared to the pictures of man's spaceship that we saw in the life recorders. The small sphere that took us away and brought me back was some kind of energy field that the Elay control with their minds. They tried to explain many things to me, but I didn't understand everything. That may come in time, with Mithdaar's help. He took from the Elay, as well as gave, I'm sure."

"But who are the Elay?" Gringers pressed.

"They're not gods, Gringers. They're a spacefaring race who have delved deeply into the matrix of our shared reality. They discovered Gatherers, crystals like

Mithdaar, eons ago, and have spent half their spacefaring years seeding the galaxies with them. Hundreds of years later they return to see what the Gatherers have learned and enter that knowledge into something they call a matrix pool, where it will be studied by others."

"To what purpose?" Gringers asked, frowning.

"Growth and understanding, is what I was told."

"And that's all? No thoughts of conquest?"

"Do you mean that now they know about us, what's to prevent them from coming back to take over?"

Gringers stepped into the tower room and started down the stairs. "That's exactly what I mean."

"I can only tell you what I felt while linked with them, Gringers, and that is that they have no need to conquer anything when they already have it all through the Gatherers. Their lives—their entire reason for living—seems to be the study of creation in all its forms, including their own part in the scheme of things."

"I don't know. It sounds too good to be true. Did they say anything about when they might come back here?"

"No, but now they've discovered us, I think it likely that they'll return periodically. But there's no use worrying about that right now. Our job is to leave Barl-gan as quickly as possible and get the rafts out onto the lake where we'll be safe from Wastelanders."

Bhaldavin pushed Gi-arobi up onto his shoulder and took his daughter's hand as they started down the stairs behind Gringers. He felt good inside. His family was safe; he had Mithdaar; and his brother would soon be returning.

Chapter 22

*P*OCO PULLED ON SCREECH'S CHAIN AS HE DUG AT THE wood with his claws. She felt it give a little more. "It's coming, Screech! I can feel it!" She pulled harder, straining until her shoulders and back protested. A buzzing in her ears warned her of a fainting spell. To stave it off she released the chain and drew in deep breaths.

"I've got to rest a few minutes, Screech."

She heard his cough of agreement as she crawled several paces to the nearest wall and leaned back against it. The tremors in her arms made her shake as if with cold. She rubbed her upper arms and rolled her head around, trying to ease cramped muscles. She had no idea how long they had been working on the chain. It seemed like days. She was hungry and so thirsty that her tongue felt swollen.

Jiam was asleep nearby, bundled in her tunic. She had fed him finally to stop him from crying. Her fear of drugs getting into her milk had faded as the reality of their situation became more and more locked in her mind. They were going to die if Screech could not break free. He alone was their only hope, for his strength plus hers might just be enough to force the door.

She looked at the wedge of light showing through the top of the door and the casing. Another day had come.

She closed her eyes. Dhalvad? Where are you? What's happened? If only you could hear me.

Her thoughts began to wander to the days she had spent as a chalk artist in Port Bhalvar, to her old friend Trass, who had taught her how to survive after her mother died. She heard Screech pick up the chain and begin to work it back and forth again, growling softly as he concentrated all his effort in breaking free. Somehow she forced herself to move, crawling back to her place beside the derkat, then fumbling for the chain.

He touched her face with the back of his furred hand, then pulled the chain in the direction he wanted her to pull.

"Got it," she said, and renewed the pressure on the chain as he continued to dig at the wall.

Minutes passed and all that could be heard was the scratching of derkat claws and the labored breathing of the two friends as they struggled valiantly to free themselves. Blood-drenched splinters dropped to the floor as Screech's claws scored deeper and deeper. Venting his frustration and anger on the wood was all that kept Screech from derkat frenzy, a type of self-destructive madness that was not uncommon among his kind. He felt the metal pin move again and gave a low growl, renewing his efforts.

The two were so intent on their work that neither heard the bar on the door slide back. It was the light from the opening door that finally caught their attention. Startled, both turned as the door bumped back against the inner wall.

Two figures blocked the light. Poco released the chain and shielded her eyes against the glare as the two stepped into the cabin.

The irises in Screech's eyes narrowed automatically, allowing him to focus on the two much faster than Poco. He growled ominously as Paa-tol drew a knife from his chest harness.

Poco's eyes finally began to adjust to the light. "Paa-tol!" she hissed softly as she stood up. Conscious of her skimpy undertunic but dismissing it as the least of her worries at that moment, she faced Paa-tol and Anwhol, her heart beating rapidly. She looked beyond them but saw no one else.

"Where's Amet and Dhal?" she demanded.

Paa-tol saw that Screech was still securely chained and slid his knife back in its sheath before answering her question. "Amet's dead. Our search was a failure. Dhalvad is dead also."

"Dhal's . . ." Poco could not finish. She felt as if someone had hit her in the stomach and she could not catch her breath.

Paa-tol saw the shock in her eyes and was secretly pleased. He had never liked her, and since there was no longer any reason even to be civil to her, he found it easy to be cruel.

Numb and still struggling to take it in, Poco asked, "How? How did he die?"

How indeed? Paa-tol thought, shivering inwardly as he recalled the light creatures. Had the light creatures gone after the others after he and Amet left? Or had they simply departed with Mithdaar, leaving Dhalvad and the others to face what was left of the Wastelanders? It did not really matter; dead was dead, one way or the other.

"How did he die?" Poco cried again, anger and grief bubbling up inside.

"The Wastelanders killed him. They're men like the Sarissans, and very efficient killers. Dhalvad never knew what hit him."

"All for nothing," Poco muttered, shoulders slumping.

Screech growled, demanding Poco's attention. When she turned to look, he signed, "*Do not trust him! He is our enemy!*"

She looked into Screech's eyes and suddenly understood what he was trying to say. A glimmer of hope sprang to life. Screech was right! Why should she trust anything Paa-tol said?

"What proof do you offer that what you say is true?" she demanded.

Paa-tol looked at Poco, grimly admiring her courage while at the same time knowing it would not be enough

to save her. The two had to die. As for the child— He
glanced to his right and saw the baby lying next to the
wall. It was fussing softly, wakened by the angry voices.
The child might well carry the talents of the father. There
was no sense in wasting such potential.

"I need prove nothing to you, Pocalina," he said,
drawing his knife again. "Because you and your friend
must quietly fade from the memories of the People."

Coldness washed over Poco as Paa-tol ran his thumb
over the blade of his knife. The time had come. I won't
give up without a fight, she thought, muscles tensing. If I
can get either of them within Screech's grasp, I can . . .

Paa-tol snapped his fingers at Anwhol. "Get the
child!"

"No!" Poco screamed, lunging forward to intercept
Anwhol.

Paa-tol stepped into her path and caught her by an
arm. He yanked her around in a sudden twisting motion
and caught her around the waist with his other arm, his
knife lying up under her breastbone.

"Leave him alone!" she cried, struggling against the
iron bands about her body, panic overriding common
sense. "Leave him alone!"

Screech was on his feet, straining against the chain,
but he could not reach either of the male Ni. His yowls
of rage were gut deep and so ferocious that Anwhol hesitated before picking Jiam up.

"Get out of here!" Paa-tol roared. "I'll take care of
these two and meet you down by the boat!"

Anwhol backed toward the door, his glance on the
maddened derkat. "Paa-tol, are you sure?"

"Yes, damn it! Go!"

Anwhol cast one last glance at Pocalina and the derkat and fled out through the door, clutching Jiam to his
chest. The child was crying loudly, disturbed by his
mother's screams.

It was all Paa-tol could do to hold onto Poco as her
frenzied struggles grew more violent. She was kicking
his legs and clawing at his arms, her nails rending his
flesh like small knives. He had come with no firm plan

for killing Poco and Screech. He had thought of poison; he had also contemplated torching the cabin with them inside, but now that the time had come, he saw that there was an easier way, at least for the female. His knife was out; all he had to do was get her in the right position for a fatal thrust and . . .

Screech backed up a step and lunged forward with all his power, throwing himself into the air at full stretch.

Paa-tol caught one glimpse of something coming at his head as he thrust the knife upward toward Poco's heart, but he could not move fast enough to get out of the way. A clawed hand raked the side of his face and caught at his neck and ear, dragging him backward off his feet.

Poco screamed as the knife slid into her body. Eyes wide in pain, she felt herself falling as Paa-tol was wrenched back away from her.

Screech pulled a struggling Paa-tol toward him hand over hand, his claws biting into tender flesh. Gasping in panic, the Ni scrabbled for another of the knives in his chest harness, but before he could get one free, the derkat was on his back, driving him flat to the floor. He thrust himself upward in an effort to overbalance the derkat and pin him beneath him, but Screech braced himself with a foot and forced Paa-tol onto his side instead.

Paa-tol screamed as Screech bit into his neck. He thrashed about, trying to free himself, as the grinding jaws released and bit deeper, this time into his jugular vein.

Poco heard Paa-tol's last gurgled cry for help, then his struggles faded. She had no sympathy for him. He had killed her and taken her child. The pain in her chest was unbearable. She could feel her strength flowing away as her heart pumped blood out of her body. Though she lay in the light coming from the open doorway, the room seemed to be growing darker.

"Screech?"

Screech released his death grip on Paa-tol and sat up, drawn out of his rage by that whispered plea from Poco . He crawled toward her, but she was out of his reach.

Her eyes were open, and she was looking at him.

"Find Jiam," she said softly. "Take him—far away. Love him—for me."

Screech spun around and grabbed the chain in both hands. Again and again he jerked against it. Poco still lived! He had to help her!

He spotted Paa-tol's knife harness. He dropped the chain and snatched a knife from its sheath, then went to work on the log, digging frantically at the wood. Finally the pin gave away.

He was at Poco's side a second later. Blood saturated her tunic front, and there was blood at her lips. She was still, her eyes open and staring.

Screech raised his head and yowled in grief, the death of his tiyah burning deep into his soul. His radg was gone! He was alone again! As his cry faded, he looked down at Poco and remembered her last words to him. *"Find Jiam. Love him for me."*

Screech pushed to his feet. Find Jiam. Take him far away. The words echoed through his mind as he reached down and grabbed up the length of chain fastened to his ankle. He growled softly to Poco, bidding her good-bye, then slipped out the door and headed down a narrow, ill-kept trail, following Jiam's scent.

A glowing ball of light bobbed down over the small cabin seconds later. It settled near the open door, shimmering in all its power. A shadow moved within the light, and a moment later Dhalvad stepped out, the aura of energy dripping from him like water as he ran into the cabin.

Another form left the sphere and quickly coalesced into the shape of an Elay. It followed Dhalvad into the cabin, drawn by the power of the Tamorlee. It bypassed Dhalvad, who knelt beside Poco, tears running down his face as he dropped into his healing trance.

Dhalvad knew he was too late, but still he had to try. He dove into Poco's body without thought for himself, his healing power radiating outward in a pulsing motion that matched the beat of his heart. He was exhausted from all he had done the past few days, the healings, the

interrogation by the Elay, the wrenching pain of leaving
Gi and his recently found brother behind—but all of that
was as nothing compared to the pain and knowledge that
he had not been able to prevent Amet and Paa-tol from
carrying out their threats.

His first task was to ease the knifepoint out of Poco's
right lung and seal the puncture, then he concentrated on
massaging the heart and lungs.

As he healed the body with one part of his mind, he
searched frantically for the life spark that was Poco, despair washing through him as the seconds passed and he
could not find her. Exhaustion slipped upon him like a
robe of darkness, and he felt his strength fading.

"Poco! Answer me! Please!"

The Elay watched from the side, observing the healing touch of the Ni. Such power was rare among the
many kinds of life he had witnessed, but it was not un-
heard of. He saw that the Ni was exhausted and stepped
closer, the Elay's creed of noninterference pushed aside
for the moment in a twinge of guilt. By preventing Dhalvad's quicker return to Jjaan-bi, he had inadvertently
caused pain and perhaps the death of an innocent. His
glowing hand came to rest on top of Dhalvad's head.

Dhalvad felt the rush of power enter his body, but
there was no time to question its source. He dove deeper
and deeper into the darkness that was beyond Poco's
mind, crying her name.

Poco heard Dhalvad's voice as if from far away. She
was warm and comfortable where she was, and she had
no desire to leave. She felt that something important was
about to happen to her, but Dhalvad kept calling her
name. She tried to remember where she was, but that
knowledge eluded her. Shadowy figures moved around
her, the feathery touch of their hands urging her toward a
light.

"Poco, where are you? Don't leave me! I need you!"

Dhalvad's voice caught at her, wrapping around her
body with invisible bonds. He sounded so lost, so frightened. She turned from the light and looked behind her,
down a long tunnel. A shadowy figure stood at the end of

the tunnel surrounded by a haze of green light.

"*Poco!*"

She hesitated, but only for a moment. *"I'm here, Dhal. I'm here!"*

A roaring rush of wind filled her ears as she fled back toward the one who had dared death's corridor to find her.

Chulu, Caaras, Tidul, and several of the city watch approached the far shore of Lake Haddrach with a prisoner in tow. As their sailboat entered the marshy cove, they spotted another boat already beached on the rocky shore.

Chulu looked at their prisoner, a young Ni named Su-gaal, one of Amet's followers. Su-gaal had several bruises on his face and was shivering, though not with cold. He was badly frightened and had lost all hope of rescue by either Amet or Paa-tol, for according to the Council Elder who now glared at him with disgust, both of his superiors were in deep trouble, the kind that carried the sentence of banishment or life imprisonment should they be found guilty.

"Is this the place?" Chulu demanded harshly.

Su-gaal nodded, avoiding direct eye contact with the elder Ni.

Chulu fidgeted as Caaras jumped out into waist-deep water and guided the boat the last few feet toward shore. It had taken them too long to learn the truth about Dhalvad and Poco. If not for Gi-arobi, they still would be complacently awaiting Amet's return. After discovering that Poco had never reached Cybury, a city-wide search had begun, and as rumors quickly spread, several of Amet's people had come forward, intent on clearing themselves of any wrongdoing. In the process of questioning, certain names had been revealed. Of the five named, three had been found and questioned; Su-gaal was the fourth, and they had yet to find the fifth, a distant relative of Amet's named Anwhol.

They all splashed the last few feet to shore. Chulu had

Su-gaal by the arm as they stepped out of the water. "Show us the way and be quick about it!"

Su-gaal nodded and started up the steep path that followed a dry streambed. The others followed behind, grabbing at branches and outthrusting roots for balance. They reached a level spot and followed Su-gaal down a narrow path to the left.

Su-gaal suddenly stopped, and Chulu bumped into him. "What is wrong with..." Chulu's words trailed off when he saw what lay on the path ahead. He pushed past the young Ni and knelt beside Anwhol. He knew the face, though it now bore a bloody gash from lip to eye.

Caaras swore softly as he stepped past Tidul, who was trying to breathe deeply in order to hold in the contents of his stomach. "He's been disemboweled," Caaras muttered as he, too, quickly turned away. "Who would have—"

An eerie yowl echoed through the woods, its wavering sound sending chills into each Ni standing there.

"Screech!" Chulu growled as he grabbed Su-gaal's arm. "Damn it, get moving! Show us where you're holding Poco and the child!"

"If Screech is free,'" Caaras said, "then Poco and Jiam have to be all right, too."

Grim-faced, Chulu hurried downtrail, leaving the others to follow. "Pray that you're right, Caaras! Pray that you're right!"

The rest was not
....
when she saw him.
"You're not going to get away with this," he per...
any word you ...
....

Chapter 23 🐟

CHULU AND CAARAS CLIMBED THE LAST FEW STEPS TO Dhalvad's porch and found their host waiting for them. A week had passed since his return and he still looked tired and gaunt.

"Sorry we're late," Chulu said as he stepped up onto the porch. "As newly appointed head of the Council, I've had my troubles today."

Dhalvad smiled. "You thrive on trouble, Chulu."

Chulu grinned. "You're right. How's Poco doing?"

Dhalvad led the way into the house. "She's still weak from the loss of blood, but she's feeling better. She wants to see you and thank you both for what you've done."

"We didn't do very much," Caaras said. "You and Screech had everything pretty much under control by the time we got there."

Dhalvad shook his head. "I don't mean that day. I mean after . . . sending searchers out for Screech."

"We still haven't had any luck finding him. No one we've talked to has seen anything of him or the baby."

"We'll find them," Dhalvad said as he ushered the two into the bedroom where Poco sat up in bed leaning against several pillows. Her face was pale, and her blue eyes were smudged with gray circles, but she smiled when she saw them.

"You're talking about Screech," she said. "Is there any word yet?"

Chulu shook his head as he stopped by the side of the bed and took one of her hands. "Not yet, but we'll keep looking."

Poco squeezed Chulu's hand. "I'm worried about both of them, but I trust Screech. He'll take good care of Jiam for me. I keep hoping that he'll come back here, but if he thinks Dhal and I are dead, he'll probably just keep going."

"Where do you think he'll take Jiam?" Caaras asked.

Poco looked up at Dhalvad. "We were talking about that last night," she said. "We think he'll head back to the plains and his own people."

"With the child?"

"Yes," Dhalvad said.

Chulu looked at Dhalvad. "You'll go after him?"

"*We'll* go after them," Poco said firmly her glance on Dhalvad. "As soon as I'm strong enough."

Dhalvad nodded. "It's together from now on, no matter what."

"What about your brother?" Caaras asked.

Dhalvad looked at Chulu. "Are the Seekers ready to travel?"

"I've lined up seven who'll travel with you."

"Good. Then while Poco is getting her strength back, I'll guide them to Bhaldavin and the rafts, and we'll work out a way for them to cross the desert, with the Seekers providing food, water, and whatever else is necessary. Once I'm sure everything is set up, I'll return with Gi, and we'll go after Screech and Jiam."

"Dhal," Chulu said, standing. "The Council members have asked me to ask you if you'll consent to be our next Speaker. When Mithdaar is brought to Jjaan-bi, it will take an experienced—"

"No," Dhalvad said, interrupting. "I'm making no promises now. It's my brother who's attuned to the other crystal, not me, and I won't commit myself to anything until I've found my son."

"Of course," Chulu said. "I understand, but as head of the Council I had to ask."

"Would either of you like some hot tea?" Poco said, changing the subject.

"Yes, I would," Chulu said.

"Caaras?" Dhalvad asked.

Caaras caught the look in Chulu's eyes and shook his head. "No. I'm fine."

"I'll be back in a few minutes," Dhalvad said, turning for the door. "Poco, you want some tea?"

"Yes, please."

"I'll give you a hand, Dhal," Chulu said. "Caaras, you stay here and keep Poco company."

Chulu followed Dhalvad out of the room, down the hall, and into the kitchen. As Dhalvad went about freshening up the fire in the stove, Chulu took a chair at the kitchen table. He waited patiently while Dhalvad put water in the kettle and placed it on top of the stove.

Dhalvad turned around, a wry smile on his face. "You were a lot of help. All right, Chulu, what is it? You didn't just come by to say hello to Poco. What's on your mind?"

Chulu smiled. "You know me too well, Dhalvad, even better than some of my friends whom I've known for years. Why is that, do you suppose?"

Dhalvad dropped into the chair opposite Chulu. "You're stalling, Chulu. Come on, out with it."

"All right," Chulu said, raising both hands in a gesture of surrender. "I've come to ask you about the Tamorlee and the Elay. I didn't want to press you about it because you and Poco needed time alone without being deluged by visitors, but the days are slipping by fast, and before you go off with the other Seekers, we must know more about the Elay, who they are, where they come from, and whether or not they'll ever return the Tamorlee to us."

Dhalvad dropped his elbows to the tabletop and rubbed at his eyes tiredly. He had known he would eventually have to explain, and had been consciously preparing a speech for the Council. He was glad Chulu had come alone.

He had told his side of the entire story to Caaras and Chulu several days earlier, only hinting about the part the Elay had played in his return to Jjaan-bi and the subsequent disappearance of the Tamorlee. Both Ni had seen the Elay for a few brief seconds as it left the cabin and returned to its module. He knew that curiosity would eventually overcome awe and they would want to know all.

"The Elay are like the Ral-jennob," he began. "They are Star Travelers who move from world to world as a Seeker moves from place to place. They are not like us in bodily form, though they can take any shape they wish, including ours. They are beings of light and energy, wise beyond our greatest scholars, but more important, they are curious about everything. It's they who brought crystals like the Tamorlee to our world. They call them Gatherers, because that's what the crystals do—they gather information through a symbiotic relationship with compatible life-forms, such as the Ni.

"As for where they come from? I don't know. Perhaps Mithdaar can tell us that, because the two crystals shared a deeper rapport with the Elay than either myself or my brother did."

"The other day you said that the Elay gave Mithdaar back to your brother after they had recorded all of the knowledge within its mind," Chulu said as he strove to understand. "Why didn't the Elay return the Tamorlee to you?"

Dhalvad looked into Chulu's eyes. "They said that the Tamorlee had broken their first law and thereby forfeited the right to continue as a Gatherer."

"What law is that?"

"All life is sacred. You shall not kill."

Chulu frowned. "The Tamorlee killed someone?"

"You can stop looking for Amet," Dhalvad said softly. "Somehow the Tamorlee managed to leave him 'between' during that last transfer. Paa-tol and Amet left

Barl-gan each using a Seeker ring. Paa-tol arrived safely. Amet didn't. Paa-tol must have recovered the Tamorlee from the transfer point; the ring setting holding the crystal was melted. Paa-tol had it with him when he died. I know I should have told you this earlier, but I knew how you all felt about the crystal. After the Elay gave me the strength to save Poco, it took the Tamorlee to its sphere. It wasn't gone very long. When it came back, it spoke to me a few minutes and explained why it couldn't leave the Tamorlee with us. It simply feared that what had happened once might happen again."

"But Amet was in the wrong in what he did!" Chulu protested.

"I know. I believe the Tamorlee did what it had to do, but that doesn't change what happened. It still killed, and that's against our laws as well as the laws of the Elay."

Chulu looked down at the tabletop and sighed deeply. "So our past is lost to us."

Dhalvad shook his head. "Not lost. The Elay have it, and during the time Mithdaar and the Tamorlee were in link, before the Elay came, I'm positive they shared deeply with each other, which means that Mithdaar might well now hold the history of the Ni-lach. Time will tell."

"What will happen to the Tamorlee?"

"The Elay struck me as being both wise and compassionate. We'll just have to trust them to do what is best for our friend."

"Did the Elay ever say how many Gatherers are seeded on each world?" Chulu asked.

"One or two to every world, each with the capacity to reproduce itself a hundred times or more if the conditions are right."

Chulu looked down at the fire stone within his ring setting. "The Seeker stones?"

Dhalvad smiled. "That's what I was told."

"But we've been using the Seeker stones for thousands of years! Why haven't any of them become like the Tamorlee?"

"One has—Mithdaar. And there will be others if we gift them as we gifted the Tamorlee, helping them to grow."

"And the Elay? Will they return one day to teach us about the worlds beyond our suns?"

"Yes, I think so. When we're ready."

About the Author

Marcia Joanne Bennett was born on June 9, 1945. Raised in a rural community, she has spent all but a few of her working years in central New York State.

After graduating from Albany Business College in 1965, she spent the next seven years in banking.

Several years ago she established a small craft shop in her hometown. While running the shop she began writing, a hobby that quickly became an addiction. Her other interests range from reading, painting, and basketry to astrology and parapsychology.